A Pious Killing

Mick Hare

Cover designs: front – Chandler Book Design

www.chandlerbookdesign.co.uk

back and spine – Rob Hare

robmhare@sky.com

Visit Mick Hare's web-site on

www.mickhr.com

Available in hard copy from www.lulu.com

Also available as e-book download from www.amazon.co.uk

To my wife Janet and my children Louise and Robert.

Mick Hare.

One

1942

The black Mercedes was the only vehicle in motion on the streets of Gerona at the early hour of 5:30am. The driver wore the distinctive uniform of the civil guard. The male passenger in the back listened absently to the zip of the tyres on the dampened streets. He was also in uniform, but it was not of the same nationality as that of the driver. He absent-mindedly stroked the Iron Cross garlanded with oak leaves that was pinned to the breast of his uniform jacket.

As they crossed Rio Onyar and entered the old city, the passenger glanced at the leather bag beside him on the seat. He tapped it gently, reassuringly. Then he sat back and spent some moments in forethought, rehearsing the task he was being driven to perform.

He was tall with the build of an athlete, which, in fact, he had been in his college days. But his well-toned physique owed more to his upbringing on the family farm where physical labour had been a part of daily life from an early age. His well-tanned face below his well-groomed, dark brown hair was further evidence of his preference for the outdoors, although his wire-rimmed spectacles invested the face with a scholarly look.

Having expertly navigated the large saloon through the narrow streets, the driver gently slid the car to a halt and racked the handbrake into lock. They were positioned outside Hotel Catalanes, the Mercedes completely blocking the narrow thoroughfare.

"Remember who you are," the driver said in English. He turned to face his passenger. His deep Iberian tones rang a note of seriousness into the exchange. "You have a maximum time limit of fifteen minutes to complete this task. You should not be disturbed, but if you remain too long, our subsequent movements could be curtailed.

"I will carry out the agreed plan. If I am unsuccessful after fifteen minutes I will abort, if at all possible," replied the passenger in heavily accented Castilian.

"If I have to move the car, go directly to Plaza de la Independencia. I will be there."

"Understood."

"Remember," emphasised the driver, "They are expecting you. They expect you to be who you are and they expect you to do what you are going to do. As long as you maintain your identity no one will oppose you.

In fact they should assist you. You are Dr Bauer of the Army Medical Corps. You are replacing your colleague, Dr Brandt and you are here to administer the General's medicine."

"Understood," repeated the passenger.

He stepped out of the car and placed his bag beside him on the flagstones. He stood erect and straightened the sleeves of his German Army uniform. He placed his hat firmly upon his head and stooped to pick up his bag. Grasping its soft leather handle in his hand, he strode confidently into the hotel.

His first sweep of the lobby informed him that it was full of men in SS uniforms. A rich cloud of tobacco smoke hovered below the ceiling. He strode up to the desk. He was about to strike the bell when a voice spoke from behind him in German.

"Herr Lieutenant! What brings you here at this hour? How can I help you?"

Although no reaction was visible from behind, Dr Bauer's face froze in fear for an imperceptible moment. But he turned to show a smiling, blue-eyed confidence to the Wermacht officer facing him.

"Good morning, Herr Captain. Heil Hitler!"

"Heil Hitler!" came the automatic response.

Dr. Bauer's German was flawless and bore the authentic hint of a Berlin accent, "I am here to administer General Zeiger's medicine."

"How so?" enquired the Captain. "I have not seen you here before."

"That is quite correct. My name is Dr Bauer and I am replacing my colleague Dr Brandt who has been given compassionate leave. His wife is unwell."

Captain Vogts was a cautious man and the General's well-being was his prime concern in life. However, faced with the relaxed demeanour of the German doctor before him and his easy explanation for the substitution, he found himself asking for the doctor's papers almost apologetically. Training and habit, however, made him scrutinise them carefully.

"It says here you were born in Cologne. I thought I detected a Berlin accent."

"You are very astute, Herr Captain. After the last war my father moved us around Germany in search of work. He refused on principle to work for a Jew. As you know, in the Weimar Republic that was not an easy principle to hold. Eventually we settled near Berlin and then I studied medicine there for seven years."

The Captain smiled without comment. The lift whirred to a halt and the Captain pulled the gates open.

"Come," he said, "Let's see the General. This diabetes is a damned nuisance to him. The Fuehrer values our General so highly that he permits these respite visits to Spain. General Franco is pleased to allow these unofficial rehabilitation visits. Of course, he must keep a diplomatic distance in order not to anger the Allies. Spain is full of English and American spies. But we need our General back in action for the good of the Fatherland. He is on course to completely break the French Resistance. The French call him "The Scourge". He has broken more of their cells than anyone else and his policy of reprisals against civilians is destroying their support."

The doctor followed along the marble corridor and stopped alongside the Captain at the door to the General's suite. He smiled reassuringly. "I will treat your General to the utmost of my ability."

As the captain studied his face in close eye-to-eye contact the doctor thought, 'I will remember this face until my dying day. Which means, of course, you will remember mine.'

They entered an outer reception area of the General's suite and the Captain went on alone into the General's private quarters.

The doctor glanced at his watch. Six minutes had passed. There was no way he could complete now within fifteen minutes. If he was going to abort, he should do it now. However, the plan to abort depended upon his being able to do so without endangering himself. His situation now meant that there was no option but to proceed. He had no choice. He would proceed. No matter how long it took. No one would get this close again.

The door to the bedroom opened and the Captain beckoned him in. The General sat up in bed. He was in excellent physical shape from the evidence of his muscular torso. However, he seemed drowsy and was obviously in need of his medication – and quickly.

"Heil Hitler, Herr General," the doctor said formally.

"Heil Hitler, Lieutenant Doctor. I am sorry to hear of Dr. Brandt's misfortune. Please pass him my condolences. Now, come on! Get me fit. There is a war to be won. Ordinary people all over the world are praying for us to win. They can't wait to be liberated from international Jewry. They long to be free of their corrupt democratic governments. They crave the success of the Third Reich to free them from their oppressors. Let us get about our great crusade."

The General's laugh was full of simple jollity as if he was planning victory in a football match. The doctor went to a table by the window, set his case down and snapped it open. As he did he heard the angry sound of a car horn from the street below. Glancing out of the window he saw his car reluctantly pull away to clear the street for the oncoming truck.

"Is there a problem, Herr Lieutenant?"

It was the captain at his elbow. The doctor turned to face him.

"No, none at all. Perhaps you will get some water. The General will enjoy a drink after his injection."

The captain retired to the bathroom.

"Now General," the doctor said, "Please relax. You will soon feel on top form again. I will give you your medicine and then I suggest you sleep some more. One hour, maybe two."

"Whatever you say, Herr Doctor. This illness has taught me the importance of taking medical advice."

The captain returned.

'Plaza de la Independencia,' thought the doctor. *'That's where I have to meet Roberto.'*

He selected a sealed packet from inside his case and tore it open. He removed the sterile syringe from inside it, then reached back into his bag and lifted out a small, round, brown bottle. He undid the black screw top. The bottle contained one lethal dose of diamorphine. It had been specially prepared for the general by British Secret Service.

Dr Bauer felt perspiration break out on his brow and found himself wishing that the vigilant captain would move away from his side. Having unscrewed the bottle top he pierced the skin across its narrow mouth. He then lifted the bottle and needle together so that the bottle was upside down and he slowly withdrew the plunger and sucked the poison into the cylinder.

"How long have you been practising your profession, Herr Doctor?" the captain asked.

"I began my studies thirteen years ago. I have been practising for six," replied the doctor.

"And where did you practise before the war?"

This part was easy. He had been carefully briefed on his history at his preparatory training in Wiltshire. It was also easy because much of it was based on the truth of his time in Germany.

"I was six years in Berlin at the Friedrichshain Hospital. I studied under Maximillian Schneider and Florian Fuchs."

"Ah," said the Captain, "Herr Fuchs is a true Aryan patriot. He is now crucial to the Reich's development of eugenics. He is celebrated by the Fuhrer himself."

Dr Bauer stepped away from the table, removing himself from the close proximity of the captain. He tapped carefully at the syringe cylinder. He then meticulously ejected a minimal amount of serum into the air to ensure the complete absence of oxygen. Turning to face the captain he said, "Now, if you'll pardon me Captain… I think the General is in urgent need…"

"Forgive me Doctor. General Zeiger says I am an incorrigible gossip. But, you know, I find it a useful habit in my line of work."

The Captain stepped aside. As he approached the bed with the murderous serum in his grasp the Doctor again felt the perspiration break out on his brow and begin to trickle down his nose. To prevent his spectacles from slipping he removed them and placed them on the table at the General's bedside.

"Now General, if you will please expose your stomach, relief is a tiny pin prick away."

"Do your worst, Doctor. I am ready."

Only the Doctor appreciated the intense irony of General Zeiger's comment as he pierced the plump white skin with his needle and began to slowly press home the plunger. *'I doubt,'* he thought, *'that a vicious torturer and murderer such as yourself is ready to face whatever awaits you beyond the grave.'*

As the plunger completed its short journey he withdrew the needle and wiped the entry point with a swab. He then went quickly to his bag and began to efficiently repack it. Speaking to the Captain as he worked he said, "Please give the General his drink now and help to make him comfortable in bed. Allow him two hours of sleep." He pulled a strip of tablets from his bag. "Sometimes these large doses can cause nausea. Permit him one of these every six hours should he complain."

"Thank you, Doctor."

"I also have two phials of the medication for the General to keep with him in case of emergencies. The war makes it difficult for supplies of medicine to be freely available. I am sure these will be sufficient until he is back under the care of his doctor in France."

"Thank you again, Doctor."

The doctor snapped his bag shut, lifted it from the table and turned to look at the man he had just assassinated. He lay there drowsily oblivious of the fate that had just befallen him. But his career of torturing and murdering

French Resistance fighters and their secret agent allies was over. The doctor put his hat on.

The Captain finished adjusting the pillows and blankets to make the General comfortable and came around the bed to the bedside table.

"Herr Doctor," he called. "Just a minute. You have forgotten your spectacles."

Damn, cursed the doctor inwardly. He froze at the door to the bedroom. He was tempted to make a run for it. But he knew he would not make it to the top of the stairs before the Captain could shoot him. He turned to see the Captain walking towards him, spectacles in hand.

At the last moment, as he was about to hand the spectacles to the Doctor, the Captain hesitated and lifted them to his eyes. As he did so he immediately saw that they were made with clear glass. Fake spectacles! The Doctor's mind raced as he saw realisation and then panic start to etch anxiety lines across the Captain's visage.

No sooner had they registered than his expression was further distorted. The Doctor, acting instinctively, slammed the heel of his hand into the Captain's top lip and upward into his nostrils. It was a move he'd learned, not from the British Secret Service, but on the college rugby fields of his youth. With the force of the blow he heard and felt the crack and snap of gristle and bone as the Captain's nose broke into many tiny pieces.

Before the Captain had time to bring his hands to the pain, the Doctor drove one pointed knuckle into his throat, instantaneously dislodging his Adam's apple. An excruciating groan escaped from the now totally overwhelmed Captain and he collapsed into unconsciousness.

He now had to kill the Captain. No sooner had he made this decision than he was forestalled by a knock on the outer door. Had someone heard the Captain's groan?

"Just a minute!" he called out.

Putting his bag down he dragged the Captain's heavy body into the bathroom, picked up his spectacles, his hat, which had tumbled off in the melee, and his bag. He checked his appearance in the mirror. A knock, this time at the bedroom door, startled him. Whoever it was had obviously grown impatient and had moved into the ante room.

The Doctor opened the bedroom door and stepped out, closing it behind him. He was standing face to face with a Sergeant of the Wermacht.

"Good morning Unterfeldwebel," he said. "Have you been sent for?"

"No Herr Lieutenant," he replied. "I was passing along the corridor when I heard someone call out."

"Oh, good fellow. However, there is nothing to concern yourself about. I have just administered General Zeiger's medication. It can often be uncomfortable for the patient. I suspect you heard the General cursing me."

The doctor smiled and the Sergeant smiled back.

"Captain Vogts is just seeing to the General's needs. He will be out in five minutes. Please do not disturb them. The General needs to rest."

"Have no fear my good Doctor. I will wait here until Captain Vogts emerges."

"Very good. Now, if you will excuse me, I must be getting back to my quarters. I will have a queue of patients waiting for me by the time I get back."

"Good day, Doctor," smiled the Sergeant.

"Good day to you."

The sergeant stood aside and the doctor stepped out of the General's suite into the hotel corridor.

Two

1941

Lilian Olivia Brett, aged twenty-eight gazed absent-mindedly out of the train window. It rumbled slowly between the backs of the north London terraces and clattered over the points on its final approach to St Pancras station.

The backs of these houses were alien to Lily. These terraces were three, four, sometimes five storeys high. There was nothing comparable in her adopted home town of Leicester. Already the train had passed through an area of urbanisation at least three times larger than the whole of Leicester. When they finally arrived at St Pancras they would still only be entering the northern part of this metropolitan monster.

She was excited and afraid at the same time. She wore a pretty fitted light green coat over a summer dress and a patterned cardigan. Her jet black hair framed her striking features. But there was no smile to ignite the beauty of that face. She looked at her reflection in the glass and was struck by the sombre expression her face took up in repose. It had not always been like that, but experience changes people.

It had been three years now since she had first volunteered her services to the war effort as a fluent German speaker. She had written to the Ministry of Defence at the outbreak of war in 1939. If she had known at the time what repercussions would follow from that letter, she would never have written it. But the passing of a certain amount of time had managed to assuage some of the pain she had endured at that time. Today, despite her experiences at the hands of the British police, she still felt as strongly as she ever had about the Third Reich. So here she was at last, on her way to the War Office, summoned to "do her bit" as the Tommy's so quaintly put it.

At a time of war with Germany she had expected to be vetted. Fluent speakers of German, German ex-patriates, might easily be enemy agents. Most "enemy" civilians in Leicester were of Italian origin and their treatment had been nothing short of scandalous. Families had been rounded up and transported to separate camps as far away as North Yorkshire or the Isle of Man. In the end, Lily had escaped that fate, initially because of her work as a theatre nurse at the Leicester Royal Infirmary but then, later, because of her letter to the Ministry of Defence.

The letter had saved her from internment but it had led to the subsequent sadistic investigation she was subjected to at the hands of Chief Inspector Peter Herbert of the City of Leicester Police Force.

Herbert was a coward who had been mightily relieved not to have been conscripted to fight. He was not quite too old for conscription, but his age plus his occupation had conspired to let him off the hook. Twenty-five years as a chain-smoker had reduced his physical prowess to the extent that His Majesty's Forces could manage without him. As a coward, Herbert was determined never to be thought as one, even by himself. To prove his great courage to the world at large he developed an over-zealousness in pursuit of his investigations. Investigations into suspected enemy aliens gave him the perfect excuse to step over the boundaries of conventional behaviour. In this way he saw himself contributing to the defence of the realm every bit as much as the private on the battlefield. When Lily's file landed on his desk it elicited one of his snake-like smiles.

Lily went to the door of her terraced house on Dronfield Street. It was situated in the respectable blue-collar district known as the Highfields. The three strong raps upon the door knocker had startled her, but she shrugged off her reaction as tiredness.

She had just returned from an all night shift at Leicester Royal Infirmary where she had participated in six emergency operations in succession. The patients were casualties of last night's bombing raid on nearby Coventry. Five times she had returned the bloodied floors, walls, furniture and instruments of the theatre to sterile cleanliness ready for the next operation. Then she had assisted the surgeons and theatre staff with the conduct of surgery.

A four year old child with a severed arm had had no chance from the start. The ambulance dash from Coventry to Leicester had seen to that. But they had tried anyway. The removal of a house slate from a young mother's skull had been completed successfully but they would not know for some time how the injury had affected her mental faculties.

With such thoughts in her mind and with a craving for breakfast and sleep, she opened the door to find herself face to face with Chief Inspector Peter Herbert. He introduced himself, formally and politely, showing his badge. Lily invited the Chief Inspector in and they sat in the front room of the house, the room traditionally reserved for special occasions and special guests; not that Lily ever had either.

"You're an enemy alien, Miss Brett," Herbert smiled humourlessly. He said it as if commenting upon the niceness of her room. The mismatch between tone and content immediately unsettled Lily and she looked at this man with increasing concern. He sat forward in his chair, back erect, elbows resting on the arms of the floral suite. His sharply creased trousers had ridden up his leg exposing pale grey socks, pulled up tight with emulsion white shins above.

"I have applied for citizenship and I am loyal to the United Kingdom."

"Nevertheless, Miss Brett, you are an enemy alien. A German!"

He got up from the armchair and moved to the mantelpiece. He reached out a hand and picked up a decoratively framed photograph.

"You see, Miss Brett, if you were a loyal British citizen, I doubt you would have a photograph of a Nazi soldier on your mantelpiece."

Lily, roused to anger, strode across to him, "Get your hands off that," she snapped. She snatched the photograph from his grasp. "It is not a Nazi uniform. That is a German army uniform from the Great War. It is my father and he was a hero in any man's language. He was not a Nazi. He was an academic and a democrat."

"Well now Miss Brett," returned Herbert, obviously affronted but still able to maintain his sinister grin. "That may be as you see it. But only an enemy alien would know the subtle differences between German military uniforms. And to an English patriot there's no such thing as a German hero."

Whenever he spoke the word 'German', he spat it out as though the utterance offended his lips.

In the face of this bigoted onslaught Lily felt her eyes begin to fill with tears. She inwardly cursed her own emotions and fought back the tears. She replaced the photograph of her father on the mantelpiece and stood between it and Herbert, as if protecting her past from his dirty presence.

"What do you want, Chief Inspector?" she asked as assertively as she could manage in an effort to bring this unpleasant encounter to a conclusion.

Herbert's serpent grin spread irresistibly across his face as he savoured his reply. "I want to find out if you're a German spy, Miss Brett."

Lily gasped involuntarily at the direct brutality of his reply.

"If you'll be good enough to get your coat, Miss Brett, we can continue this interesting chat at the police station."

"But Chief Inspector, I was working all yesterday and last night and I have eaten nothing for twelve hours." Lily was aware of the uselessness of her protest even as she spoke it.

Herbert enjoyed rebutting her, "I'm afraid I can't help that," he grinned. Then, with deliberate abruptness he lost the grin and assumed an expression of aggressive seriousness. "Stop stalling! Get your coat!"

Lily stepped into the hallway to get her coat. As she slipped it on she heard a crash from inside the room. She dashed back in just in time to see Herbert in the act of lifting his heel from the broken frame of her father's photograph.

Lily's introduction to wartime security at Leicester Police Station was brutal and swift.

Having signed for her possessions at the front desk she was suddenly seized by two uniformed officers. With her arms clasped painfully behind her back she was pushed through a swing door into an area of the station which contained the cells. She screamed out in pain but her protests were useless. She felt a floor fall in her stomach but she refused to be overwhelmed. She experienced dislocation resulting from a feeling of complete defencelessness. In here they could do what they liked with her.

Inside a cell she was confronted by Herbert and four uniformed officers.

"Take your clothes off!" hissed Herbert.

"You can't make me do that," gasped Lily, her voice catching in her throat.

"That's where you're wrong Mrs Fritz," yelled one of the officers, his bellow resounding off the walls of the hollow cell.

"German spies have no rights – and we have all the rights we want."

The shouter walked forward and stood face to face with her. Lily brushed the tears away from the corners of her eyes and held her abusers stare.

"All right," said Herbert, stepping forward. "We can't waste any more time. Undress her!"

What happened to Lily then and was repeated more than once over the next fourteen days was, she knew, tantamount to rape. It happened here at Leicester Police Station and it happened repeatedly at Leicester men's prison, where she was transferred after three days.

Her clothes were ripped from her and she was intimately searched. Each of the five men took it in turns to effect their own intimate search of her. All the while humiliating insults were hurled at her. They discussed her shape, size, proportion, all as if passing judgement on an animal for sale. They spoke disparagingly of her Teutonic breasts and pubic hair. They accused her repeatedly of spying for Germany.

All alone in her Leicester prison cell she had to endure the taunts of the male inmates. Each night the guards told her that they would be bringing a few prisoners along to her cell to keep her company. Fortunately, each night they failed to keep their word; as they did in all things.

She was interviewed daily by Herbert, who seemed to have no other case-work to pursue. Every two or three days Herbert would decide that it was necessary to strip search her again, as if she could have acquired something to hide from them in her cell. She always knew when that was about to happen because Herbert would be accompanied by one of his companions from the first night of her interrogation.

During this period Herbert seemed to believe that he was getting somewhere. He established that Brett was not her real name but that it had been anglicised from the German, Brecht. That her father had fought in the German Army in the Great War, that he had been an elected member of the Reichstag in the Weimar Republic but that he had stood down from political activity in early 1934. Mysteriously, she and her father had emigrated from Germany to Britain in 1936. In 1938 her father had died of a burst spleen and resulting complications.

"And now you are here," concluded Herbert triumphantly, "successfully insinuated into English society, ready to spy for the country you love."

Lily repeatedly countered that, yes, all those facts were true, but they did not add up to a cover story for a sleeping spy.

"My father was a true patriot. He was a Social Democrat. He believed in the Weimar Republic. He did not believe the lies about the Jews being to blame for everything. My father suffered repeated beatings at the hands of the Nazi thugs. In the end he could take no more. He quit political office. He hoped he could settle to his academic work at the university. But by 1936 he could see the way things were going and he knew we had to escape. In the end we came here as fugitives from Hitler's brutal government. The same government you accuse me of spying for. That same government would have killed me by now as an enemy of the Fatherland. It wanted my father dead too. Yes, I love Germany. I am German. But I loathe Nazism and I want to see it defeated every bit as much as you do."

So it went on. And it might have continued in this way for the duration of the war if intervention had not come forward from an unexpected place.

After her fifth day of incarceration, her best friend and colleague, Janet Collins, became concerned. Janet worked alongside Lily in the theatre. She had never known Lily be absent before. She could not conceive of her taking this much time away from work without informing Sister.

One night, on her way home from work, she had called at Lily's house. She did so again the next night, to no avail. On her third visit a neighbour opened her front door and said, "It's no good knocking there, duck."

"Why, what's happened?"

"She's been arrested. Nazi spy! That's what they say. Shootin's too good for her if you ask me."

"Oh my God!" gasped Janet as she turned and raced to the bus stop to get straight back to the hospital.

Janet had explained everything to Sister and Sister had spoken immediately to John Barberis, an experienced surgeon in his early thirties and a trusted colleague. He had been a Cambridge man. Once a Cambridge man, always a Cambridge man. That trite expression was in his mind as he picked up the telephone in his hospital office and dialled the number of his old college friend, Andrew Trubshaw.

He was waiting on the phone to be put through to Andrew before it occurred to him that he had not stopped to consider if the accusation against Lily might be true. Perhaps he was being naïve. But no sooner did it occur to him than he angrily dismissed the idea.

"John, you old dog. What a pleasant surprise. How are you old chap?"

Andrew's voice was immediately reassuring to John Barberis, who realised he was nervous now about what he was about to ask.

"I'm fine, Andrew," he replied. "Overworked, underpaid, just like everybody else. What about yourself?"

"Oh, you know, just about keeping flesh and spirit together. We live in exciting times John, but you know, I'd give a lot to have a few of those college days back. What do you say?"

"You bet!" John replied with genuine longing.

John allowed the conversation to roam over past times and old friends for several minutes. John and Andrew had been room mates for the last of their undergraduate years and had shared a strong bond of friendship. It was only since the declaration of war that they had become remiss in maintaining contact. Until then they had regularly visited each other and had had whisky and beer drenched weekends in either Leicester or London.

Although they had studied medicine together only John had had the ambition to practice. Andrew, although a brilliant student, had moved straight into military intelligence on leaving Cambridge. Recruitment for MI5 and MI6 had been pretty active during those years and John had also been approached. For himself, he considered the idea a preposterous waste of his training. But that hadn't been the case for Andrew. He had leapt at the chance. "No more sterile butchery for me," he had joked. "A brolly, a bowler and a desk, that's the life for me."

Until now the two friends had never discussed the work Andrew was involved in. Now John was about to presume to seek Andrew's support and influence in solving the mystery of Lily's disappearance. After listening to

Andrew describe in detail the action of a college rugby match he had seen the previous weekend, John took the plunge and began.

"Andrew, I need your help," he said.

"Just name it old friend. I can refuse you nought!"

"No, Andrew," John stumbled. "This is serious. If you are unable to help I will fully understand. It involves... your work... as it were."

"I see," said Andrew, a note of seriousness entering his voice for the first time. "Well, until you tell me, I cannot decide can I?"

And so John began the tale of Lily, or as much as he knew of it. He told Andrew about the best, hardest working theatre nurse he had ever encountered. He spoke of the endless hours she worked, often to the point of exhaustion. He painted a picture of a dedicated professional nurse without whom many English lives would have been lost within the walls of Leicester Royal Infirmary. He then told what he knew of her background. Yes, she is a German. But she is an implacable enemy of Nazism. Her father came here as a political refugee from the Nazis. His life was ruined by them.

Then John went on to explain her disappearance and the terrible rumour that had found its way back to him. That she had been arrested as a spy. As he talked, John realised he was sounding more and more desperate. When he finally got to the end of all he could think of to say, he concluded with a comment he knew to be overly dramatic, but one he was unable to resist; "My God, Andrew. They are hanging spies, aren't they!"

Suddenly Andrew was businesslike, "Righto old chum, I've got your drift. Now listen carefully. I'm going to say two things. First, I will investigate Lily Brett for you and find out what has happened to her. Second, if she turns out to be a spy I will do my best to see to it that she does hang. Leave it with me. I'll get back to you within the week."

The line went dead as Andrew hung up. John looked at the mouthpiece in his hand in shock at what his best friend had just said and at the thought of what he might have just initiated.

Three
1942

By the time Dr Bauer reached the Plaza Espana in Gerona he was at the limit of his endurance. His fight with Captain Vogts, swiftly followed by the encounter with the sergeant had left him drained. As he had walked down the carpeted stairs of the hotel to the lobby he had felt like a lamb walking into the wolf's lair. Wermacht, SS and Gestapo officers filled the lobby, smoking, playing cards and joking loudly. At any moment he expected the sergeant to come chasing after him and that he would be seized by this Nazi mob. His knees were water but his wits were sharp. At the turn in the stairway half way down, he slipped a piece of paper from his pocket and let it fall to the floor by the skirting board. It was a receipt for an aeroplane ticket from Barcelona to Madrid. It was a forgery and a false trail. But it was one the Germans would have to follow up even if they suspected its falsity.

He made it safely across the lobby and out into the street. The sun was warming the early morning and one or two people were out and about attending to their daily business. Franco's Civil Guards patrolled in twos, armed with rifles. They acknowledged Dr Bauer with a salute and he saluted back. Crossing the footbridge he was approached by two SS men. As they drew level with him one stepped in front of him and stopped his progress. However, the man just smiled and asked him for a light. Clumsily the doctor found his lighter and lit the man's cigarette. He was sure his nerves would give him away. The man thanked him and walked off to join his companion.

Entering the colonnade surrounding Plaza de la Independiencia he spotted the Mercedes. He was distraught to see that his driver was standing beside the car being questioned by two Civil Guards. At least, it appeared he was being questioned. Maybe they were just having a chat and a smoke to pass the time. What should he do? If the alarm had been raised and they were looking for him it would be suicide to approach. On the other hand, if they were idly killing time the longer he hesitated the sooner the assassination would be discovered and the hue and cry would begin. He moved out of the shade of the colonnade and called to his driver. On hearing him his driver looked towards him and called back. He then said something to his companions and they moved off across the square. Restraining the urge within himself to run to the car, he approached as slowly as he could as his driver stubbed his cigarette out with his foot and moved around the car to the driver's side.

Within minutes they were pulling away from the Old City and approaching La Plaza de Toros.

For several minutes Doctor Bauer was overcome with relief and he slumped in his seat like a dead man. They glided through the city streets, passed the train station and turned south onto the Barcelona road. It was only when he found himself looking out of the windows onto fields and farmhouses set well back from the road that he realised his driver was talking to him.

He tuned into the driver's words.

"When you are ready you must tell me what happened!" the driver was saying.

The doctor recounted the action in the hotel as his driver listened intently. The act of retelling the events served to further revive him; as if his brain was telling him that de-briefing was procedure. He had trained to de-brief. Things were becoming normal again.

"Is the General dead?" asked the driver.

"Definitely!"

"No doubt?"

"None at all!"

"What about the Captain?"

"No. Definitely not! But he is severely injured. His active participation in the war might well be over."

"Yes," came back the driver, "But if he is alive he may recognise you."

"That's true."

"And so might the sergeant."

"Also true," said the doctor. "It's a bit messy, isn't it!"

"This is a messy business. The important thing is you achieved your main objective. If we get out of the mess alive, that's a bonus. If we don't – well we were expendable anyway."

The driver slowed the car down as they reached the outskirts of a small town called Llagostera. He drove slowly through the quiet streets, careful not to draw the attention of any conscientious Civil Guards. He ignored a signpost indicating Barcelona to the right and drove straight ahead and then left following signs to San Feliu de Guixols. Once through Llagostera he pushed the accelerator to the floor and within twenty minutes they were skirting around San Feliu and pulling into a cove beside a tiny fishing village called San Agaro. Parking under a group of trees, as close as he could get to the beach, the driver got out and went to the boot of the car. From inside he got out a pair of fisherman's boots, a jumper, an oilskin and a pair of corduroy trousers.

"Go over there into the trees and put these on. Bring your German uniform back to me."

When the doctor returned he had also dipped his head in a trickling stream and rubbed his hair clean of the black theatrical hair colouring he had used to darken it. His blond locks were not fully restored to their former glory, but he did look quite different with this new crop of fair hair.

"Look down there!" ordered the driver pointing to the beach.

It was a beach of tiny white stones and was empty except for a small rowing boat sitting upright at a gentle angle.

"That's your escape out of here."

The doctor looked at him questioningly. The driver hesitated in his delivery and asked, "Will you be able to launch it?"

The doctor thought about his watery limbs. "I don't know," he replied. "Maybe."

The driver scrutinised him and seemed to be pondering a decision, "Okay," he said finally. "Come on, I'll launch you on your way."

He took off the jacket and hat of his uniform, threw them in the car and set off down to the beach ahead of the doctor. The sun was well into the sky now and by the time they had walked across the beach to the boat the doctor was feeling the heat.

The driver checked on the oars and between them they dragged the little craft to the shoreline.

"Time for my final instructions, I think," said the doctor.

The driver pointed to his left up the coastline. "Row to the north around the headland. You will be met by a fishing craft. It's called 'Mas o Menos'. The captain is called Miguel Massanet Gomilo. They are out of Mallorca. They will set a course for Cork in Ireland. They will go about their business, which is fishing. They are not wealthy men and they need to feed their families. Also, they need to act as fishermen act and not arouse the suspicions of Axis shipping. You will have a long journey home but I am sure you will make it. They will expect you to work alongside them hauling in the nets."

The doctor nodded as the driver went on, "The captain will call out to you these words. First in Spanish he will say, 'Hola Irlandesa'. Then in English he will say, 'A cork floats well in stormy seas'. You must reply, 'An Irish cork never sinks'."

The doctor looked at the face of a man he would never see again. He was not a tall man but he had big features. His shiny, jet black hair framed a handsome face. His upper body was broad and strong. To this man, this

Spaniard with whom he had shared a life-threatening mission, there was nothing meaningful he could say. He set his oars and pulled away from the shore. The driver walked back up the beach, put on his uniform and drove away.

As he reached the headland the Mas o Menos was already rounding it towards him. The coded exchange was delivered and the doctor climbed aboard. Within twenty-four hours he was rested and fed and embarking upon a new career as an Atlantic fisherman. By the end of that same week he was landing, exhausted, at the fishing port of Cobh, just beside Cork City, Eire and emerged into the Irish daylight as Dr Sean Colquhoun, General Practitioner.

As he stepped ashore onto the concrete quay, the wild Atlantic wind whipping his blonde fringe, he caught sight of his wife, Martha standing beside their car. She was waving to him standing on tiptoe. Her strong-featured, handsome face was framed in a tightly tied headscarf, shielding her long strawberry locks from the weather. As soon as he caught sight of her, he broke into a run and did not stop until they were embracing in greeting.

He looked into her lightly freckled face and felt a strong emotion wash over him. They kissed until she broke away. In that breaking away Sean had felt the emotion drain out of him. There had been too much reluctance in Martha for him not to notice. He suddenly knew that what he had hoped for had been unrealistic; that his absence would have healed the wound and they could get back to normal. But there had been something icy about her withdrawal. It was an iciness he was all too familiar with; an iciness he knew his own deceit had helped to create.

As if reading his thoughts Martha seemed to relent and said, "Come on, I'll take you home before that pilot's eyes pop out of his head."

After his six week absence it was wonderful to hear her Irish voice again. Martha had never been overtly romantic or publicly affectionate. Sean would have liked that sometimes. But she had been passionate. She had saved her displays of passion for when they were alone and that had been Sean's absolute joy and delight. She had always had a slightly gauche, intensely private, rural manner, but it had only added to her appeal as far as Sean was concerned.

She pushed him in the chest, offered him a weak smile and walked around to the driver's door. Unlike most women of her generation, Martha Grady was an experienced driver, a skill she had acquired driving her fathers tractors on their County Clare farm. Unknown to Sean, Martha had experienced as great a disappointment as his to her reaction. She had sincerely believed that on his return the love and passion would return to overcome the resentment that had crept into their lives. She was struggling to cope with the knowledge that it had not.

Four
1936

When Sean met Martha in Dublin in late 1936, she was studying for a Bachelor of Arts Honours degree in modern languages. She was specialising in nineteenth century German theatre. A woman undergraduate in Ireland at this time was a rare specimen and as such Martha O'Grady attracted interest, particularly, but not exclusively, amongst her male acquaintances.

Sean was newly returned from Berlin where he had studied medicine at the Friedrichshain Clinic. He had been there since 1930 and was six years into his studies when he sought and achieved a transfer to complete his qualification. He had in fact achieved professional status whilst in Germany but he needed to spend two semesters at Trinity to validate his qualification. He was steadfastly reticent about his experiences there and had decided to see his return to Dublin as a new beginning.

They had first met at a tea party held by Martha's tutor. His name was Brian Hagan and he had a pretty, little, if somewhat plump, Austrian wife, Eva. Hagan was a fanatical Germanophile and his tea parties were his way of recreating a little corner of Germany within Dublin's Celtic environs. Meeting the Hagan crowd and especially Martha would help Sean create the kind of persona he wished to become.

Hagan's wife, Eva, fed the guests, usually about eight or ten in number, on sausages, sauerkraut and apple strudel. Hagan arranged these gatherings for a Saturday evening following one of his frequent trips to Frankfurt where he guest lectured at the University College. He always returned with a plentiful supply of bottled German beers, schnapps and sausages to oil the party conversation. Martha was a regular guest.

Sean first met Hagan through a colleague at the hospital, consultant, Mr James Callan. Callan had become acquainted with Hagan through his own guest lecturing in obstetrics to medical students at Trinity. Although Callan had no German connection, he and Hagan had hit it off. When James Callan mentioned to Hagan that his new colleague, Sean Colquhoun was recently returned from five years of study in Berlin, Hagan immediately fired off an invitation.

And so it was in the autumn of 1936 that Sean found himself in the dining room of a well positioned house on Grafton Street, inside a tiny German colony, immersed once again in the staccato music of the German tongue.

"Your German is flawless, Mr. Colquhoun," Hagan remarked formally.

"I never found it a problem. I took to it the moment I encountered it at school in Cork. One of our Christian Brothers, Brother Peter, was obsessed with all things German. Except Martin Luther, of course."

The company laughed heartily.

"I have to admit that six years in Berlin has helped a bit."

They laughed again.

"Forget Luther," Hagan retorted taking control of the topic. "Germany has a rich seam of Catholicism running right through its beating heart. Why Mr. Hitler himself is a devout Catholic."

And so it went on. Most evenings the party would break up by 9.30. Every so often it would drift on past that hour and a second schnapps bottle would come out. As the clock crept on past ten and the schnapps loosened tongues, the conversation would tentatively turn to the subject of Mr. Hitler and the fate of Europe. Hagan would be provocative.

"Sure he's a great man. Didn't even Ghandi say so? What better judge of character is there?"

Whenever this topic emerged, Eva would become agitated. Sean kept his counsel. The rest hooted at Hagan's parlour talk.

After his third visit to the Hagan's, Sean suspected that Martha was taking a shine to him. All the signs were there. They had been introduced on the occasion of Sean's first visit. He had enjoyed talking to her but there were no strong feelings. He'd thought her fresh-scrubbed face a little too rural and her big smile too immature. He was also intimidated as well as intrigued by her academic prowess. There was nothing unfeminine about her; quite the opposite, but she did not fit in with the other women in the company. She could lead conversations on many topics and could often dominate an argument. However, by the end of his second visit he imagined that she was looking at him whenever she thought he was distracted. He realised he was beginning to find that fresh-scrubbed face and that toothy smile quite provocative. Sean could not help remaining partially detached, whilst at the same time feeling the natural thrill of unspoken attraction. He could be immersed in the moment and, simultaneously, view it all as if watching two other people go through the motions. But he did not do anything to discourage Martha. Before long they were spending lots of time together in one to one conversations. To Sean's surprise they could talk effortlessly to infinity.

Leaving the porch one night and descending to the pavement, Sean and Martha for once found themselves alone together. Taking the plunge Martha ventured, "It's a fine, warm night. Too fine to be going home. Do you fancy a walk through the park? You can leave me at my bus stop on the far side."

Even as she was speaking Martha was wondering why she was the one to be making this move. She did not mind taking the lead but what was it within Sean that made him so reticent about moving their friendship forward. Eventually after a long moment's thought Sean replied, "That would be grand."

After that they began to meet by convenient co-incidence. It amused Sean and again he did nothing to halt the development of their relationship. He did nothing to correct the notion amongst their mutual acquaintances when it was starting to be assumed that they were a couple. He was attached elsewhere, emotionally at least, if not in reality. It was in this respect only that he was not completely open with Martha. In all of Ireland, at that time, he could think of no one he would rather spend his time with.

And so they were soon meeting on a daily basis by prior arrangement. Lunch. Tea. Supper. Whichever time suited Sean's hospital commitments best. They tried every café in Dublin. Each became obsessed with the other. Martha knew instinctively that Sean liked her. But why was he always holding back. Why did she always have to take the lead in the making of arrangements? Who was this Sean Colquhoun and why was he so damned self sufficient? How could he always give the impression that if he never saw her again that damned composure would not even be dented. If that was the case, why did he always agree to meet her and why did they have so much fun together? And why was it that his independence was so attractive to her? However, because of her own determination, the relationship was developing well. Sean always walked Martha to the door of her flat now. When they parted they kissed. Gently, formally at first. But gradually they succumbed to nature and their passion. Like all lovers before them, their kisses spoke distinct messages to each of them. Three weeks after they took their first walk through the park together, Martha made a bold move.

>"I'm preparing a meal this Saturday night," she said.

>"Who for?" asked Sean

>"You if you like," she whispered.

For a moment Sean hesitated and Martha instantly regretted her impetuosity. Her regret and embarrassment showed on her face. Sean could not help but see it and he quickly put his arms around her shoulders and said, "I'd love to."

It was something that could never have occurred had they been living in the places of their births, surrounded by family. But, as two independent students in a strange, big city, they not only had every opportunity but they were also subject to the sense of bohemian freedom and implicit danger that the city possessed.

Neither Sean nor Martha had ever considered themselves devout, but as products of early twentieth century Catholic Ireland they found themselves much too uncomfortable with the idea of contraception. The physical side of their relationship was a major proportion of the attraction between them in those days and thus it became a major source of frustration and dissatisfaction. Worries about an accident leading to a rushed wedding were a further consideration.

Out of a logic of its own it emerged that to get married seemed the only sensible thing to do. Sean had planned for none of this. It had come about the way Friday comes about at the end of the week.

To the world they were deeply in love, obsessed with each other; marriage solved so many of their practical problems. Sean had other reasons for wanting the relationship to follow convention. Convention could be conveniently slow and even though he had no doubt that to love Martha would be the best kind of life he could hope for, he knew that there was a basic reservation within him and for that he bitterly regretted deceiving her. He knew that Martha could never compensate for the loss he had endured. It was unfair to Martha to let her walk unknowingly into the mess of his emotions and the secrecy of his activities but, with determination he believed he could make her happy. There was no other happiness he could aim for. Germany had left him with doubts about the man he was and the life he had chosen. Did he have the right to take Martha unknowingly into that life?

His recent experiences in Germany had battered his self image. Love and marriage with Martha were his way of returning his life to blessed normality after the chaos he had so recently stumbled through. For himself, this relationship was perfect, but for Martha, how could that be when he was concealing so much of himself from her?

Meeting each other's families took time. There was the need for Sean to formally ask Martha's father for his permission. This was necessary despite the fact that Martha would have married Sean with or without her father's blessing. He did not refuse. He was delighted to have a doctor as a son-in-law. As a farmer it could only have been bettered if Sean had been a vet.

All the while Sean wondered if he should put a stop to the whole affair. He often believed that he would if a suitable opportunity arose. But as time drifted on, no obvious obstacle to their progress towards marriage offered itself to him and so he went along with the plans.

Then there was the wedding itself and all the attendant arrangements. Although demanding of their time, skill and patience, ultimately the whole process went smoothly. And so it was in the spring of 1937 that Martha stepped gracefully to the sound of her wedding march to stand by Sean's side, there to share their wedding vows. Their first son, Cornelius (after Martha's father), was even then beginning to grow within her.

Five

1938

"Will there be war do you think?"

The question came from James Callan and he addressed it to the assembled company in Brian Hagan's dining room. It was the evening of March 13, 1938 only one day after German troops had marched into Austria and united it to Germany as a province. Hitler, who had accompanied his troops, had received a rapturous welcome, particularly on his home ground of Linz.

Hagan had somehow acquired some small red, black and white Nazi flags boasting swastikas and had bedecked his mantelpiece with them celebrating the "Anschluss" with Austria. He grasped his wine glass as he stood up from the table, thus signalling to his guests that they might adjourn with their drinks to the sitting room where schnapps and cigars lay waiting. As they moved between rooms the question hung in the air.

"Never in a million years," Hagan finally responded as he lowered himself into his favourite armchair. "Herr Hitler is much too clever for that."

"What do you mean by that, Brian?"

It was Martha Colquhoun, who submitted the follow-up enquiry as they settled themselves around the blazing fire. Hagan almost successfully erased the smug look stealing onto his face, but not quite. He settled himself deep into his armchair and looked at the faces of his guests – all awaiting his expert response. There was James Callan, senior consultant in paediatrics at Dublin University Hospital. Probably Dublin's most eligible bachelor, and a man who had proven himself in the troubled twenties. A patriot and hero of the Anglo–Irish War and the subsequent bloody Civil War.

There was Martha and her husband Sean. Martha, was attending her first Hagan soiree since the birth of her son; Martha Grady of pure Irish rural stock; a child of the Catholic landowning class; the repository of Ireland's future; Martha of the County Clare Grady's; niece of Patrick Grady, trusted lieutenant of Michael Collins himself. And her husband Sean, the son of a man who had fought alongside De Valera at the Dublin Bakery in 1916 and now an official of Fianna Fail. Sean Colquhoun, reputed to be a veteran of the Anglo-Irish war, though this was something he refused to confirm or deny.

Beside them he saw Martin Beatty and his glamorous wife Peggy. Martin and Peggy were both in their early 50s but Peggy had retained her youthful looks and health. Martin was a junior minister in De Valera's new administration. He had allowed the Guinness and the whisky to expand his figure. His suit jacket rolled around his rotund waist like a sail before the wind. His beetroot complexion could not hide the handsome face of his youth or the ready smile that preceded his generous laughter. His portfolio was currently education and as such he was an important contact for Hagan to cultivate. Hagan's most recent visit to Germany had seen him return full of enthusiasm for Nazi education policy. He had reported to Martin on the amazingly rapid re-writing of children's reading books that had been carried out to incorporate Nazi attitudes and to inspire children with admiration for Germany's Nazi leaders. Martin had been very keen to introduce this approach to the Irish education system. He wanted to be the man to successfully inculcate Catholicism and republicanism amongst Ireland's fledgling readers. Martin had been a supporter of De Valera throughout the Civil War and had suffered politically during the years of Dev's exile. He was reaping his reward for loyalty now that De Valera was back in favour and back in office. He was ambitious and he wanted to make a name for himself. The significance of the connection between Beatty and Hagan was mutually advantageous.

Like the rest of the company, Beatty was an implacable enemy of England, or the British Empire as they sometimes referred to it. Having experienced first hand the brutality and evil of the British army abroad in their own home towns, villages and cities they were reluctant to be swayed by England's denunciations of Hitler's Germany. How could it possibly be as evil as the British Empire? Most of those present could recount an incident involving the infamous Black and Tans. None of them could stomach morality preached at them by England.

The only exception to this was Sean Colquhoun. Sean was indeed a republican and also an Irish nationalist and a fierce supporter of Irish independence from British rule. He also believed in a united Ireland and accepted that Northern Ireland was a bastard state and an example of Britain's reluctance to release any of its dominions from subjugation to its control. But Sean had had his views re-positioned by his first hand experience of living under a Nazi administration in Germany during his time at the Freidrichshain Clinic in Berlin. The sight of the little swastikas in Hagan's apartment had put Sean into a bad mood; made him sick to his stomach in fact. However, Sean had good reason not to voice his views in this company. Reasons he could not tell them. Reasons he had not even told his wife.

The company was completed by two of Hagan's university colleagues and their wives plus Father O'Shea, a man from County Clare and known to Martha from her home village. Father O'Shea was returning from a visit to Rome and had contacted Martha on his way through Dublin to renew their acquaintance. O'Shea had a welcome delay before being transferred by the Church to Cork to take up his placement as curate at Sacred Heart Parish. Hagan had been delighted to add him to the guest list.

Six

Brendan O'Shea had been born in Birmingham. His father was an immigrant building worker from Galway. His mother, from Catholic Derry, had moved to Birmingham along with two of her sisters. They had found work in Birmingham's outdoor market selling fresh fruit and vegetables. Brendan's mother, Mary Clinton, had supplemented her meagre earnings by working as a barmaid at the Birmingham Catholic Men's Club. It was here that she met Brendan's father.

Arthur O'Shea turned up at the club every Friday and Saturday night. After a long week on the buildings he would bathe and shave and dress in his best blue suit, grease his hair and set off for a night of drinking and good Irish company. He was a humorous, charmer of a man and he found it easy to chat with women. In the male environment of the club Mary stood out like a beacon. Arthur was drawn to her and would spend many an hour propping up the bar chatting to her and cracking jokes as she served the members. They would also encounter each other at mass on Sundays. It did not take Arthur long to ask Mary to go out to a dance with him.

They first met for an official date outside the Assembly Ballrooms in Sparkbrook. They were married in February 1908. Brendan was born in March 1910.

The news of the death of Arthur's uncle in County Clare in 1915 at first seemed nothing more than a sad reflection back to a former life. But when three weeks later news arrived of the will Uncle Michael had written reached Birmingham, Mary and Brendan could hardly believe it when Arthur told them both the news.

"I'm to be a farmer," he cried. He danced a jig in his bare feet and he swept Mary and Brendan into his arms.

"What on earth are you talking about?" asked Mary.

But Arthur was into his thoughts.

"That'll show the bastards. That'll show the Galway bastards!" And through the wide-eyed laughter Mary and Brendan perceived a venomous contortion in his expression.

"Arthur," insisted Mary. "Please tell us what is going on."

So Arthur explained. As a young boy Arthur had been shipped out of his family home in Galway to become an unpaid helper at his Uncle Michael's farm in County Clare. Uncle Michael and Aunty Peggy had had no children. Managing an Irish farm without children was as difficult as it was unusual. Arthur had interpreted the move as a rejection by his own parents and family but, thanks in some small measure to his aunt and uncle he recovered. He developed a fake outer shell. When his homesickness receded he had made a deliberate decision to shut his parents, brothers and sister out of his mind. In their own way Uncle Michael and Aunty Peggy loved him like parents and he came to respect them and appreciate their goodness.

When he reached the age of fifteen his own parents woke up to the notion that if they left Arthur with his aunt and uncle they might do something ridiculous – like leaving the farm to him. Arthur's parents had always assumed that, in the fullness of time the farm of the childless couple, who were considerably older than themselves, would come to them. To remove him as a rival for this inheritance they suddenly decided that they had better whisk him back to Galway.

Arthur once again found himself torn away from the comfort of his home and the relationships he had forged. He was desperately unhappy, more so than he had been to be sent away in the first place. He bitterly resented his parents and his siblings. They were strangers to him but strangers with the power to make life changing decisions over him. At first he had blazing rows with his parents and vicious fights with his brothers. Later he learned the trick of switching off his emotions. He took pride in the fact that there was nothing they could do to enrage him; at least not on the outside. He may burn with anger inside, but outwardly he laughed in the faces of his tormentors.

He learned to mimic the people he judged the happiest and most successful and cultivated an air of confidence. He became the convincing charmer who would woo and marry Mary. Inside, however, the storm continued.

On the day of his sixteenth birthday he woke at the crack of dawn. He slipped a chunk of bacon and a loaf of bread inside his coat. He went out to the barn and collected the bag of clothes he had hidden there the night before and he set off to walk to Dublin. In two weeks time he arrived in Birmingham.

"The farm is mine. Uncle Michael has died. He's left the farm to me. It's ours."

Thus, Birmingham born Brendan was destined to grow up in County Clare. The boy who might have been a city bred Englishman instead became a farm bred Clare man.

Brendan was seven when his father first abused him. His mother was away in Birmingham. Her oldest sister, Betty, had died and she was attending the funeral and spending some time with her other sister, Catherine. It was the third night of her absence when Arthur came back from the village dead drunk. Brendan had put himself to bed and was asleep when his father woke him from his dream and used him.

Arthur experienced almost unbearable guilt following this act as he did following every subsequent repetition. But once he had crossed the line he could not stop satisfying himself at the expense of his son whenever he was drunk. It did not take much to frighten his son as to what might happen if he ever told anyone about their secret times together. Some perversity of thinking caused Arthur to believe that his son was in need of penance. To achieve this for his son he insisted that Brendan become an altar boy. Arthur took Brendan to the church and asked Father Haggerty to take Brendan under his wing. When Father Haggerty began his own serial abuse of Brendan, the boy could come to no conclusion other than it was normal behaviour.

When Brendan entered early adolescence he did not see himself as calculating but it was not a coincidence that with his proclivities he unconsciously endeavoured to conceal them by working to develop female friendships. It was thus that he cultivated an acquaintance with Martha Grady, the serious-looking tom-boy from the Grady farm that lay seven or eight miles away beside the coast. Neither of them would consider their friendship close, but there were days when they came across each other and tagged along side by side over the fields and streams, looking for trout to tickle or haystacks to climb. Martha found herself easy in his company. Although physically well-developed by the age of twelve she was not sexually mature by any means. There was something about Brendan that seemed to free her from the self-consciousness she felt when in the company of other boys. So it was, years later, when they met again in Dublin, Martha was delighted to renew her acquaintance with this boy from her childhood.

Brendan's relationship to Father Haggerty became the closest in his life and it became the determining factor in his decision to aim for the priesthood.

Brendan began his own abusive behaviour at the age of thirteen. By this time he was the senior altar boy in the parish and responsible for instructing the other boys in the procedures and routines of the mass and benediction and the rites of marriage and burial. He began to be able to spot and develop likely victims. He was eighteen when a parent first complained about him to Father Haggerty. This time Brendan had miscalculated in his choice of victim and the distressed boy had rushed straight home and told his mother how Brendan O'Shea had played with his private parts. Brendan had denied the whole thing and Father Haggerty had told the woman to go away and pray for forgiveness and give her sick-minded son a good telling off. For good measure he gave her a penance of two 'Our Fathers' and three 'Hail Marys'. The woman went off soundly rebuked and very confused.

Meanwhile however, Father Haggerty realised that they had had a close call. He arranged for Brendan to enter a seminary in Athlone, many miles away. Thus did Brendan's decision to study for the priesthood finally come to pass.

It was a complaint by a fellow seminarian in the last year of Brendan's training for ordination that led to him being transferred to Rome to complete his studies. Brendan, despite continuing his abusive activities whenever the opportunities arose, developed a sound reputation amongst the clergy he came into contact with. Although rumours inevitably emerged around him, Brendan was protected by the unshakeable reluctance amongst the clergy to entertain thoughts of such matters.

Seven

"Herr Hitler has a bigger world view than his detractors," continued Hagan, slipping comfortably into an argument he had used many times before. "Look at Italy and Germany; look at Spain – soon to be under Franco's fascist leadership; look at the rise of the fascist right in France. Look, for goodness sake at the welcome Hitler has received in Austria. You've only got to look at England and the rise of Mosley. Mark my words, in our lifetime all of Western Europe will be part of a prosperous and powerful fascist concert. Mosley will be Prime Minister and Edward VIII will be restored to the throne. Now the crucial power is America and in less than two years there will be a presidential election there. And who's going to win that? Charles Lindbergh, that's who! His running mate will be Joseph Kennedy, an open admirer of Hitler and an implacable enemy of that warmonger, Churchill. Lindbergh is a holder of the Iron Cross presented to him by Hitler himself and he's already campaigning on a pro-Germany platform," he paused for breath.

"The point I am making is that Hitler knows there is no need for war. In a few short years the democracies will crumble of their own accord. We all know they are rotten to the core. England and its empire is ripest of all. Just waiting to collapse in upon itself. Calls itself a democracy yet an aristocracy owns ninety-nine percent of all wealth and fiercely excludes other sectors of the community from power with its public schools and old boy network. And what about the British Empire? Well we don't even have to leave this room to find first-hand evidence of the brutality and murder practised by that so-called democracy. Murderers and robbers wherever they went; India, Africa, the Middle East."

Hagan paused in his soliloquy as he went about the room replenishing glasses and offering cigars to the men. He had loosened his tie about his broad neck and he wiped a bead of sweat from his red brow with the forearm of his shirt.

"I can feel the tide of history rising up to carry us forward," he continued. "Soon the democracies will fall apart and the fresh face of fascism will spread its sunlight into all nations. The world will then no longer be held hostage by corrupt Jewish finance systems – nor will we be corrupted by Jewish and Negro art forms. What need of war when the tide of history is running your way?"

Hagan sat back, immensely pleased with himself, with his company and with the way history was unfolding just as he expected it to. His plump wife, Eva swished across the room to him, leaving a whiff of expensive perfume in her wake and sat proudly beside him on the arm of his chair.

As the company sipped their schnapps, Father O'Shea shifted slightly in his seat and then spoke up.

"I wonder," he said hesitantly, "...I mean, I get the drift of your antagonism towards modern art. God knows it's almost beyond comprehension and also often downright obscene. And I accept what you are saying about the hypocrisy of states like Britain criticising others as uncivilised when we all know what crimes she has committed. But... I wonder... I mean I've never understood the point about Jewish financiers ruling the world in a great big conspiracy. I'm sure I know a lot more poor Jews than rich ones and I just don't see where that's coming from. When I was in Italy I saw none of the anti-Semitism there that we hear from Mr Hitler. And no one can deny Mussolini's fascist credentials. In fact he led where Hitler followed."

Sean pricked up his ears at this careful contribution from O'Shea. This was the kind of Catholicism he thought he had been raised in. Looking at O'Shea, Sean realised he had committed his usual act of bias and dismissed O'Shea as a non-person until now. He found he often did this with priests. It was as if their celibacy removed them from the arena of true human interaction. As O'Shea spoke, Sean studied him and tried to stop himself thinking here was the waste of a good man.

Most of the company shifted uncomfortably in their seats. Eva got up from the arm of Hagan's chair with an irritated shuffle and began fussing with a cheese board at the sideboard. This was a subject the company preferred to take as read; a subject that had to be dealt with but not thought about too much.

O'Shea sensed the discomfort he had caused and shrank back into his chair. Hagan let out a laugh. A warm, comradely laugh aimed at dispelling the atmosphere that O'Shea's question had created.

"Now then, Father," Hagan said reassuringly. "Like a good man of the cloth you are always prepared to think the best of people. But you must not be hoodwinked by your Christian principles into allowing evil to prosper. Suffice to say that in serious quarters it is no longer disputed that the murderers of Our Lord and Saviour," and here he blessed himself, causing the rest of the company to do likewise, "control banking throughout the western world. Where they don't do it openly with their names above the door, so to speak, they do it secretly, pulling the strings of dupes and knaves from behind their conspiratorial cloaks. And yes, we know there are poor Jews. But to a man, woman and child they are a hard-hearted breed. Whatever disparagement they suffer they bring upon themselves. Which other race so hard-heartedly refuses to welcome the Saviour into their hearts? And that Saviour predicted by their own scriptures. It is a wilful, sinful, hard-heartedness."

Sean squirmed as Hagan patronised the young priest.

O'Shea was cowed and nodded in agreement. It was not an alien thought to him that the Jew denied the divinity of Jesus Christ out of sheer hard-heartedness. Maybe that carried over into their business dealings. He was content to concede to Hagan.

Sean was disappointed that O'Shea did not take up the argument, but his opinion of the young priest remained decidedly improved. The rest of the company were pleased to let this distasteful subject drop. The conversation went on to consider the resurgence of Germany under the Nazi party and the relative merits of Hitler and Mussolini. The inevitable success of Franco's rebellion was also discussed, as was the fabulous reception Hitler received from the Austrians following his pre-emptive surge across the border.

Later on, Martin Beatty brought them back to James Callan's original question, "If I understand what you're saying Brian, then your real answer to James' question is that we are already at war. The democracies are in a fight for survival in the face of the successful rise of fascism."

"Exactly," pounced Hagan. "And let's not forget – my enemy's misfortune is my opportunity. Everyone here knows who our inherent enemy is – England. While England struggles to survive we can grasp a powerful advantage. No one in this room has forgotten that we still do not have a united Ireland. We could be on the threshold of momentous times."

"But," came back Beatty, "are we not one of the democracies, and if so are we not therefore also under threat from rising fascism?"

"Ah, but there is the beauty of Ireland's position. We hover between democracy and theocracy. We are a fledgling state. We are at the birth of our freedom. We are flexible enough to move with the times. We have a Blueshirt movement of our own growing in numbers and confidence every day."

"Wait a minute," said Beatty. "The Blueshirts are a bunch of dangerous jokers. Most of them have criminal records. They couldn't hold the end of an ass' rope, never mind the reins of power."

"That's what they were saying about Hitler's Brownshirts not so long ago. Mark my words. Anyway, look no further than Spain. Franco will inevitably win his crusade and overthrow the degenerate Republican Government with its scandalous policies. Legalised divorce, abortions, men no longer the bosses in their own homes – I ask you. What would Mother Church say to that in Ireland, Father? Catholic Ireland will mirror Catholic Spain. We will evolve into a theocratic dictatorship."

It was here that Sean made his one contribution of the evening to the political discussion.

"Franco is illegally attempting to overthrow a legitimate republican government. I thought we were all republicans here."

"We are indeed republicans, Sean. But there are new kinds of republics coming into being in this revolutionary age we live in."

"So," came back Beatty, "Would you have us align ourselves with Hitler and the dictatorships and work towards the collapse of the western democracies?"

"I would," retorted Hagan. "And don't we have the ideal motive and opportunity? We are not long out of a state of war with England. We have won our independence by force of arms. We have given the world's mightiest empire a bloody nose. Now we have men willing and easily armed, who will carry the fight to the heart of their cities. We also have who knows how many loyal Irish men and women living and working in every British town and city. We could be their Trojan horse."

As they walked home to their apartment across the Liffey, just north of O'Connell Street, Sean and Martha were out of sorts with each other.

"What was the matter with you tonight?" asked Martha, obviously irritated. To her it was that secret, independent Sean that so irritated, yet so attracted her.

"What do you mean?"

"Well you hardly spoke a word to anyone and when you did it was that silly comment about republicans."

"I don't think it was a silly comment. Men and women have fought and died over many centuries for the cause of republicanism in this country."

"Yes, but it was obvious in your tone. You were annoyed. It sounded spiteful, as if you were just trying to make Brian look silly."

"Make Brian look silly? I'd have to be very good to do a better job than he does himself."

Martha stopped in her tracks, causing Sean to halt and turn to look at her. He put his hands in his pockets and shrugged against the cold. Martha looked perplexed. She walked to catch him up, staring at him.

"What's the matter, Sean? You sound odd. I thought you liked Brian. He's been a good friend to us."

Sean seemed about to speak, then as if he had second thoughts he pulled his hands out of his pockets and put an arm round Martha's shoulder.

"Come here," he said. "We are not going to argue about this."

Martha did not relax into his embrace.

"I don't want to argue either. But I don't understand why there is a Sean Colquhoun that I don't know. I am your wife. I don't want to be able to read your mind but this feeling of not knowing you is growing more and more uncomfortable. We've been a part of Brian's German group for a long time now. Why, that's where we met! I always thought we were like-minded about Germany. I thought we shared adult views that could see through the vicious propaganda coming out of London. But I just sense you haven't been wholly honest with me."

"Look," Sean sighed. "There's nothing to discuss. You know I'm a Germanophile every bit as much as the others."

"But," urged Martha. "There's an unsaid 'but' in your sentence."

"But," hesitated Sean.

They stood face to face, close to the base of Nelson's column. Sean seemed to be searching for something elusive in Martha's face. Some empathy that would give him the confidence to speak his thoughts. 'She's my wife,' he was thinking. 'She has to know.'

"But," went on Sean, "I have lived in Germany. I saw the rise of Hitler. I watched Nazism take power. I lived beside the people and I saw what it did. I'm sure of one thing; I could never live under Nazism. I am also sure it is a far worse evil than Britain ever was. Brian is a dangerous fool. Dangerous because he has influence. Martin Beatty sits at his feet as if he is some kind of sage. And Martin Beatty has the ear of De Valera, God help us!"

Martha was dumbfounded for a moment.

"Sean, I am shocked," she said eventually. "I never guessed you felt like this. I am also hurt. Why have you not shared this with me before? I'm your wife! It's as if you have hidden your real self from me. It's not that your views upset me. What I can't understand is why you've kept them secret. Nobody has to agree with Brian and his opinion of Hitler, but it is as if you have pretended to do so. If you feel this way why don't you come out and say so. Your experience is the most valid of everyone in that group. They would listen to you. Why Sean? You're not a deceitful person so why deceive me over this? Why do you allow them to believe you are pro Nazi – because that's what they infer from your silence? And why did I not know this about you until now?"

She turned away from him to hide the tears that were filling her eyes. Sean put his arm around her again and said, "Come on now. This is not the time. We're tired and we've been drinking. Let's go home. We can talk again in the morning."

But the next morning they ate breakfast in silence.

Eight
1942

From his office window high above the Thames, Andrew Trubshaw could survey the damage inflicted by the previous night's Luftwaffe raid. Down river he could take in the Palace of Westminster and, later that day, he knew he had an appointment with the Prime Minister to update him on the Norwegian project that he was currently running.

He watched for a few moments as a young woman in her twenties, face smudged with dirt and a toddler on her hip, picked her way over smoking rubble searching for something. Reluctantly, he turned back to his desk and picked up the internal telephone.

"Mrs Kitson, please bring me everything we have on the following two subjects; One, Lily Brett, works at Leicester Royal Infirmary. You could look under enemy aliens. Two, detective inspector Peter Herbert of Leicester City Police Force."

He replaced the telephone in its cradle.

Large-framed and loose-limbed Trubshaw gave off an air of casual indifference. His boyish face exaggerated this demeanour. However, when he set to work he was transformed into a well-focused and decisive man of action. Mrs Kitson was not the only female won over by this endearing trait. Within minutes she entered and placed two files in front of him.

"There you are, Sir. Would you like a cup of tea to accompany your reading?" she asked.

"You're a mind reader, Mrs Kitson. And a couple of biscuits if we have any."

"Of course, Sir." She then added, "I recognised the name Lily Brett when you said it. She has passed across my desk recently. I have slipped a note inside the file informing you of our knowledge of her."

"Thank you Mrs Kitson. You are amazing."

Two hours later, a cold cup of tea left forgotten at his elbow, Trubshaw closed the second of the files and leaned back into his armchair. In front of him a coal fire crackled healthily but it produced insufficient heat in the large office to persuade Trubshaw to remove his suit jacket.

After a moment's pensive hesitation, he leaned forward and picked up the note Mrs Kitson had left in the file. A paper clip attached it to the letter Lily Brett had sent to the War Office volunteering her services to the Government. He reached for the internal phone and spoke to Mrs Kitson.

"Mrs Kitson, will you please reserve a seat for me on the morning train to Leicester. Get me a compartment on my own if you can. One at about 10:00am. I'm seeing the P.M. this afternoon. After that, cancel all of my appointments for one week. I will speak to you from Leicester tomorrow evening with an emergency contact number." He then swapped phones and dialled.

"Trubshaw here. Yes. My number is 4967E and my codeword is Derwent."

There was a short silence as the security codes were verified.

"All correct, Mr Trubshaw. How can we help?"

"I need one of our agents to get some information out of Germany. I need information on subject Lily Brett, formerly Brecht. Her father was a member of the Reichstag until the Nazi takeover. I will have her file transferred to you. It contains all we have on her. My question is, can we take her as genuine? If not, is she a sleeper?"

"How urgent is this request, Sir?"

"Well," replied Trubshaw sarcastically. "If the war ends tomorrow you can put it on a back burner. If not, I'd like your reply yesterday."

"Got you, Sir."

The Coach and Horses was a large rambling inn containing a warren of tiny rooms. Men only; ladies only; skittles; a bar with darts and dominoes being played; a music room with a tinkling piano rattling out songs about Hitler; and a snug; a lounge where the clientele spoke in quieter tones. The rooms were linked by a maze of corridors, themselves filled with uniformed soldiers, Home Guard members, and Air raid wardens. The atmosphere, although just this side of manic, was not in the least threatening. Laughter peeled out, cutting through the thick blue smoke that had filled the whole interior from the ceiling down.

Trubshaw elbowed his way to the bar and ordered his pint of foaming bitter. Pint in hand he withdrew to a relatively peaceful corner of an end room. He took his raincoat off and removed a crumpled newspaper from one of its pockets. As he pretended to read he paid close attention to detective inspector Peter Herbert. He had followed Herbert from the central police station on Charles Street when he had come off duty. In the gathering dusk and the faint but persistent drizzle, Herbert had ignored the bus stops close to the station and headed left, over the steel bridge on Swain Street at the back of the railway station on foot. Trubshaw kept a steady distance behind Herbert, even as he disappeared within a swirling belch of steam from a train passing below the bridge. As the steam cleared, there was

Herbert treading wearily up the cobblestone hill towards the inner city suburb of Evington.

When he stopped at the gate to the garden of his small semi-detached house Trubshaw walked on by. Herbert did not notice him. He was engrossed in a rose bush beside the gate that was beginning to flower. From the next corner Trubshaw watched Herbert enter his house and saw lights coming on. He knew he might have quite a wait and that he would become quite conspicuous if he continued to hang around this corner. Net curtains would start to twitch. Fortunately, he saw that half way down the next block there was a bus stop. There is nothing suspicious about a man standing at a bus stop, and from there he would still have a clear view of Herbert's house.

He waited an hour. Luckily, in that time only one bus came. He saw it from a fair distance and managed to contrive to miss it by disappearing around the nearest corner until it had passed.

Eventually, Herbert re-emerged and walked off towards the Coach and Horses. Trubshaw tailed him long enough to be sure where he was and then hot-footed back to the Herbert domicile to further his enquiries.

For a police officer, who should have had a keen awareness of crime and crime prevention, Herbert's house was a very easy nut to crack, especially for an experienced burglar such as Trubshaw. As he let himself in through the back door he reflected that the skills he had acquired at the hands of his Secret Service trainers were much more practically useful than anything he had learned at Cambridge.

The smells of cooking lingered. Trubshaw guessed that Herbert had eaten liver and onions for tea. It was a lonely smell; loneliness echoed in the sight of the single plate, knife, fork and cup lying clean and upturned on the draining board.

Trubshaw was not altogether sure why he was burgling the house of a detective inspector of the local constabulary. He knew that he had always been a belt and braces man. He also knew that "research" was always his favourite part of the job. Lily Brett's house was the one he really needed to search. But he would do that later.

By now he was entering Herbert's bedroom. Like the other rooms it had a bachelor's Spartan quality. A single bed, neatly made, stood in one corner. Diagonally opposite there was an old wardrobe. Inside there hung one dark blue suit, quite worn, and four white shirts. There were two built-in cupboards, chest high, filling two alcoves. In the first there was a gas meter and a bottle of whisky. In the other there were socks folded in pairs, underwear, some letters, several packets of photographs and a scrapbook. The scrapbook caused Trubshaw's eyebrows to rise on his forehead. The first page was a large portrait of Oswald Moseley. The rest of the book recorded incidents in the progress of the British Union of Fascists. There were newspaper and magazine articles and pictures. Occasionally, in the margins, there were annotations in what Trubshaw guessed was Herbert's precise hand.

September rally, East Hampstead – I am just out of picture to right of pillar box.

Leicester march – you can just see me four rows behind the leader. I am on duty today, getting paid for guarding the Leader

Birmingham – just before the communists attacked us. They certainly got the worst of it.

Trubshaw closed the book and carefully placed it back on its shelf. He was sufficiently satisfied to conclude his search of Herbert's house. What he had discovered was not conclusive in any way about Herbert. However, it gave Trubshaw two things. One, he now had a good grasp of Herbert's character; solitary, lonely, slightly obsessive, attracted to extremism. Two, it gave him an excellent lever over Herbert should he need one. A serving police officer with secret membership of the British Union of Fascists had broken his disciplinary code, could be dismissed from the force and would forfeit his pension rights.

Trubshaw finished his pint and folded up his damp newspaper. All the time he had been there Herbert had sat alone. The only person who had spoken to him had been the waitress, who from time to time replenished his whisky glass. Trubshaw put on his overcoat and walked out into the night. He had another burglary to complete before he returned to his hotel.

Lily Brett's house on Dronfield Street was one of those tiny terraced houses in an endless row of identical houses that Trubshaw had rarely been inside. It was just as easy for him to gain entry as before. The atmosphere, however, was entirely different. Of the two houses, although this one was a lot further down the social scale, it was the one Trubshaw would have preferred to stay in or visit.

He could relax into his search of Lily's house as he knew she was not going to escape from Leicester Prison and disturb him. His first approach was to look for any of the obvious possessions an enemy agent would be likely to have. He started in the small, dank cellar and systematically made his way into the rooftop attic. He missed nothing. He looked under floorboards; he investigated ceiling spaces. He went from the butter basin in the pantry to the fireplaces in the bedrooms. He moved all free-standing cupboards, peered into the lavatory cistern and shone his torch around the inside of the cooker. When he had finished he was satisfied there was not a space he had not investigated. He had found no wireless transmitter/receiver; no weaponry; no code books; no unlikely messages.

However, there were several items of interest, although he did not consider them incriminating. First of all, and the one that engaged him the most, was again a scrap book filled to bursting. It had a beautifully embossed hard cover and thick extravagant pages that were filled with letters, photographs and newspaper cuttings. As he handled it he had the feeling that he was in possession of something extremely precious. Turning the pages he saw unfolding before him, the lives of Lily and her father.

At first there were the pictures of Herr Brecht and his pretty young bride Renate Hofmann. Easter, 1907, in the tiny church at Pirna in Saxony; with family and friends beside the Elbe, celebrating the wedding breakfast; Herr Martin Brecht in the grounds of Dresden University, where he was studying Classics, standing beside Renate; another outside the university library where Renate worked. Other pages showed the christening of Friedrich, Lily's older brother and later of Lily herself. Later, the scrapbook would reveal to Trubshaw much more about the Brecht family history.

There were pictures of homes and gardens and holiday outings. Then, unusually, there was a picture of a gravestone. The engraving was clear and it showed two names. Trubshaw decided to steal the scrap book and take it with him for closer inspection.

Back in his room in the Grand Hotel, close to Leicester's Clock Tower centre, Trubshaw sat at a mahogany desk to make notes.

Martin Brecht, born 1886 in Luckan in the province of Niederlauritz - Small town

Father is local doctor

Moved to Dresden to study Classics at the university October 1904

Met and married Renate Hoffmann Easter 1907

Renate is from Pirna - Small town on the River Elbe in Saxony

Father is local doctor

Common factors - small town natives in the big city for first time – both children of doctors – similarities in backgrounds may have first attracted Martin and Renate to each other?

Friedrich born August 1908

Martin graduates and accepts post at Munich University as lecturer in Classics.

Lily born in Munich 1914

Martin recruited into army 1916. Distinguished record. Wounded in action. Decorated. Discharged on compassionate grounds January 1918 due to death of wife and son.

Notes suggest Renate and Friedrich killed in accident whilst travelling to Freiburg in Alsace to visit Renate's dying mother. No information about how Renate's mother (Lily's grandmother) had ended up living in Freiburg.

1918 Martin returns to his post in Munich. Brings up his daughter alone. Does not re-marry.

Promoted to professor of Classics, Munich University, 1926

Enters Reichstag, 1928 as Social Democrat

Admitted to Berlin hospital 1931 with ruptured spleen and broken ribs following a vicious assault by SA Brownshirts after he delivered a stinging attack on Hitler and his Nazi party and the deals that he believed the Wiemar authorities were making with them

1933 Hitler comes to power

1934 Martin Brecht and his daughter Lily leave Germany and set up home temporarily in Northern France before being granted asylum in England in 1936.

1937 Martin Brecht dies in Leicester Royal Infirmary – the result of the damage to his spleen which had never fully recovered.

The Clock Tower bell chimed one in the morning and Trubshaw sat back in his chair tossing his pencil onto the pages of his notebook.

"Here's a woman with every reason to hate the Nazis," he mused aloud as he undressed.

With a mental note to himself to introduce himself to Herbert, interview Lily and then get seriously drunk with his old mate, John Barberis, he settled his plan for tomorrow before falling into a deep sleep.

Nine
1928

Sean Colquhoun had been a celebrity of sorts back in his student days in Dublin. It was 1928 and he had come up to Trinity from his home town of Cork to study medicine. He was in his twenty-sixth year having been distracted from his career ambitions for sometime by his involvement as a soldier in the Anglo-Irish War. His aim though, had always been to become a General Practitioner and return to Cork. Their own local family doctor, Dr Townley, had hinted very strongly that he would be needing an assistant doctor in his practice in a few years time and eventually, of course, that could lead to a partnership. Dr Townley was no fool. A young man with Coquhoun's reputation as a patriot and a fine republican would enhance the attraction of their practice immeasurably

Sean took to university life like a duck to water. Although Trinity had opened its doors to Catholics as long ago as 1794, the nature of Irish society under British rule had been such that few Catholics had ever been able to afford the cost of tuition there. Thus when Sean entered those hallowed gates he was not just a new fresher, but a representative of the new independent Catholic Ireland. Being a novelty he attracted attention, and being an attractive personality he soon found himself at the centre of a large circle of friends. He had been a star Hurley player as a junior, when his soldiering had allowed, but in Trinity there was only one prestige sport for an ambitious student to play, and that was rugby.

He was a natural athlete and before Christmas at the end of the first semester he was a regular in the first fifteen. This was unheard of in college rugby club annals and although his age obviously helped him, it was still quite a feat to break into the clique that surrounded the first fifteen. A great future in the game was predicted for him. His sporting prowess made him a very popular man. It also gave him the opportunity to travel to other college cities in Ireland and the other parts of the British Isles to play rugby fixtures. This success and experience of travel gave Sean the confidence to widen his horizons and when a notice appeared on the medical students news board that applications were invited from first year students to transfer their studies to Berlin University he went straight back to his rooms and wrote a letter of application. He was not the only applicant and there were rumours around Trinity Green that Sean Colquhoun would never get the placement. As if Trinity would let its best ever rugby prospect disappear to a non-rugby playing country. Some hopes!

Despite such rumours, by Easter 1929 Sean knew that he was going to be moving to Berlin the following September.

Back home in Cork he received mixed responses to his decision. Brother Peter of the Christian Brothers was delighted. They spent many afternoons together going over Brother Peter's own experiences there as a young man before the Great War. He had been a regular visitor there ever since and spent several weeks each year at a Catholic convent in Munich. His enthusiasm for German culture and the German people was such that Sean's desire to go grew and grew. Between them Sean and Brother Peter only spoke German, which was to serve as a refresher course for Sean. Brother Peter gave him a contact name and address for when he had settled in Berlin. It was for one Hugo Strasser, a long time friend of Brother Peter. They had shared rooms together in Berlin in 1910 when Peter was studying for the priesthood and Hugo was a philosophy student.

Sean Colquhoun emerged from the bustling Alexanderplatz railway station into the middle of a packed and noisy Berlin. He stood with his back against the brick façade, dwarfed by the recently constructed majestic vaulted roof of this magnificent terminal building, away from the surging river of humanity and watched in awe.

His blood surged with excitement and his eyes could not feast greedily enough on the vision that lay before him. His nostrils filled with the scents of Germany, in this year of 1929, of coffee and onions and pickle, so sweet, so enticing and so alien to the scents of his homeland. Brother Peter had filled his head with expectations and his heart with longing but nothing could have prepared him for the vista that was now spread out before him. Here he was in the midst of the beautiful, beating heart of a struggling but vibrant Germany and he was staggered to comprehend that it had all been going on without him and for so long.

He was awakened from his reverie by the touch of a hand on his arm. He jumped slightly and turned to look at the stranger.

"Brother Peter describes you well," said the man in an aristocratic German accent. "Forgive me but you are Sean Colquhoun and I am Hugo Strasser. I am delighted to welcome you to the Fatherland and Berlin, our capital city."

Sean recovered himself and reached out to take the man's offered hand. They exchanged a vigorous handshake and then Hugo said, "Come on, the car is here. There are people waiting to meet you."

Hugo gestured towards an enormous, shiny Mercedes Benz that stood beside the pavement. Sean reached down to pick up his suitcase but Hugo beat him to it and headed off with it towards the vehicle. A driver jumped out of the front seat as they approached and relieved Hugo of the case. The two men climbed inside the car and as soon as the driver had deposited the case they drove away into the traffic.

Strasser, like Brother Peter, was in his mid to late thirties, but he welcomed Sean with all the enthusiasm of a first year student meeting his room mate for the first time.

"If you are a friend of Peter's, you are like family to us, Sean. With your blonde hair you have a touch of the Aryan in you, but your ruddy complexion made it easy for me to identify the Irishman on Alexanderplatz."

Sean watched the avenues and boulevards flick past until they arrived at a large house in the Berlin suburb of Wansee. A boy opened the gates as the car approached and the driver crunched up the gravel to the front door.

By the end of his first evening, Sean had met Hugo's wife, the stunningly beautiful Magda Strasser and her parents Josef and Anna. They had treated him like one of the family and Sean could imagine himself recounting his experiences to his own family of the generous and unselfish kindness of these Germans towards a lonely Irish boy adrift in Berlin. He could almost hear his mothers "Ah, God bless them," as she heard his tale.

He also met Maximillian Schneider. Max worked at the Friedrichshain clinic and was going to be Sean's immediate superior at the hospital. Sean liked Max immediately. He was open and funny. His humour was often self-deprecating and he was a good listener too. He seemed genuinely interested in Sean and asked him to describe growing up in Ireland and his experiences at University in Dublin. He asked all about Sean's family and about his plans for the future. For Sean, at that time they were purely to do with qualifying as a doctor. With his wife, Johanna, Max helped him to settle into his new life in Berlin. They invited him to their house for meals and social gatherings and they took him along with them to the theatre, cinema and to football matches. Football was Max's passion.

Sean's life as a German medical student began in a whirl of introductions and parties. His days were divided between the University and the Clinic where Max looked out for him and guided his development as a doctor. The Senior Consultant in charge of their department was a big man named Florian Fuchs. He was a humourless man with a literal train of mind. When Sean was introduced to him he remained seated but held out a hand to offer a soft handshake.

Fuchs' office was a very plush affair with a carpet; the first carpeted office Sean had ever seen, and a large, ornate, gold-leaf mirror above a marble mantelpiece. The whole interior seemed like it didn't belong to the more utilitarian Friedrichshain building at all. Sean also noticed the twin pots that stood at each end of the mantelpiece. He noticed them because they each contained two miniature flags on twelve inch sticks. The flags bore the crooked cross insignia of the Nazi Party.

"Now Mr Schneider," Fuchs continued after the introductions had been completed, "Where are you going to put Mr Colquhoun?"

"He'll be directly below me, Sir. I intend to lead his instruction personally."

"And where will you give him an office?"

"I thought he could share with Meyer on the first floor."

"Well he could," said Fuchs. "But why not have him in with you?"

"That would be ideal but unfortunately I share with Hildberg and there is not room for three desks in our room."

"Hildberg," said Fuchs, his tone expressed disgust. "Hildberg," he repeated. He rose slowly from his chair, his bulky figure dominating the space between mantel and desk and he turned to look towards the mantelpiece. Sean could see the man's face reflected in the mirror and watched his dark gaze fall upon the twin swastikas at each end of the mantel.

"One day we will sort out the Hildbergs of this world for good and all."

He turned around to face them, one of the miniature flags now being toyed with in his big hands.

"Move Hildberg to the first floor and put Mr. Colquhoun in with you," he ordered.

"But, Sir," Max rejoined, "What about Hildberg's seniority?"

"As far as I am concerned Mr Schneider," Fuchs replied taking obvious pleasure in his own rejoinder, "Seniority and Hildberg are mutually exclusive concepts."

And so, later on that day, with extreme discomfort, Sean stood by as Hildberg first heard from Max that he was to be moved to a new office on the first floor and then had to stand witness to the removal of Hildberg's desk and effects from the office that he had, until now, occupied.

Hildberg protested to Max. He wanted to know what he had done to deserve this humiliation. Why had he been singled out for this treatment? His protest was not made in anger. Throughout the procedure he remained in control and respectful. But Sean saw the humiliation and frustration in his eyes and he wished he had stayed at home in Ireland rather than be the unwitting cause of this man's distress. He felt a strong resentment towards Fuchs for using him this way to achieve some internal victory at Hildberg's expense. He was also fascinated by the process in a dispassionate way. He could not imagine this happening at home without Fuchs finding himself in a blazing row or even a fist fight. But here, although the emotions were at flaming point, on the surface everything remained calm. Was this the famous German national characteristic that he would have to learn to accept?

"Look Hildberg," Max said, beginning to show a little impatience with Hildberg's continuing protest, "If you want to take this further you'll have to speak to Fuchs. It was his decision; he ordered the change."

"Fuchs," said Hildberg nodding in resignation. He removed his spectacles and wiped the lenses with a white cloth he had drawn from his pocket. "Well, why am I not surprised!" he said. With that he carried the last of his belongings and left the office.

After a week and a half had passed and Sean had settled into more permanent lodgings near to the Alexanderplatz railway station, he made the decision to approach Hildberg and offer his apologies for his role in his humiliation. The after-taste of the incident was spoiling all other experiences he was encountering. If he was going to enjoy Berlin with an untroubled conscience he would have to lance this particular boil. He had found it impossible to approach Hildberg at work to resolve the issue that he worried was hanging between them.

After a large dinner at the family table of his hosts he lay on his bed only semi aware of the clattering trains running by outside his bedroom window. After his first night in the bedroom he had been startled awake by the first train to leave Alexanderplatz at 6.30am. He had thought the noise of the trains would drive him insane. But within a few days he found he hardly noticed them at all.

He had a piece of paper in his hand containing Hildberg's home address, which he had acquired from one of the receptionists at the hospital. He fingered it gently and re-read it as he waited for his decision to get up and go to arrive in his brain.

He turned his collar up against the cold as he entered the U-Bahn station and caught the subway car to Hildberg's district. When he reached the address on the paper, he was impressed with Hildberg's location. He had a first floor residence in an eight courtyard complex known as the Hakesche Hofe in Berlin's Mitte district.

Sean let himself into the apartment block and mounted the stairs to number four. After a moment or two he heard someone withdrawing bolts inside the door in response to his push at the bell. Then he thought he heard the sound of someone saying "hush."

The door crept open a couple of inches and a female face appeared in the crack that had been revealed. The face was half in shadow but nevertheless Sean could see that it was an extremely attractive face; possibly beautiful in the full light of day.

"Excuse me, Fraulein," he said in his most formal German. "My name is Sean Colquhoun. I am a colleague of Mr Raul Hildberg at the Friedrichshain Clinic. I believe he lives here."

"Just a moment," she said, and the door was closed in his face, leaving him to wait on the landing.

After a long two minutes, the door opened again and there stood Hildberg. He had removed his necktie and collar and he had apparently been eating as there was some slight evidence of food stains at the corners of his mouth.

Hildberg's face filled with anxiety as he recognised Sean Colquhoun at his door. Defensively and without a hint of warmth he said, "What do you want?"

Before Sean could answer this was quickly followed by, "You shouldn't have come here."

"I'm very sorry if this is inconvenient but I really did want to speak to you."

"You can speak to me at work."

"Well I have tried," said Sean, "But it has not been easy. So I resolved to come here and speak to you tonight. I didn't want any more time to pass."

Suddenly Hildberg was surprised as a hand came from behind him and pulled the door fully open. He turned to see the attractive woman who had initially answered the door standing there. There was a sadness and a reproach in her voice as she spoke to Hildberg.

"Raul," she whispered. "What are you doing? What has happened to you? Is this how we welcome visitors to our home?"

Ignoring Hildberg's attempted reply she turned to Sean and said, "I am so sorry Mr Colquhoun. Please forgive my husband. He forgets his manners. Please come inside and make yourself at home."

Under his wife's insistent gaze Hildberg stood aside and allowed an uncomfortable Sean to pass along the passageway into the family sitting room.

The room was very tastefully furnished with a welcoming sofa, a rocking chair with ornate wooden arms, and two matching armchairs in rich floral fabric. A large golden and black rug lay before a blazing fire in the hearth and on it sat two children who, by their looks were obviously the offspring of Mr and Mrs Hildberg. Against the far wall stood a tall bookcase with every shelf full to bursting with books and framed photographs. The children looked up as Sean entered but they did not speak. The elder of the two was a girl of about eleven years. She had the striking good looks of her mother with high cheekbones, a delicately curved nose, full lips and a flashing white smile framed within dark wavy locks of hair which tumbled down to her shoulders. 'Mother and daughter could be twins,' thought Sean. The other child, a boy of about eight years, was also dark and had strong, good looks and a serious expression.

In the absence of any attempt at introductions by Hildberg himself, his wife did the honours, "I am Raul's wife," she began. "My name is Grete. These are our two children. Lisa is eleven. She is studying music at the Academy. Her instruments are the voice and the violin. This is my son, David. He is seven years old and in first school."

'Pretty good guess,' thought Sean

"Hello Lisa, hello David. My name is Sean and I am very pleased to meet you."

By this time Hildberg had followed them into the room and Sean turned to speak to him. But before he could begin Grete insisted on making coffee and providing cake.

"I came to apologise to you for the way in which I was moved into your office and you were forced to leave. I want you to know that it was not my doing. If I could have prevented it I would have. It was my first day in the hospital. I am a visiting student from a foreign country. I was powerless to affect the decision-making that went on. I want you to know that it was not Max's doing either. He protested to Dr Fuchs when he suggested the arrangement, but Fuchs was determined."

Hildberg and his wife looked at each other. Eventually it was Grete, his wife who spoke, "Sean, you must forgive Raul. He takes everything so seriously." She reached over and stroked Raul's hair playfully like a mother with a sulky child. Raul was embarrassed but the gesture began to bring him out of his mood.

"Grete is right," he said. "I am over sensitive. If it was not for my lovely wife I would have been crushed under the weight of my own resentments years ago."

They sat around the table drinking coffee and eating cake and they asked questions of each other the way people do when they have first met but have formed an instinctive liking for each other and expect to go on to develop a close friendship.

"So," asked Raul, "How does Berlin compare to Dublin?"

"Well, there are differences. Berlin is more like London than Dublin. Dublin has had a history of subservience to London, so it has not had time to develop as a capital city. Dublin also has a much worse housing situation. Much of the population lives in appalling conditions in slum areas. However, we have not been so badly affected by the Wall Street crash as you have here in Germany. We're still very much a rural economy. I miss the pubs and I miss my sport. You don't play rugby here, or hurling."

Hearing this, seven year old David got up from the rug in front of the fire and approached the table. "What is hurling?" he asked.

Both David and Lisa listened intently along with Raul and Grete to Sean's vivid descriptions of hurling and Gaelic football. Sean had them laughing as he recounted some anecdotes from his experiences on the Hurley field. By the end of his account the children at least saw him as some latter day northern warrior. Perhaps Raul and Grete did too.

Grete decided it was bed time for the children, despite Lisa's complaints that it was not fair for her to go to bed at the same time as her brother, and she escorted them through the apartment to the bedroom they shared.

Raul said, "Come on, Sean, "Let me show you a Berlin bar. Perhaps then you will not miss your Dublin pubs so much."

As they sipped strong German beer from pint pots Raul said, "It's because I am a Jew."

Sean put his pot down and looked at Raul seeking further explanation.

"Fuchs. He hates me because I am a Jew. He is a member of the Nazi Party. They have a paranoid hatred of Jews. That's why he took the opportunity of your arrival to humiliate me."

"Do the hospital authorities allow him to practise his anti-Semitism in his post?" asked Sean.

"Technically no, but in practice, yes. Oh don't misunderstand me, his anti-Semitism is not allowed full rein. If it were I would not have a job there. But he has his little victories on a day by day basis."

"What can you do about it?"

"Well, if I took my wife's good advice I would grow up and forget about it."

He took another sip of his beer and considered how to explain himself to this foreigner.

"You see, Sean, we Jews are as German as the Germans. I fought in the Great War. I was seventeen years old when I was captured by the French at the Marne. We are fully integrated into German society. But at the same time we have always suffered anti-Semitism. I expect it is the same in Ireland."

Sean gulped at the directness of Raul's question. As he thought about attitudes in Ireland he was well aware of the presence of anti-Semitism in his native country.

Raul continued, "As a minority group we have so much experience of dealing with prejudice that it's like water over a stone; it erodes, but so slightly you think you hardly notice. This Hitler fellow; He's a joke. The German people will never allow him to come to power. We will ride out Hitler like we have ridden out surges in anti-Semitism before. And when he has retreated into the obscurity he has come from we will still be here, loyal Germans working hard and living our lives."

The two men sipped their beers for a few moments in silence.

"My problem is," ruminated Raul, "I take it all to heart. I am too sensitive. It does no good to be sensitive and a Jew."

"I'm not sure if I should say this," ventured Sean. "I mean no offence by it."

"Say what you are thinking Sean. You will not offend me, I promise you."

"Well, you don't look… that is, I mean, I would not have thought you were Jewish."

Raul spluttered into his beer with laughter as he looked into Sean's embarrassed face.

"Relax Sean. You're right. In the sense you mean we are not Jewish at all. Grete and I converted to Protestantism in our university days. Hence, no pigtails, no skull caps!"

Sean looked even more nonplussed now, if that were possible.

"So, what exactly is Fuchs' problem?"

"It's to do with Hitler's teachings about blood and race. As far as Fuchs is concerned - once a Jew, always a Jew. To him I'm as Jewish as the most devout Rabbi."

"So you mean he's been through your files to investigate your background?" Sean asked.

"Absolutely. Make no mistake. He's been through yours as well. You must be free from the taint of Jewish blood. But look, let's not dwell on this anymore. I am very grateful for your kind gesture in coming to see me and my family tonight. Let's make it the start of a lasting friendship. Like I say, my problem is mainly paranoia and soon the Nazis and their Herr Hitler will blow away with the dust of history."

As good as their word, the two men became firm friends and Sean was a regular guest in the Hildberg household. At least three times a week Grete would save Sean from the dreariness of his digs and invite him to share in their family meal. On Sundays Sean would sometimes offer to take the children out to the Tiergarten or for a boat ride along the Spree.

Lisa loved to walk in the Volkspark Friedrichshain and to play tag around the Marchenbrunnen fairy tale fountain. She loved to dodge between the animal sculptures and the figures from Grimms' Fairy Tales. She also loved to visit Museum Island in the middle of the Spree River. Her favourite outing was to the Old National Gallery, where she would happily view the paintings for hours. On day when he knew the choir would be practising, Sean took the children to the Lustgarten, beside which sits the Berlin Cathedral. Lisa would be happy listening to the heavenly choral singing, but David would become restless after half an hour.

However, David was usually happy to go along with Lisa's preferences. Happy, that was, until two Hurley sticks and a Hurley ball arrived from Sean's father in Cork. Sean had written home requesting the items as a result of David's fascination with Sean's stories of hurling. Once the Hurley equipment arrived, all David wanted to do was practice his shots and catching skills. It was a difficult skill for a young boy to learn, but within a few months he was striking the ball a good twenty metres distance and twenty- five into the air. Sean would run and catch the ball and strike it back. At the end of a good hour-long session of this, with curious passers-by watching in amused puzzlement, Sean would end the session by agreeing to David's request to strike the ball as far as he could. Making sure that the area of the ball's destination was clear of people, Sean would launch massive shots high into the air and well over one hundred and fifty metres distant. David would run, laughing, after the ball and Sean would pretend to race him to it.

On their walks home, sweating and happily exercised, David would say, "You make it fly like a bird, Uncle Sean."

"Well, you're nearly as good as me already. One day I can see you playing in an All-Ireland final. But when you do you must promise me that you will play for County Cork."

"But I'm a German, Uncle Sean," David laughed. "They won't let me play for County Cork."

"When they see the way you can hit that ball they'll snap you up in a minute!"

Usually, when they arrived back at the Hildberg apartment Grete would let them in and provide drinks and biscuits and listen to David Raul's excited retelling of their sporting exploits. Often Raul would be at work. The work load for both doctors was heavy and it was a lottery when trying to synchronise rota duties so that they could be free from work at the same time.

As Sean watched mother and son, so obviously happy and secure in their relationship, he would try not to look at Grete and think how beautiful she was. The more he saw of her the more he was becoming fixated on her beauty. The landscape of her face was instantly attractive; her pale smooth skin, her high cheekbones, her curved nose and her full lips. When she smiled, laughed or frowned it was as if a light came on in the room. 'In fact,' Sean thought, 'she would light up even a summer's day with her smile.'

Whenever he reached this state of infatuation he would thank Grete for the refreshments and arrange to pick David Raul up again the next time he was free.

Ten

1930

One Sunday, on his walk home from mass, for he had kept up his Catholic obligations, he was hailed by a passenger in a car, which pulled up at the curb beside him. When he turned to look in the direction of the caller, he saw that it was Magda Strasser. He had been thinking about Grete and he laughed inwardly when he was immediately struck by the blonde beauty of Magda.

'I'm beginning to think this is a Sean Colquhoun psychiatric syndrome,' he mused silently. 'Everywhere I look I see beautiful women.'

Hugo had climbed out of the driver's side and was coming around to the pavement towards him.

"Sean," he called warmly, "I knew it was you when I saw that rustic Irish gait ahead of us on the pavement."

They both laughed and clapped each other on the arms.

"Come on, Sean," insisted Hugo, "Climb in. We haven't seen you in so long. That is the trouble with our busy lives these days. The days and weeks slip by and we don't have the time to keep up our contacts. You must come to lunch and spend the afternoon with us."

"Oh, thank you so much Hugo, but I can't."

Sean broke away and moved to the car to greet Magda who was leaning out of the window.

"But you must Sean. Wait 'til you hear who is joining us for lunch and then you'll change your mind."

"I am sure it will be tempting, Hugo, but I am expected at the Hildberg's apartment. They have invited me for lunch and I have promised to take the children to the Tiergarten for a stroll."

"Adolf Hitler."

"I beg your pardon?" said a perplexed Sean.

"Adolf Hitler."

"I thought you said that. What about him?"

"That's whose coming to lunch!"

"Adolf Hitler?"

"That's what I said!"

"You're having Adolf Hitler for lunch and you want me to join you?"

"Let me explain," Hugo said. "Look, jump in the car and we'll explain on the way."

Without having intended to let Grete, Raul and the children down, Sean found himself being ushered into the limousine and swept towards the grand suburb of Wansee with its big family residences and its limousines on the driveways.

On the way there Magda had explained about the lunch party and how they were entertaining Adolf Hitler, the enfant terrible of German politics, as she described him. The Vatican Secretary of State, no less, one Cardinal Eugenio Pacelli was eager to affect a meeting with Hitler given his growth in support throughout Germany. He did not really expect the Nazis to make a great deal more progress but Pacelli is a careful man who likes to anticipate all the possible options well ahead of time.

"But why have they chosen your house as a meeting place? Surely an office in the Reichstag or at the Papal Nuncio," Sean enquired.

"Tempting as it is to pretend so, they are not in fact coming to see us, although we have known Cardinal Eugenio for some time. He often came to our country estate and rode during his time here as the Vatican's representative to Germany. He is a very fine horseman. He does his best to get back here at least once a year since his return to Rome to become Vatican Secretary of State. He still likes to ride and enjoys retreating to a Catholic convent in Munich. We are merely acting as facilitators. As you know, Hugo works in the secretariat at the Reichstag. Through his work there and his own Catholicism he has become close to the leader of the Catholic Centre Party, Ludwig Kaas. Ludwig is an unusual individual. He mixes politics and religion being a politician and a Roman Catholic priest. Over the last few years Ludwig has become devoted to the man who, until recently, was the Papal Nuncio here in Berlin; one Cardinal Pacelli. Pacelli was recalled to Rome earlier this year and is now Cardinal Secretary of State for the Vatican. Previously he was in Germany since 1917. He worked furiously to preserve peace and to defend Germany against Bolshevism. He is already being talked about as the next Pope and some even declare him to be a saint."

"Yes," said Sean, "I have heard of him. Brother Peter admires him greatly."

Reflecting on Magda's reference to "the country estate" Sean realised the Strassers were much higher up in German society than he had realised.

"Brother Peter is close to Cardinal Pacelli. They worked together often and they still meet up at the convent from time to time."

"I did not know that!" returned Sean.

"So what is Cardinal Pacelli's business with Adolf Hitler?" Sean asked.

Here Hugo took over from Magda, "The Cardinal is a serious minded diplomat. In the last thirteen years he has negotiated concordats with most of the German states. It is his aim to reach a concordat with Prussia and with the Reich itself. He is probably hedging his bets by wanting to get to know Hitler. Realistically there is little chance of Hitler gaining power. But it may become necessary for the Christian parties to do a deal with him to keep out the Bolsheviks and the Social Democrats. Pacelli works himself to exhaustion to ensure the security of Catholics within the Reich."

"But isn't that dangerous?" asked Sean. "Surely Hitler is a demagogue. A man of violence. Hasn't he threatened the Jews with extinction?"

Magda and Hugo laughed.

"You don't understand German politics, Sean," said Hugo. "It's all only talk. Hitler will temper his talk and his objectives when he gets a sniff of power."

"But I read only this morning in my newspaper that the Catholic Bishops of the Reich have denounced Hitler and the Nazis. They have withdrawn the right of the sacraments from any Catholic who joins the party or votes for it. Are you telling me there is a split in Catholicism between Rome and Germany?"

"In part that is why Pacelli is here. He has the bigger picture. Perhaps he wants to get a better grasp of Nazism first hand. Anyway, at three o'clock this afternoon they will meet in our humble home. And you my Irish friend will be there to see history as it happens."

Despite his concerns, Sean was now excited at the prospect of the afternoon to come. He had heard reverential talk of Cardinal Pacelli and now he was to meet him. Hitler was famous and infamous throughout the world. To some he was a clown; to others he was a god; to still others, he was a devil. Now Sean was going to meet him too. Which would he turn out to be?

That night when he recounted his tale to Grete and Raul there were two aspects of the afternoon that stuck in his mind.

"Oh, Sean." It was Grete as she opened the door of the apartment to him. "We had given up on you. The children are in bed."

"I know," Sean answered as he walked along the hallway to the sitting room. "I feel terrible for letting you down, especially the children. But wait 'til you hear where I've been today and, more to the point, who I've been with."

As he told his tale of the afternoon, he was still trying to form his judgements about what he had seen and heard. He had waited with Hugo and Magda for some two hours before the esteemed guests had arrived. Sean could sense the nervous anticipation within his hosts. They obviously felt they were facilitating some great historical moment.

The first to arrive was Ludwig Kaas, the leader of the Catholic Centre Party. Hugo introduced him to Magda and then Sean and the three of them participated in a light conversation while Hugo went out into the hall to welcome a married couple who were special friends of the Strassers and fellow parishioners at their Catholic Church.

There were two servants and they offered wine and canapés. Gentle and polite conversation continued until Cardinal Pacelli arrived with his entourage of three assistant Monsignors. He swept in, his invisible feet beneath his flowing robes making no sound on the thick carpet. It was as if he floated on air.

Sean studied the man as he was introduced to the others in the room. He could not help but be impressed with the man's air of saintliness. There was an indefinable gentleness that he exuded, which was to do with his ascetic aquiline face and the calmness in his voice. There was also an unmistakeable authority that surrounded him. When he was introduced to an individual he did not offer a handshake; rather he presented his ring which each person dutifully kissed. When Sean bent to kiss the man's ring he felt close to the Mother Church he had been born and raised within.

Pacelli's German was excellent and his knowledge of German Catholicism was comprehensive. Sean began to consider the effect Hitler's arrival would have on the holy atmosphere that had overtaken the room since Pacelli's arrival. He began to fear that the whole occasion might degenerate into a horribly tasteless mistake. And then, with a shocking suddenness, a servant stood at the door to the room and announced the arrival of "Herr Hitler."

As this infamous character emerged into sight and strode into the room, Sean felt as if a spell had been broken. The holiness he had been experiencing popped like a bubble. It seemed now as if it had been childish imaginings and here was the real world again. Hugo, playing host, stepped forward and reached out his hand to greet his new guest. Before taking it and shaking it vigorously, Hitler raised his arm in the Nazi salute Sean had often seen on the newsreels. He almost laughed but restrained himself in time. Then Hugo led him straight to Cardinal Pacelli, who did not rise from his seat but offered his ring hand for the politician to kiss.

Sean found himself numbed by the incredulity of the man's persona. It was a jumble of contradictions. He strode in, obviously well practised in a military style step and in maintaining an erect back and repeatedly whipped at his boots with a riding crop. Yet he brought with him an intangible emptiness. Sean kept thinking, 'here is the human manifestation of the mathematical zero.' Yet his pasty face, his raisin eyes and his oily hair gave a simultaneous image of complete ordinariness. Here was the epitome of the school teacher or the bank clerk who had repeatedly failed to achieve advancement.

As Hitler was being introduced to the assembled company, Sean could smell the fresh polish on his knee-length boots. Hovering around him like a faithful collie dog was Gregor Strasser, an administrative official of Hitler's Nazi Party and no relation to Hugo and Magda. Yet Hitler was obviously awed to be in the presence of Cardinal Pacelli and he dutifully stooped to kiss the proffered ring.

All light conversation immediately ceased and Sean felt an intensity of oppression fall on the room. Pacelli opened the greetings by blessing the assembly and then gave a special blessing to Herr Hitler for the burden of leadership that he carried and a prayer that he could fulfil it to the greater glory of Our Lord and Saviour Jesus Christ and his Holy Mother, Mary.

With that the company regained its seats and the conversation opened. It immediately became apparent to Sean, and from the look on his face, to Hugo too, that the idea of an informal gathering to add a lighter air to this introductory meeting was not going to succeed. The two main protagonists immediately proceeded to serious discussion.

Hitler perched forward on the edge of his armchair, looking like a naughty schoolboy summoned before an all-powerful headmaster and hoping for a light punishment, listening intently as Pacelli began to explain how the Holy Father in Rome bore a deep, loving and lasting concern for his flock in Germany and for all of the German people. The Holy Father had entrusted his humble Cardinal with the task of agreeing a concordat with the German Reich and with its individual state legislatures.

Hitler nodded and concentrated on the Cardinal's words. When he spoke, he at first made conciliatory noises and spoke fondly of his own Catholic upbringing in a devout family. Pacelli rejoiced that Hitler was indeed a member of the one, true Catholic and apostolic faith.

Hitler went on to assert his belief that too many churchmen misjudged their true purpose. By this he meant that they failed to concentrate their energies on the saving of souls and meddled too readily in matters of social policy. This was none of their business, he asserted, and they should be guided by the Holy Father in Rome to attend to spiritual matters and leave politics to the politicians.

To Sean's shocked amazement, Pacelli wholeheartedly agreed with Hitler and boasted that the concordat he had negotiated with Mussolini, the Lateran Treaty, had dealt successfully with just such matters. He also guided Hitler to the concordat he had recently concluded with Croatia in Yugoslavia as evidence of his clear policy of separating spiritual and social activity.

Sean cast his mind back to the worker priests in Ireland and the political role many of them had played in bringing about Ireland's independence and wondered how they would react to this definition of their mission by the Holy See. But Hitler went on to argue that removing the clergy from the political stage was only part of the issue. All the time he kept glancing at Ludwig Kaas who was a stereotypical example of a politicised clergy; an ordained priest and the leader of the Catholic Centre party.

"There must be no political parties with religious allegiances," Hitler asserted. "All allegiance must be to the state."

"We may be able to find agreement on the first part of your statement, my Herr Hitler," expounded Pacelli, "but as a child of the Roman Catholic Church you know that there are much higher allegiances than the state. There is a greater Kingdom that has been revealed to us through the blood sacrifice of the Creator's immaculately conceived Son."

Hitler nodded wisely.

Sean was in disbelief. Had he just heard correctly? The representative of the Pope himself had just agreed that political parties with a religious stamp had no place in politics. What did that mean for the millions of Catholics in Germany who voted for their representatives in the Catholic Centre Party? What did that mean for traditional groupings that might be able to provide opposition to the likes of Hitler and his Nazis? What about the political parties at home in Ireland and their ties to the Church? But while he was thinking this Pacelli was continuing.

"The Holy Father wishes to remind the world that the message of Christ is one of love, charity and forgiveness. Hatred has no place in the Kingdom of Heaven."

'This is better stuff,' Sean was thinking. Now we will see how Hitler explains his message of hatred towards the Jews and all the other minorities and ethnicities he pours his vitriol on. 'Hitler's response began,' Sean thought, 'with the duplicity of a skilled politician.'

"We are filled with a love for the German people and race. The Aryan inspires us with love and we generously extend that love to others. Our aim is to improve the lives of all of our people. But to truly love our brethren we must protect them from the poison that floods the waters of their minds. The Bolshevik, the Jew with their lewd, lascivious, bestial natures would destroy our people. To shrink from the fight with these forces would be to run from the responsibilities of love and to hide like cowards in the forests of the night."

Here was the moment when Sean Colquhoun's life might have taken a different turning from the road he was to eventually travel. He knew what he expected Cardinal Pacelli to say. He was almost prepared to mouth the words with him as he spoke, so certain was he of the reply to come. But when Pacelli spoke they were the wrong words and Sean felt the walls of his life fall away into a bottomless pit.

"The Bolshevik is the true enemy of Christian civilisation. He is the anti-Christ. I have seen with my own eyes the results of Bolshevism during my time as Papal Nuncio in Munich during the Red Terror there. You will have no greater ally than the Holy Father in Rome in your fight against Bolshevism. Now the Jew. The poor misguided Jew. The Jew is a victim of his own hard-heartedness. He closes his heart to the great good news of the Saviour's birth; the Saviour prophesised in their own scriptures. With this hard-heartedness he brings his problems upon himself. He carries on his hands the blood of *deicide*. There is nothing more to say about the Jew."

Sean sat back in his armchair in amazed disbelief. He doubted the evidence of his own ears. He looked around the room at the faces of the other witnesses to this shocking interchange. All he saw were pious faces nodding sagely in agreement with the sentiments expressed.

Suddenly Hitler was on his feet and launching into a speech. Sean could see the confidence surging through him. He praised the Cardinal for his modern views and drew parallels between the authoritarian structure of the Church and the State he intended to create when he was Chancellor, which he asserted was inevitable. He whipped his boots with his riding crop several times and then stepped forward to grasp the Cardinal's ring hand. He stooped stiffly, kissed the holy icon and then strode theatrically from the room. Gregor Strasser jumped to his feet and ran out after him.

Everyone, including the Cardinal, sat in silence for a long time. Eventually, Hugo stood up and threw open the French doors that led into the garden. There was the tangible bursting of a dread atmosphere and people got to their feet and wandered outside.

Everyone there took their turn to approach the Cardinal in the garden and offer their congratulations for the way in which he had put the upstart in his place. Everyone except Sean. Sean could not see how they drew that conclusion. Or was it just a form of German politeness? To his mind, Hitler had totally dominated the exchanges and was fully justified in walking out of that house confident that the Roman Catholic Church had no issue with his plans for governing Germany.

He found himself beside Magda as they strolled alongside the floral borders.

"Are you all right, Sean?" she asked.

"Why do you ask?"

"Well you are pale. You look as if you've seen a ghost."

'How appropriate,' Sean thought with intense irony. 'I have just seen a ghost. The ghost of all my beliefs and certainties evaporating into oblivion.'

"I'm fine," he said.

"Well," Magda concluded as she moved away to join Hugo with Pacelli. "We can take comfort in the thought that that little horrible man will never gain power in Germany."

Raul and Grete sat in stony silence as Sean finished his tale. Eventually Grete spoke. "Magda is right, isn't she? He will never come to power. Germany is far too mature for that!"

"I'm sure you're right," said Sean. "But it's not Hitler that worries me, it's the Catholic Church. I am shocked to my core with the things I have heard today. They go against everything I was taught to believe in. I was taught Christianity at the hands of Catholic priests. I know they didn't always practise what they preached – especially when they were beating the living daylights out of us. But I always gave them the benefit of the doubt. I always believed they were acting in our best interests. Now I have none of that belief left. I know the Church has always dallied with a certain amount of moderate anti-Semitism. But what I've heard today frightens and appals me."

Raul and Grete sat in silence for a long time.

"Maybe I'm not the over-sensitive one," commented Raul at length. "Perhaps I've been reading the runes correctly all along!"

Eleven
1938

In the days and weeks following their disagreement on the walk home from Hagan's, Martha and Sean failed to heal the small breach that had appeared between them. In the morning Sean cursed himself when he remembered his part revelation. He could not understand how he had allowed himself to do it. Pure irritation at Hagan's smugness – that's what had done it. But even so, how could he have allowed such a trivial thing as that to get under his skin so much so that he would blab in a way that might ultimately endanger his beloved Martha.

For her part, Martha decided to wait for Sean to volunteer the full truth of his views. She wanted him to explain why he had allowed others to believe that those views and opinions which he expressed, or allowed to go unchallenged, were not in fact his own. And she wanted him to do it of his own accord. She did not want to badger him into telling her. Sean's mistake was to believe that Martha had woken up the next day and dismissed their discussion as a silly tiff. This was a mere hope, but he clung to it until it seemed to convince him.

Eventually they returned to themselves, but this gap lay between them. Martha prayed and asked for guidance. She rationalised that she loved Sean and he was her husband until death. Therefore she would accept this…. well, what was it? She found it hard to call it a betrayal. But it sure felt like one. Whatever it was, she would accept it. She would accept that it had inserted a splinter into their relationship which had spoiled something so precious that she had considered it to be as near perfect as made no difference. She mourned the loss of that perfection but told herself to grow up and asked herself - who ever told you to expect perfection on earth?

Although never devout, she found that the church and personal prayer had given her the means to achieve a kind of peace of mind and so she was drawn closer to it. Meanwhile Sean was mightily relieved to believe that the squall was over and hoped it would stay that way until the day came when he would have to tell Martha his whole story.

It was at about this time that Sean took to visiting London. This was something Martha had been vaguely aware of in Sean's life before they had married. But since the wedding he had ceased the visits, until now. It was not just one visit but many, and some of them lasted for many days. The longest was for three weeks. Sean was now fully qualified and had a temporary post at Dublin University hospital alongside James Callan. James had reassured Sean that the post would become permanent but Sean told

Martha he could not be sure of that. His visits to London, he explained, were to seek a permanent post. Other times he said it was for crisis management and for training in the treatment of victims of explosions.

Martha had no idea why she did not believe Sean, she just knew that she didn't. However, her lack of trust in Sean was becoming a burden. So much so that whenever he was away she would go to the church of St Peter and say her confession to Father O'Shea, the young curate who was attached there as he awaited his transfer to the Parish of the Sacred Heart in Cork. At first she just sought forgiveness for her lack of trust in her husband, which she saw as a venial though potentially dangerous sin.

Father O'Shea forgave here her sins and counselled her to put her doubts behind her. If she could not do that then in the interests of a lasting marriage she should voice her concerns to her husband.

But then the visits to London seemed to have stopped and soon Martha and Sean were preparing to leave the capital city and their student days behind them for good as Sean moved into general practice in Cork with Dr. Townley.

Martha was thrilled. She hoped for a new beginning. She convinced herself that getting away from Dublin would free them from the friction that had arisen between them there. She could not completely reconcile herself to the loss of her academic life but she had found ways of compensating for that. 'Deferred gratification' is how the middle classes labelled it. She also drew pleasure from the knowledge that Father O'Shea would soon be transferring to the Sacred Heart church in Cork and that she would be able to retain him as her confessor.

Twelve

This truly felt like the beginning of their lives together. They bought a cottage with an acre of land on the Cork side of Cobh, just a fifteen minute drive to the downtown surgery of Townley and Colquhoun. Like every general practitioner in the late 1930s, Sean found that a motor car was an essential symbol of solidity and success. With enthusiasm, they threw themselves into a complete renovation of their first property with its spectacular views out over the southern coastline across the broad Atlantic Ocean.

With the cottage refurbished and redecorated, 1938 turned into 1939 and Martha found herself pregnant again. There was much joy at the news in the Colquhoun and Grady families. There was a Christmas visit to Clare to the Grady's and a New Year stay over at the Colquhoun's farm in County Cork. Sean and Martha were both feeling closer again and that brought back much of their original happiness.

As January crept its painful way into the new year, Sean returned to work at the practice and Martha spent her time with her first born son, Cornelius, whom they called Conny. She also made herself active in the little community around that side of Cobh, particularly in the local church. She took to attending Mass on most weekdays and then sitting in the church hall with other mothers and spinsters of the parish, discussing the state of the world and helping to organise fund-raising activities for the missionaries in Africa and the Far East. She became closer to Father O'Shea, the popular young curate who often joined the ladies for their morning sessions and also rolled up his sleeves to help when they polished the altar rails and changed the flowers in the vases.

Although she was reluctant to admit it to herself, Martha, a well-educated young woman, was not fulfilled by the activities a married woman in Ireland of the 1930s was expected to confine herself to. She maintained her academic reading, sketched out plans for articles and even a book, which she would return to once the children were older. Her subject being German theatre in the late nineteenth and early twentieth centuries she did not find it easy to discuss her ideas with Sean. His ambivalence towards modern Germany made her self-conscious whenever the subject was raised. She became all too quickly aware that there were boundaries they must not cross if the equilibrium their relationship had achieved was not to be disturbed. On the other hand she found Father O'Shea more than willing to listen to her ideas and views and he provided her with an outlet for her intellectual needs.

Sean had just finished dealing with a young man of twenty-two who was in the early stages of tuberculosis. His coughing had rattled the shelves in the surgery. The blood on his handkerchief was of a startlingly bright shade. As Sean bade him farewell with a bottle of useless medicine in his pocket, he knew the man's days were numbered because he would never be able to afford the treatment he so desperately needed. A porter on Cork's riverside railway depot, his wages were insufficient to feed his young family properly.

He was at the sink in the corner washing his hands, his back to the door, when he heard the next patient enter his surgery.

"Good morning," he said without turning as he dried his hands on a white towel.

The absence of any reply caused him to turn out of curiosity before he had finished the act of drying his hands. The figure he saw before him made him stop his hand drying instantly. His face lit up in bemused recognition.

"Well in the name of all that's holy! What are you doing here?"

The man opposite Sean still did not speak. He was a small man, maybe five foot six but with a wiry physique that made him look taller. He had a shock of dark brown hair and a wild red beard. He wore a workman's clothes of corduroy trousers, a dark blue shirt and an old suit jacket stained with earth and oil. His face beamed with pleasure and he spread his arms out, inviting Sean into a manly embrace.

The men grasped each other powerfully and then stepped back and scragged each other's shoulders.

"Well say something, for Jesus' sake," complained Sean.

"Ah will you look at you. By God I'd say you've put on a few pounds since we were last together," the man at last said.

Sean looked the other up and down. "I can't say as much for you. You're as much a whippet now as you were in the old days."

"Well you know now I stayed in the field. None of your idle university ways for me."

"Eamonn Brodie, you were always the laziest sleepy-Joe I ever knew. You just burn up energy without moving. I swear you burn it in your sleep. You'll never have an ounce of fat on you."

Thirteen

1921

The window pane clattered fit to break as a cluster of grit collided with it. Seventeen year old Sean, already out of bed and dressed, crossed his ice-cold bedroom and lifted the flimsy curtain to peer out into the impenetrable dark of the County Cork midnight. He saw a match flare and he knew that Eamonn was outside in the yard. Tiptoeing to his door he pulled it open a crack and listened. There was the sound of his father snoring, and that meant his Ma was asleep too, for if she had not been he would have heard her ordering her noisy spouse to rollover off his back and give over that terrible row.

Noiselessly, he closed his bedroom door and went back to the window. Pulling aside the curtain, he slid the sash upwards and climbed astride the sill. Standing on the outhouse roof he slid his window closed again and then jumped down into the yard.

"Over here ya big eejit," he heard Eamonn call in his famous clandestine whisper.

As Sean reached Eamonn's side he said, "Will you shut your gob before you wake up every Black and Tan between here and Galway Bay!"

"Enough o' that," said Eamonn, suddenly business-like. "Come on, lead the way. You know where the artillery is."

Sean picked his way faultlessly across the yard, despite the thick black of the night. He led Eamonn to the barn and once inside they were able to light an oil lamp. Beneath a bed of hay Sean lifted a set of boards and brought out two rifles and a package wrapped loosely in sacking. He handed one of the rifles to Eamonn and then reached into the gap once more and pulled out a leather satchel.

"Here," he whispered. He gave Eamonn several rounds of ammunition and Eamon immediately loaded his rifle. Sean did the same and then, with rifles broken, they stashed the sacking parcel into the satchel. Sean threw the strap of the satchel around his shoulder and they hurried away from the barn yard into the night.

They moved in silence over the fields away from the roads until they came to a cluster of houses, a pub and a tiny church. On the far side of the church from the houses, about a quarter of a mile from the centre of the village, they could distinguish a black outline informing them that they had reached their objective. It was the Royal Irish Constabulary barracks where they knew a small detachment of Black and Tans were billeted this week.

News of the Tans arrival in the village of Ballyslevin had sent a wave of fear around the immediate area. The Tans always arrived in a location when the Crown demanded revenge for some deed perpetrated by the patriots. Three weeks earlier, a squaddie in the British Army, a local lad who had joined up to beat the dole queue, had returned home to see his mother, father and family members. His father was recovering from a mild heart attack and the lad had been obliged to come home. Unfortunately, the local Republican battalion had got wind of this and on the evening before his planned return to his barracks in North Yorkshire he had been abducted on his way home from the local pub and summarily executed as a traitor to Ireland.

Sean, a veteran of the Anglo-Irish guerrilla war, had been angry about the execution, although he had to accept that the presence of a serving member of His Majesty's Armed Forces did constitute an insult and a provocation. It just seemed a pointless waste of a young Irish life to prove a bleak point. However, when the Tans had arrived three nights ago and rounded up all of the men from the families who lived nearest to the scene of the execution and murdered all eight of them, he was in no doubt about what action should be taken.

So here he was with Eamonn to carry out his part of the night's action. Their unit had planned three separate actions and each depended on the other for their timing.

Eamonn and Sean crept to the edge of the field and emerged onto the road beside a large personnel truck in front of the tiny barracks. It belonged to the Tans and was used for carrying them to and from the scenes of their atrocities. With silent expertise they set about booby trapping the truck. Sean taped the gelignite to the chassis of the truck and inserted a detonator. They then backed away into the field, playing out a line of cord as they went. Now the action depended upon unit one completing their mission.

Just when it seemed that time would stretch into an eternity they were jolted from their thoughts by a massive explosion coming from the direction of the pub. The crashing of glass and slate roof ripped apart the silence of the night and the flash of light illuminated the sky. Then came the sounds of screaming, crying and groaning as men stumbled out of the bar into the night.

The only villagers were those who had not received the warning not to fraternise with the enemy. The rest of the casualties were Tans and coppers. They had no idea haw many lay dead and wounded inside. Unit one had successfully completed. Now Sean and Eamonn, unit two, were about to go into action. Within seconds of the explosion the barracks door burst open and the rapid sound of orders being barked could be heard across the black silhouetted night. As they had anticipated, the officer considered the distance to the pub necessitated the use of the truck. He screamed at the men to get on board.

As Sean put his hand on the detonator Eamonn crept swiftly to the right, slightly ahead of the truck. When Sean considered that the last man was on board and he heard the sound of the engine starting up he plunged the detonator with a swift, smooth push. There was an agonising instant of silence just long enough for Sean to think, "It's not worked". It happened every time. But then the night was ripped apart for the second time. Screams and cries; the roaring of flames; the splintering of glass; the clatter of metal crashing to the ground. All of these sounds in a chaotic maelstrom echoed the earlier explosion that had sliced through the infinite peace that had reigned over the village.

Sean immediately crept to the left of his position and crouched behind a hillock. Tattered and bloody, survivors began to fall out of the burning truck, some with their clothes on fire. At that moment Sean and Eamonn, from their different angles, began to pour bullets into the wreckage. The stumbling survivors were riddled with the incoming fire and they fell, some still consumed by flames.

After several long bursts of fire, Sean and Eamonn stilled their guns. They lay in the flickering night and listened and watched. There was no movement. Still they listened and watched. Then one of the Tans, the officer who had been barking orders started to lift himself from the ground. He got onto all fours, and then pushed himself up into a kneeling position. Just as he moved to put one foot on the floor to begin the painful effort of getting to his feet, first Eamonn and then Sean, let loose one round each. The officer jerked one way, then the other before falling forward onto his face. Just then the petrol tank succumbed to the intense temperature engulfing the vehicle and exploded, spewing flaming liquid into the air and onto the dead and dying, ensuring a one hundred percent fatality achievement. Sean ran back to the detonator, disconnected the leads, stowed it into his shoulder bag and slung it across his back. Eamonn was by his side now. The nervousness was gone and a glow of excitement suffused his expression as Sean caught flickering glimpses of it in the light of the burning truck.

"Okay Sean, me bucko. Let's make ourselves scarce."

They turned and ran back across the fields they had come over. After a two mile scramble they saw a gate ahead of them, which stood about five hundred yards from a farmhouse. They stopped and crouched low. Eamonn lifted his head and whistled. He had a good strong whistle and it pierced the night. The tune he whistled was The Camptown Races. They lay back down and stared into the blanket of night. Then a confident whistle came back. The Camptown Races. They jumped to their feet and ran to the gate. "The

Camptown ladies sing dis song," was going round in Sean's head. As they approached the gate a car drew up and a man stepped out of the shadows beside the gate and came towards them.

"Mission accomplished, Michael," said Eamonn as they met.

"Well done, boys," came the reply from Michael, a small man with a black crombie and a trilby hat. "Get in the car and we'll have you in a place of safety before the empire can get its dreaded claws into you."

As they pulled away there came the distant sounds of more explosions; one, two, and then three.

"Unit three are making sure the roads are impassable. We'll have you in Dublin by daylight. When the bastards have finished their reprisals in this part of the world we'll have you back home with your families."

And they drove across the broad plain of central Ireland to Dublin, where they would remain in hiding until the heat died down and they could begin planning for their next operation.

Fourteen
1939

Eamonn and Sean completed their warm greetings and talked briefly of old times and people they had known, but then Sean had to remind Eamonn that he had a waiting room full of patients and he would have to get on. They arranged to meet that night in a bar in Cork City. Eamonn said his farewells and left.

Sean explained to Martha that an old comrade in arms from the Anglo-Irish war had turned up and he was going out to meet him. He did not expect to be late, but that she shouldn't wait up.

Eamonn became a regular visitor to Cork over the next few weeks. Each time he hit town Sean would meet up with him. They often went out drinking but occasionally, they would take in a hurling match. At other times they would head off on bikes around the coast towards Blarney.

They could laugh and joke like only old friends can, but at some point Eamonn would always bring the conversation around to "the cause" and how the situation in Europe might be a great opportunity for Ireland. Eamonn would sometimes come and stay with Sean, Martha and Conny for a couple of nights at a time. Martha sometimes found it a little tiresome to have two men to look after, but deep down she was delighted to see Sean so happy. They were like brothers when they were together. And she smiled at Sean's attempts to include her in everything they got up to. His consideration for her made her feel loved. For the most part she let them get on with their male pursuits unhindered by her company. She also loved it when they took Conny off with them on one of their jaunts. As they set off on their bikes, Conny sitting astride the crossbar seat Sean had attached for him, she would say to herself, 'there go my two men,' and the thought would fill her with contentment.

When September came, the German Reich inflicted its Blitzkrieg upon unsuspecting Poland and the outrage of the Nazi-Soviet Pact became common knowledge. Britain and France declared war on Germany and her allies and the world held its breath. The kitchens and pubs of Ireland were filled with conversations about the rights and wrongs of the international crisis and whether DeValera would take the new Republic into the war.

That same month, Sean announced to Martha that he had another appointment in London. The University Middlesex Hospital was providing up-to-the-minute training for general practitioners on how to treat injuries sustained during air raids. That old chestnut again.

Martha had in fact been dreading this announcement. It was her habit to check through Sean's surgery once or twice a week to make sure that their cleaner, Mary, was maintaining the appropriate levels of hygiene and tidiness. On her last visit some five days earlier she was clearing up some paperwork when a letter fell to the floor. She had glanced at it before she realised what she was doing. And then it was too late. It was from an Andrew Trubshaw – an old rugby acquaintance from university days. A rival from matches between Trinity and Cambridge. It was a harmless letter really. Andrew talked about mutual acquaintances he and Sean had had and he recalled one or two typically undergraduate incidents. But Martha was uneasy because Sean had never mentioned this Andrew Trubshaw to her. And towards the end of the letter the tone altered, but it became obscure.

"The time is coming close, Sean, old buddy," he wrote. "Old Albion needs the men of the west now."

To Martha this was not obscure enough. The 'men of the west' were famous in song; fighting men who fought the invaders. Now this Trubshaw fellow was suggesting that they would help Albion. Well, Sean lived in Cork. Cork was south, but it was also west. An Englishman might be forgiven for not knowing that Connaught was the Wild West in Ireland.

"And what would a GP in Cork, Ireland be doing with training like that?" she asked sarcastically. "Or have I missed Dev's declaration of war?"

"It's only a matter of time, don't you think?" Sean asked tentatively. "Surely to God we cannot sit by while Britain and France face this nightmare alone!"

"I sincerely hope we can and do," Martha asserted. "What good would it do to anyone in Ireland to take up arms against Germany alongside the greatest enemy Ireland has ever had? The British Empire has enslaved Catholic Ireland for centuries. For God's sake Sean, you and your father before you took up arms against the hated British."

"This is different, Martha. Hitler and the Nazis represent something very different; something the like of which we've never encountered."

"Now you're sounding like a British propaganda broadsheet. I don't know how you can say that. You've seen the real Germany. You know about German civilisation. You've been a part of Brian Hagan's cultural group. We're not ignorant anti-German bigots Sean. There is absolutely no reason for Ireland to enter this war."

"Don't talk to me about that little snake Hagan. He is nothing but an apologist for Nazi imperialist and racist doctrine. Look, Martha, I lived in Germany. I experienced the rise of Hitler. And yes, I did fight the English in the twenties. But we were fighting to gain freedom. We were fighting for an Irish democracy. We wanted a humane society. Now Britain and France are standing up for humanity and democracy, surely we can be mature enough to know on which side we belong."

Martha suddenly burst into tears. There was nothing new in these opinions. But they belonged to Dublin and the distance that had grown up between them there. She had hoped they would not re-surface out here in Cork. This was not a new Sean. But it was one she had tried to forget. Why was she married to a man who did not trust her enough to reveal himself openly to her? Why was he tearing down something she thought they had held in common; something she thought had helped to bind and strengthen their relationship? It gave her a feeling of worthlessness.

She couldn't bring herself to admit she had read the letter from Trubshaw, but she found herself able to say, "You lied to me about your visits to London, didn't you? You weren't looking for a job. And you've lied to me about this University Hospital training. You're not going to London to learn how to apply a bandage to a wound. You're involved in something and as your wife, I think I deserve to be told."

Sean approached his wife and tentatively reached out to embrace her. She accepted his embrace but there was no submission or forgiveness in her stance. He kissed her hair and whispered, "I can't tell you, Martha. For the sake of you and Conny, I can't tell you."

As his words reached her, he felt her stiffen. He held her shoulders at arms length.

"Martha, please don't do this. I love you. You know I love you. But I cannot bury my head in this Irish haven and pretend that the world out there does not matter. If Britain falls, how long do you think it will be before the Gestapo is up there in Dublin castle? What will our lives be worth then?"

"I can't believe you," said Martha in a cold distant tone. "Here we are, newly set up in our married life. A baby son who adores you. A new baby on the way. There is no compulsion for you to take one step away from here. And yet you are prepared to risk everything. Everything! For what? Tell me that, Sean! For what?"

Sean could find no other answer, and at the end of that week he took the Cork to Swansea crossing and the onward train to London.

Sean went and a week later returned. Christmas 1939 came and went and the family enjoyed all the traditional festivities. The war that had been declared in September still hadn't started. Perhaps everything was going to be all right after all.

They met in Mannix's bar beside the river and they settled down behind two pints of Guinness. Sean's delight in Eamonn's visits had diminished now. The regularity with which he appeared was becoming a concern. Although the campaign for full independence was dormant at the time, it was obvious that Eamonn was still active in the movement.

During Eamonn's previous visits they had covered all the old ground and there was little catching up they had left to do. Sean and Eamonn had been partners in an active team for fourteen months. To Sean they would always be brothers in arms. Fourteen months might not seem long in the grand scheme of things, but in active combat it was more binding than a lifetime of normal friendship. Britain's declaration of war against Germany had excited Eamonn and Sean knew what was coming. Knowing the commitment he had made with Andrew Trubshaw, being around Eamonn made him nervous.

"What's the matter, Sean?" asked Eamonn. "You've hardly touched your pint."

Sean gave a faint smile and sipped at his Guinness.

"War is coming, Sean, make no mistake. England and France will be facing up to a taste of their own medicine at long last. That bastard Chamberlain and his men are already cosying up to DeValera. If we're not careful we'll be declaring war on Germany soon and Irishmen will do the fighting and dying for bloody England all over again."

Sean did most of the listening. He had to be careful about what he said. This old comrade of his had shared the most dangerous of times with him. They had saved each other's lives more times than they could count. But if Eamonn knew fully what Sean was now involved in, he would have him executed.

Eamonn continued, "We should never have let DeValera back into the country after we drove him out in the civil war. Now is the best chance we will ever have for uniting the whole of Ireland. We must act now against England. Lots of us are active and we have big plans. We haven't forgotten you Sean. You are well remembered. You have a lot of admirers in the hierarchy. They want you back in. What do you say?"

Sean took a long swig of his Guinness. This was the moment he had dreaded since Eamonn first appeared back in his life. He looked at Eamonn and his bright optimistic face. His eyes said, 'We can change the world' and the temptation to become active again was a powerful draw. But then he thought of Martha and his son, Conny. He thought of his new child on the way. He also thought back to his days in Germany and to Raul and Grete and their children Lisa and David Raul. He had to find a way to decline this poisonous invitation without giving fatal offence. He also thought of his secret commitment. But he quickly pushed that out of his mind.

"Eamonn," he said carefully. "You and I shared great danger together and there is no man on earth I would trust my life with more than you. But I am different now. I am a doctor. I have to be a man of peace." He felt the irony of these words as he spoke them in the light of his current affiliation. "I have a wife and son and a new child on the way. Also, I have been inactive since the end of the war. I took no part in the civil war."

He stooped to his pint again, looking into the eyes of his ex-comrade. He was saddened to see the obvious disappointment there.

"I'm afraid you've got the wrong man, Eamonn. Those days are behind me. I'm sorry but my answer is no!"

Eamonn said nothing for a couple of moments. He sat back in his chair staring into Sean's face. Always one to wear his emotions on his face, Eamonn could do nothing but let Sean see the disappointment turning to annoyance then anger and dislike. Eventually he spoke. "Patriotism isn't a fashion accessory, Sean. You can't pick it up or put it down when you feel like it. You're either for the cause or against it."

Sean knew he was on dangerous ground here. "We all have to find our own way of expressing our patriotism, Eamonn. I do it the best way I can. My way now is to heal the sick. Tell your masters I have nothing to be ashamed of. I carried arms in defence of this country. I have no ill will towards them. But I am now seeking my own way to do my patriotic duty."

Eamonn put down his still half-filled glass. "I would not have believed it of you Sean. Sean Colquhoun of all people. I'll drink no more with you. Let me give you a friendly warning before I get out of your hair. You will upset some mighty powerful people with this answer. Watch your back is all I say. Watch your back!"

With that Eamonn threw back his seat, toppling it to the floor as he stood.

"For the love of God, Eamonn," Sean began. "You'd throw away all we went through together over this?"

But Eamonn had turned his back and left the bar.

Fifteen
1943

"This is London, St Pancras," announced the tinny wall speakers as Lily stepped down from the Leicester train. She looked at her written instructions once again and confirmed that she was to take a taxi to Onslow Gardens in Kensington. There she must ring the bell of apartment number one delineated by the name Mr Belshaw.

Lily stood at the top of the steps leading up to the door from the pavement. She stood between the grand pillars that held the porch and pushed the bell. A middle aged woman in a floral print dress answered the door and invited her in.

Lily was shown into a large carpeted room fronting the street. There were two large sofas either side of a low table and a fire blazed encouragingly in the grate. Above the grand mantel there was a full length oil painting of King George VI in ceremonial dress. After studying it for a moment Lily walked to the large bay window and observed the desultory activity in the street below. From here, London looked unaffected by the war, but her journey across town in the taxi had shown her some of last night's damage caused by the Luftwaffe. However, life and work continued unbowed by the devastation.

Lily wondered if Goering knew that his efforts were not denting English morale but perversely drawing the people closer together. If anyone dared tell him she wondered if he would believe it.

The smart woman re-appeared and invited Lily to follow her upstairs. They went as far as the first landing where Lily was shown into the room directly above the one she had waited in. There were two men in the room; one she knew, one she didn't.

"Welcome Lily," said Andrew Trubshaw warmly as he came around a large solid desk to greet her. "Allow me to introduce a valued colleague of mine."

Lily let go of Andrew's hand and turned to face the stranger. She saw a tall, blonde, handsome man who was reaching out a hand to greet her. Although his smile was strong there was something missing in his eyes which meant they were not illuminated as they should have been. It was as if some tragedy shadowed his expression.

"This is Sean Colquhoun," Andrew said. "We are hoping you will get along together. We have high hopes for you."

The man said, "Pleased to meet you Lily. I've been hearing all about you."

Lily had been in Britain long enough to recognise his soft lilting accent as Irish. She felt his hand encircling her own. It was weathered but warm and she warned herself not to be fooled by first impressions even though this one was very positive.

"I have been telling Sean about your recent experience of British justice."

Sean gave an ironic snort. "It comes as no surprise to me. We Irish are well versed in the behaviour of our next door neighbours."

"Joking aside," said Andrew. "I want you to know that what happened to you is unacceptable and that Peter Herbert has been dealt with. He has been dismissed from the force for gross misconduct. That was as much to do with his treatment of you as with his inappropriate membership of a banned, fascist political party. He is currently interned in Norfolk as a potential threat to the safety of the realm."

"I'd rather not think about Mr Herbert," said Lily.

*   *   *

Trubshaw had visited Lily in Leicester Prison. After his second visit she was released to his custody and was allowed home. He visited her every day in her home and interrogated her. He had queried every detail of her past. He had attempted to flush out any latent Nazism that might have remained within her whilst feigning liberal attitudes. He argued in favour of eugenics; he suggested that all Christians were anti-Semites and that Hitler was just more honest than everyone else; he introduced discussions on race policy and put forward convincing proofs of Slavic and Negro inferiority. Lily could not be trapped. She was consistent in her beliefs. She became vehement in her opposition to his loathsome attitudes.

Finally, one afternoon as Andrew was putting on his coat to return to his hotel, he said, "But the trouble is Lily, you and I both know this is all play-acting. Your position in all of our arguments could be just as false as mine."

"I know," she said. "I wish I had never volunteered myself for His Majesty's Service." Tears pricked her eyes as she went on. "I truly wanted to help. I thought my inside knowledge of German and Germany might make a small contribution to helping win the war. Now I wish I had kept my head down."

She put a handkerchief to her eyes and could not look at Andrew. "Why don't you forget about me?" she asked. "If you cannot be sure, why not just go away and leave me to go back to nursing."

Andrew looked at her realising that here was the nub of the situation. Yes he could easily go away and let her get on with her nursing. But then he might be turning down the opportunity of deploying an agent of incalculable value; a woman whose activities might save hundreds or even thousands of British soldiers' lives if used in the right way. It was then that he decided to give up on the routine he was employing and to put her through a final test.

He had left saying nothing more than, "I will be in touch."

When the test came, Lily proved herself in a way that Trubshaw could not have expected. Her instructions had arrived in sequence. First, the local lamplighter had knocked on her door and handed her a note that he said a stranger had paid him to deliver. The message was in an encrypted code which she deciphered using the book Andrew had provided for her. Go to London Road Station, it said, buy a platform ticket and wait under the clock on platform 2.

Watching travellers disembark from the recent arrival from Sheffield, she was approached by a young woman in a military uniform and handed a ticket, an envelope and a small brown package. The woman briskly walked away.

Lily had opened the envelope and read, "Go to Central Station and catch the 2.40pm to Coventry. Do not open the package until you arrive in Coventry. Visit the Ladies on Coventry station and open it there. Further instructions will follow."

Lily went out of London Road Station and walked across town to Central Station. It was a sunny but cold spring afternoon and she wondered at the birds singing in the trees lining New Walk as if it was a normal day.

Her train to Coventry took over an hour and had no heating. In the Ladies convenience she locked herself in a cubicle and opened her package. She was not altogether surprised to find herself holding a service revolver, the handle cold in her hand. She opened the barrel and examined the six bullets. An ironic smile twisted her lips. 'If this is a game' she thought 'it's getting damn silly.' But if it is not she would show them she could go through with it.

Strapped to the barrel of the revolver with an elastic band was another note, "The bus station cafeteria. Buy a pot of tea and a piece of toast. You will be met. Treat stranger as a close friend."

The walk across Coventry could not have been a greater contrast to the walk across Leicester. Here was a war zone. The remnants of the destroyed cathedral stood against a greying sky like the ruins of a medieval castle. There were ragged children in the street in flimsy clothes that would provide no protection against the cold.

The bus station cafeteria was deserted apart from one grizzled old man in a corner beside a wall heater. Lily was waited on by a woman in her fifties who dangled a cigarette from her lips as she took the order for tea and toast.

Lily was finding it difficult to squeeze another drop of tea out of the pot when finally the door swung open and, along with a bitter draught from the street, in swept a man in his late twenties. He was clean shaven and wore a belted brown gabardine mac and a brown trilby. He approached her table removing his hat, exposing some premature hair loss.

"Mary," he called out attracting as much attention as he could from the grizzled tramp and the smoking waitress. "How good to see you."

Lily rose not knowing what to say except, "It's good to see you too."

To her horror he threw his arms around her and kissed her full on the mouth. She caught the intimate smell of beer on his breath and felt his hands caress her back. She pushed herself carefully but forcefully away. He had a wicked grin on his face as he looked into her eyes. "Come on, love," he said. "We must get going. We'll miss our bus."

Lily paid her bill and they exited into the gathering gloom of the cold dusk. They sat upstairs on a number 33 bus and her companion smoked without offering her a cigarette. They left the city centre behind and came to a downtown housing area with row after row of terraces. Some children played in the streets between the houses and women stood on doorsteps, smoking and chatting with neighbours. On every street there were houses splintered in ruins. Sometimes whole rows were missing, only rubble providing an adventure playground for the children. Miraculously, some houses stood out unscathed. They could not help appearing proud and disdainful of their absent neighbours.

They came to an area where tall factory chimneys belched out smoke that hastened the black of night and Lily's companion stood up. They went downstairs and jumped off at the next stop. As they walked along the street Lily felt her arm gripped by her companion and they strode along like any couple. Suddenly he pulled her into a factory doorway and leant up against her.

"Okay Mary. Listen well! Your job today is to assassinate a German agent who has been guiding the Luftwaffe to the most sensitive areas of this ravaged city. He is responsible for hundreds of lost civilian lives. This is how we are going to do it. He works as a clerk in the offices of this factory. We are going to enter the offices and I will show my counterfeit papers which declare that I am an undercover military policeman. We will request a tour of their stockroom to check that their supplies agree with the paperwork they have submitted. We are investigating black marketeering. We will insist that this agent accompanies us. When we reach the stockroom and are away from the rest of the workforce I will offer him a cigarette. I will ensure that he has his back to you as I light his cigarette. At this point you will call out in German. You will say, 'This is a trap. That cigarette is poisoned.' If he refuses to smoke the cigarette we will know that he has understood your German. He will not want us to know he is a German speaker but he will die if he smokes the cigarette. If he does not smoke – you kill him." He stared into Lily's eyes looking for a reaction. There was none.

Everything went just as her contact had said it would, except, that is, for Lily's part. Her partner was extremely convincing. His papers and his authoritative manner convinced the office receptionist immediately of their credentials and when the factory manager came out to the front desk he too was immediately cowed into agreeing to their demands to see the administrative clerk. The clerk looked confused and flustered but agreed to take them to the stockroom and bring his files along with him. On entering the stockroom Lily's partner made sure they would not be disturbed by locking the door. He then took out his cigarettes and lighter and offered the increasingly anxious clerk a smoke. He manoeuvred himself so that he was facing Lily. The man stooped to put his cigarette to the lighter flame and Lily raised the gun. Her partner glanced at her over the clerk's shoulder. His eyes screamed 'get on with it!'

In a calm, clear voice Lily called out, "Dies ist ein Witz. Die Zigarette ist Kandi." As she expected, the clerk's face dissolved into panic and he threw the cigarette away from him across the storeroom floor. Lily strode across the room towards them, her gun held at shoulder height. Her partner stepped to one side, out of the line of fire. He studied her closely. Why was she approaching? Why did she not fire? She had a clear shot! His eyes began to widen in non-comprehension and the clerk turned fully to face her. He found himself staring into the barrel of Lily's gun, now held an inch from his face. The clerk fell to his knees and began pleading. In that instant, Lily pulled the trigger. The stockroom echoed to the empty sound of a resounding click. The barrel had been empty. The clerk and the agent stared at her in shocked silence. Before they could recover their wits, Lily threw the gun to the floor. Then out of her other hand she let the six cartridges spill, she had removed them before entering the stockroom.

"Tell Andrew Trubshaw, if that's who set up this farce, that I wanted to be involved in serious work against the German Nazis. I do not want to take part in ridiculous charades. If this is the best he can come up with, tell him I'll get back to nursing."

Lily strode out of the stockroom. She knew that the cartridges were blanks and she became convinced that the whole thing was a set up when the clerk threw his cigarette away in horror when she informed him in German that his cigarette was made of candy. The smile on her lips was more satisfaction than humour.

When John Rigger, for that was the security agent's name, reported back to Andrew, he could not keep the enthusiasm from his voice when he described Lily's behaviour.

"She had us both going for a minute. Poor old Peter. He knew we'd got blanks in the gun but when he saw how close she was to his face he nearly shit himself. She was cool Andrew. Cool as a cucumber. If you take her on I'll work with her anytime you say."

Andrew Trubshaw spent a long time considering Rigger's report. He was pleased that Rigger was so positive about Lily. An experienced agent's gut feeling is often the best guide a spy master can have. But he knew it was not conclusive. He played out the options in his mind. If Lily was a Nazi agent she would have had no problem in eliminating another Nazi if her mission was to penetrate the British Secret Service. However, if she had guessed the ruse, why not go ahead with the fake assassination? What impressed him the most, as it had Rigger, was her honesty. Taking on Lily would be a judgement call. But all of his work was. Despite his strong desire to enlist her he might have erred on the side of safety and sent her back to nursing in Leicester if a certain project folder had not landed on his desk while he was still considering her potential value. He knew she was ideal for the role; it required and tilted the balance of his decision-making.

Andrew Trubshaw began to explain the nature of the mission they were being asked to consider, "The first thing I have to say is that neither of you are under any obligation to carry out this mission. As well as extremely dangerous, with strong possibilities that things could go wrong, you may find the proposal extremely distasteful. Even in the context of the work we do the proposal might repel you."

Lily and Sean looked at each other, neither quite knowing what to say.

"What I must say is that you will need to keep the bigger picture in mind as you delve into the details of this proposed operation. I also, in fairness, have to tell you this. If you two do not agree to go operational on this, the whole project will be shelved. It is not possible for us to find another two people with your unique qualities and experiences to be able to continue. In the truest of senses, this is *your* mission."

"When can we stop going around the houses Andrew?" asked Sean. "We need details if we are ever going to make a decision."

"Yes, you're right Sean, but we must take things in order. There are some important facts you must know before I disclose the nature of the mission; facts which might lead you to turn the job down anyway."

"Well," said Lily. "Let's hear them."

Andrew gave her a satisfied look, pleased to recognise the cool rational approach which he had come to expect from her.

"Number one," he said, "you will be behind enemy lines for up to three months."

He waited for them to take that in.

"The time could be shorter, but we have to prepare you for the possible limit."

He stared at each of them in turn. When he got no reaction he went on.

"You will be living in Munich. Think about that," he emphasised. "Bomber Command will not be ceasing operations for the duration of your stay. You will have to take your chances with the rest of civilian Munich."

Sean dragged one side of his mouth into a stoical half smile. He looked at Lily. Her face was immobile.

"You will have to live together as man and wife. And I mean convincingly."

Lily said calmly, "I take it you will leave *how* convincingly up to us!"

"Of course," replied Andrew, "As long as convincingly is *very* convincing!"

Sean felt himself beginning to blush and he brushed his scalp in an awkward effort to distract his own attention. Lily turned and smiled for the first time. She looked at Sean and said, "I am sure I will find Mr Colquhoun a very considerate husband."

Sean could find nothing to say, so Andrew rescued him by saying, "By the way Lily, it is not Mr Colquhoun but Dr Colquhoun. You will be Dr and Mrs Hermann. And that fact is crucial to your mission."

Andrew then allowed a silence to fill the space. Eventually he said, "Lily you need to know that Sean has completed missions for us before. It has involved him using his skills as a doctor in what we refer to as a combative function. Do you understand what I am saying?"

"I think so," replied Lily. "You mean that Sean has made some compromises with his Hippocratic oath in the light of current hostilities."

Sean turned to look at her. There was a look in his eyes that might have been hurt, or it might have been curiosity. She met his gaze and her eyes held his.

"I'm sure he is not the only one in this barbaric age we live in who has been forced to step down from the pedestal of high principle in the struggle for survival."

Her delivery left them to decide whether she was being earnest or disparaging. Sean's mouth twisted again into a half smile. He had squared his actions with his conscience and had no need for her approval.

"Okay, enough for today," said Andrew. "You need time together and time alone together. You need time away from here. You must consider your positions. If either of you wants out – that's enough for me. You must want to do this mission if I am going to let it proceed. There will be no pressure from me and I hope neither of you will pressurise the other."

"Andrew," said Sean. "You haven't told us what the mission is."

"I don't need to until I know you can make a convincing couple."

Lily and Sean looked at each other again; both trying to imagine what it would be like living as man and wife.

"I expect you're both thinking that you need to get to know each other. Well we've made some arrangements that we hope you will find acceptable."

He opened a drawer in his desk and reached into it. He retrieved something from it and closed the drawer.

"Here," he said, dropping a key on the desk in front of them "is the key to your home for the next two weeks." Ignoring their surprised expressions he continued, "Living the role begins now. We need to find out if you two will find marital bliss."

"But surely you can give us some idea about the mission?" demanded Lily.

"It will be an assassination! I will tell you that much. But until we know that you two can work as a married couple we have no need to inform you further. We may find that you are incompatible as a team and this project can be aborted. I probably shouldn't say this, but part of me hopes you two prove incompatible."

The existence shared by Sean and Lily over the next two weeks was a strange mixture of independence and confinement. Andrew had arranged for them to live in a semi-detached house in Highgate. It was close to the tube station. They spent their days wandering around the city visiting interesting sites, and most of their time was their own. But each morning the postman would deliver a list of suggested visits or activities from

Andrew that he expected them to carry out that day. Thus they had tea at the Ritz and took in a matinee at the Windmill. They watched the Woolwich Arsenal play against Tottenham Hotspur, which was a very competitive game, despite the fact that the League competition was suspended for the duration of hostilities; they toured St Paul's Cathedral and even sailed on the Serpentine. Wherever they went, they were followed.

In between scheduled visits they found a little café called the Carlton Tea Rooms on Drury Lane which they repaired to each afternoon. They were both self-conscious of the fact that they were trying to construct a friendship out of necessity rather than desire, but to their relief and pleasure the friendship came along easily. Sean made Lily laugh effortlessly. But there was no laughter in his soul. His slightly sideways view on life tickled her and she found herself often giggling helplessly like a schoolgirl. Whenever this happened she realised he was watching her humourlessly, as if intrigued by the very mechanism of laughter itself. She was aware that some part of this man had closed down. He was acting a superb part but it was not him. Should she be afraid of this? Was she being tested again? Or was this man concealing his true intentions? Well she would do her best to discover the truth over the next two weeks. If it did not happen, she could tell Andrew she wanted out of the whole mission.

Their favourite activity and one which they took to repeating on most days was to attend the music concerts that were held around London at lunchtime.

On their fourth day together they went along to a C of E church in Earls Court where a string quartet and a German pianist, a Jewish refugee, were performing two Mozart piano concertos. Lily and Sean arrived in good time and found seats in the second row of pews right in front of where the musicians would perform on the altar steps. It was their first such concert and they had not known what to expect. The first thing that struck them was the crowd that gathered. It was small and not representative of anything much at all. Although made up of predominantly older people, most escaping from work during a lunch break, there were some young men and women. It was stimulating just to look at them and to wonder what their lives were like and how they had been affected personally by the war. The off-duty fighter pilot, alone, no girlfriend in tow; the three women factory workers all in headscarves and bib and tuck uniforms; the young soldier and his adoring girlfriend, clinging to each other as in the last throws of a final goodbye. The music brought a oneness upon them, forming their mood and demanding their attention.

Three young women and two elderly men had taken to the altar. The women and one of the men carried their instruments with them; a violin, a viola, a cello and a double bass. The second man was obviously the pianist. The women were striking in appearance and their confidence, obviously drawn from their musical accomplishments, gave them a powerful attraction. All five were dressed in black, the women in long dresses and the men in somewhat faded dinner suits.

As they played, Sean found his gaze settling upon the lead violinist. She led the group in with strong movements and Sean could not help but be attracted to the physicality of her playing. She wore her jet black hair in a short bob. Despite that stark difference, she reminded him of Martha. Her high cheekbones glowed under the intensity of her smile, which she could not prevent lighting up her face from time to time as the music triggered her emotions. Her joy revealed a white-toothed smile that could have been Martha's.

To his embarrassment, Sean became aware that she had been returning his stare for some time and that her smile was directed towards him. He looked away and saw that Lily was smiling at him too.

At the end of the first concerto the musicians left the altar to enthusiastic applause. After a moment, the lead violinist returned, followed by an elderly black man wearing a guitar around his neck. He was tall and good looking and was dressed in jeans and an open-necked shirt. The lead violinist introduced him as Moses Abraham, a folk singer from Southern Oklahoma.

Moses Abraham stepped forward and spoke about his life in America. His father had been born a slave but had been emancipated by Abraham Lincoln. He himself made his living playing and writing folk songs. He had joined a group of folk singers including Woody Guthrie, Cisco Houston and Hudie Leadbetter, who supported America's entry to the war on the Allies' side during the heyday of the America First movement, which was headed up by Charles Lindburgh. Lindburgh and his crew had campaigned to keep America neutral. Their support for neutrality was a front for their pro-Nazi sympathies.

Moses Abraham then sang two songs, accompanying himself on the guitar. The first was called Little Charlie Lindburgh and talked about Lindburgh's trip to Berlin and the Iron Cross that Hitler had awarded him. The second was a song about dust bowl refugees and the terrible injustices they encountered at the hands of Californians. Moses Abraham sang in a deep, soulful timbre which filled the church with emotion. He enhanced his singing with his simple but effective guitar playing. Sean was enchanted and moved by his performance. He turned to look at Lily, expecting to see her smiling in appreciation but instead caught a stony cast to her expression which surprised him.

When Moses Abraham left the altar the musicians returned to play the second Mozart concerto. The church was filled with the most unexpected beauty by this tiny group of musicians and as they left, Sean and Lily were at first reluctant to break the spell by speaking.

When they were seated at their usual booth in the Carlton Tea Rooms drinking hot, strong chicory essence, Lily was the first to speak, "I think the lead violinist took a shine to you back there."

Sean almost ducked in embarrassment. Then he smiled self deprecatingly.

"Oh I don't know," he said. "Perhaps I let myself get carried away by the music. I have a feeling the poor girl was staring back in self defence."

"Don't be so modest," laughed Lily. "You are a good looking man. Any woman would be glad to attract you."

As soon as the words were out of her mouth there was a joint realisation of the implication of her comment. After a momentary sheepish surprise they both laughed out loud and looked for something to divert the conversation in a different direction. It was the first time Lily had seen Sean laugh.

"What did you think of the American folk singer?" asked Sean.

"You mean the Negro?" replied Lily. "I don't see how a Negro can claim to be American. He is obviously African."

A bit taken aback, Sean said, "If you're going to say that, the only Americans you would give the name to are the Indians."

Lily seemed to realise the impossibility of her position and laughed at herself.

"Did you not like Moses Abraham?" asked Sean, remembering her expression as she had listened to him.

"Oh, very much so," she answered, but not altogether convincingly. "I thought he had a beautiful singing voice, although his guitar playing was primitive. But I thought he was hard on Charles Lindburgh. That poor man and his wife lost their son to kidnappers. I didn't like the way he criticised him."

"I thought the accompaniment enhanced the emotion of the songs," Sean replied slightly non-plussed by her comments, but he decided to let it go.

On the way back to the tube station Lily slipped her arm into Sean's as they were now used to doing, and to the world at large they were like any other happy couple. In fact, the world might have concluded they were in love.

There were moments when their intimacy made Sean feel guilty. He would think that he should be sharing moments like these with Martha, not with Lily. But then he would think that if he was with Martha, there would not be these moments. He knew that the time for moments such as these with Martha had passed forever. His new daughter was a stranger to him and probably would remain so. When Martha had told him to get out of her life for good there had been no equivocation in her command.

Out in public there were times when individuals would look at them disapprovingly. One old veteran had reported them to the local police station. His accusation was that they were obviously enemy agents. When asked why, he had said that the Irish accent of the man had alerted him, but when the German accent came from the woman he had been convinced. A phone call to Andrew Trubshaw had swiftly sorted the matter but the incident was a constant source of amusement to them and they would often seek out a likely looking codger, put on the thickest accents, resort to speaking in fluent German and make obscure references to security in the hope that they might trigger another similar reaction. They were amazed how often they were completely ignored. "Maybe it is not so difficult to be a spy in England," Lily had said.

Since moving into the semi-detached house they had stuck to agreed, though unspoken routines. Lily always left the living room first to prepare for bed. Whilst she was moving between the bedroom and bathroom Sean always remained downstairs. Sometimes he would read; sometimes he would listen to the wireless. Once he left the house and went to a call box. He dialled Martha's number but he did not wait to be connected.

When he could hear that Lily was settled he would go upstairs himself and wash before getting into bed. On their fourth night together he was dismayed to find himself picturing Lily as she lay alone in her bed. He wrestled the thought from his mind and fell into a dream-filled sleep.

By the end of the first week they both knew that they liked and were comfortable with each other. Sean could not be sure but he had started to believe that when Lily slipped her hand into his as they walked along the street, the touch was more meaningful, more urgent than it had been at the beginning. One thing he was sure of; he liked it more and more each day. But he liked it the way he would enjoy observing something pleasant happening to someone else.

Twice Lily had asked Sean leading questions about his past in an attempt to get him to open up to her about the climate of sadness that enveloped him. She intuitively believed there was another man inside. There had been fleeting glimpses of him on occasions when some humorous event had surprised them both. But Sean had not been ready to share his tragedy with her.

"You are a very well house-trained man," Lily laughed on their second Saturday evening together as Sean got up from the dinner table and began clearing away the dishes.

"We Irish are a domesticated breed," he asserted. "We would make excellent housewives if only the women would let us stay at home."

Lily stood to help him and Sean found himself looking at her bare neck and arms, and the tiny glimpse of cleavage as she stooped to rise. He went quickly into the kitchen and began to wash the dishes at the sink. In due course Lily followed him through with the rest of the pots and, after placing them on the bench beside him, moved to stand behind him. She leaned over his shoulder and peered at the dishes in the bowl.

"Let me see how well an Irishman washes dishes," she teased.

Sean said nothing, just carried on washing, but his back could feel the firm pressure of Lily's breasts. He had no notion of what to say or do. All he knew was he did not want to move and bring this sensation to an end. The smell of her perfume faded as she went back into the living room to wait for him.

Later, as they sat playing cards, Sean knew that a decision had been made for him. No matter how hard he tried to bring Martha into his mind he could not do it. She remained faint and distant.

The greatest surprise to Sean was how easily he had accepted unfaithfulness. No matter how deeply he searched he could find nothing within him to encourage him to resist. He even wondered if he was being unfaithful to Martha. The strangest twinge troubled him when he thought of Grete, however.

It was at the moment when she said, "I think I'll go up to bed now," that Sean felt another person take control. He got up too and said simply, "Me too."

Lily turned at the door. Her face held a mixture of surprise and triumph. When Sean reached her they embraced immediately like lovers. There was no preparatory exploration. Her lips sought his and her tongue darted into his mouth. A thousand walls came crashing down inside Sean. He returned the pressure of her body against his and before he knew it he had her skirt up above her waist and his hands were caressing the whites of her thighs above her stockings. She placed her hands upon his shoulders to gently restrain him and whispered into his ear, "Not here, come with me."

Sean followed her up to her room, his mind a wild tornado of imagery. Martha was there, flashing in and out of his thoughts, and her presence made the passion for Lily all the more erotic. Grete was there too. He was ashamed and the shame made his desire more powerful still. As he followed Lily to her room he could not keep his hands from her. By the time she had drawn the curtains they were unable to control themselves even long enough to undress. She pulled his belt free as he raised her skirt and pulled her panties aside. She lay on the bed as he rubbed her triangle, but she stopped him as he attempted to enter her with his fingers. She pulled him onto her and guided him inside. The dark, wet heat made him groan uninhibitedly. As he penetrated her he lifted her blouse over her head and removed her bra, exposing her full breasts. He kissed the proud, upright nipples before she rolled him over to be on top. Drawing her legs up either side of his trunk she rode him like a girl on a pony. His big hands roamed over her back, her breasts, her buttocks. He reached up and caressed her cheeks. He drew her down to kiss her lips and he whispered, "I must come out. I am ready to finish."

"No!" she screamed as she rode him harder. "You must come. You must come!"

"But we're not protected," Sean said breathlessly.

She leaned down, her wide mouth on his face, her vagina parting wider to take him further in. "It's all right," she moaned, "It's my fifth day."

As the words entered his consciousness, Sean fell off a cliff. His mind roared with the image of the forbidden and the unclean and the contradiction of the purity of love. And in the drowsy aftermath Sean opened his soul to Lily and cried his heart out in her naked embrace. Lily cried too to hear of the terrible tragedy that had stricken the Colquhoun family and washed this man up here preparing to wage a one man war against Nazi Germany.

Sixteen
1933

Sean and Max were in the theatre prep room where they were scrubbing up prior to a day's programme of operations they were to assist in. Fuchs, as senior consultant, rarely dirtied his hands in actual surgery, but today he was leading one of his occasional bursts of activity. Raul would be supporting too and Sean was looking forward to working alongside him for once.

When Sean had first read through the day's list he had been surprised that Fuchs was going to lead. There was no one special on the list and it had not taken Sean long to realise that Fuchs generally only became directly involved when someone he considered to be important was to be treated. It was in fact a pretty mundane selection of operations; three caesarean sections, two gallstones, three stomach ulcers and two appendectomies. The only thing unusual about the list was that all patients were female, but that could just be chance.

"Good morning gentlemen," chimed Fuchs in an upbeat manner as he entered the prep room. He joined them at the basins and began his own preparation. Raul came in just then, but before he could join them at the basins Fuchs said, "Ah, Hildberg. I noticed blood on the floor of the theatre just now. Go in and clean it before we start!"

Sean could not believe what he was hearing. Raul was a senior surgeon. It was not his role to clean the theatre floor.

"I beg your pardon," Raul stammered.

Fuchs straightened himself up and turned to stare at Raul. Sean felt the intimidation in the stare.

"Which part of my instruction did you not understand Hildberg?"

"I understood the instruction, Sir," began Raul in reply, "It's just…"

"Well get on with it then and stop wasting this hospital's precious time!"

Raul turned and went through to the theatre. Hurrying to finish his own preparations, Sean followed him through.

"Here," he said, "I'll give you a hand."

Raul looked up from his position on the floor, scrubbing brush in hand and smiled at Sean.

"No," he said decisively. "You've already scrubbed up. You'll have to do it all over again if you help me. Anyway, that's the last of it gone now. I'll go and scrub up myself."

The nature of the day's activities was revealed during the course of the first operation. The first patient was one Lisa Brauer; 25 years old, Jewish, married, no children. Reason for operation – appendectomy.

The operation was straightforward and Sean was very impressed with the skill and efficiency of Fuchs' work. He dropped the appendix into the receptacle and the theatre nurse wiped sweat from his forehead.

"Shall I finish off?" Max enquired, thinking to give Fuchs a breather before starting the next procedure.

"No thank you Max. I wish to move on to the second part of the procedure for this patient."

"Oh," replied Max. "My apologies. When I read the notes I only saw appendectomy specified."

"Don't worry about it," replied Fuchs and Sean thought he had never seen him in such good humour before.

He began his incision as he spoke. "I will now effect a hysterectomy. This patient is a classic example of the undesirable elements within our society which it is our great task to control. The new government under the Fuhrer will regenerate the health of the volk with careful policies that ensure the reproduction of only the racially hygienic and healthy of our race."

With stunned silence Sean, Max and Raul watched as Fuchs removed the patient's womb. As the nurse turned away with the debris to dispose of it she stopped and said, "Pardon me, Herr Fuchs. There was a foetus present."

"Thank you nurse," Fuchs replied. "Not a moment too soon, hey, gentlemen." And he walked through to the preparation room to ready himself for the next procedure.

Nine more operations; nine more hysterectomies. With each one Sean felt more sickened until, by the end, he felt damned by association. With each cut of the knife Fuchs would explain the need for the procedure with a word or two about each patient.

"Asocial."

"Gypsy."

"Criminal alcoholic."

"Jew."

"Asocial."

"Prostitute."

"Jew."

"Asocial."

"Asocial."

At the end of the day Max, Sean and Raul left the hospital together and walked across Volkspark Friedrichshain to a coffee bar on the east side. None of them felt like coffee. They all ordered beer.

"Well," ventured Raul. "There are three babies who will never play around the fountains in the Volkspark."

In total three of the women had turned out to be pregnant and been the recipients of involuntary abortions in tandem with their involuntary sterilisation. The three men drank in silence, each finding it as hard as the others to put their experiences into words. Eventually Sean found something to say.

"If we were in Ireland we would go to prison for this day's work."

The other two men looked at him. Max was the first to respond.

"Thank God we're not in Ireland then is all I can say. Germany is very different to Ireland as I am sure you know Sean. We have pretensions to modernity. We look to science to guide our policies. And, let us not forget, today we have a National Socialist government."

"Today we assisted a butcher in carrying out crimes against humanity," interjected Raul in a depressed, resigned tone.

Sean looked at him, waiting for him to continue but Max responded swiftly curtailing any development by Raul of his point.

"Oh come on, Raul. Let's not get too melodramatic. This country has been developing a policy of eugenics for several decades. And we're not the only ones. Eugenics is a feature of the social policy of most Scandinavian countries and much more developed than here in Germany. Parts of America are well ahead of us in this field."

"If you don't mind me asking," interrupted Sean, "What is the aim of this eugenics policy?"

Max took a deep drink. He looked in two minds as to whether to attempt an answer, being only too aware of where the conversation might lead. But, looking from Sean to Raul and back again, he plunged on.

"Eugenics is about the health of the volk. Many scientific studies have been carried out investigating the worthiness of certain types within the volk. Some families have been tracked back as far as the seventeen hundreds. These so-called "asocial" families are shown to have traits that lead to criminality, work-shyness, prostitution, dishonesty, mental illness, you name it. These traits recur in all branches of the families in all generations. The eugenics standpoint is that these weaken the blood of the nation. Ironically, they breed more prolifically than other sectors of society, more healthy sectors, and therefore their blood is spread ever more widely throughout the volk. When their children go to school they are slow learners and they disrupt classes. As adults they create large mismanaged and dysfunctional families. They are a drain on the state. Their high reproductive rate weakens the blood stock of the volk. A eugenics programme would improve the blood stock by first encouraging more stable, respectable sectors of society to increase their rate of reproduction and to gradually eradicate the "asocials" or "undesirables" through a policy of sterilisation. That is what we saw in action today – a sterilisation programme."

Raul leaned forward and in a quiet voice asked, "Max, will you tell me how Lisa Brauer was dysfunctional or asocial? According to her notes she was a recent graduate of Berlin University. She achieved first class qualifications in Physics. She is married to a young man who is a qualified veterinarian and she was expecting her first baby. She lived with her husband in a good area and she paid her taxes and rent without fail."

Max looked crestfallen knowing that the only truthful answer he could give would be highly provocative. Nevertheless, he knew he could not duck the question or the answer.

"She was Jewish, Raul, that makes her an undesirable. You know that."

A couple at the next table and a group of young men just beyond them turned to look at the three men who were inadvertently raising their voices. There was a long silence at their table as they sipped occasionally from their pots. But both Sean and Max knew that there was more brewing within Raul. Just as Sean thought he would break this hideous spell by calling for more drinks Raul spoke, "So this is where we are at, is it? Our Germanness is no longer good enough? The Iron Cross in my father's chest of drawers counts for nothing? The men he fought alongside in the Great War were German enough, but not him? Are you telling me Max, that the great and good German public are going to buy this anti-Semite message from their new Chancellor? Are you going to stand by and watch as we are - what was the word you used? Eradicated, from the blood stock?"

The table of young men again stopped to turn and observe the doctors in debate.

" No," protested Max. "Of course not. You must not get paranoid Raul. There have always been these theories and there have always been those more inclined to try them out. We are just unlucky that our Senior Consultant is a fanatical Nazi. But they will never become mainstream because the people wouldn't stand for it."

"Who will stop them?" asked Sean.

"What do you mean?" asked Max in return.

"I mean, who will stop them? Where is the political power to stop them?"

"My dear Sean," replied Max. "You do have such a naïve view of German politics. Hitler will be a nine-day wonder. Hindenberg will keep him as a pet poodle on a tight leash for a few months at best, and then we will have a new centre right government and all of this turmoil will fade."

"I might be naïve, ignorant even, but are you sure you know where this centre right group will come from?"

"Well for one thing," replied Max, "There's the Catholic Centre Party. It is massive and has almost complete support from Germany's Catholics."

"And where does the Catholic Centre Party stand on this notion of the eugenicists that sterilisation and abortion are good for the bloodline?"

Max was hesitant. "Well, it's not so easy for them. They have to look to the Vatican for many of their policies."

"Yes," said Sean triumphantly, "And that's the whole problem isn't it. We all know the Vatican has been negotiating with Hitler and his chums for years. The powers that be in the Vatican don't care what a state gets up to so long as they keep their schools, their churches and their financial grants."

Raul, who had been silent throughout this exchange, called the waiter for more drinks. He turned in his chair as the waiter walked by ignoring his request. His face flushed angrily and he began to rise from his chair. Sean put a hand on his arm and restrained him.

"Leave it Raul," he advised. "It's not important right now."

Max raised his hand to attract the waiter and he came over immediately.

When the drinks had been served Raul spoke, "I can feel myself separating in two. My Jewishness and my Germanness are splitting apart. The life, the fatherland, the friends, the places I have been attached to since birth, they all seem alien to me now. I don't know what to do."

Sean felt helpless. He was impressed with Max, who seemed to have a better understanding of how Raul was feeling and did his best to console him.

"Raul, listen to me," he said. "This is all transitory. You must not let them force you into behaving in a way that is not natural to you. You must keep your self confidence. You must keep your pride and esteem intact. If you do not they will have won. They will have made you into what they say you are. You cannot allow that to happen."

Almost simultaneously the three men realised that their light was being blocked by the four young men who had been sitting nearby. As one, they looked up at the intruders.

For the first time Sean noticed that they were wearing armbands on their shirtsleeves carrying the insignia of the Friekorps. The one who stood nearest the table fixed his gaze on Max and said, "There is a very noisy Jew on this table. Why do you spend time with him? I assume you are a good German, but I will begin to doubt that if I think you befriend noisy Jews."

Instinctively Sean was on his feet. He was a good four inches taller than the stranger and he looked down into his face.

"You are interrupting a private conversation," said Sean quietly, his face in close proximity to the other. "My recommendation to you is that you return to your table."

There was a moment's hesitation and Sean realised that the Friekorps thug was doing a rapid calculation about Sean, Max and Raul and what odds they presented to him and his comrades in a fight. That hesitation was enough to give Sean the ascendancy. In one swift move he took the thug's shoulders and spun him around. With a push and a kick he propelled him into his comrades. In a moment Max and Raul were standing beside Sean. The Friekorps group were taken aback, and having lost the initiative decided to vacate the scene. As they headed for the door the spokesman turned and looked at Sean, "We'll be back," he threatened. And then he looked at Raul. "As for you – your days are numbered." With that they left.

Re-seated at their table, the three doctors now felt uncomfortable. They felt under a microscope, being stared at by all the other customers. Max drained his pot and said, "Well, I must be going. I'll see you boys in the morning. Good evening, Sean. Good evening Raul."

As Max walked to the exit the waiter approached him and blocked his path. He fixed Max with a cold stare and simply said, "Your behaviour has been noted." He then moved on to serve drinks at a table by the window.

Sean and Raul had one more drink and then they too left for home. Raul insisted that Sean join him and his family for the evening meal and Sean consented.

Max emerged from his Metro station and set off to walk the remaining mile to his home where his wife and children would be waiting for him. As he turned off the main thoroughfare he turned his collar up against the cold wind that was blowing in off the River Spree and just watched his feet as they took him homeward. The lights were on in the windows of the middle class houses he was passing and he felt warmer inside as he anticipated arriving home.

As he turned the corner of his avenue he glanced absent-mindedly over his shoulder at the sound of footsteps just behind him. He was immediately startled as a hand grabbed him by the shoulder, spun him around and pushed him into the hedgerow at the edge of the pavement. His eyes darted around taking in the scene. There were four of them and their Friekorps armbands confirmed for Max that they were the same four from the bar.

Max expected the worst. The two nearest to him punched him in the chest and then took hold of his arms and held him spread-eagled against the hedge. The third knocked his hat off and took hold of his hair whilst the fourth, the smallest of the group but obviously the leader, stepped up close and pushed his face to within an inch of Max's.

"Jew-lover."

Max instinctively tried to shake his head but he was too fiercely constrained. He could smell beer and onions on the man's breath and he could see, as if magnified, the pores and pock marks on his face. Without warning the man gathered a large goblet of spit in his mouth and spat it into Max's face. The revulsion almost made him retch. The odour assailed him and the taste and texture of the tiny amount that had entered his mouth caused him to recoil reflexively. The three others holding him snapped him back into an upright position, his face again within an inch of his tormentor's. The saliva was running down his nose from his eyes onto his lips.

"That's what we think of Jew-lovers, Herr Doctor. We are very disappointed in you. You have a privileged position in the Fatherland. Why would you want to jeopardise it by befriending a specimen from the most despicable race in existence? Why befriend a despoiler of our greatness as Germans?"

98

Abruptly, he punctuated this speech by ramming his knee into Max's crotch. Max's breath was stolen from him and he struggled to groan in agony.

"We don't want to hurt you, Herr Doctor. We are just here to provide you with some friendly advice."

Just then the front door of the house they were outside opened and a man and woman in their late forties came down the drive calling, "What's going on there? What's happening?"

For a moment Max's heart lifted. But he was soon disabused of his optimism as the goon holding his hair let go and moved towards the concerned occupiers.

"I thank you for your concern," he said in a most calm and reassuring tone. "You are obviously good citizens doing your civic duty." He reached out and gently took their arms, turning them back towards their front door. "But you need not concern yourselves here. We are dealing with an anti-social individual. We are providing him with some corrective advice. It will not take much longer and then your peace will be restored. Please, return to your home."

As the goon returned and grabbed at his hair, Max heard the front door of the house click shut and he was once again alone with his assailants.

"I wonder how your concerned neighbours would react to your situation if they knew you were a Jew lover."

The two who were holding him by the arms now raised them so that he was forced to stoop lower and lower until his head was level with their leader's knees. His shoulders screamed in agony and he made pathetic cries of pain that made him feel ashamed.

"Now, what I am wondering is if we have had any impact upon your love of Jews. Perhaps you would like to tell us what you think of Jews now."

To help Max in his thinking processes, the Friekorps hero swung his boot into Max's face. Max managed to turn it slightly at the last moment ensuring that the steel toecap shattered his cheekbone, but this probably saved the sight in his left eye.

"Well?" encouraged the leader.

Max spat out blood and saliva, and to his great shame cried out, "I hate all Jews. They are sub-human. They are vermin. You are attacking the wrong man here. Today, in my work I sterilised three Jews and seven other undesirables. I am a true patriot. I revere the Aryan. I hate the stinking Jew."

Simultaneously and without warning the goons released him. Max toppled to the ground and lay clutching his face.

"We're so glad to find that we now concur," said the leader. "We will say goodnight and hope that from now on you practice what you profess to believe."

With that they took turns to kick him in the chest and stomach and then they turned and walked away.

As the sound of their footsteps faded into nothingness Max was overwhelmed with first relief and then disgust. He began to cry uncontrollably and as he choked on his tears he vomited bile and blood. As he cried he was assailed by treacherous thoughts. He thought of the Germany he loved; the Germany of his childhood, his parents, his wife and children. He thought of the Germany he hated; the Germany of division and violence, the Germany that had left him behind in its move towards a brutal greatness that he was not fit for. He thought of the self he despised for his weakness and treachery; but he thought too of the weakness that had allowed him to be seduced into friendship with a Jew. He blamed Raul for the beating he had received. And then he hated himself again for thinking that thought.

In the weeks that followed Max's return to work after the insertion of a plate in his cheek, Raul was in no doubt as to why Max no longer spoke to him. If he could avoid it he was never in the same area of the hospital as Raul and he always avoided eye contact if caught unawares. Raul felt that Max blamed him for the assault he had suffered. In truth Raul did feel guilt for the treatment Max had been subjected to. Every time he saw Max's face, the feeling came over him. Max's eyes never sparkled nowadays as they had once. The insertion of the steel plate which had been used to reconstruct his face had left him with an exaggerated asymmetry that unmistakably robbed him of his good looks. The surgery had also turned down one corner of his mouth, leaving him with a permanent expression of negativity.

Although, nominally still in post, Raul was now only permitted to treat Jewish patients and these were becoming ever scarcer. In truth, Raul was correct in all of these suppositions, but there was one overriding factor he could not be aware of. This factor rendered Max incapable of associating further with him. He was burdened with an unbearable shame for the things he had said that night. His crushed psyche had the notion that Raul had heard his cowardly pronouncements. Indeed, perhaps the world had heard him. Ironically, his face and his eyes now accurately reflected his inner self.

Events in the world had moved on significantly during his convalescence. Issues that had, a few short months ago, been a matter of bigotry and prejudice, were now enacted in legislation. The Friekorps, the SA and the SS were off the leash and everyone was walking in fear. A whole nation was quickly learning to adopt attitudes and behaviours it had once looked at askance from a respectable distance. Each and every one had to prove his or her loyalty from scratch.

"Germans defend yourselves! Do not buy from Jews!"

This was how April 1 had been organised – The National Boycott of Jewish shops and businesses. Max had lain in his sick bed and listened to his wife Johanna describing the events of the day. One of her old Jewish school-friends, whose father owned a grocery shop, had been visited by Nazi activists. Any members of the public attempting to buy from the shop had been driven away. Those who objected had been beaten. What had been so upsetting was that one of the activists was a neighbour who had always bought his groceries at their shop.

"What's happening, Max? Julia was beside herself. I've never seen her so upset. She said she had never seen her father so humiliated. You know what he's like Max. He is always bursting with confidence and so optimistic."

Max felt his shame and depression expanding as he recalled his own humiliation at the hands of the members of the Friekorps who had attacked him.

"I don't know, Johanna. The whole situation is just too depressing."

Johanna looked down at him and her heart was filled with a momentary dread; as if the Max she had married had vacated this man in front of her. She sat on the edge of his bed and leaned her face to kiss him.

"Listen to us," she said mockingly. "Getting all worked up about the actions of a few thugs. Don't you think Hitler had to agree to something as gross as this to satisfy the lunatic fringe that has helped him win power? Now that they cannot say he reneged on his anti-Semitism he will be able to sideline them and get Germany back on track. I'm sure it was just a morsel to them to prove his credentials."

"I hope you're right, Johanna."

But Johanna's concern was not assuaged by the indecision in Max's voice and the distant look in his eye.

Sean's April Fools' Day had been eventful too. As he had walked to the Metro he had called as usual for his newspaper and a packet of mints at his local shop. This morning however, as he had stepped into the doorway, his path was barred by two men in full Nazi regalia.

"Not today mein Herr," one of them said politely. The other touched his shoulder and directed his gaze to the poster that had been stuck onto the glass in the doorframe.

"Germans defend yourselves! Do not buy from Jews!"

Sean read the poster and then looked back at the two Nazis. The one who had spoken to him was about nineteen years old and had traces of acne along his chin and forehead. He had mouse brown hair, which he wore with the limp fringe of his beloved Fuhrer. He was shorter than Sean but was in good physical condition. The other was a good four inches taller than Sean and he was a man of big proportions, weighing about two hundred and forty pounds.

Having taken them in, Sean slowly and deliberately said, "Fuck off!"

As he spoke he barged between them, knocking them both off balance as he entered the shop.

"Good morning, Gunther," he said to the man behind the counter.

Gunther looked extremely worried.

"Good morning, Sean," he replied. "Are you sure you want to buy your paper and sweets here today? It could get you into trouble."

"What, with those two specimens of Aryan superiority? The day people like that tell me where I can and cannot spend my money, is the day I give up the ghost. My paper and sweets please, Gunther."

Gunther's gratitude at this display of kindness and support was painful for Sean to observe. What was going on in the world to reduce such men of experience to these childlike levels of gratitude?

"Thank you so much, Sean, thank you. You must accept them with my compliments today."

"I will not," retorted Sean. "I'll pay for them the same as I do every day. Otherwise those bastards out there will have won."

"Well, all right," conceded Gunther. "But at least you can let me throw in an extra bag of mints."

Sean laughed and Gunther made an attempt to laugh along with him.

"I never could say no to a bag of mints. Listen, are you going to be all right today? What will you do if those bastards turn nasty?"

"Don't worry about me," said Gunther. "I am an old soldier. If they come in here I'll show them my Iron Cross. That will put the young thugs in their place."

"Well just take care and don't let them get to you. Remember, you've done nothing wrong."

As Sean stepped out of the shop the Nazis were not in the doorway barring entry. They were at the far side of the pavement looking back into the doorway. He stood opposite them. The younger of the two raised his finger and shook it at Sean.

"You have made a grave mistake today Herr Jew-lover. We will not forget you. You will have to answer to the party one day."

Sean felt his anger rising but made a powerful effort to control it.

"Is that so?" he said, advancing on them. "Well listen to me spotty. You've made a big mistake too." As he advanced they retreated half a step, informing him that they were not prepared to back up their arguments with force. "I won't forget you. And I know where you live," he added, inventing the fiction as he spoke. "Be certain my young friend, if anything happens to the man inside that shop today, I will hold you personally responsible."

He stared at them, inviting their response, but they had nothing more to say. With a disdainful look he turned on his heel and continued on his way to work.

By mid-day Sean had completed his shift for he was due to commence a week of night duties from the following evening onwards. As he left the hospital he decided to go round to see Raul and Grete. The nature of the day had placed a dead hand over his feelings and he needed to reassure himself that everything was fine with them.

On reaching their apartment he was met at the door by Lisa.

"Hello, Lisa," he said. "What are you doing here? I thought you'd be at school." You're not ill are you?"

"No I am not ill," replied Lisa. "We were at school but we were sent home."

Just then Grete emerged from within the apartment and welcomed Sean.

"Come in Sean. I am so pleased to see you. Lisa, let Sean come through. You go back to your room and continue your studies."

"Yes Mama. But can David and I come through and talk to Sean before he goes?"

"We'll see. Come through Sean."

Through all of this interchange, Sean could see that Grete had been crying. He had never seen her face so reddened by tears before. When they were alone in the sitting room he asked, "What on earth is the matter?"

Grete looked at him as if dreading to answer in case she was overcome with sobbing. And then as her mind played over the morning's events she burst into tears. Sean instinctively went to her and put his arms around her, attempting to soothe her. Eventually she regained control and began to recount her morning's experiences.

That morning Raul had not been going into the clinic. As Sean knew, Fuchs was not including him in the rosters unless he was forced to by an unexpected level of cases coming through the door. So the day had begun well. The children got up and the family breakfasted together. Then, because he was free, Raul volunteered to walk the children to school. They left the apartment together at about 8.15. By 9.15 Raul had returned and after about twenty minutes he had decided to go out for a walk in the Tiergarten. He hoped to bump into some old acquaintances, share experiences and talk politics.

About five minutes after he had left, Grete was surprised to hear the key turn in the door to the apartment. When she walked into the hall she saw David and Lisa coming in, she was puzzled but not worried because, although she could not understand why, at least the children were here.

"Lisa," she asked. "What are you doing here? Why are you not at school?"

Lisa simply replied, "We've been sent home."

"Well, what for? Who sent you home?"

"Our teachers."

"Well what for?" Grete repeated. "Have you done something wrong?"

"I don't think so," replied Lisa.

"Well then, tell me," asked Grete again, trying not to sound impatient.

"Our teacher said that today the whole class will be practising for Family Day celebrations. She said we could not take part because ours is only a Jewish family. So she sent us home."

Grete felt herself go hot and cold. She was dumbfounded. She could not find an instinctive motherly reaction to shield her children from the experience they had had.

"Come in and close the door," was all she could find to say.

As she helped the children out of their coats she hugged each one and told them not to worry about their teachers, who must be very ignorant individuals if they could behave in this way.

However, before the children were out of their coats, Grete made a sudden decision. She knew she had to go to the school and confront the teacher. She was sure that the Principal would be outraged when he heard what had happened to her two children. If people like her did not stand up to injustice, how far would things go?

"Put your coats back on children," she said. "You're going back to school."

"But Mama…" began David.

"No buts," interrupted Grete. "We're going to sort this out straight away. Come along – coats on."

And so they had walked back to the school. Some of Grete's confidence had waned as she passed the shops with SS men outside and the big posters telling Germans to defend themselves. But at the same time her indignation grew. Besides, the Principal had always been kind and respectful to her and Raul. And he had always praised her children as intelligent and diligent pupils.

When they arrived at the school, Grete presented herself at the administration office. As she stood at the reception desk she was not sure if the receptionist had seen her or not but she had made no move to come to the desk and deal with her. Grete waited patiently for a couple of minutes. Then she coughed. Still no response. Eventually she called across the desk, "Excuse me, please."

Reluctantly the receptionist stood and came towards her.

"What do you want?"

Shocked by the abruptness of her tone, Grete politely asked to see Frau Schulze.

"Frau Schulze is teaching right now."

"Nevertheless, I need to speak to her."

"Wait one moment."

The receptionist disappeared through a door at the back of her office while Grete, Lisa and David waited. And waited. After five minutes Grete said to Lisa, "Come on, show me the way to your classroom."

"But Mama…"

"Lisa! Now!"

Lisa reluctantly led the way along a corridor and up one flight of stairs. As they were ascending, a group of boys were coming down. As they passed the family they started a low chant of , "Juden, Juden, Juden, Juden."

Grete was horrified. As she turned to upbraid them they ran away laughing. What hurt her most was the way her children seemed to be unaffected by the abuse – as if it was something quite normal.

On an upper corridor they stopped at the door to Frau Schulze's classroom. Grete knocked and went in. Frau Schulze was seated at her desk and she turned to look at the group shuffling into her classroom. The children who had been working when the Hildbergs entered stilled their pens in mid-sentence and raised their heads to witness the interruption.

Frau Schulze rose, "What are you doing here? You have no right…"

"Oh but I think I do," interrupted Grete. "You turned my children out onto the street after I entrusted them to your care. I have the right to know why. I want to know the reason for your outrageous treatment of my children."

From the back of the room a child called out, "Juden!"

Frau Schulze ignored the call and turned on Grete. "How dare you burst into my room lecturing me about your rights? You have no rights. You are an undesirable presence and we have tolerated your like for too long. Now get out of my room and get out of this school. I will be informing the Principal that I will no longer agree to your offspring being under my tutelage."

"But what has my child done? I think you owe me at least the courtesy of telling me."

"I think you know very well what this is about. Your children don't have to do anything. It is what they are. It is what you are. This is a new era. Your time is gone."

"How dare you speak to me like that? What makes you so superior?"

Frau Schulze did not answer. She looked past Grete and the children to the doorway where two security guards had appeared.

"Security," she called. "Remove these Jews."

Instantly Grete was grabbed by one of the guards and the children by the other. As Grete tried to pull her arms free of the man's grasp, he seized her around the neck and holding her in a headlock, dragged her from the room. The class full of children all began to cheer and chant, "Juden, Juden!"

Tears of humiliation sprang from Grete's eyes. Her children were dragged behind her also in tears. As they passed the reception area the Principal was there to observe their ejection. The guards paused beside him and Grete was permitted to stand upright and face him.

"You and your children will not be welcome here again." Then turning to the guards he ordered, "Remove them."

Grete, Lisa and David were taken down the steps of the entrance onto the street.

As Grete finished her tale she began to cry again and Sean found himself comforting her in his arms.

"Where is Raul?" Sean suddenly asked.

"I don't know. Soon after we got back from the school he returned from the Tiergarten and I told him what had happened. Well you can imagine his reaction. He went mad. He stormed out. He's gone to make a formal complaint to the police. I don't know when he'll be back."

"What will his complaint be?"

"I don't know. Assault? Negligence? He was just so angry. He said that Hitler might have taken power but there were still laws in Germany and they had to be obeyed.

Sean, I'm frightened. What will happen?"

"Look, don't worry Grete. You stay here and look after the children. I'm going to the police station to find Raul. I'll bring him back soon."

Sean took a shortcut to the police station through side streets and alleyways. He dodged pallets that workers were unloading from trucks outside factory entrances and he hurried past bales of rags. Nearing the police station he emerged from an alleyway onto the haupstrasse. Anxiety rose in him when the sound of shouting and jeering invaded his ears. In the distance he could see a crowd shuffling slowly along towards him. It was lining the pavements and seemed to be watching the middle of the road as if a parade was passing by. As he drew nearer his pessimism was confirmed. The crowd would be more accurately described as a mob. And the parade was Raul.

By the time Sean had jostled his way into the crowd and got himself in a position on the pavement where he could see Raul clearly, the damage was irretrievable. Walking alone down the centre of the haupstrasse was Raul. He wore a hastily improvised poster around his neck made out of cardboard and string. In black letters the board read: This Jew dared to challenge the behaviour of an Aryan. Never again!

His jacket was covered in spit and he was stained from the tomatoes, eggs and rotten vegetables that had been thrown at him. All the time men and women stepped out of the crowd and approached him in the middle of the street. Some spat in his face. Some kicked his legs or pushed him in the back. Many dropped items of litter and the police who were escorting him forced him to pick them up. One well-dressed woman dragged her dog, which had begun to defecate at the side of the road. She dragged the reluctant terrier into Raul's path and allowed it to complete its bowel movement in front of Raul. When it had completed its movement the woman screamed, "Now pick that up!" The police escorts forced Raul to pick it up with his bare hands and put it into his jacket pocket. The mob screamed in delight.

If Sean had been able to step out into the street and machine gun the mob and the police down into the dirty gutters, maybe the rest of his life would have been different. But in truth he never got over the feeling of absolute impotence he felt in the face of that mob. He never forgave himself for standing by and watching Raul's utter humiliation.

Eventually, when the police had had enough of this sport, they dispersed the mob, not without some difficulty, and then with a kick in the back they dismissed Raul the way a child discards an old toy. Sean rushed over to Raul and assisted him to his feet.

"Come on, my friend," he encouraged. "It's over now. Come on. Let's get you home."

He walked along beside Raul, holding him upright with an arm across his shoulders, ignoring the stares and sneers of strangers they passed. Raul did not speak. All the way home he did not speak.

When they arrived at the apartment and Grete answered the door still Raul did not speak. Grete let out a gasp of horror and threw her arms around him. She took him into their bathroom and Sean was left alone for over an hour.

Grete came through to the sitting room saying that she had put Raul to bed. She believed he was in shock. Sean suggested that he take a look at him but Grete shook her head.

"I suggested that to him," she whispered. "He can't stand to see anyone. He has prescribed himself a relaxant and a sleeping draught. He will sleep now. He will need help in the next few days Sean if he is to overcome this."

"Don't worry. I will be around."

Grete, overcome with gratitude came forward to embrace Sean. They hugged and gave each other comfort. Then, from out of nowhere it was more than comfort. Their bodies moved together and Sean was kissing Grete's neck. It was not something he had decided to do. It was something that happened to him. Grete did not pull back. She leaned her head back, opening her neck and inviting Sean's passion. Suddenly Grete pulled away and looked to the doorway. Sean looked over his shoulder and saw Raul standing there in his pyjamas. Raul looked down and walked out of sight back into his bedroom. Sean moved to follow him but Grete restrained him.

"No," she whispered. "It will be all right."

That was the last sight Sean ever had of Raul. Two days later he killed himself whilst Grete and the children were out attending a church service. David found his father lying in the bath, his wrists opened and the water blood-red. There was an envelope lying on the bath mat beside him.

David ran out of the bathroom with the note and gave it to Grete saying, "Papa's having a red bath and he sent you a letter."

Whilst Grete started to open the envelope, wondering what game Raul was playing, Lisa went into the bathroom, saw her father and screamed. Grete dropped the letter and ran to the bathroom.

It turned out to be much later on in the day, half way through the evening in fact, that Grete opened the envelope and read her husband's last words. "I am not strong enough to be a Jew in today's Germany. I love you. Goodbye."

Sean's mind drove him insane as it repeatedly ran over the events in the apartment on his last visit there. He could not be sure how much Raul had seen. There were times when he could convince himself that Raul had seen nothing. Grete had pulled away in time. There were other days when he squirmed in the full knowledge that Raul had witnessed every last moment of his and Grete's passionate embrace. Anyone seeing that would have been left in no doubt as to the feelings being expressed. If that was the case then the cause of his suicide was possibly nothing to do with his treatment by Nazis earlier on that day, and everything to do with what he saw happening between his wife and his friend.

The guilt for the betrayal of Raul was worsened by the knowledge that part of him was rejoicing in the knowledge that Grete was in love with him every bit as much as he was in love with her. Even if he had wanted to he could not have prevented himself from following up the love he had felt being reciprocated by Grete during their brief embrace.

When the news of Raul's suicide reached Sean he had been at work. It was Max who informed him. He threw off his doctor's coat and ran out of the clinic. He ran all the way to Grete's apartment.

She answered his knock and when she saw him standing there she stepped back into the hallway and he followed her in. All the way there Sean had fought against a feeling of triumph. He was ashamed to feel it. It clashed with a terrible sadness he felt for Raul, for Lisa and for David. For Grete too! It mingled with a shocking feeling of responsibility for something too immense to grasp. But always coming round again on the cycle of feelings was an unbelievable elation. Grete was his. She was his and he was hers.

"Where are the children?" he asked as they stood together in the living room.

"They are in their bedrooms doing some school work I have set them," she replied.

She stood leaning against the back of a chair, her arms folded. She looked cold. Instinctively, and with no sense of inhibition Sean walked around the chair towards her and reached out to pull her into his embrace. To his surprise Grete pulled away in horror.

"What are you doing?" she whispered. "Please, don't touch me."

Sean's arms fell to his side. He froze. Something like fear ran through him. He shrugged it off. He had been inconsiderate. He should have known better.

"I'm sorry," he said.

Grete looked at him over her shoulder. Her eyes were wet but she was not crying.

Eventually she said, "What have you come for, Sean?"

"I came to see you. I have only just heard the terrible news. I came straight here."

He moved towards her again, but again she stepped away. She walked across the room and seated herself in an upright chair against the wall. Sean stood in the middle of the room and stared at her.

"I have been… thinking about you," he said, leaving much unsaid.

The intensity of Grete's response was a shock to Sean.

"Stop! I will not listen to you. I know where you are trying to take this and I want you to stop."

She got up and paced the floor to the door and back before she spoke again.

"What did we do, Sean? Did we kill Raul? Are we to blame? I know I blame myself."

Her tears fell now and her ribs shook with bitter regret.

"I had no right to respond to you the way I did. On that day of all days. You are a man and you have no ties. You have made no vows. But you were his friend. You and I are both guilty of betrayal."

Sean's pulse was pounding in his temples.

"You are right," he said. "We did betray Raul. But it was because we could not help ourselves. You know and I know what passed between us during that short moment."

"Stop!" Grete whispered again. "I will not listen to this."

"No," shouted Sean in retaliation. "I will not stop. What has happened is tragic. But it was not just about us. Raul experienced humiliation and degradation in the street that day. That was what turned his mind."

"Yes," interrupted Grete, "and when he came back to the one place where he should have felt safe and loved and wanted, what did he find? His wife enjoying the kisses of his best friend."

"Grete," pleaded Sean. "Everything you are thinking and saying is right. But you did not intend it. I did not intend it. But I love you and you love me. That is the surviving fact. You can't deny it. If you reject your true feelings now we will both suffer for the rest of our lives."

Grete listened to Sean's words and seemed to be considering them in great detail.

"If we suffer for the rest of our lives it is because we deserve to. I did love you Sean."

The use of the word 'did' sent a shock wave through Sean. He felt his knees waver.

"I started to love you many months ago. When you reached out to me the other night I succumbed to my feelings. But now, after what we have caused, when I see you I feel nothing but guilt. The appalling circumstances of our coming together make it impossible for us to ever be a couple."

"But…"

It was a hopeless interjection and Sean knew it.

"Being with you Sean, will mean a lifetime condemned to feel permanent guilt, betrayal and regret. I can't do it. I can't ever be with you. Being with you reminds me of what I am capable of. You showed to me a side of myself I cannot bear. Your presence will always make me into someone I don't like. I cannot be with you. If you love me you will go now and not come back."

Sean did not reply. He replaced his hat upon his head and walked out.

Sean, however, took every opportunity he had to call on Grete. He had not given his word not to come back and he lived every minute of every day in the hope that Grete would emerge from her self-loathing and her loathing of him and accept her true feelings. If he had not been so sure of the feelings between them he would have been less determined. But he was desperate. He had been given a glimpse of a rare chance of love and his certainty and determination surprised even himself.

Whenever Sean visited the apartment in the next few weeks it was rare that they were not interrupted by so-called Aryan or kindereich families who were interested in acquiring the apartment. The authorities had told Grete that she would be required to vacate the premises. This would have happened with or without her husband's suicide. His suicide was just convenient in hastening the re-acquisition of this property for an Aryan family. Sean helped Grete with her preparations for the family to move to Rome, where she had relatives who had agreed to take her in following the recent tragic events.

Although Grete became less intolerant of his presence he could not move her. She refused to engage with him on any personal issue. It was a gradual process of withering hope which was conducted within Sean's spirit that eventually eroded his self belief. Ultimately he just gave up. Whatever it was that left him at that point, he knew he would never regain.

On the last day of May 1933 he waved them off from Alexanderplast Station as they headed for a new life in Rome. Sean had considered Rome an odd destination for Grete to choose and had said as much to her. Why not London, or Dublin, or Amsterdam? Better still, why not America – New York or Boston?

"I have relatives in Rome," Grete had explained. "My aunt Ruth and her two children. Anna and Josef are two years older than me. They are twins, both married with children of their own. Their children will be companions for Lisa and David. They are doing well there. They say that the fascists have no extremes of anti-Semitism. We will be safe in Rome."

Sean had pulled her into his arms. But his embrace met no warmth. Grete accepted it coldly. Looking away from his eyes Grete had said,   "You must not worry about us. I don't want you to."

It was as clear a statement as Sean had feared hearing from her in his worst nightmares. Without hesitation he had released his hold and stepped back. He realised he was now actually scared of Grete. He dreaded what she might say next that would live to haunt him.

In the bustling throng of Alexanderplast, Sean watched the three figures, each with their own suitcase, as they disappeared into the crowd along the platform. They seemed so fragile and vulnerable that his heart was breaking. 'Rome it is then,' he thought. 'At least, they will be safe from all of this madness in Italy.'

During the following months Sean walked around like a man in silt. He went about his daily routine but his mind was somewhere else. His feet moved in slow motion and his thoughts floated in a vacuum. He became increasingly disinterested in his work. He hardly ever spoke to Max outside of the topic of work. Max himself had become withdrawn and uncommunicative.

Sean had begun to visit a nearby general practice surgery run by a Jewish doctor. Peter Abramovich had known Raul vaguely but had lost touch when Raul and Grete had converted to Protestantism. Peter's practice was shrinking, along with his income. A recent law enacted by the new Nazi government dressed up in some title about the restoration of the professions, was in fact about nothing more or less than removing Jews from the Civil Service and other professions. All of Peter's non-Jewish patients had been re-allocated to other practices and he was now only allowed to treat Jews. The Jews who came to him were often now out of work and, therefore, could rarely pay his fees. Sean asked Peter if he could come and work alongside him sometimes. He saw the worried look on Peter's face and knew it was because the income from the practice was barely enough to keep Peter's family in food.

"I don't want you to pay me," Sean reassured him. "The Friedrichshain does that. I can't give that up because I need to complete my studies. But working there nowadays leaves me feeling worthless; dead even. When I come here I get back some old feelings of well-being."

Peter had agreed and Sean spent many of his off-duty hours there restoring his psychological health.

It was to be the Friedrichshain, however, where the life-changing moment occurred. He had not immediately recognised the difficult patient when she began to rant and rave at one of the nurses.

"Get this undesirable away from me. Get your filthy hands off me."

Drawn by the commotion, Sean had entered the ward to see nurse Hilden attempting to administer a pain relieving injection to the patient."

"What is the problem here, nurse?" he asked.

Before the nurse could answer the patient screamed at him.

"How dare you speak to this asocial and ignore me? She is a nobody. I am the patient."

Sean looked at her and said with firm insistence, "Just a moment!" and he drew nurse Hilden aside and repeated his question.

"I don't know doctor. I think she objects to who I am."

At the sound of these words Sean felt his blood begin to rise. He recalled how Grete had recounted the words of Frau Schulze.

"Okay nurse. Don't worry. It's not your fault. I'll deal with her from now on."

"If you say so doctor."

Sean moved closer to the patient and drew the privacy curtains around the bed. Nurse Hilden had left the syringe in a kidney dish on the bedside table.

"Now madam," he asked "What seems to be the problem?"

The woman's manner changed immediately. She smiled up at him.

"At last," she said. "Someone I can speak to at my own level."

'If you knew which Irish bog I grew out of you'd soon change that tune,' thought Sean.

"I am a true Aryan German. I am the grandmother of an award winning kindereich family. I cannot be left in the hands of undesirables and asocials like that nurse who was in here a minute ago."

"I'm sorry but I do not understand. What exactly is your problem with nurse Hilden? She is not Jewish as far as I am aware."

Sean choked on these words but he spoke them in order to draw the patient out.

"Jewish," she shrieked in horror. "Don't tell me you still employ Jewish nurses here. It's against the law."

"But she is not Jewish. I have just told you that."

"No! She may not be Jewish but she is undesirable nonetheless. I know her. I knew her mother. I knew her grandmother. They came from the east. They say they are German but they are most likely Poles. A more dysfunctional, asocial, workshy, mentally infirm family you could not meet. They should be purged from the workplace and sterilised."

It was as she spoke that Sean realised he knew this woman. It was in the turn of her lip as she proclaimed the need to purge the undesirable nurse. That expression! Where had he seen it before? And then it came to him. It was exactly the same expression she had worn when demanding Raul to "Pick that up!" after her terrier had defecated at his feet.

His decision-making was instantaneous and instinctive. He immediately calculated how to assassinate this abomination of a woman who epitomised for him all that was wrong with Germany; the Germany that had caused Raul's suicide and driven Grete and the children away to Rome.

Reading her notes he saw that she was admitted in order to have several painful cysts removed from her ankle and groin. He also noted that the cysts were the result of extremely poor blood circulation. Her Doctor's referral suggested suspicion of heart disease. The hospital had not yet run the necessary tests to confirm this prognosis but from the woman's facial pallor and the swellings and lesions on her legs and ankles Sean suspected that her Doctor had made a pretty accurate guess.

Whilst he examined her ankle and observed faint traces of injection pricks on the skin he estimated the time it would take for her to die and concluded that by the time she entered her final trauma he could be back in his office sitting at his desk.

"Let me reassure you Frau Hahn, you will never be bothered by nurse Hilden again."

She gave Sean her sweetest smile and thanked him.

Sean lifted the syringe to the light coming in from the street and tapped the cylinder. He made absolutely sure that the top of the cylinder contained a bubble of air and he carefully omitted to expel it from the tube.

Finding a vein on her ankle he located a suitable entry point, one which duplicated a previous injection. He presented the glistening needle to the spot. The oxygen and the fluid hovered at the entrance to her vein.

"How is she?" said a voice. Sean almost dropped the syringe in shock."

He turned to see Max at the curtain looking inquisitively at him. Sweat ran down Sean's face and he stepped back from the bed and Frau Hahn. Max came to his side and took the syringe from Sean's hand. There was something in the movement that told Sean that Max knew.

"Here," he said. "Let me."

Max held the cylinder up to the light and studied the liquid. He looked at Sean briefly before expelling the bubble of oxygen with a sharp squirt. He then administered the injection to Frau Hahn.

"There you are, "Max said to Frau Hahn. "The pain will be all gone in a moment. Now, please excuse me. I must go to another patient. I will call back shortly to see how you are."

With that he opened the privacy curtains and stood aside to allow Sean to walk ahead of him out of the ward. They walked together to the office they shared. Sean was just lowering himself into his chair and waiting for the interrogation he expected from Max when they heard the emergency calls coming from the ward where Frau Hahn was apparently experiencing cardiac arrest. He remained in his chair as Max turned and ran out of the office door towards the unfortunate Frau Hahn. Eventually he jumped up to follow Max.

In the days following the death of Frau Hahn, Sean suffered extremes of emotion. Frau Hahn had been on the point of death at the very moment he had decided to murder her. If Max had not intervened he would have become a murderer, broken his Hippocratic oath, for nothing. His execution of her would have preceded her natural death by mere minutes. At times he experienced intense elation. He felt like a god, the electricity of power pumping through his veins. She was dead and he had willed it. His only regret was that he had not physically carried out the act before Max had come in. His elation was stunted by the fact of not having acted. However, his delight in this demonstration of poetic justice at times overwhelmed him. When he drank he experienced a powerful regret that he had not managed to insert the needle before Max's intervention. To have done so would have represented his rejection of passivity in the face of overbearing Nazism.

But when he awoke after nights of drinking, if he had slept at all, he was always consumed by guilt. Guilt mixed with relief. He knew he was guilty because in the moment before Max intervened he had decided to commit murder. The fact that he had not become a murderer was purely accidental. In principle he had accepted murder as a legitimate course of action. His mind ached with the contortions his thinking embraced. Was he a murderer or not? The philosophical implications left him dizzy. His face in the mirror as he shaved was a black hole. There was nothing he recognised. What kind of a god celebrates the crushing of an insect? Who was Frau Hahn that she should be the victim of his criminal vengeance? What kind of man was he to break his oath, betray his professional code? And what was his justification for this wilful, murderous intent? Frau Hahn had insulted his friend. His friend had committed suicide. He was in love with his dead friend's widow.

Was he not as guilty as this arrogant woman? His friend's widow and her children, the only true friends he had in this increasingly oppressive city, had been driven to move to another country for their very lives' sake. But Frau Hahn's insult was not the cause of his friend's death. Frau Hahn was not a power to be reckoned with in the Nazi scheme of things. The great god Sean had planned to lash out at, an insignificant nobody. It would not have dealt a body blow against Nazism. It would have been a cowardly swipe at the nearest available easy target. It all added up to a story of Sean that he could no longer bear.

Looking back at his time in Berlin, Sean knew that events there had been the driving force in his subsequent actions; actions he came to regret once he had met and married Martha, but by then it was too late for him to go back.

Berlin gradually became a nightmare for Sean. Too many things had gone wrong. Raul's suicide; Grete's departure for Rome; the loss of his friendship with Max; the death of Frau Hahn. He was also becoming a marked man. There were several Nazi Party members who had him identified as a troublemaker because of his inability to avoid a confrontation with them as they carried out their bullying behaviour. Most of all he despised Nazism now for making him despise himself and the person he had become. He knew he had to get out of Berlin and Germany and get himself back to Ireland.

One evening at the end of a long day at the Friedrichshain, followed by an additional shift with Peter Abramovich in his surgery, Sean sat down to write a series of letters. The first of these was to the Dean of Medicine at Trinity College, Dublin. He explained the difficulties of practising medicine, even as a student under Nazi rule, and asked to be considered for re-admission to Trinity to complete his studies. Next he wrote to his parents, explaining his plans to them. Then came the letter to Rome. He explained his plans to Grete. It was his intention to detour through Rome on his way back to Ireland and he hoped that he would be able to meet her. Finally he wrote a letter to one Andrew Trubshaw at the Ministry of Defence in London. In this letter he explained that he intended to pass through London on his way back home to Ireland from Berlin and might there be an opportunity to meet and discuss important issues as he passed through?

It was with a mixture of relief and sadness that he closed the door on his apartment for the last time in July 1936 and headed for the Alexanderplast Railway Station to begin his journey home.

The streets were crowded. Hitler was attending the Olympic Stadium today. There was a genuine air of celebration. This new regime, the "enfant terible" of Europe, was starting to believe that the world could accept it. Here were the Americans, the British, the Russians and the Chinese. Forty-nine nations all giving their stamp of approval to the Thousand Year Reich by their attendance. The nations of the world had come to the Nazi party. The newspapers were full of boasting about how the great Aryan sprinters were going to thrill the Fuhrer by humiliating the lowly black American runner with the improbable name of Jesse Owens, who dared to challenge their superiority. Today Hitler would participate in a clear illustration of racial superiority when he presented the Gold medal to an Aryan sprinter.

Before closing his apartment door for the last time he made one last search through the mail that lay on the occasional table by the door. There were letters there for three of the apartments, but none for him. His letter to Grete in Rome remained unanswered. He told himself that this feeling of emptiness would leave him when he arrived back in Ireland. His old spirit would return. Germany had worn him down, but Ireland would revitalise him. He was not very good at telling lies, even to himself.

At the Alexanderplast, Sean bought a ticket on the Amsterdam Express. From there to Ostend, London and then home to Dublin.

Seventeen

1939

On the day that Sean was meeting Eamonn O'Brodie and turning down his overtures to rejoin the IRA, Martha was going through Sean's surgery. When Sean went out on his visits she was always attacked by guilt. He was a good man; a good husband. Why did she hold him at arm's length when he was near? Why was she so resentful of him? Wasn't he entitled to his own opinions about the political crisis in Europe? Then the spiteful nagging voice would whisper – but what is he hiding from me?

At the same time she was mildly annoyed with Mary, the cleaner, because she found a dirty dishcloth lying on a trolley beside some surgical instruments and this led her to absent-mindedly busy herself with a flurry of tidying up. She started to gather up Sean's papers on his desk and to sort them into separate piles; medical cards, letters, bills, anything else. It was an item in the anything else pile that caused her to catch her breath and drop into his chair. It was a note on his reminder pad. It was in Sean's handwriting and it ran thus: ring AT at HMG. This was followed by a telephone number.

Martha recognised AT as the Andrew Trubshaw of the earlier letter she had found. She knew instinctively what HMG stood for. The telephone number was preceded by the code for London.

Martha had to be sure. There was an outside hope that this was a perfectly innocent message connected to his medical practice. She dialled the number. Her heart beat against her rib cage as she listened to the ringing tone.

"Hello," a female voice suddenly spoke. "You are through to the Ministry of Defence. How may I help?"

Slowly, silently, like a thief discovered, Martha gently replaced the handset in its cradle.

Martha went upstairs to her bedroom and cried for an hour. Her heart broke to think that this marriage, which she had perceived as a perfect partnership, was in fact a web of deceit. Not the normal web that wives traditionally dreaded. There was no mistress or unfaithfulness here. But there was secrecy. And she was angry. If Sean had to have this secret, why was he so careless about keeping it safe? If Sean had been there he would have told her that his trust for her was so total that he could not in a million years imagine her reading through his papers.

When she had exhausted her tears she rose from the bed with a firm plan of action in mind. She went downstairs into Sean's surgery and conducted a meticulous search of his papers. For an hour she found nothing to confirm the worst fears that had coagulated in her mind. It was as she was about to give up and sneak out of there in shame that she dislodged an old, battered wooden vase from the top of the filing cabinet as she slammed a drawer shut. As it fell, a key tumbled out of it. It was a key she had never seen before. With it in her fingers she prowled about the surgery looking for the lock it must fit. She found it inside his writing desk. She lowered the drop down leaf and felt along the facia, which held four drawers. Between the drawers on a blank stretch of polished wood there was a small moulded iron gargoyle. When her hand brushed it it swivelled upwards and revealed the missing keyhole. She slid the key into it and turned the lock. A large drawer slid open exposing a brown, unlabelled, manila folder.

The contents spilled out onto the desk as she tipped it and her first emotions were curiosity and surprise. There were no incriminating letters or plans for secret rendezvous. Instead she found documentation of identity; Two identities to be precise. There was a German passport in the name of Dr. Bauer. But the photograph showed a dark haired, bespectacled Sean. There was a birth certificate, a marriage certificate and a bank book for a Berlin branch. There was another passport. This time it was for Dr Schneider. The photograph was a red-haired Sean with a beard and moustache. Dr Schneider also had a birth certificate, but no marriage certificate. With her German fluency Martha had no difficulty understanding the contents of the file.

There was no doubt in her mind that her husband was an officer in the British Secret Service. She carefully slid the file back into the drawer, locked it and replaced the key in the wooden vase.

She went into the nursery, awoke Conny from his afternoon nap and washed and dressed him for a trip to the church. Even the presence of Conny with his loving touches and his innocent questions could not bring her out of her mood that day.

As soon as he caught sight of her coming along the lane, Father O'Shea closed his missal, got up from the graveyard bench he favoured for his afternoon prayers and went to meet her at the gate. He wondered at the physical, ticklish sensation in his throat as he watched the boy and the woman hurrying towards him. The excitement he felt caused him to crave approval from this woman. As she drew near he could see at once that she had been crying.

"Martha," he soothed as they met. "What on earth is the matter?"

He reached out to touch her forearm.

"Can we go inside?"

"Of course, of course."

He stopped to allow her to enter a row of pews, but she kept on walking and entered a confessional.

O'Shea was taken aback but he quickly gathered his wits and knelt down at the altar to prepare himself to hear confession. When he entered the box Martha was speaking softly to Conny. She took her keys and rosary beads out of her handbag and gave them to Conny.

"Here, Darlin' take these. Mammy's going to confession. You know what you have to do. Sit on the bench there outside and play quietly with these. I won't be long."

Conny was always good in church and he lay himself out along the pew and played with the keys and rosary whilst his mother made her confession.

"Bless me Father for I have sinned. It is one week since my last confession."

Martha felt herself filling up as she spoke to the priest. She restricted herself to her own sin at this first occasion. She asked for forgiveness for being a deceitful, untrusting wife. O'Shea's curiosity was awakened. He sensed a chink in the idyllic front the Colquhoun's displayed to the world. As a priest he could not pry too deeply. But as a man he was determined to find out more.

"For your penance I order you to take a stroll down to the harbour right this minute. Conny can stay with me and help me put out the hymn books for Benediction."

"Thank you, Father," whispered Martha. "You are very good to me."

"And on Sunday you must take communion," continued O'Shea.

"I will, Father,"

O'Shea's hand rested on Conny's shoulder as they watched Martha set off for the harbour. As she disappeared beyond a curve in the road O'Shea reached down, took Conny's hand and led him into the Sacristy at the side of the altar.

O'Shea was not to be disappointed for, as the weeks passed, Martha's confessions became more and more explicit about Sean and his secret activities. She always asked for forgiveness for being a prying and jealous wife. Through gentle questioning O'Shea garnered the details of Sean's secret folder and the correspondences contained within it. O'Shea's self satisfaction was complete. The secrecy of the confessional protected him like a shield. His possession of this knowledge about Sean Colquhoun excited some manipulative gene inside him that craved control over people and situations.

Soon Martha's confessional sessions had metamorphosed into the rights and wrongs of Sean's behaviour. Should an Irish citizen act for a foreign government? Like a good confessor he counselled her not to be too hard on herself. She had not deliberately searched through Sean's correspondence. She had not gone to his surgery with evil intent. She must forgive herself and then she must require of herself that she believes only the best of her husband and to always give him the benefit of the doubt. Her penance was always to take a reviving walk to the harbour and to pray for God's forgiveness as she walked, to say three Our Fathers and three Hail Marys and to attend communion on Sunday. O'Shea was always happy to mind Conny while she took her reviving walk.

O'Shea's guidance as her confessor was that she must always be prepared to act in her husband's best interest, and to that end she should continue to monitor his correspondence with the British.

Like many a Catholic before her, whenever Martha walked home after making her confession she would always feel so much better about everything. Father O'Shea would always say exactly the right things. O'Shea's advice was always such that she was bound to return to him for further support when things got worse – as they were destined to.

Eighteen
1936

A reply from Andrew Trubshaw to Sean in Berlin had arrived faster than by return. Andrew had forwarded his response urgently through the British Embassy. A hand delivered note invited Sean to call at the Ministry without appointment as soon as he was in London. Andrew would make sure he was available.

As his train rumbled out of Alexanderplast, away from this darkening continental dictatorship and towards the coastline of mainland Europe, he fingered the note in his hands and thought about Andrew Trubshaw, the friend he had acquired in his early university days. Not only had they encountered each other whilst playing against one another in university rugby matches, they had also met playing representative rugby for English and Irish universities respectively. Andrew and his closest friend John Barberis had struck up camaraderie with Sean that had reached across the rivalries of the rugby pitch. When playing in Cambridge, Sean would bed down on the couch of either John or Andrew in their rooms, and when they played in Dublin he would return the compliment. Their post match celebrations were legendary. The friendship became more than just rugby and drink. There arose a genuine trust and affection between them. The fact that so recently in their countries' pasts they might have been conscripted to kill each other somehow made the friendship more precious. The friends were open with each other and soon learned about each other's pasts and hopes for the future.

Although they would have been enemies if thrown against each other during the Anglo-Irish War, John and Andrew retained a genuine admiration for Sean and the active service he had known. They acknowledged that if they had grown up in his shoes they would have seen his path as the only honourable one to take. Sean too became aware that Andrew's ambitions were not medical. He did not hide from his friends his intention to be recruited to the secret service once his studies were completed. It was not an issue as he had no intention of ever being a field officer.

The friendship between Sean and Andrew came close to breaking point only once. Whether it was the level of intimacy the friends had achieved or the amount of drink they had consumed following Trinity's narrow victory over Cambridge that afternoon makes no matter. Almost without realising what he was doing Andrew was suggesting to Sean that the British Secret Service would be very interested in a man of Sean's ability, knowledge and contacts. It did not take a moment for Andrew to realise his mistake. Sean's expression collapsed into disappointment and disbelief. Before Sean could regain himself sufficiently to respond, Andrew was apologising.

"Oh my goodness, Sean, please forgive me. I know what I have done with that crass comment. You would be quite right to infer that I am suggesting you turn traitor to your former comrades. I can't believe I could impugn your character and honour so disgracefully. I don't know what to say. I beg you to forget I ever spoke. Please don't let it overshadow our friendship. I think I would rather give up all my plans for the future than to give up your friendship. If you can see your way to forgetting I ever opened my stupid mouth, I promise I will never insult your character again."

Andrew then fell silent, realising that, all told, he had said far too much. It was an early lesson that he would never forget in his future career as a spy master.

Sean smiled inwardly. It was the formality of Andrew's language that amused him. When stressed he reverted to the mores of the upper class from whence he came. Not knowing that an ominous portent of their future had just flickered across there lives, Sean got up from his chair and walked across to where Andrew was slumped on a sofa. He put his hand on Andrew's shoulder and said, "I've already forgotten it."

Nineteen

It is a cold man who is not moved by a feeling of insignificance when entering the Ministry of Defence Building in Whitehall, London. For an Irishman, the feeling is intensified by the knowledge that so many life and death decisions have been made within these walls affecting his countrymen and his forebears. The stone façade reaches to the blue London skyline and the immense proportions of the oak doors impose a physical as well as historical perspective on the insignificant figures that scurry in and out.

Andrew was not "at home" when Sean arrived, but his receptionist had obviously been briefed and Sean was prevailed upon to make himself comfortable with tea and biscuits whilst Andrew beat a hasty return to meet him. Andrew had been at Downing Street but had been instantly dispatched by his superiors to see what the "interesting paddy with kraut connections" might want.

When Andrew arrived he put down his bag and went directly to Sean and embraced him.

"My God, Sean, it's good to see you."

He guided them both to a pair of leather sofas and then called for Mrs Kitson and asked her to bring tea and toast. When she had done that he instructed her that he was not to be disturbed.

Andrew began with pleasantries. He mentioned old acquaintances and occasions they had shared, but he could see that Sean was only half interested. Something was preoccupying him.

"Andrew," he stuttered. "I'm sorry to be rude but I've come here to do something and until it's done I can't join you in reminiscences."

"Sure," said Andrew, Becoming immediately attentive. "Go ahead."

There was a long pause as Sean sat weighing up his words. He had a powerful sense that the next few sentences would change his life forever. He was about to step off the edge of normal life out into the abyss of chaos. But then he thought back to Frau Hahn and knew that his life had been deserted by normality already. When he did begin it was slowly.

"Once upon a time you said something to me Andrew that was an insult any Irishman would take exception to."

He raised his palm to silence Andrew's attempted interruption.

"If that insult had come from anyone else I think I would have chinned you. I want you to remember that so that you will have some understanding of the struggle I have had to arrive at the decision I am here to implement."

He stopped and took a sip of his tea. The rattle of the cup as he replaced it in its saucer was amplified by the silence that filled the high-ceilinged office.

"For the last few years, as you know, I have been working and studying in Germany. I have seen the rise of Nazism first hand. I went there with an open mind. Well to be quite honest I was well-disposed to Mr Hitler and his party, believing a lot of the criticisms of him from this side of the Channel to be typical British arrogance and bigotry."

A look from Sean into Andrew's eyes silenced any protest that might have been about to emerge from him.

"My experiences have fundamentally altered my thinking. In fact, whilst your Government here procrastinates with a policy of appeasement hoping to avoid war at all costs, I, to my great shame, have already declared war on Nazism."

Seeing Andrew's puzzled look, Sean recounted the story of Frau Hahn. Andrew's face betrayed no emotion.

"So, Andrew, right now you see a changed man before you. Here I sit in the Ministry of Defence where all your bloody campaigns of slaughter in Ireland were planned and approved; here I sit offering my services to the bloody crown."

After a long silence, during which neither man moved, as if trying to absorb the full significance of the words just spoken, Andrew finally cleared his throat and said, "Let's go out."

He then surprised Sean by putting his finger to his lips beckoning silence. He got up from the sofa and walked across to his enormous oak desk. Opening a drawer he took out a recording device. Sean saw that it was turning and must have recorded everything that had been said. He watched Andrew switch it off and remove the cylinder from the machine and slip it into his jacket pocket. He replaced the machine back into the drawer and repeated, "Come on, let's go out."

Andrew led Sean to a set of stairs at the rear of the building and down into a basement area. They entered a dimly lit room where Andrew called "Hello Gordon!" to an elderly man clad in blue overalls. "It's only me, sneaking out the back way again."

The man looked up from his Daily Mirror and called back.

"Not to worry, Mr Trubshaw, Sir. Your secret is safe with me."

Andrew winked at Sean and led him across the basement. He stopped at a large furnace and, using an iron poker that lay beside it, he pulled open the door. The intense heat from the interior flowed out and washed over their faces. In the dancing glare, Andrew looked into Sean's eyes. He took the recording from his pocket and held it up. Sean watched Andrew throw the recording into the furnace and heard its agonising crackle as it disintegrated.

It wasn't until they were seated inside the cocktail bar of the Grosvenor Hotel in Victoria that Andrew explained his actions.

"Listen Sean, I can't tell you how pleased I am that you've made this decision. I agree with you about Hitler's Germany. I am positive that soon his bunch of gangsters will bring about war. Unfortunately, when that comes we will not be warring against a bunch of gangsters but against the whole might of the Wermacht. Our problem is we are a divided house. Every department of state is embroiled in a virtual civil war between the appeasers and those who have seen through the illusion of Nazism. You have been brutally honest with me and I credit you for that. But if the story of Frau Hahn fell into the wrong hands in my Ministry there are those who would see it as their duty to expose you. If, as you say, the woman died, they would find no difficulty in implicating you in her death. They would find a way of returning you to Germany as a criminal. They would see it as a marvellous way of proving to Hitler that they wanted to do legitimate business with him and his administration."

Sean's face fell into a sad grimace.

"I'm not proud of what happened."

"No Sean, that is wrong. Those of us who have allowed reality to re-enter our lives know that the normal rules of law and civilisation no longer apply in Germany. It is because of Germany's magnificent history and culture that so many of us are unable to believe the evidence of our own eyes. As I have said, your honesty does you credit, but it is dangerously naïve. No one else must know what you have told me today. If they did not have you extradited to Germany they would use it as a lever to pressurise you into doing their bidding whatever your own feelings might be."

Sean drank his whisky down and called for another. The waiter replenished Andrew's glass at the same time.

"Well I can't go back to medicine, that's for sure. Not after what I've done."

"That's exactly where you're wrong," interrupted Andrew. "Medicine is the very thing you've got to get into. You must get back to Trinity and finish your course there. In any case, you have only a few months validation to complete. Then we must get you away to a gentle practice somewhere out in the west of Ireland; somewhere where intermittent absences won't be too alarming. But your occupation must exempt you from military service should Eire declare war on Germany alongside Britain when the time comes."

"The country practice won't be a problem. I've got one lined up."

The men downed their whiskeys and Andrew called for two club sandwiches.

"Sean," he began hesitantly after they had both finished eating, "I want you to know I do appreciate the extraordinary courage it has taken for you to make this decision. Some of us are not blind to the crimes of the past committed in the king's name in Ireland. You and your kind are greatly admired in military circles for the tenacity of your campaign. I know this decision of yours has caused an intense struggle within your conscience and I recognise the morality of what you are doing."

"Well, you may be right," replied Sean thoughtfully, "but sometimes I think I really have no choice. Deep down I'm a fighting man, a soldier, and that's all there is to it. All of this doctoring, studenting and rugby playing has been a vain attempt to deny the undeniable truth."

"Well, if that's the case," said Andrew, "you're exactly the man for us."

There would come a day when Sean would look back upon this conversation with morbid regret. He would come to see it as the day when his whole life turned and led directly to the day of his greatest and most tragic loss.

After spending a week in Leicester with his other close friend, John Barberis, Sean returned to London to undergo his induction programme. Despite the best efforts of the department's psychiatrists, no reason could be found to doubt Sean's anti-Nazi convictions, nor his determination to work with his new masters to help engineer the downfall of that odious regime.

On completion of his induction he was sent back to Dublin where he would meet and marry Martha Grady, and quite soon become the father of her son.

Twenty
1939

Eamonn Brody stepped from the shadow of an ancient horse chestnut tree as Martha left the church with Conny. Father O' Shea was sitting in his room in the sacristy drinking a large glass of red wine. He was feeling drained, overpowered by his complex relationship with Martha and the intensity of feeling the proximity of the boy aroused. Whenever he spent time in her company her departure left him feeling like this. In another life she would be his ideal partner. He liked her. She made him feel good about himself. She made no secret of her admiration for him. She trusted him implicitly as her confessor. But he knew his desires led him elsewhere. Unspeakable desires that drew him to the very place that would make her abhor his very existence if ever she were to discover them and the deeds they drove him to. His self-abasement was disturbed by the scrape of a sole on the stone floor. He was startled and shot his glance over his shoulder to catch sight of Eamonn Brody entering the sacristy.

"Pardon me Father," whispered Brody. "I didn't mean to startle you. I see you're having a wee sample of the altar wine. How about pouring a comradely glass for a poor pilgrim such as meself?"

O'Shea rose suddenly from his chair and approached Brody aggressively.

"Get out of this house of God you. You have no place…"

Before he could finish his sentence Brody had him by the throat and had slammed him against the wall. O'Shea banged his head on a coat hook and a splash of blood fell onto his white collar.

"Now don't be getting preachy Father," hissed Brody. "You might be the priest here but I'm still your senior officer."

Brody released him and O'Shea slid to the floor.

"What do you want?"

"That's more like it," grinned Brody. "Your church walls are not thick enough. I heard that woman make her confession. She's found something out about Sean Colquhoun that she doesn't like. We need to know what it is. You're the only man who can get that information."

O'Shea dragged himself to his feet. "How do you expect me to do that?"

"A good father can find out most things."

O'Shea looked as if he had taken another blow. His worst nightmare since being recruited to the IRA was coming to fruition.

Twenty-one
1928

Eighteen year old Brendan O'Shea had been sent to a Catholic seminary in Athlone. It was not long before he encountered a young priest who was happy to step into Father Haggerty's shoes in Brendan's life. Father O'Lally described their relations as "what men do together". O'Lally was the youngest teacher priest and everybody wanted to be in his class. Brendan was lucky to have been allocated a place in the dormitory that O'Lally supervised as Housemaster.

O'Lally used a similar strategy with all of his boys. In his third week Brendan was invited to O'Lally's room after seven o'clock mass in order to discuss his last written assignment. After a cup of tea and a brief explanation by Brendan of his academic efforts, O'Lally commenced to demolish the boy's work. Manifesting impatience and temper, he ridiculed Brendan's essay until the boy was reduced to tears. It was then that O'Lally made his move. Embracing Brendan he whispered soothingly into his ear that he should not take this criticism so seriously. Then O'Lally was kissing his face and wiping away the tears. Brendan now knew what to expect and when O'Lally took him by the hand and led him to the bed, he followed without reluctance.

"We men know how to help one another. You and me are going to become best friends."

And so they did.

It surprised no one when Brendan confirmed to his teachers that he felt he had a vocation for the priesthood. A vow of celibacy held no fears for Brendan. He knew he could never sustain a physical relationship with a woman. He would of course strive to battle and defeat his demons. But if he could not, he had the example of Father O'Lally to comfort him. Blessed father O'Lally had been humbled before his own demons, but he was revered by all and talked of as a saint. Surely he could not expect to aspire to greater holiness than such a godly man.

He caught a glimpse of the precipice his life was to be acted out upon during his third year in the seminary. One of the work experience roles allocated to him was the preparation of boys and girls for their first holy communion. This was in the local primary school not a five mile walk from his seminary. One afternoon as the children were leaving at the end of their instruction, a sweet young boy named Jimmy walked back into the chapel hall holding his knee and crying. He had fallen over and there was blood coming from the scrape on his knee.

"Lord save us!" exclaimed O'Shea. "Whatever's happened to you, Jimmy McShane?"

"Laura pushed me over and I've scraped me knee."

"Ah she's the devil in her that wee Laura. Never mind Jimmy. Come over here and I'll fix you up."

As O'Shea washed the boy's knee he felt a stirring within him. He felt it at first like a curse he had come to dread. But in a moment it transformed itself into an intense pleasure. His hand wandered above the boy's knee and stroked his thigh. Before he knew himself he had slipped his hand inside the boy's pants and was caressing him passionately.

"What are you doing, Father?" asked Jimmy.

In a breathless whisper he replied, "I'm making you better."

"You are not," yelled Jimmy. "You're rubbing me johnny, that's what you're doing."

And with that, little Jimmy lashed out with his fist and thumped the distracted Brendan on the lip. It caught between the tiny fist and his teeth and it split, spilling blood onto his chin. Jimmy pulled himself away and ran from the hall.

"Come back, Jimmy," called O'Shea. But Jimmy had no intention of coming back. He ran straight home and told his big brother, Seamus what had happened.

Eighteen year old Seamus put down the sledgehammer he had been using to break stones for the wall he was repairing and set off for the church. He met O'Shea half way to the chapel and gave him a fierce beating.

When O'Shea got back to the seminary for supper he was bleeding and bruised, and on the advice of his mentor, to whom he had told his tale of an unprovoked vicious attack, he reported the assault to the police. Seamus McShane served nine months in Dublin Gaol and Jimmy was expelled from the first communion class and never took the sacrament.

O'Shea knew that his black garb had saved him. He also knew in his own mind that he had done nothing wrong and had not harmed the boy at all. He had no prescient knowledge of the jagged gorge his desires would plunge him into as he stepped out along his own personal precipice.

It was not long after this incident that he made a clumsy attempt to seduce a fellow student. The boy's detailed complaint led to Brendan's transfer to Rome to complete his studies. It had been during his first placement as a curate in Dublin that his chickens had come home to roost. He was serving in a parish just beyond Westland Row station in an area of slum housing. He resisted the temptations available to him in the primary school, the confession box, the communion classes and at altar boy training classes. He was reading and praying. It was in the years following the civil war and he was a fierce republican.

One evening he attended a play at the Abbey theatre, which opened up into a debate about the play and the issues of colonialism, republicanism and Irish socialism that the play had dealt with.

As he was preparing to leave, having thoroughly enjoyed this intellectual stimulation, he was approached by a face he vaguely recognised.

"O'Shea," the man said, "I thought it was you. You don't remember me, do you?"

O'Shea did not wish to be impolite. He knew the man's face but could not remember his name or where he knew him from.

"It's Dougal Lennihan. I was at primary school with you. We were both altar boys."

O'Shea stopped his face from falling. His past always made him uncomfortable.

"Good God!" he exclaimed. "Lennihan. Yes I do remember you. You were in my class. I don't remember you as an altar boy though."

"I'm not surprised. I soon got out of that crowd when that bastard Haggerty tried to get his filthy paws on me. He tried getting his hand inside my pants once. He didn't try again. Did he never try it on with you?"

"Not likely. I don't know what you're talking about."

Lennihan paused and looked O'Shea up and down.

"I see you've found a vocation," he said with a sneer.

"Yes, I have," said O'Shea starting to feel embarrassed and hoping it wasn't coming across as humility or piety.

"What brings a man of the cloth to an event like this? I thought the church stood outside of politics."

Surprised and relieved by this swift change of topic, O'Shea responded with the enthusiasm the play and follow-up debate had engendered.

"Well the Church in Ireland has always been close to the state. 'Church and State as one' is how I like to think of it. Just because a man dresses in black, does not mean he has no political principles."

"So you're a patriot, are you?" asked Lennihan.

"I am that, and proud of it too."

"Well there's many a good precedent for you. Father Murphy led the men of Wexford and many a good priest has joined the movement."

O'Shea immediately regretted his previous statement.

"Don't get me wrong. I have no intention of joining any organisation other than Holy Mother Church. I am not politically active. I simply meant to state where my sympathies lie."

A cold expression came into Lennihan's eyes.

"Sympathy's not much use to the patriots of Ireland. It's action that's got us where we are today. And now we need more of it. The priesthood is a crucial factor in the success of our movement. Friends of mine will be very disappointed to hear that you are not a man of action."

"Well, I'm very sorry for that, but there it is. Saving souls is my calling." O'Shea laughed with nervousness and relief as he found the courage to state his position and hopefully extricate himself from an unwanted, possibly dangerous entanglement.

But he laughed too soon. Lennihan leaned forward. He leaned so close that O'Shea could smell his dinner on his breath.

"Saving souls, you say," breathed Lennihan into O'Shea's ear. "And I thought it was saving little boy's arses that interested you most."

Within a month O'Shea was a sworn-in member of the IRA with the honorary rank of Sergeant.

Twenty-two
1942

Sean Colquhoun was enjoying his life with Martha and Conny in County Cork. He had an immense feeling of satisfaction following his recent successful mission as Doctor Bauer in Gerona and it intensified his feeling of well-being as country Doctor Colquhoun as he made his rural rounds to deliver babies, mend broken bones and treat his tuberculosis cases.

The intensity of his reunion with Martha had been spectacular. They had recaptured all of the physical passion that had burst into life at the beginning of their relationship. The fact that it had waned slightly over the months since his return did not trouble him at all. He smiled to himself at the thought that he would have needed to be super human to keep it up at the pace they had set in the first few weeks of his return.

He had no idea that Martha's cooling had nothing to do with exhaustion and everything to do with her discovery of his file containing false identities. Her growing reluctance to be intimate with him was a withdrawal from this man who deceived her by omission. He omitted to tell her what he was involved in; what risks he was taking. Her anger and annoyance were driven by a feeling that her husband could not trust her. To be kept out of this crucial part of Sean's life was to be slapped in the face. She could only grow colder towards this man. Although her mood grew into an almost permanent sulk, she maintained civility and was as responsive as she could be when he made love to her. Because she had not immediately confronted him on discovering his file, she felt unable to subsequently. It was as if she had been deceitful by not admitting to her discovery at once. She determined she could not now raise the issue with Sean. He would have to come clean about his secret life of his own volition.

In the meantime she sought solace in the confessional. Gradually she found it possible to reveal more and more details about Sean to O'Shea. Each time she revealed a little more it was no great thing. But each item added up to a bigger picture. Whilst Martha was secure in the sanctity of the confessional, O'Shea was feeding back everything he knew to Eamonn Brody. Soon Martha had told them of his absences and the identities he had adopted. Pretty soon it was clear he was active for the British Secret Service in their fight against Nazism.

Brody delivered all of his information to High Command South West and argued that any active officer of the British Government was an enemy of Irish nationalism and must be eliminated.

Amongst those on the High Command there were those who remembered Sean's active service during the Anglo-Irish war and harboured a deep reluctance to eliminate a former comrade; a particularly courageous one at that. They ordered Brody to bring back some more compelling evidence before they would issue the order to take out Sean Colquhoun. Annoyed, but not defeated, Brody headed off to County Cork and the company of Father O'Shea.

Stepping off the train at the village station outside Cobh, Brody hired a trap to take him up to the church. As they trotted along he ignored the stubbly old driver who chatted in Gaelic about the price of bread and whisky and the state of the world. He paid particular attention to the doctor's house as they sailed past and caught a glimpse of a tall, straight-backed woman astride a fine stallion, just turning her mount into the field at the rear of the cottage and urging the steed to an increasing canter out of it. Martha Colquhoun was out for a gallop along the cliffs. If Brody wondered for a moment who might be looking after the boy, his curiosity would have been satisfied on arriving at the church.

At first Brody thought he must have arrived at a bad time. The church seemed empty, with no sign of activity. Reluctant to have wasted a journey he wandered up the centre aisle, automatically going through the rituals of blessing himself with holy water and genuflecting before the altar. Even in the sacristy there was no sign of any one and he was just about to leave when he heard what he thought was a gasp of breath and a faint knocking sound like a table on a wall. It came from beyond the back of the sacristy where he could now see a wooden door, partially hidden from view by the number of holy vestments hanging from several hooks screwed into the timber. He tiptoed across the sacristy towards the door and as he did so the sounds from inside became clearer.

A man's voice was whispering in soothing tones. The words were indistinguishable at first, but as he drew closer he could make some of them out.

"Conny… everything is good… God loves you… this is our secret with God… your daddy would be angry if he knew… he might leave you…"

By now Brody had silently opened the door and was watching O'Shea as he pleasured himself on the dumbstruck boy. The boy's pants and undergarment lay discarded on the floor and O'Shea had opened his cassock to allow himself access. His urgent to and fro movements were grotesquely mimicked by the boy's painful jerks.

"Enjoying yourself there are you, Father?" enquired Brody casually.

The shock of his voice shot through O'Shea like a thunderbolt. He clumsily disengaged himself and the boy fell to the floor. O'Shea turned in horror to see Brody grinning at him.

"God forgive me Father, but you're an evil bastard!"

Conny began to cry as he scrambled into his clothes.

"No need to cry son. The nasty man has had his fill for today," sneered Brody. He then turned to O'Shea. "Sort the lad out and then come in here."

Brody went back through the door into the main sacristy. He heard O'Shea reassuring Conny and eventually the sobbing subsided. O'Shea came into the sacristy.

"Brody," he began, "It's not what you thi…"

Before he could finish Brody slapped him across the mouth.

"Don't trouble yourself, Father. Who am I to question the ways of the Lord?"

To his great dismay, O'Shea found himself crying uncontrollably. Ignoring his wracked sobbing Brody took him by the throat and spat into his face.

"No excuses, O'Shea! Get up to that house and get all the documents relating to Sean Colquhoun; the ones that disloyal bitch of his has been discussing with you in confession. Get them today or you'll find yourself exposing more than your wee todger in the middle of Cork City before tonight is through."

About a quarter of an hour after Brody left, Father O'Shea and Conny set off hand in hand on the short walk between the church and the cottage. O'Shea knew that Sean was out on a long trip into the county to visit two old patients and would not be back until quite late this evening. He knew because Martha had told him. Martha would be out for a good three hours on her ride.

When they reached the cottage they had no trouble gaining entry as the doors were not locked. It was very unusual for anyone to lock their doors in this part of the world.

*   *   *

Mannix's bar was busy that night. Mannix had the radio turned up so that everyone could hear the commentary on the big fight from Dublin. The contender was a Cork man and he was battling for the All-Ireland Heavyweight Championship against a man from Monaghan. There was little attention paid to the individuals entering the room at the back of the bar. The south west High Command was in session.

Eamonn Brody stood before them and said, "You asked for more evidence." He dropped a large file on the table. "Here it is."

The file was passed between the six men around the table and they scrutinised every document there.

"What happens when Colquhoun finds this file missing?"

"He won't. Holy Mother Church will see that it is returned to its place tomorrow with nobody any the wiser."

Captain Doyle glanced around at his comrades. He received a nod in return from each of them. He closed the file and handed it back to Brody.

"Get it done," he said and closed the meeting.

Martha placed a plate of smoked mackerel in front of Sean at breakfast and he took up the bread knife to cut a thick slice.

"Is everything all right, Martha?" he asked.

"Why wouldn't it be?" she replied a bit too sharply, arousing his concern. He put down his knife and got up to go to her.

"What's the matter?" he said attempting to reach his arms around her.

Sensing his approach she pulled away leaving him open armed and empty.

"It's nothing. I'm a little worried about Conny," she said, more as an excuse to avoid the real issue.

"What about Conny?"

Now that she had said it she realised she *was* worried about Conny.

"I'm not sure," she said. "He's just not himself recently. He's become withdrawn and moody."

Sean approached her again and this time she did not move away. He took her in his arms but there was no embrace in response.

"I'm sure it's nothing. Probably a phase. I'll check him out tonight."

Sean sounded reassuring but his concern was triggered. So much so that when he returned to his breakfast he slipped and cut himself with the bread knife. The cut was small but drew blood and he had to wash it at the sink.

"What are you doing today?" he asked his wife.

"Oh, I'm not sure. I'll probably go up to the church. Conny seems to like it up there. Father O'Shea is very good to him."

"I'm married into a very religious family all of a sudden," joked Sean, but Martha was not amused.

Sean finished eating, washed his hand again at the sink because the cut was still bleeding and then kissed Martha goodbye.

"I'll get off," he said. "The Lennon baby is due at any time. I promised Joe I'd call up and see Mary today. I'll try not to be late."

"Bye Sean," said Martha. "Send Conny in from the yard. Tell him we're going out now and he needs to wash his hands and face."

Sean stood in the yard and looked across at his son. He was sitting against the wall talking to himself. He wasn't chasing the hens or swinging on the gate as he often used to.

"Hey there, Conny. Come and give your dad a kiss."

Conny jumped at the sound of his father's voice. Slowly he got to his feet and walked over. His father picked him up and kissed his cheek. Conny pulled away. Sean put him down trying to make nothing of it, but he couldn't help agreeing with Martha. There was something wrong. Now, however, was not the time to go into it. He put his son down and said, "Go in now, Conny, your mother wants you. You have to get ready to go up to the church."

Conny's face darkened but he said nothing. Sean put him down and watched him walk into the house.

Sean drove out of the yard, along the drive and stopped to climb out and open the gate. He drove through the gate, stopped again, and got out to close it. He then drove in to Cobh where he had two calls to make before driving up country to the Lennon's farm.

His first call was not a good start. Mrs Flynn had asked him to call to see her daughter, Josephine. She was complaining of stomach pains and vomiting. She was refusing to go to school. It took Sean less than a minute to decide the young girl was pregnant and no more than five to confirm it. Fourteen year old Josephine with the mind of a six year old had been taken advantage of. When Sean questioned her about whom the father might be he got little sense from her. Poor Mrs Flynn was distraught.

"We are ruined! What will we do with the child? We'll all be damned to hell!"

"Now, now Mrs Flynn. It's not as bad as all that. I'll guide Josephine through the pregnancy and then we'll find a good home for the baby. I meet many a childless couple in my line of work who would love to adopt a healthy baby. In the meantime, I'll fill out the forms for the school so that no one will pry into why Josephine is absent."

"Oh Doctor. You're a good man. Let's hope it is a healthy baby. The stupid girl has no more sense than a monkey. I hope the baby doesn't take after her."

Sean left the tiny house and headed for his next call. He was irritated that the cut on his hand had re-opened whilst working with Josephine. Realising it was not best practice for a doctor to turn up for house calls with blood coming out of his hand he decided to divert his route back home to deal properly with the cut before going on.

As he turned into the lane that led to the cottage he glimpsed two figures way up the top field going over the brow towards the church. Martha and Conny looked so beautiful, in such an idyllic setting that he felt water come to his eyes. Conny would be five soon and starting school in the following year. That would be good for him too, Sean thought.

When he reached the gate to the yard he could not be bothered with all the opening and closing involved so he switched off the engine and decided to walk up to the cottage. Coming around the wall of the stable he was surprised to see a figure ahead of him right up at the cottage door. He was just about to call out when he stopped himself as the figure pushed the door open and walked in. The figure was a priest, if his garb was anything to go by, and if he was not mistaken, Sean was pretty sure the priest was Father O'Shea.

Sean reached the front door and tiptoed in. The door into his consulting room was open and he could hear the sounds of someone rummaging around. Soundlessly he went to the door and watched as O'Shea placed a brown folder, one Sean recognised as his own, on the table and began to feel around in his writing bureau. In a moment O'Shea had opened the drawer which Sean believed to be known only to himself, and turned to pick up the folder from the table. It was as O'Shea turned that he saw Sean watching him.

O'Shea froze. His groin turned to water. His chest lurched in fear.

"What's going on O'Shea?"

"Hello there, Sean," croaked O'Shea, dragging his tongue across dry lips.

"Put both hands flat on the table," ordered Sean in a suddenly cold tone.

O'Shea did as he was told. Sean walked towards the table. He picked up the folder and flicked through the contents. He knew that whoever had read this would know of his activities and involvement with British Secret Service.

"What were you doing with this? Who else has seen it?"

About to answer, O'Shea seemed distracted and glanced behind Sean towards the door. Sean instinctively looked behind him. There in the doorway, armed with Thompson rifles, stood Eamonn Brody and a comrade soldier of the movement. Brody was confident and assertive. His partner was no more than seventeen years old and he was red-faced and nervous. His eyes darted here and there and his head jerked from side to side. Sean knew immediately what this meant.

"You can go now Father. You can catch up with the rest of the Colquhouns and continue your filthy practices."

It was Eamonn who spoke. He wore a triumphant grin and he stared at Sean. Something jarred in Sean's mind as he digested Brody's obscure comment.

"What do you mean –'filthy practices'?" he asked.

"Maybe you should ask your wee boy, Doctor Colquhoun. If you were an anyways decent father you wouldn't have to ask. If we had more time the Holy Father here would enlighten you, but unfortunately for you your time has run out."

Sean made an instinctive lunge towards O'Shea. Brody raised and cocked his rifle and stepped towards Sean.

"I wouldn't do that if I were you," Brody threatened.

Sean stopped himself.

"Go on, get out of here priest," yelled Brody. "Before I set the British secret agent on you."

O'Shea scurried around the table almost crashing into Brody's nervous comrade and ran out of the room without looking back. Sean was now backed up against the table with Brody's rifle barrel at his throat. His eyes studied those of Sean. He looked puzzled.

"I don't get it Sean. You of all people - a traitor. How could it happen?"

"I'm no traitor to Ireland, Eamonn Brody, and you know it." Sean rasped his reply into Brody's face. Brody did not flinch. He was enjoying Sean's impotent rage.

"You're the traitor to everything that is decent, Brody. You use an abuser of children to further your own ends. God help Ireland if you people ever succeed in your twisted aims. If you had any decency in you, that bastard priest would be dead with your bullet in his sick brain."

Brody was ruffled by the vehemence of Sean's denunciation of him.

"At least I have good reason for my behaviour. Look at you Brody, fighting yesterday's war."

"It makes no difference what you think or say," shouted Brody. "We are here to carry out a sentence of death upon you as an agent of the crown and a traitor to Ireland. That will happen here, today, no matter what." Brody paused and backed away slightly, lowering his rifle barrel from Sean's throat. "But go on," he added. "Tell us your twisted reasoning."

"I wouldn't waste my breath except I know you Brody. You came into this movement through the Irish Citizen Army. Your father was a lieutenant of James Connolly. Your roots are socialist. The people I am fighting are committing mass murder against the socialists in all the countries of Europe. If they win this war you and all your comrades will be wiped out. There will be no more socialists; there will be no more socialism. They are your enemies too, Eamonn."

"England and the bloody Empire are my enemies. And that means you are too."

Brody took a step backwards.

"Jimmy," he shouted.

His young comrade stepped forward to join him. The boy's face was as white as a sheet and sweat poured from his scalp.

"I'm sorry it has come to this, Sean. Orders are orders and traitors are traitors."

They lifted their rifles to their shoulders and took aim. Sean's mind went into freefall. He had to get out of here. He had to get Conny in his arms. He had to get to O'Shea. With seconds left in which to think the infinite range of thoughts available to him, he plunged into a spinning vortex. It was then, as if a hand had reached into the physical matter of his brain and scraped it with a stone, that he heard a distant, echoing call. It was his name. Someone was calling his name. It was a voice he recognised. It was Martha. But Martha was not here. She had gone to the church.

Walking past the window Sean could hear Martha talking to Conny. "Daddy will be pleased to see us. You were a clever boy spotting his car. We don't have to go to the church if you don't want to. You run on ahead and surprise him."

"No Conny! Martha, no!" Sean's mind flashed back to his meeting with Trubshaw in London in those days just after his return from Berlin. He screamed at the top of his voice.

Sean watched helplessly as Jimmy's nerve went. He shook with fear as he turned to face the door and began firing. The wood splintered and the door creaked open. There on the other side was Conny. He lay face down crumpled in a motionless heap.

Brody screamed in the chaos, "What the fuck are you doing?" and he swivelled round to try to make sense of Jimmy's action.

In a melee of screaming from Martha and the resounding echo of the gunfire, Sean launched himself at the assassins. He seized Jimmy from behind and with a vicious wrench he broke the boy's neck and snatched his rifle from him. As Brody turned towards him, Sean knew he did not have time to raise the rifle and fire. He twisted the full trunk of his body and slammed the butt of the rifle into Brody's face. Martha came running into the room and fell on Conny. Sean walked over to the unconscious Brody and shot him through the temple.

The boy was pronounced dead on arrival at Cork City hospital.

Twenty-three
1943

On hearing Sean's heartbreaking tale, Lily believed that their relationship was sealed. Although wracked with guilt, this was a good man. His commitment to the cause he now espoused had directly led to the dreadful abuse and death of his son and the break-up of his marriage. But it had made his resolve as strong as iron. He would be a good man to work with.

From the moment of their first intimacy it had no longer been a struggle to act as man and wife when in public. In fact, whenever they met Andrew or any of his aides, the struggle was to not act in such a way as to make it obvious to them just how intimate they had become.

At the end of a wild fortnight of passion, Sean and Lily found themselves with Andrew in his office in Onslow Gardens again. Andrew could see from their invisible body language that they had made a couple. He was confident that they would be able to carry off the disguise of man and wife behind enemy lines. To be sure he did not know exactly how well they could carry it off; Only Sean and Lily knew that. It was now time to brief them on their mission. Only if they agreed to it would the project be taken forward.

"Before I go into details I need to ask you both whether you think you will be able to be convincing as man and wife if you undertake this mission."

Despite himself Sean felt a blush beginning to spread upon his face. Lily distracted Andrew by speaking up first.

"Sean must answer for himself, but as for me, I am certain we can do it."

"No problem at all, Andrew," Sean said and then coughed several times.

"Dear chap," said Andrew. "Here, have some water."

Sean gratefully gulped a glass of water and then sat back to listen to what Andrew had to say.

He opened a file and then began speaking in a business like fashion, "Ironically, for this mission, the fact that you are both Catholics is important to us." He paused.

Lily and Sean looked at each other. 'Where is this leading?' was the expression on their faces.

"The powers that be don't want this to appear sectarian in nature should anything go wrong."

Sean shifted in his seat. "Look Andrew, you don't need to prepare the ground any further. We've had two weeks to think about this. We are both here because we want to play our part in bringing down Nazism. We want to be involved. We doubt there is anything you can ask us that is so morally repugnant that we will want to back out. If there is we might have to ask why we want to work for you at all. But now is the time to tell us."

Andrew looked up from his file. He closed it and looked from Lily to Sean and back again. Then he said, "We want you to assassinate the Pope!"

Twenty-four
January 1944
Munich

Dr Robert Hermann opened the door between his consulting room and his receptionist's office and enquired, "Was that the last one?

"Yes Herr Doctor," she replied.

"Thank you, will you please ask my wife to come in."

"Certainly, Doctor."

A few moments later Frau Hermann came into the consulting room carrying a hot cup of onion soup. It was the only vegetable she had been able to get hold of in the shops that day.

"Here you are my good Doctor. Something hot to put the strength back in you."

She smiled as she handed the cup to him. She rubbed her hand gently over his close-cropped hair. It was thick and spiky but, being fair; it was so short that his smooth scalp showed through. It had the desired effect of altering his appearance for anyone used to his normally abundant locks. As she leaned forward to place her lips upon his she became Lily and he became Sean. But only for the duration of the kiss.

Dr Robert Hermann sat back in his chair and sipped his soup. Frau Lily Hermann smiled as he grimaced at the taste. As the new incumbents of this south Munich surgery, they were settling in nicely and getting to know their patients. Things had gone smoothly since their arrival. Their patients were thrilled to have another doctor so quickly after the loss of the previous incumbents; the unfortunate Dr and Frau Troost.

Dr Troost and his wife had been the victims of an allied bombing raid. Their bodies had been found in the ruins of a bar in central Munich. It had been a daytime raid and there had been some odd features about the deaths. For example, they had told friends that they were travelling to the Bavarian Alps for a few days leave and their bodies were found in the middle of Munich. Also, people who knew them remarked that they had never been known to frequent bars.

Robert and Lily knew that their support cell had been instrumental in the removal of the Troosts and had arranged for their bodies to be found after a bombing raid to avoid suspicion. Why would the authorities worry about two more fatalities of a bombing raid! Robert could not decide if it really mattered that they were high profile Nazis who had unashamedly used their positions in the party for their own gain. Maybe they would have been removed to facilitate this mission whether or not they had been Nazis?

"We must be ready for this evening's meeting," said Lily.

"I have everything I need," replied Robert.

"We just have to be careful," said Lily. "Especially when walking to and from the rendezvous."

Robert leaned over and kissed her forehead.

"We'll be fine," he said. "Stop worrying."

"I'm not worried. I think I'm just getting excited at the prospect of meeting our comrades at last."

"I wouldn't get too excited about that. If we get caught by the Gestapo, knowledge of the others could be our undoing."

As she left the consulting room to get her coat, Lily's face fell into an expression of annoyance, frustration and concern. Her relationship with Robert (she had successfully forced herself to refer to Sean as Robert, even in her thinking) had burst into life during their days together in London and they had quickly become a pair. But the longer they had been together, the more she knew that there was a deep inner pain in Robert that she was not reaching. Within himself he shouldered all of the blame for the terrible fate that had overtaken Conny. Although a consummate actor in his role as Doctor Robert Hermann, she could see that he was a man crippled with guilt. He was driven by personal motivation to complete this mission and she was not sure that would be a good thing. When the mission was not engaging his thoughts there was an increasing tendency for him to recede into a dark inward contemplation that did not include her at all. It irked her that she had to literally remind him of her presence by a physical touch before he would give her any attention. Ironically, Martha Colquhoun would have been the one person most able to empathise with her feelings.

Two hours later as the October dusk began to smudge the Munich skyline and the streets began to empty in anticipation of tonight's pounding, Robert and Lily Hermann walked arm in arm out of their home, which was attached to the surgery, and walked along the tree-lined suburban streets to their rendezvous. Robert carried his doctor's bag with him and he wore a trench overcoat and a black trilby. Lily wore high heels and a plain dress below a fur collared fitted overcoat. Her hat was pinned to her hair and it was plain also, apart from a green band.

They walked directly to their meeting place. They were spoken to once by one of two policemen from the opposite side of the street.

"Hurry along home now, you good people. The bombers will be here soon."

Robert had just tipped his hat and Lily had smiled.

Although the sign on the apothecary's shop read "closed" the door sprang open when Robert pushed it and they both walked straight in. A woman sorting bottles on the shelves turned and said, "We're closed!"

Robert replied, "Surely not to co-religionists."

The woman recognised the phrase and said quietly, "Come through here and go up the stairs. The door you want is directly facing you at the top of the stairs." She lifted a flap in the counter and they went through. Robert felt comforted by the familiar smells of a chemist's shop.

The room was blacked out and a faint bulb glowed dimly from an overhead light fitting. Robert had expected a table with figures seated around it, but there was no table. A variety of chairs, some upright, some easy, were scattered around the walls of the room. Five of the seats were occupied. No one rose to greet them. There were no formal introductions. There were two women and three men. The women were both in their early thirties. One had long, dark hair which fell well below her shoulders, the other was altogether smarter, wearing a fitted suit with a knee-length skirt which she pulled down to cover her thighs as she crossed her legs. She was the only person smoking. Two of the men were dressed similarly in formal suits of thin dark cloth. The third wore the white smock of an apothecary. It was he who began proceedings.

"Welcome," he gestured with his delicate hands. "Have a seat. There will be no formal introductions here. The less we know of each other the safer we will all be. We are pleased to have you working with us. There are people in London who hold you both in the highest esteem." The apothecary took a deep breath and then continued. "The people in this room have taken the decision to oppose the current regime of Adolf Hitler and his party. We have sworn allegiance to the resistance. We are not strong within the Fatherland. The Fuhrer has used his charm, his charisma and every tool of terror known to man to command an unswerving loyalty from the vast bulk of our compatriots. If we are discovered there will be no one to speak up for us. Our fates will be terrible."

Again he paused for breath.

"Having come to this position we are agreed that anything which might hasten the end of the war and the defeat of the Nazi terror is a legitimate activity. We have therefore agreed to participate in the current mission. On face value it appears to be a bizarre one."

He looked around the room. The smart woman lit another cigarette.

"Our mission," he went on, "is to assassinate the Pope. Pope Pius XII. I am briefed to go over the rationale behind this mission to ensure we all accept the need for such an undertaking. However, I do have to say that the fact that we are here now means there is no going back for any of us."

Again he looked around the room at each of them in turn. They each nodded faintly as his gaze met theirs. Before he could continue Lily asked, "Who were you briefed by?"

He looked at her with surprise.

"That is not the concern of anyone here. It surprises me that you would ask such a thing."

Lily shrugged, looked down at her hands and fell silent.

"It is the view of many that this Pope has contributed to the rise of Nazism. He has assisted it in gaining a camouflage of respectability by refusing to issue Papal statements denouncing its extreme cruelties and anti-humanitarian actions. At first, throughout the 1930s it was hoped that he would mobilise Catholic anti-Nazi feeling and at least provide a brake on the rapid rise of Hitler. He acted to the contrary. As Cardinal Pacelli he ordered the Catholic Bishops of Germany to refrain from any criticism of Hitler and his gang. The Catholic body politic, which until then had been a significant factor in German political life, was withdrawn from active participation. Then when the anti-Semitic laws were enacted it was assumed that the Vatican would issue strong condemnations. Pacelli was instrumental in silencing any criticism that was emerging. After the collapse of Italy earlier this year, those of us who cared were in no doubt that Pope Pius XII as Pacelli had become on his ascendancy to the Papacy, would take this opportunity to condemn Hitler's criminal gang. But no! For some inexplicable reason he remained silent. When the Wermacht went to the rescue of Mussolini and set him back up as a puppet dictator it was hoped that Pacelli would protect the Jewish community in Rome when Germany moved against them. But his failure of leadership was as apparent in practical issues as it was in broad policy."

Here the apothecary paused and looked at Robert and Lily.

"Our access to information under the Nazis is seriously curtailed. I will ask our friends from England to provide further details."

Robert looked at Lily but she nodded that he should speak. As he began, thoughts of Grete came to him. David and Lisa came to him too.

"It is now common knowledge in the Allied territories that the Nazi's have embarked upon a policy of mass extermination of the Jews. It is murder on an industrial scale. If there are any Jewish populations left alive it is purely because, logistically, the Nazi's haven't got round to them yet. So it became the turn of the Jews in Rome. In a cruel and deceitful prelude to the evacuation, the German Governor of Rome announced that the population would be spared evacuation to the death camps on payment of a ransom. Gold in the amount of fifty kilograms was demanded. We don't yet know the exact figure demanded. Most right-thinking people assumed that the Pope would simply hand over the gold and take the Jewish inhabitants of Rome under his personal protection. But Pope Pius could not be prevailed upon to make any comment or any contribution. So the people of the ghetto and Italian civilians all over the country dug into their own pockets and collected the enormous ransom fee in gold. The German Governor took the money and then proceeded to break the agreement and ordered the mass evacuation of all Jews in Rome to Germany. Once again, Pope Pius XII disgraced his office. As the Storm troopers moved in and drove the Jews onto the cattle trucks he closed the windows of his Vatican Palace and turned his face away. These were innocent men, women and children who had lived out their peaceful lives within view of the walls of the Vatican. They were to be exported to Germany and Poland as slave labour or to be murdered never to be seen or heard of again."

Robert sat back in his seat suddenly aware that he was shouting in barely controlled rage. Lily reached out and touched his hand where it rested on the arm of his chair.

"So the record of Pope Pius XII is indisputably a disgrace to the name of Holy Mother Church," said the apothecary, quietly taking up the thread where Robert had left it. "But why, you may ask, should we act against him now. What possible good could it do to our cause? Well here is our argument. Intelligence sources are aware that a Papal encyclical has been prepared and is ready to be issued. As you know, a Papal encyclical is a document which elucidates what the Pope declares to be an article of faith. The Pope is infallible. His word is the word of God. This encyclical is a rejection of the race and blood doctrines of the Nazis. Scholars in the Vatican have studied the race laws and subsequent actions of Nazism and have mounted a wholehearted rebuttal of them. The encyclical calls on all Catholics, *as a matter of faith*, to reject them and condemn the perpetrators."

The apothecary paused, played with the cuffs of his smock and sat forward in his easy chair.

"I can anticipate your next question," he said with a wry grin. "Why target the Pope now just as he is finally coming down from his ivory tower of wilful ignorance?"

Nobody spoke, but one or two in the room displayed a flicker of agreement with this question on otherwise expressionless faces.

"I'll tell you why. This Pope has read the encyclical and made the unilateral decision to shelve it. He refuses to issue it. He is behaving true to his past form."

There was a silence as this news sank in.

"We have strong reasons to believe," went on the apothecary, "that a new Pope would immediately issue this encyclical. It would come as a dagger to the heart of Nazism within Germany. Every Catholic in the country, and that's about thirty per cent of us, would have to re-think their allegiance to this odious regime. The effect on Catholics throughout the rest of Europe and the world would be as stunning. The Nazi edifice could crumble. We could shorten the war by years."

The silence that followed left the apothecary's words echoing in the room.

"There is one more thing I have been instructed to tell you. Everyone in this room is a Roman Catholic. We are not anti-Papist bigots. We undertake this mission from a Catholic position."

Robert was the first to respond.

"You have explained the rationale very clearly. I am in no doubt as to the validity of this mission. I suggest, unless anyone has some objections to raise, that we get on with the practicalities."

"Thank you, Doctor."

The apothecary then enquired of each person there if they were entirely in agreement with the mission.

"You might think this a pointless question. If you answer 'no' how could we let you leave here? However, arrangements have been made to evacuate anyone who cannot go along with this plan. You will be airlifted to Sweden and, from there, processed to the destination of your choice. Some of you might play only a minimal role. But your involvement provides a support structure that might become vital to other operatives."

The apothecary could have saved his breath. Each one present answered in the positive.

"Our access to the Pope will be via the Convent of Our Lady of Perpetual Succour," and he paused here to acknowledge the nun to his left hand side. She nodded at him and glanced around the room at the others without smiling. "...and the school that is attached to it," and again he paused to acknowledge the smartly dressed smoker. "Helga is a teacher in the school. Our objective is to get Robert and Lily accepted as regular visitors to both the school and the convent so that no one will wish to apprehend them when the time comes to act. As most of you know, both institutions fall within Dr. Robert's responsibilities. However, we cannot await the vagaries of fate to call upon him to visit. We must engineer the immediate commencement of his visits. Sister Fatima has bravely volunteered to facilitate this objective. In a moment I will administer a small dosage of herbal poison to Sister Fatima. It will be extremely unpleasant but will leave no long-term effects. Later tonight, the good Sister will experience extremely unpleasant gastric symptoms and Dr. Robert will be sent for. It will be the first of many visits this week, during which it will be up to Robert and Lily, Sister Fatima and Frau Helga," he nodded at the teacher, "to develop the relationship to ensure that Robert and Lily's visits continue until Pacelli arrives."

"Why will the Pope be visiting the convent in Munich?" It was the first time either of the men had spoken.

The apothecary looked at the man who sat forward in his chair and leaned his elbows onto his knees.

"This is Adolf," said the apothecary to the room. "He is our latest recruit. Adolf is from Hamburg. He was wounded on the Russian front and has been invalided out of the war. He is now with the Munich police force. Most police activities nowadays come under the jurisdiction of the Gestapo."

Sensing the unease this announcement had brought, the apothecary went on quickly, "Adolf has been vetted thoroughly by our people. He can be trusted totally. He will prove a very useful contact for us. In answer to your question, Adolf, the Pope has been a regular visitor to our little convent ever since he was Papal Nuncio to Bavaria in the early 1930s. He comes for rehabilitation and contemplation and he comes at least once a year. He has a passion for horse riding, which he can pursue in the convent's extensive grounds. The war has not prevented him from maintaining this habit. Our information is that he will be here sometime within the next six weeks."

Doctor Robert recognised the reference to horse riding in connection with this Pope. Adolf sat back in his chair, satisfied with the response from the apothecary.

Suddenly everyone jolted forward in their seats as there came a knock at the door. The third man, who was seated nearest the door jumped up and put his hand on the knob.

"Who's there?" he called.

"Me! Ilsa." It was the voice of the girl from the shop.

With a nod from the apothecary, the man opened the door and Ilsa entered. She had a pretty face, with jet black hair and a good figure, but her shoulders stooped as if the result of too many hours bent over a counter. Rubbing her hands together to stave off the cold she leaned into the room apologetically and said, "I'm sorry to interrupt but I thought you ought to know that there are two policemen who have walked past the shop front three times now. I know they have seen me and I'm worried that they are getting a little too interested in me and why I am still here."

Adolf stood up and said, "I'll deal with this. Ilsa, come with me." And they went downstairs together. Adolf led Ilsa by the hand back into the shop and they crept to the window to survey the street.

"There they are," whispered Ilsa. Adolf followed her gaze and saw them just moving away from the corner at the top of the street back towards the shop.

"Well, Ilsa," whispered Adolf. "I suppose I should apologise to you first but, you know, there is only one way out of this predicament. I know those two. They're not bad sorts. Just not very bright! I know what will satisfy their under-developed curiosities."

By now the two policemen were almost outside the shop. Quickly, Adolf pulled Ilsa to him and moved them both in front of the glass door. As the two drew level, he pulled Ilsa into his arms and kissed her passionately, apparently oblivious of the two onlookers. They kissed like this, Ilsa suppressing her shock, until there came a tap on the glass.

Adolf and Ilsa sprang apart in mock surprise. Then Adolf's two colleagues recognised him and he feigned surprised recognition of them.

"Look Sepp," said one to the other, "it's Adolf."

The one called Sepp beamed from ear to ear. "Adolf you old dog. What are you up to?"

Adolf just put on an embarrassed grin and shrugged, as if to say, "What do you think?"

"Hey, Adolf," called the first policeman whose name was Heinrich, "Open up, let us in. It's freezing out here."

Adolf looked at Ilsa and gave her a reassuring nod. He opened the door and the two pushed their way in.

"Are you on duty then Adolf?" asked Heinrich. Sepp and Heinrich looked at each other and burst out laughing. "This is a fine way to police the Fatherland, I must say!" They guffawed again.

"No I am not on duty," retorted Adolf, and he went on, "and please do not embarrass my good friend here."

"Many apologies to you and your Fraulein," said Sepp with mock seriousness.

"So why is the young lady working so late?" asked Heinrich becoming business-like.

"She wasn't working late," answered Adolf. And before Heinrich could contradict him and take it further he added, "But *we* were!"

Looking at each other and slowly getting his meaning the two of them burst into rude laughter once more.

"Well you sly old fox, Adolf," taunted Sepp. "I never thought you had it in you."

Just then a scraping sound came from behind the door at the back of the shop.

"What was that?" asked Heinrich as the four of them froze.

Ilsa spoke for the first time. "It's the cat. She's waiting for me to put her out. Don't tell me you're frightened of a little old pussy."

"No, I'm not," replied Heinrich. "I'm a cat lover. Let me have a look at her."

So saying he moved across the shop to go behind the counter to the door. Behind the door Robert held his breath. In his hand he held a nine inch dagger and he caressed the handle with nervous fingers.

Adolf shot across after Heinrich and took hold of him by the shoulder. He spun him around so that they faced each other.

"Look, Heinrich my friend," he growled with a murderous expression on his face, "If you don't get out of here and let Ilsa and me get on with our *work*, I will not be responsible for what I might do to you."

Just at the exact moment that Heinrich thought he might genuinely be in danger, Adolf gave him an outrageous wink. With nervous relief Heinrich let out a great bellow of laughter and he and Adolf clapped each other about the shoulders.

"Come on Sepp," called Heinrich, "we must leave these two citizens to their patriotic war work."

He looked at Adolf again, thumped him on the shoulder and laughed raucously. Adolf saw them out of the door.

"Don't be too long with all this overtime Adolf," said Sepp. "The British bombers could be well on their way by now. You don't want to get caught with your trousers down when the bombs start falling."

The pair of them walked off highly pleased with their own jocularity.

Upstairs Sister Fatima was swallowing a glass of water following the dose the apothecary had just administered to her.

"Now you must move swiftly," he said to Sister Fatima and to the third.man. He, in fact, was the gardener-come-caretaker at the convent and he got to his feet, took Sister Fatima by the arm and led her out of the room. Frau Helga accompanied them.

154

"God speed!" called the apothecary after them. Only Lily noticed how Robert almost winced to hear the expression.

Robert and Lily followed the directions the apothecary had given them in order to get back home whilst avoiding the main boulevards. They scurried down lanes and across waste ground. Twice they had to hide in alleyways to allow patrolling SS and regular policemen to pass by. The night was now black and the air raid siren struck up its infantile scream. Robert and Lily ran the last few blocks home and got inside just in time.

"English bastards," muttered Robert ironically. "They could make tonight difficult. Why couldn't they bomb Nuremburg or Essen instead?"

They sat in the dark in their parlour listening to the thud and boom of the exploding bombs. They had no compulsion to seek safety in a shelter, nor even in the cupboard below the stairs. They knew that they had already damned their fate and they had no incentive to attempt to thwart it, whatever it might bring. They shared a drink of whisky. Flames danced on the window from the results of a direct hit on a home two streets away.

Occasionally, above the whine of the bombs and the crackling of flames they could hear the cries of casualties. As a doctor, Robert knew he should go out there and join the rescuers and fire-fighters, but tonight he had more pressing business.

One of the longest waits of their lives transpired to be no more than two and a half hours. But when the gardener finally knocked on their door it seemed to them that they had waited half a lifetime. He spoke as if he had never seen them before.

"I have a message for you from the convent." He handed Lily a note. She unfolded it and read it.

"Robert," she said, re-folding the note. "You're needed at the convent. She turned to the gardener, realising for the first time that he was not alone. The realisation shocked her and she checked back over her actions and words to see if anything she had done or said could have given away the fact that this was all a set up.

"Come in," she said. "Come in quickly. Oh," she said with feigned surprise, "there are two of you. Well come in before we all get bombed."

Robert came along the hallway and tried not to betray any surprise when he saw the stranger.

"What is it?" he asked.

"It's one of the nuns doctor," said the gardener. "She's terribly sick. I've never seen anything like it. The Mother Superior sent me. They're afraid the Sister might die. Hans here," he turned to acknowledge his companion, "saw me leaving and kindly drove me here. He is the Mother's chauffeur. Luckily her car is well known to the authorities. It is one of the few cars that would not be stopped for being out during a raid."

Lily turned to Robert. "This is ridiculous. Send them away and tell them to come back in the morning after the raid."

"Please mein Frau," said the gardener. "I don't think the Sister will be there in the morning if the doctor does not come with us now."

Robert smiled down at Lily. "I'll have to go. There's no need for you to worry. These two good men will look after me."

Lily walked down the hall and picked up her coat. "If you're going, I'm coming with you."

And before anyone could object she had walked out of the house and let herself into the back seat of the Daimler Benz that stood beside the pavement.

It was a hazardous journey without headlights and avoiding newly cratered roads, but they finally arrived within the grounds of the convent and were ushered in by a trio of anxious Sisters.

Twenty-five

Both Robert and Lily experienced a sense of unreality as they entered the dark, high-ceilinged reception area of the convent. For so many months now they had prepared for this. Most of their waking hours had been spent imagining this very moment. Now that it was here, it held a faintly surreal quality.

The gardener and the chauffeur evaporated from view and the Doctor and his wife were greeted with relief and gratitude by the Mother Superior herself and a small, handsome man in light coloured flannel trousers and an open-necked shirt. It was inappropriate clothing for early November but Robert guessed he was making a statement about his robust health. He was in late middle age but looked to be in excellent physical shape. Before Robert and Lily could speculate on his identity the Mother Superior introduced him as Herr Todt, the headmaster of the convent school. As headmaster he occupied a house within the school grounds. Sister Fatima was a member of his teaching staff. In her concern for Sister Fatima, the Mother Superior had called him for his advice and he had hurried over.

All introductions were effected on the move as Robert and Lily were ushered towards the cells occupied by the nuns. They knew they were heading in the right direction from the lonely sound of retching they could hear coming from along the corridor.

The convent itself was laid around two quadrangles that sat either side of a central chapel. The corridors were lined with doors to offices, sleeping cells, communal rooms and punishment cells. Tributary corridors ran off the main thoroughfare leading past private quarters and stairways leading to the upper floor.

"Here we are, Doctor," gasped the Mother Superior breathlessly as she ushered Robert and Lily in through a small doorway. Robert bumped his head on the door frame just as the Mother was about to warn him to duck. The stench of vomit assailed their senses as they entered and it was only years of discipline and training that enabled Robert and Lily to override the nausea.

"Forgive me, Mother," said Lily, "But it will be better if you wait here, or go back to your quarters. The doctor and I can deal with this."

"As you say, my dear," replied the Mother trying not to sound too relieved. "The headmaster and I will wait for you in my quarters."

She opened the door to the cell and called in, "Sister Gemma, come here a moment."

The Sister who had been attending Sister Fatima emerged from the cell.

"Sister Gemma, wait outside here until the Doctor has finished and then show them both to my quarters."

"Yes Mother," replied the exhausted nun.

Inside the cell Robert and Lily set to work. Robert knew exactly what antidote he had to administer and he had it with him already prepared. Meanwhile Lily set about restoring the cell to a habitable state. She stripped the bed of its meagre rough blanket which had been covered in vomit, and she tossed it out into the corridor.

"Sister Gemma," she said to the exhausted nun who leaned against the wall to prevent herself from total collapse. "Show me where to take this soiled blanket and where to get hold of cleaning materials and then you can go and rest."

"Oh I can't do that," she protested, "Mother wouldn't…"

"But you must," interrupted Lily. "Doctor's orders."

Together they set off down the corridor, turning right at the end and then, halfway along this side of the quadrangle they took a left into a side corridor. Eventually they came to an area containing a kitchen and a communal dining room. Sister Gemma led Lily through to a room at the back of the kitchen where she found buckets, mops and cleaning materials.

"Right. I will find everything I want. Now you must go to your bed… and that's an order."

Reluctantly, but with a faint smile of gratitude, Sister Gemma turned and disappeared into the dark, shadowy network of corridors.

Meanwhile, Robert had administered the medicinal antidote to the poison and injected a re-hydration solution. The poor girl had suffered more than the rest of them so far in pursuance of their mission. He tried to re-assure her with soothing words.

"I know you feel terrible and probably, right now, death would be your preferred option, but I can assure you there will be no lasting damage. You will recover your strength soon. You have done a magnificent thing. It's up to the rest of us now."

Lily took a circuitous route back to the cell in an attempt to acquire as much knowledge of the convent and its layout as she could. She heard voices coming from a room at the end of a side corridor and, placing her cleaning equipment carefully on the floor, she tiptoed along the corridor towards the sound. A polished-wood double door screened her from the owners of the voices and so she leaned her ear against it and listened. Without being able to decipher all that was being said she heard enough to know that the voices belonged to Herr Todt and Mother Superior. These must be the Mother's private rooms. One or two fragments informed her that they were discussing the arrival of the Pope, but not enough to garner much more.

Lily began the process of cleaning out the cell whilst Robert carried Sister Fatima in the direction of the Mother Superior's quarters. He knocked on the door with his foot and Todt opened it for him. He walked in and laid Sister Fatima on a couch that stood under a large window.

Looking non-plussed Mother Superior asked, "Pardon me Herr Doctor, but what is happening?"

Robert rose and turned to face her.

"I cannot permit Sister Fatima to stay in that cell whilst her health is in such a poor state."

The Mother Superior stared at him for a few seconds as if deciding whether to attempt an explanation of the life of a nun. Seeming to think better of it she merely said, "Of course! She will stay here with me until you say she is fully recovered Doctor."

Robert was relieved to hear this. The poison had had a much greater effect on the hapless Fatima than he had anticipated. He had also noticed a significant rise in room temperature on entering the Mother's quarters. She obviously exempted herself from some of the more stringent privations expected of the ordinary nuns.

"I have done what I can to deal with her symptoms but as yet I cannot say what has caused her malady. With your permission I would like to return in the morning and probably again over the next few days, firstly to check on Sister Fatima but also to take some samples away and run some tests on them."

"What sort of samples?" asked Todt.

Robert looked at him as if he had just appeared. When he answered Todt's question he addressed himself to the Mother Superior, "I need to test your drinking water for impurities. I must also take samples of the food you have stored here. If I do not isolate the cause there is no guarantee that other members of the Sisterhood will not be affected in the same way. I cannot express too strongly the danger Sister Fatima has been in."

Mother Superior looked at Todt and then back to Robert.

"Of course, Doctor. I bow to your judgement. We will see you in the morning. By the way, where is Sister Gemma?"

Robert answered without thinking.

"I ordered her to her bed. The poor girl was exhausted. When I return tomorrow I would like permission to check her out too."

"Of course Herr Doctor. Whatever you say."

Back in the cell Robert assisted Lily in restoring the cell to a safe, habitable condition. When all was completed they stopped and looked at each other. A smile passed between them.

"I think we've accomplished all we can here tonight," whispered Lily.

"I think you're right my precious one," answered Robert as he leaned down to place a kiss on her lips.

"Back off Herr Doctor," laughed Lily. I don't think a convent is the place for what you might have in mind!"

They both laughed and set off for home. Each knew, instinctively, the elation the other was feeling at the ease with which this initial success had been achieved. The danger had excited the basic elements of their natures and it was a commentary on their emotional make-up. But knowing this did not affect their enjoyment.

Over the next few weeks Robert and Lily became regular visitors to the convent. Fortunately, an outbreak of scarlet fever amongst the nuns kept Robert and Lily busy in a more legitimate way. On Sundays the doctor and his wife attended mass in the convent chapel and afterwards they were always invited into the Mother Superior's quarters for coffee or sherry and biscuits. They were usually joined by Herrr Todt and his plump but very pretty wife, Julia.

"Tell me Herr Todt," asked Lily during one of these pleasant social gatherings. "How are the schoolchildren surviving these brutal times we live in?"

Herr Todt paused in the act of sipping his sherry.

"We bring them up to be good patriots. They understand the justice of Germany's fight. We also teach them to fear and honour God. They are good Catholics. Their faith is their greatest gift."

"What about their health, and their hygiene? Before the English and Americans committed their war crimes against us we enjoyed the best health and hygiene in the world."

"Well," hummed the headmaster, prepared to concede some shortcomings here, "Shall I say, things have been better."

"Headmaster," said Lily enthusiastically, "Why don't you let me come into school for regular visits. I can provide medical inspections. I can check for things like head lice, scabies, and ringworm as well as malnutrition."

The headmaster looked at her over the rim of his glass.

"You know, Frau Hermann, I think that is a wonderful idea."

He turned to Mother Superior and called across to her, "Mother Superior, listen to this new idea Frau Hermann and I have come up with. And he related Lily's idea to the mother as if he had just thought of it himself. Such was his enthusiasm that the Mother too agreed that it would be a marvellous service for the children, not to mention a protection for the poor nuns and teachers from infection.

Twenty-six

As a skilled surgeon, Robert had to work three days each week in the casualty department of the University Hospital, Munich. In some ways working there reminded him of his days in Berlin at the Friedrichshain Klinik. There were the political Nazi appointees. However, the difference was caused by the amount of work everyone had to do. Allied raids on Munich were regular in occurrence and devastating in effect. Even the Nazis had too much to do to worry much about the niceties of dogma. Besides, the issue that had confronted him in Berlin was solved now. There were no Jews. If there were, they had become invisible.

Robert finished his shift at the university hospital and walked briskly towards Marienplatz. He had become accustomed to cutting through a warren of narrow lanes before emerging onto the approach to the square. It was quicker and it gave him a good feeling – as if he was a true native of the city. Miraculously, few of the buildings here had been hit by the bombers - Yet! And he loved the sounds and smells that spilled out of the cramped homes onto the walkways as he passed through. Sporadic voices, sometimes so close as to be almost intimate; a dog yapping; the clatter of a knife or spoon on a plate as a table is set for dinner; scents of cabbage and potatoes cooking in a pot and, very occasionally, the aroma of meat.

So familiar was he with his route now that he barely paid attention to where he was. He could navigate himself automatically whilst indulging in a relaxing reverie. But tonight his thoughts were splintered by a sudden scurry of footsteps behind him which startled him from his daydream. Too late! He had just begun to turn towards the source of the sound when a thunderous blow landed on him. A jagged length of timber bounced off his shoulder and caught a glancing blow on the side of his head. As he stumbled beneath the blow he retained enough survival instinct to glimpse his attackers: two or maybe three men, each with lengths of timber, closing in on him. Comically, his only thought at the time was, 'if they kill me, who will assassinate the Pope?'

The glancing blow to his head had not connected sweetly enough to deprive him of consciousness and, in the moments it took his assailants to follow through, his adrenaline rush gave him sufficient awareness to raise his hands above him to protect his head from further blows. He could feel his shock turning to aggression and as the next blow landed he succeeded in grabbing the end of the club he was being beaten with. As he entered a tug of war with this particular assailant the other one (he could now definitely see that there were only two) landed two blows upon him; one on his back and one to the back of his legs. He knew his only hope of gaining ground was to concentrate his aggression on the one attached to the other end of the club he now had firmly gripped in his two bloodied and splintered hands. With a vicious wrench he pulled the timber towards him and then as the attacker fell forwards he reversed it into his oncoming face. He knew he had the upper hand with this one attacker when the accomplice landed a mighty blow across his shoulders bringing him down to his knees, again close to a loss of consciousness. All the time his assailants were shouting at each other.

"Get his wallet, get his watch, take his case, kill the bastard!"

Flailing wildly with his arms to protect himself, not really sure now where the next blow was coming from, Robert began to realise that he was beaten. As he was sure the final blows were about to be delivered he was surprised to hear a cry of pain burst from lips other than his own. Dimly, he became aware of some other body having entered the fray. This stranger had grasped the raised club as it was set to be delivered and wrenched it from the second assailant's fists. He then used it to deliver a sweet blow to the crown of the assailant's head, rendering him completely unconscious. Turning to the other assailant, who was still bloodied and bruised following Robert's successful counter-attack, he chased him out of the lane. By the time he returned the other attacker had recovered consciousness, got to his feet and made good his retreat. Robert watched him go.

Robert's rescuer returned. He was a little out of breath after his exertions but he helped Robert to his feet.

"You let the other fellow go. A pity! They have both escaped now. We'll never find them in this rat hole of a place."

As he talked Robert took in his saviour. He wasn't a big man but he was heavy-set. His face was round and sat atop his bull neck without the seeming delineation of any chin to speak of. His bushy moustache rose and fell animatedly as he spoke. He was flushed with the excitement of the fight but his face was lit with a kind of innate joy.

Although small and substantially overweight he gave the impression of enormous strength. As he stood face to face with Robert and examined his injuries he exuded a generosity of spirit that Robert found very appealing.

"Well," he said. "What's it to be; hospital or my local bar for a strong drink?"

Despite the pain it induced, Robert could not help but laugh. "I guess I'll take the drink," he said and with the aid of his new comrade he made his way to a bar he had passed many times but never entered before.

Friedrich Lehmann, for that was his name, placed Robert at a table in the corner of the room and stomped to the bar to order drinks. As he came back to the table men from all parts of the room called to him and he called back friendly greetings in return. Everyone asked him what had happened to his companion and he delightedly informed them of the attack in the lane.

As he returned, Robert took in more of his new friend. Most significantly he observed the Nazi insignia armband he wore. The barman brought over a tray containing two enormous tankards of beer and one large glass of brandy.

"Here, my friend," said Friedrich handing the brandy across. "For the shock, yes."

He watched Robert intently as he took the brandy and raised it to his lips. From the intensity of Friedrich's stare Robert knew he was expected to down the large measure in one swallow. He obliged to be greeted by a roar of approval from Friedrich and the sight of the beer tankard being handed to him.

"Now we begin the rehabilitation, yes."

Both men drank deeply from their tankards. Wiping a mountain of froth from his moustache with the back of his hand, Friedrich began the conversation.

It took many weeks for Robert to find out all about Friedrich and his life, but it took only a couple of moments to realise that he was in the company of a man he thoroughly liked. It was something he reflected on often. What was it that drew individuals to one another? Here was this fireball of a man with that hated armband proudly worn at all times. A man who loved his Fuhrer; a man completely incapable of finding anything disagreeable in any of Hitler's domestic policies or in the conduct of the war. Someone Robert would argue with day and night if he was at liberty to honestly share his own views. Someone he would kill in the line of duty. But still, a man he liked more than most he had met. He thought back to many comrades in arms he had known during his fighting days in the Republican Army. Men who shared his vision of the future for Ireland. Men who had stood back-to-back with him in desperate shoot-outs. Most of them he would cross the street to avoid having to speak to. Friendship, like love, was a mystery to him.

Twenty-seven

Working all the hours sent was no bad thing for Robert. The scorched, blackened hole that sat right at the core of his being could be more easily skirted around if he was too busy to think. When he did get time to stop Lily was always on hand to give him the physical love he craved in order to retain some semblance of belief in himself as human. When they fell apart he was saved from the emptiness by the rock-like sleep he plummeted into.

A large part of his work involved picking up the patients' list left behind by Doctor Troost. Some of this involved going into the avenues and boulevards of Munich to visit housebound patients. Quite often he would set off to see a patient only to find the address no longer existed but had been replaced by a massive bomb crater. Another name to cross off the list; sometimes several.

A substantial number of his patients lived in the poorer districts of the city. In wartime poverty is magnified. Robert, who had developed his detestation of the Nazis during his days in Berlin, had however retained a lot of his admiration for the Germany he had first fallen in love with at the feet of father Peter. One of the aspects he had always admired and compared favourably to the situation in Britain and Ireland was the health and social services that had been developed since the days of Bismarck. They had lifted the German population far above the privations of poverty and illness experienced back home. The German troops had laughed at their British adversaries when first encountering them in battle. Who were these malnourished, growth-stunted, bad-toothed warriors? What chance could they possibly have of victory?

On entering the square-block apartments of some of his patients he could see that almost ten years of Nazism had undone much of that work. He encountered levels of poverty the like of which he had never seen before. Tall apartment blocks, cheaply built to house the asocials. Here was the starkest reminder that there were two Germanys. This was the worst poverty he had witnessed, and coming from Ireland that was some statement to make.

Katerin Tring was a ten year old with tuberculosis. Different country, different age-group. But the same killer he had encountered in Ireland. She lived with her mother, grandparents and six siblings. Her father and two older brothers were infantrymen in Russia. Here was an asocial family, not much better than the Jews to the Nazis and here was their reward for fighting in the *drang nach osten* for the greater glory of the Third Reich. A damp, cold flat in a paper thin apartment block with two bedrooms for nine people and a child with tuberculosis. It was only a matter of time before the girls' younger siblings contracted the disease.

A framed picture of the late Pope hung above the mantelpiece. They obviously couldn't afford one of the new Pope yet.

Robert administered what he knew to be useless medicine and dispensed some equally useless advice about the living conditions and the effect they were having on the girl's chances. What could the Tring family hope to do about the conditions? The only people likely to effect any lasting change were the British airmen who paid nightly visits to drop bombs on people like this. Robert took consolation in the fact that his own mission would not inflict indirect damage on the likes of these. In that sense he could think of his mission as pure.

Grandfather Tring walked with Robert to the end of the aerial walkway and they stood talking at the head of the stairwell. He explained to Robert that he had no money and could not pay for the home visit. From behind his back he pulled the picture of Pope Pius XI, the old, dead Pope.

"For you, Herr Doctor," the old man said. "It is the only thing of value I have to offer you. I know you are a good Catholic and will value this. It is not a painting. It is a genuine photograph."

Robert began to protest, but when he saw the silent plea in the old man's eyes he reached out, took the painting and murmured his thanks.

The old man turned and walked back along the walkway to his apartment door. For a moment Robert watched him and then turned towards the stairs. Out of the darkness towards him came a figure. Only slowly as it emerged towards the light of the opening could Robert begin to make it out. With coat and hat too big for him, this man had experienced a decline in fortunes. He walked with the assurance of an ex-soldier, upright and stiff, but there was a sense of defeat or disappointment in his bearing.

Robert looked down at the papal face in his picture and headed towards the stairs. It was only as he came alongside the approaching figure that he glanced up and met his eyes. As their glance connected Robert felt a rod-like shock shoot through him.

And then he was in the stairwell and descending through the darkness. If he had looked over his shoulder he would have seen ex-Captain Vogts looking down into the darkness after him with a puzzled expression on his face. Ex-Captain Vogts, once staff Captain to General Zeiger, the scourge of the French Resistance, assassinated in Gerona by one Doctor Bauer.

Twenty-eight

As they were finishing their evening meal the air raid sirens started up. Robert and Lily continued their meal. Having been upbraided by the apothecary for their irresponsibility to the mission by being careless with their own lives they then wrapped up warmly to make their way to the nearest public shelter. Robert had told Lily of his encounter with Captain Vogts.

"I don't think he recognised me. It was a fleeting encounter."

Lily's impatience with this comment was evident in her response.

"You recognised him, didn't you!"

"Yes!"

"Well we must assume that he recognised you. If he did it means our days are numbered. It means our mission must be aborted."

"Hang on," protested Robert. "Think it through with me. Suppose he saw someone he thought he recognised. Well, that happens to people all the time. So he will dwell on it for a while and then forget it."

"Robert," said Lily. "You're not thinking straight."

"No," pleaded Robert. "Give me a chance, bear with me. If he recognised me as the Dr Bauer who assassinated General Zeiger, he knows I'm an enemy agent and we would already be inside Gestapo headquarters."

"Well," joked Lily ironically, "Any minute now."

"But," continued Robert, "If he thought he knew me and wanted to find out who I was, he would have to ask the Tring family. Remember, he only saw a stranger walking by. He doesn't know I'm a doctor or why I was there. To get that information out of the Tring family he would have to make some door to door enquiries and hopefully, from his point of view, alight on the Trings during the course of his investigation. So I need to go to the Trings and find out if Vogts has been there."

"Robert, you are being ridiculous. Listen to yourself."

"No, Lily. I will call tomorrow on the pretext of checking up on the young girl and I'll make some general enquiries of my own."

Lily was silenced by exasperation. Eventually she spoke.

"All right, Robert. I'll go along with your plan, but only on one condition."

"Good woman! Now what's your condition?"

"I go to the Trings. Not you."

"Oh no…"

"For pity's sake Robert, open your eyes. If he saw you there once, he could see you again. Suppose you're clutching at straws is right and he hasn't been able to place you, do you want to give him another sighting to help jolt his memory?"

Robert looked downcast. He knew she was right. But he did not want to accept it.

All through their night in the shelter he argued the point. But Lily didn't need to respond. They both knew she had won. When Robert dozed off Lily stared at his sleeping face. What was it about this man that made him so elusive? There were times when she thought she knew him, only to feel him slip away again. She knew that he no longer cared about his own fate. It was as if the war was incidental to some personal mission of his own. Perhaps this was what drew her on towards him ever more desperately despite her best intentions. Finally, she too dozed off, leaning against him in this damp, smelly place. Above them the sky snapped and boomed like a taut black sheet and Munich wondered if the morning would ever come.

Twenty-nine

The next day was Sunday and Robert went off to the convent chapel to hear mass. He was alone. He explained to those who asked, that last night's raid had left Lily with a severe headache and she was at home trying to sleep it off. In reality she was on her way to the home of the Tring family ostensibly to administer care to the tuberculosis patient; in reality to find out how much Vogts had discovered.

Lily went straight to the Trings front door and was immediately ushered in when she introduced herself as Dr. Hermann's wife. Her pretext for calling was to drop off some more medication for their daughter and she carried out an examination of the girl.

"There are blood stains on this pillow," she said accusingly to Frau Tring. "Why have you not replaced the pillow case with a clean one?"

Mrs Tring looked ashamed.

"That case was clean this morning Frau Hermann. As soon as I give her a new one she coughs up more blood. I cannot keep up with her."

"There is no excuse for poor hygiene Frau Tring," Lily replied coldly.

On her way from the child's bedroom to the front exit she passed by Herr Tring sitting in the living area

"I believe someone was asking about the Doctor after he left here yesterday."

It was a stab in the dark but it paid off.

"That is correct," replied Herr Tring. "It was quite odd actually. He is a man I've seen about the area. Apparently he lives at the far end of the next block. But I cannot say I know him. He asked if a man answering to the Doctor's description had called here. When I told him yes, he asked a few questions and then thanked me and left."

"What sort of questions did he ask?" Lily interjected.

But Herr Tring paused and looked closely at Lily.

"How did you know someone had called here?" he asked.

Lily almost blushed and for an instant she was stuck for an answer. Then she quickly recovered herself and said, "A woman in the stairwell said a man had asked her about the doctor and she had directed him to you."

It was an instantaneous lie of some ingenuity and it seemed to satisfy Herr Tring.

"Well," he said, "he asked who the Doctor was and how long he had been in practice here. He then asked where the Doctor's surgery was… and things like that."

"Did the man say who he was?" asked Lily. Then to justify Frau Tring's curiosity she quickly added, "Perhaps he needs the Doctor to treat him."

"He said his name was Vogts; and he is an ex Wermacht Captain. Like I said, he lives at the end of the next block, but he didn't say exactly where."

"Oh well," Lily said, deciding she had garnered all the knowledge she was going to from this source, "If he needs the Doctor I'm sure he will know where to find us."

"Oh yes," said Frau Tring, "He'll be able to do that all right. We told him exactly where to find the surgery."

Lily did not return home immediately. Instead she wandered from the Trings' block amongst the other apartment blocks towards the one Herr Tring had indicated Captain Vogts was living in. On some notepaper she wrote down the address of the block and was about to leave when an apartment door opened and out stepped what seemed to be an elderly man. When he turned so that she could see his face she saw that he was not elderly but in early middle age. It was the air of defeat about him that suggested old age and Lily knew that it was the effect of her doctor husband's actions that had broken this man in far off Gerona.

After mass, the holy Mother invited Robert back to her quarters for coffee and biscuits. Headmaster Todt was there along with his wife, Julia. The holy Mother was in sparkling form, taking Robert by the arm and leading him ahead of the others back to her warm rooms, although there was some aspect of pre-occupation in her manner. She talked about one of the children who had been with the school choir at mass

"Did you see little Angela?"

Robert looked at her quizzically.

"The little tot in the big ribbon," she added by way of explanation. "The one who tripped over on her way up to communion."

"Ah yes," nodded Robert, smiling at the memory.

"And again at the altar!" added Mother. "I suppose we should feel sympathy for the poor unfortunate. She is the clumsiest girl in Germany.

She is always stumbling and tumbling, bless her. She often has us in fits of laughter. But it can be so infuriating. I mean this very morning. Did you see the way she fell against the altar rail? Father was most put-out."

Robert was surprised to hear Mother sound so irritated at such a little thing. He had been vaguely aware of a stumble but had dismissed it until now. Mother was showing a side he had not seen before. He had only experienced her formal side before today. But today she was excited, yet disproportionately annoyed by an insignificant accident.

"I've asked her mother to bring her to my quarters for a moment before setting off for home. I hope you don't mind."

"Why, of course not, Mother. I shall be very pleased to see her and her mother."

"Let's hurry along before the headmaster and his wife catch us. Herr Todt is a marvellous teacher, but he is a bit humourless. I want to deal with this without his presence."

She laughed again, nervously, and they hurried along the corridors to her rooms. Angela and her mother were waiting outside when they arrived. Angela looked even smaller beside the giant oak door than she had done in the church; her ribbon giving the illusion that she was a wrapped parcel.

"Frau Rusbech, thank you so much for calling. Come along in."

As they all entered, the Mother took Angela's face in her two hands and fondled it. But there was little affection in the gesture. Angela smiled and giggled nervously.

"Your dughter is an angel, Frau Rusbech. You named her well. Come here, Angela," said the Mother as she beckoned Angela to join her beside a tall cupboard against the far wall.

As Angela moved across the room she lived up to the reputation Mother Superior had boasted for her and tripped. She fell to her knees but jumped up just as quickly. Mother Superior laughed and Frau Rusbech chuckled knowingly. "That's my daughter," she seemed to be saying in a form of ironic pride.

Robert was not smiling. In his frown, which he immediately did his best to disguise, lay the recognition of an extremely rare muscle wasting disease. His medical mind executed an instantaneous diagnosis before his consciousness told him not to be so stupidly melodramatic. Still, he was sure there was evidence there worth investigating.

"Here you are Angela," Mother Superior was saying as she handed a large chocolate biscuit to the beaming Angela.

As Robert watched the scene his thoughts roamed over morbid ground. Part of him longed to be here, not just in the role as doctor but as a real doctor. He cursed his mission and wished he could intervene in this little girl's fate. But then he asked himself, what would be the point? He should be back in England in a few weeks, two months at the latest. This young girl would probably have been blown to pieces by an allied bomb by then. Her chances of surviving until hostilities ceased were virtually nil. Why should he destroy this passing happiness with some diabolical diagnosis; always supposing, of course, that his depressing assumption had any basis in fact.

"Now go and wait outside the door Angela, while I have a quick word with your mother."

Frau Rusbech looked nonplussed as her daughter went into the corridor. Mother turned to speak to her in a quiet but deliberate manner.

"Your daughter caused disquiet during this morning's service." She paused, her eyes fixed on Frau Rusbech. "Her clumsiness," she went on, "is beyond a joke. She distracts the other children. They were giggling at her at the very moment of communion when they should be experiencing the most sacred and profound holiness."

Frau Rusbech looked too shocked to respond. Her face blushed with embarrassment.

"We cannot have the mass turned into a comedy every week. I have decided I do not want you to bring Angela to mass for the next two weeks."

Robert was as shocked to hear this as Frau Rusbech. He said nothing. He thought that Mother's behaviour was telling him something. Something he was pleased to hear. However, pleased or not he could not help a rising anger swelling up inside him to hear Frau Rusbech spoken to in this way.

"But..." began Frau Rusbech. But her words dried up as she found Mother's hand, palm out, in front of her face.

"Please do not but me, Frau Rusbech. I have made my decision. Now, please go!"

Ashamed and humiliated, Frau Rusbech turned, glanced briefly at Robert before quickly averting her eyes and exiting the room.

Outside in the corridor she found Angela in the company of Herr and Frau Todt. The Headmaster put on a mock serious face and said, "Angela, have you been naughty again? I hope Mother didn't have to slipper you."

Angela laughed but there was a strong hint of nervousness in it. Herr Todt was her headmaster and she had a healthy fear of him.

"You have a very special daughter here Frau Rusbech. I hope you are very proud of her."

"Thank you so…" ventured a wet-eyed Frau Rusbech before being interrupted by the holy Mother who had appeared at the door to her office.

"Ah! There you are Herr Todt. Come along in. The doctor and I have been waiting for you. Goodbye Frau Rusbech," she added as an afterthought.

As they settled to their ersatz coffee and malt biscuits, Robert noticed that they were not treated to Mother's secret supply of large chocolate biscuits. It was probably the exchange he had just witnessed that provoked Robert to introduce a topic of conversation that would normally not be touched upon. However, given the situation in Germany it was surprising to Robert that a discussion of politics never entered their conversation. But he was coming to realise that in this Germany the political situation was the last thing anyone spoke about. The nearest they came to the subject was some brief reference to the state of the war and what the allies might have in store for them that coming night.

In an attempt to provoke his host and fellow guests Robert raised the issue of the Weisse Rose. He regretted doing this almost at once. Herr and Frau Todt looked most uncomfortable and it was the Mother who rescued him.

The movement, which had become known as The Weisse Rose, was one of the very few public protests against the Nazis in Germany. Someone was organising a propaganda effort to counter the Nazis. Graffiti and leaflets appeared around the city criticising the regime and exposing some of its evil activities. The authorities issued dire warnings against this group which they labelled mentally deficient, pro-Jewish and communist conspirators at various times.

"God works things out in his own mysterious way. It is not for us to pass judgement on those misguided souls, the Lord forgive them."

And thus, in her dismissal of even this most pathetic act of opposition to the might of the Nazi terror machine, Mother summed up the attitude of the church to the current conflict at large.

Robert's clumsy fumbling towards some glimpse of the attitudes of his companions had almost misfired and he silently thanked the Mother for putting the issue to bed.

Frau Todt who, in her late forties was five or six years younger than her husband, uncrossed her legs exposing an expanse of elegant thigh and got up from her seat. She crossed the room to the window and looked out.

"It's funny," she said, "When we look at the sky these days we rarely comment on the weather. Instead of clouds we look for planes." She turned and faced the room. "I hate this war," she said. "I think it could go on for another twenty years. Our lives will have been totally wasted. The man I blame for all of this destruction is Winston Churchill."

She lit a cigarette, returned to her chair and continued, "What did Germany do to deserve this onslaught? Can anybody tell me?" She paused to allow a response but nobody took up the offer. "Well," she continued. "I'll tell you what I think. Germany was surrounded by enemies and agitators and our brothers and sisters across neighbouring borders were being persecuted. Austria, Czechoslovakia, Poland. All the Fuhrer tried to do was right a few wrongs and to give Germany some pride back. And what happens? The warmonger Churchill, with his lust for blood and destruction, refuses all reasonable approaches for peace; even against his own cabinet and the rightful king of that horrible little island. And so what do we have now? A permanent state of war, that's what. And that's what will remain. The so-called allies will never defeat Germany. Our fighting men are invincible. The allies will soon fall out amongst themselves. But, unfortunately, as long as Churchill wields his evil power over the English this war will never end."

She leaned forward to stub out her cigarette.

"Do you know what I think?" she said in conclusion. "I think someone should assassinate Mister Winston Churchill and then all of our problems would be solved."

Robert, Mother Superior and Herr Todt chuckled and nodded agreement.

"I will write at once to the Fuhrer," declared Herr Todt, "And tell him of your solution to the world's crisis."

Unable to rid himself of his provocative mood, Robert heard himself asking of the Mother, "What is the Church's position on political assassination in a time of war?"

Mother took her sherry glass away from her lips and wiped a rich ruby liquid from them.

"The commandment says, 'thou shalt not kill!'

Realising, as her companions were staring at her in anticipation of some further development of her statement, that in the context of a world war that particular commandment was somewhat redundant, she hid her embarrassment behind a sip of her coffee.

"Well now," she answered with more confidence having swallowed, "I think Holy Mother Church has enough to do guiding and leading us in prayer without getting into a debate about assassinations."

Thirty

As dusk fell late that Sunday afternoon and the city braced itself for another pounding, two trucks pulled swiftly out of Gestapo/SS Headquarters and raced along the cobbled streets of the Marienplatz out along the Theatinerstrasse, past the Max Joseph I and the lion statues out towards the residential apartments on the edge of the old town.

The Tring family were shocked at the sound of jackboots pounding across the courtyard below their flat. But they kept their door locked and prayed, along with every other resident, that the jackboots were not heading to their door. To their relief the scraping sound receded slightly and they went back to their time-filling activities expecting the air-raid siren to sound at any time.

Captain Vogts had hardly reacted to the sound of boots pounding on the stairwell of his block. Another traitor discovered and captured was his first thought. Like that doctor he had encountered. He was going to investigate that man further in the morning. He wanted to be sure he knew his man before informing the authorities of his suspicions. Tomorrow, after a visit to the surgery, he would be certain.

The sound of his front door splintering shocked him out of his reverie. Before he could even get to his feet two of the six guards who had crashed in had grabbed him and were already dragging him away to Gestapo/SS Headquarters.

On Wednesday afternoons Frau Helga was permitted some free time from the school. The girls all took part in physical education programmes and Frau Helga did not number physical education as one of her areas of expertise. She paid her time in lieu back each Saturday morning with advanced English and Latin lessons.

Her first activity each Wednesday was to inspect the "dead letter box" used by the group. It was her intention to always vary her routine but invariably she was too curious to postpone her visit to the central municipal library where the "dead letter box" was situated.

In the late autumnal afternoon Frau Helga decided to walk the short distance into the centre of Munich. It was a mild afternoon with hardly a breeze and the occasional flickering of sunshine through the thin clouds. She was intermittently aware of the odour of cordite and dampened ash in the air as it drifted around the city streets following last night's raid. Sometimes a gust of unnaturally warm air would caress her as she walked past a still smouldering ruin.

In the library foyer she queued at reception to show her papers and to have her handbag searched. The receptionist, a local Nazi Party official smiled at her in recognition.

"Good afternoon, Albert," she whispered with a friendly smile. "How are you today?"

"Today I am good. I glory in last night's great success. Four allied bombers shot down."

"That is wonderful," replied Helga.

She moved away from the reception desk and the bedraggled line of old and injured men and women behind her.

Forcing herself to take her time, Helga first went into the main reference library and sat down at a desk with a recent copy of the official Nazi Party publication. She read two articles; one about Hitler's promise of new opportunities in the east for loyal Germans. There would be land and work and untold riches for the brave and the daring once the war was won. She read a second about how Aryan blood was already enriched thanks to the blood and race policies of the Fuhrer. Eventually she left her station, returned the magazine to its position at the front of the stand and then wandered slowly through the main reference hall to a side room labelled anthropology.

Anthropology was housed in a large, high-ceilinged room with grandiose coving echoed by carved dado rails. The walls were lined with bookshelves twice a man's height and they also stood in lines at right angles to each other carving the room into a maze. Helga could not help noticing with disapproval, as she did on every visit, that many of the shelves were bare; the result of enthusiastic Nazi book-burning frenzies. The volumes that remained were those produced by Nazi pseudo-scientists who had managed to re-structure anthropological knowledge in the image of the Fuhrer's dogma.

At the end of a deep corridor between bookcases, which dead-ended before a redundant, ornate fireplace, she stooped and reached to raise a short floorboard adjacent to the wall. As a loose floorboard it had eluded detection because, at the end of this corridor and against the wall, it was never walked upon.

Her hand came away with a tiny piece of note paper. She unfolded it, read it and memorised it. Then she quickly shredded it in her fingers, ensuring that each letter on the paper was torn in two. She then spent the next fifteen minutes in deep concentration wandering around the main reference section once more browsing through the shelves. At each wastepaper bin that she came to she deposited one of the scraps of paper in her hand until all the scraps were gone. Finally she selected a book from the history section and sat down with it at a reading station. With the aid of this book she de-coded the message.

With her heart in her mouth she returned the history book to its shelf and walked out of the main reference section into the reception and towards the exit.

"Mein Frau!" she heard the receptionist call in a voice inappropriately loud for the library. Her heart stopped as she turned to face him.

"I fear you have forgotten something," he said sternly.

Frau Helga looked at him hoping that the frozen terror she was experiencing was not illustrated by her expression.

"Your bag?"

Her mind blank, she looked down at the bag on her arm and then back at him.

"I must search it before you leave – as I always do."

The release of tension made her laugh a little too loudly, but he did not notice and in a moment she was outside on the Munich streets hurrying towards a rendezvous with Adolf.

"We are blown!"

The words reeled in her head as she walked as quickly as she dared to without attracting unnecessary attention.

As she entered the Englischer Garten she saw Adolf at once. He was seated on the bench where they met. Usually relaxed, Helga could tell from Adolf's rapid scouring of the park that today he was very agitated. This only heightened her own anxiety.

She sat at the other end of the bench to him and he began speaking at once.

"You got my note?"

Helga nodded.

"They know about us."

On hearing the words she most dreaded her stomach tightened in a spasm of fear.

"What do they know?"

"Everything."

"What do you mean, everything?" Helga could hear the irritation in her own voice. "Do they know who we are?"

The sensation of fear she experienced as she anticipated the reply she dreaded was almost overwhelming.

"I don't know."

"For God's sake , Adolf, what *do* they know?"

"They know of the plot. They are monitoring the convent. They are waiting for their moment to strike."

He searched his pockets for a packet of cigarettes, although he knew he had none.

"We must get the message to the others. It's every man for himself now. If we're caught you know what will happen. You saw what they did to the White Rose students."

"Adolf," Helga interrupted. "Slow down. Tell me exactly what you know."

Adolf looked to the sky where a sheet of gun metal grey loomed above them. Two mothers walked past pushing their prams and glancing at the two strangers sitting in the cold.

"It was about ten minutes before I was due to finish my shift and the sergeant sent me down to the cells with drinks for the two men on duty down there. There's a new prisoner; a Captain Vogts. He's become a bit of a sideshow because of the unholy row he's been making. He has this hideously twisted scream; the result of a war wound. He screams at anyone who goes near about his innocence; how he served in France; how he was invalided out; all about a doctor who is a British agent."

Adolf stopped and stole a glance at Helga. He could see the horror in her eyes.

"They know about the doctor?"

"Well that's what I thought was odd to begin with. If they know about the doctor, then why is Vogts in a cell? But then, as I delivered the coffee to the guards there were two Gestapo men discussing Vogts. Basically they were saying that he would have to stay where he was until the assassins – that's us – had been rounded up."

"Oh my God," breathed Helga.

They sat in stunned silence for a while. Then Helga said, "Wait a minute. If they know so much, why didn't they take you there and then? And why would they carry on talking in your presence if they didn't feel secure?"

Adolf looked at her waiting for her to continue.

"Don't you understand? This means they don't know that you're involved. Which means they might not know about the rest of us."

"They must know something. Otherwise how would they know about an assassination plot? How would they know about the doctor?"

Helga did not reply. When Adolf glanced across at her he could she that she was crying. Sensing his glance, Helga shook her head and took a handkerchief from her bag. She wiped her eyes and blew her nose.

"I'm not brave enough for this," she stuttered.

"What shall we do?" asked Adolf.

"It's simple," said Helga regaining her composure. "I will go back to the convent and warn Sister Fatima and the caretaker. On my way there I will call at the surgery and warn the doctor and his wife. You must go to the apothecary and warn him. Do not use the dead letter box again. When we have warned the others we must escape as best we can. Goodbye, Adolf and good luck."

With that she hurried away.

Although Helga had formulated their action plan it had been dredged out of her rational mind which, even as she spoke was being swamped with fear. As she walked out of the park and towards the surgery she walked along war torn streets passing stoical inhabitants doing their best to live a semblance of normality during the brief daytime respite between air raids.

Women queued outside shops and walked away with meagre rations. Young and old walked about with a driven sense of purpose. People rarely looked at each other. Few stopped to chat. To Helga everyone was a potential Gestapo informer. She felt her guilt was a flag waving to the authorities. Since her friend Sophie Scholl and her brother Hans had been brutally executed for their Weiss Rose activities she had been determined to resist the Nazis in whatever way she could. When she had gained the confidence of Sister Fatima and risked sharing her hatred of the Nazis with her it had been an easy matter for Sister Fatima to recruit her to their group. But she had always, since being a little child, been terrified of authority.

The particular brutality of the Nazis terrified her beyond reason. Even as she accepted recruitment to the group she had promised herself that at the slightest possibility of discovery and capture, she would flee. If flight would not be possible she would kill herself rather than be caught. Now her worst nightmare had come true. She continued on her way to the surgery even as her brain screamed at her to leave Munich; get the train to her aunt in Austria; then get to Switzerland.

Before she knew it her feet had carried her to the gate at the entrance to the small garden fronting the surgery. She had to let Robert and Lily know. There could be no danger here – could there?

She rang the doorbell and the receptionist opened the door and invited her in.

"Good morning," she said. "Is the doctor available? It is most urgent that I see him."

"Please wait here. I won't be a moment." The receptionist left the waiting area and disappeared through a door at the back."

Helga's anxiety would not allow her to sit still. She paced to and fro in the waiting area, fighting the desire to run out of the building and disappear forever.

The door at the back opened and the receptionist held it open for her saying, "Please come through."

Helga pushed hurriedly past her intensely relieved at last that she would see Robert. The receptionist guided her to the doctor's surgery and once again held the door open for her. Helga opened her mouth to speak as she was entering but it froze into an unattractive gape when she saw that it was Lily who was there to meet her, not Robert. Well, she thought, what difference does that make? She turned to watch the receptionist leave before speaking.

"Where is Robert?" for an instant she feared the worst. Maybe Robert was already in custody.

"He is out on a call. What did you want him for?"

"May I sit down?"

Of course you can," Lily answered beckoning towards a chair beside the desk.

Helga sat. A moment later she was on her feet again and walking towards the window. She stood for a moment scanning the street from end to end.

"Helga?" asked Lily, concern rising in her tone, "What is it?"

Helga walked back to the chair and sat down. She opened her handbag to get a cigarette but found she had none. 'Damned war,' she thought. 'You can't even get cigarettes.'

Lily had come around the desk and was leaning against it right in front of Helga.

"Helga, will you please tell me why you are here?"

"Where is Robert?"

As she asked the question she knew she had asked it already.

"I've told you."

"When will he be back?"

"I'm not sure but I'm not expecting him to be long. Will you please tell me why you are here?"

Lily's tone now told Helga that her patience was running out.

"You know you're not supposed to call here except in an emergency. If this is an emergency don't you think you should tell me? And quickly!"

Helga realised she was in dread of hearing from her own lips the words she had to say.

"I met Adolf today. We are discovered."

Lily shifted uncomfortably on her feet. She began to move around the desk but stopped herself and came back to face Helga.

"What do you mean, 'discovered'?"

Helga blurted out the details of her encounter with Adolf and the conversation he had overheard at headquarters about Captain Vogts.

When she had finished Lily went to a drawer and lifted out a bottle of brandy and a glass. She poured a measure out and handed it to Helga.

"Drink this!" she ordered. "You are in a state of shock. Don't let it turn into panic."

Helga drank the brandy in one gulp and then had a mild coughing fit as it caught on the back of her unaccustomed throat.

"Right," said Lily. "We have been trained to deal with this. Let's face it. You don't get involved in something like this without expecting the enemy to try and stop you. So we just have to think rationally and follow a logical path. We need to plan to keep ourselves and our mission safe."

Helga reacted violently to this.

"Keep our mission safe? What the hell does that mean? Our mission is blown. We're the ones who have to find safety. We must abort the mission and escape. If not we will be captured and tortured."

She stopped and began to sob painfully.

"What you have told me does not necessarily mean that our mission is affected at all."

"What?" screeched Helga. "Are you mad?"

"Keep your voice down, you fool," hissed Lily. "The receptionist will hear you."

Helga gulped down her sobs but her face was still filled with anger.

"What Adolf heard could be totally disconnected to our mission. For example," she went on, "who is this Captain Vogts? I've never heard of him. What's his connection to us? What's his connection to the Pope? As far as we know there is no connection."

Helga stared with disbelief into Lily's eyes.

"Of course it's connected to us. Why would Adolf say it is if it isn't?"

"Because he thought it was. But maybe he jumped to the wrong conclusion. Listen, Adolf is no different to the rest of us. He may be under the Gestapo but despite the propaganda it doesn't make him a superman. He's just as anxious and paranoid about being found out as the rest of us. When he stumbled halfway into a conversation he assumed it was about us. But the Gestapo are always hunting dissidents. It's their job. There must be a hundred such conversations going on at any one time; probably right at this minute. They can't *all* be about us."

Lily moved away from the desk and went to the window. There was a startled look in her eyes as she saw Robert turning at the end of the street on his way back. She turned quickly back to Helga.

"But having said all that, which I am sure is true, we must take all the necessary precautions to protect ourselves."

She went back to the window. Halfway along the street she could see that Robert had stopped to pass the time of day with a neighbour. They were looking up at the sky. Probably weighing up the chances of another raid tonight.

"Listen, Helga," she went on. "You've done really well. You've reacted properly and made the right decisions. I want you to carry on with your plan. You must get to the convent and warn Sister Fatima."

Lily came around the desk and took Helga by the elbow. Helga rose and allowed herself to be guided to the door.

"You must leave by the rear exit in case you are seen."

Lily guided Helga through the hallway that led to the kitchen and out into the rear garden.

"Go quickly, Helga, tell Sister Fatima what you know and then wait until I contact you."

Lily leaned towards her and kissed her on the cheek. Helga hesitated for a moment and then turned and ran down the garden path to the gate and was gone. Lily hurried inside and went straight back to the window at the front of the house. Robert was just ending his conversation with the neighbour and coming on towards the house. She picked up the telephone and dialled. The other end picked up immediately.

"This is Black Rose," she said. "This is Code Red. I am about to intercept a dissident before she can communicate with anyone else. She has been informed that we are onto them. Helga Rathaus is a teacher at the convent school of the Sisters of Perpetual Succour, and will attempt to communicate with a fellow dissident there. The fellow dissident is a sister at the convent. Her name is Fatima. I will go now to the convent and ensure that Helga Rathaus does not communicate with Sister Fatima. Do you understand?"

A voice replied, "Yes."

"Tell Captain Netzer to meet me there with support in case anything goes wrong."

"Yes."

"You must also intercept a police officer named Adolf Stern. He is the dissident who has alerted her to our knowledge of them and must be apprehended.

"We are active," the voice replied and the phone went dead.

Lily replaced the receiver and hurried to the entrance area where she could hear Robert coming in. "Hello Inge," she heard him say. "Have there been any call…"

"Robert," Lily interrupted sharply. "I need to speak to you. Will you come through please?"

Robert gave Inge an apologetic smile and followed Lily into the surgery. As he entered he put down his bag and removed his hat. He slotted the hat onto the rack in the corner and hung his overcoat below it.

"Who was on the phone?" he asked as he turned to face her.

"I beg your pardon?" asked Lily, colour coming to her cheeks.

"I heard the receiver bell as I came in."

"Oh that! I don't know. I picked up the receiver and the person rang off."

"Oh. Well what did you want to see me about?"

Lily went to him, her demeanour softening. She reached her arms up and around his neck. Robert pulled her to him, his arms around her waist. They kissed.

"That's better," she said. She led him to the seat Helga had occupied and motioned for him to sit down. She sat on his knee. "This war gets in the way of too many of life's pleasures," she said and kissed him again.

"I don't want to sound ungrateful," Robert whispered, "But what was it you needed to tell me?"

"Helga has been here. She says she thinks she can find out when the Pope will arrive. She overheard a conversation between Mother Superior and Herr Todt. They didn't reveal the date in the conversation but she is pretty sure that Todt wrote details into his school log book. I told her I would go up to the school as soon as you got back to help her locate the information."

"This is excellent news. But why don't I go?"

"No Robert. You don't have a genuine reason to go. It could arouse their suspicion. I am a regular visitor. I can claim to be updating my files on the children. Helga and I can move around up there with much more freedom than you can."

"You're right. When will you go?"

"Right away."

She kissed him again and he kissed her back with rising passion. She slid from his knee and whispered, "Later." He looked at her as if for the first time. He tried to understand his feelings for her. He measured them by attempting to compare them to the feelings he had had for Martha. But his mind could not do the work. He knew he was no longer the kind of man who had feelings in that way. Where they had once been, there was now just a dark space. Physically he could imitate the effect of those feelings but he was not sure that that was the same as having those feelings. He thought of Grete and although he could no longer resurrect the feelings he had had for her, he knew they had existed. He thought of the anger that had consumed him when Raul had committed suicide – so much so that he had attempted his first clinical murder – the obnoxious though innocuous Frau Hahn. A seething hatred for the evils of Nazism had driven him then. Now, he had no rage left. He was about to commit the most outrageous assassination in the history of civilisation but he had no strong emotion about it. It was a task he had set himself. He knew it was right. It was a cold emotionless, rational decision.

He thought all this as he watched Lily leave the house. When she came home he would make love to her. Physically he would be demanding and demonstrative, but inside he would be empty.

Helga Rathaus walked as quickly as she could without actually running or drawing attention to herself from passers-by. The effort was exhausting her much more than she knew it should be. As she hurried past the rail terminus she experienced an almost irresistible urge to rush in and buy a ticket to anywhere. Almost, but not quite, irresistible. Lily's reasoning had been persuasive. But her thoughts of Sister Fatima were the strongest argument against succumbing to her urge to escape. She had to warn Sister Fatima. She would be unable to live happily anywhere if she thought Fatima was being subjected to Gestapo torture techniques. Her resolve was to speak to Fatima, ask her to inform the caretaker, and to subsequently disappear.

There was nobody at the main gate as she entered the grounds. She left the main drive and took a narrow path that led around to a side entrance used by the nuns. If she encountered the gardener here she would inform him. If not, she would find him after speaking to Sister Fatima.

As she approached the entrance she saw the gardener in the distance at the bottom of the vegetable garden. He had paused in his work to speak to two men who were standing at the edge of the plot he was working. They were men in working clothes and she made a mental note to come straight back to the garden when she had finished informing Sister Fatima.

The crunching of her shoes on the path ceased suddenly as she stepped into the gloom of the interior through the low, arched doorway. On tiptoes she ran silently along the corridors until she reached the door of Sister Fatima's cell. She knocked and hissed, "Sister Fatima." She heard a sound from within and footsteps padding across the cell floor. The door opened slowly and she hurried inside.

Thirty-one

When Mrs Kitson entered Andrew Trubshaw's office she was half into her coat. It was a warm, unflattering, belted coat that matched the functionality of her flat, laced shoes. It was seven o'clock and today, so far, there had been no emergency to cause her to miss her normal going home time. She approached Andrew's desk with a printed sheet in her hand.

"This has just come up from communications. They say it is urgent"

Mrs Kitson waited as he read it. She knew if she had any sense, she would exit as quickly as she could and get on her bus home. But she had a feeling that this message from communications was going to involve her in some extra hours work. She watched Andrew's face as the contents of the message sank in.

"the monastery has been invaded - the monks endangered – not all aware of threat – need to be informed - need sanctuary – chapter completion unlikely."

"Cup of tea, Mr Trubshaw?" Mrs Kitson asked as Andrew's head fell into his hands. The sound of her voice seemed to bring him back to reality. He looked up at her as if just becoming aware of her presence.

"Tea?" he reiterated. "Yes, Mrs Kitson, tea! And after that a return ticket to Leicester on the next train."

Entering the house on Dronfield Street in Leicester at midnight, Trubshaw realised that if his hopes came to fruition here, he would have to book the boat train to Ireland tomorrow and begin a thorough investigation of Sean. Every mission carried with it the danger of entrapment; possibly a double agent at work to expose the people involved. He had to check out the two under his control. If they were in the clear it would be someone in the dissident network. His heart would not let him believe that Sean was the double agent. He had worked so brilliantly on previous missions. But Trubshaw knew his heart could not be allowed to affect his thinking. He must investigate every angle.

On the journey northwards he had re-read the notes he had made when he first investigated Lily.

The Dronfield Street terraced house felt and smelled like a house that had not been occupied for many weeks. Cold, musty and empty of spirit. He made sure the blackout curtains were drawn tight before switching on the lights. He then set about a systematic search of the property. His problem was that he had already conducted a search of this property and it was hard for him not to skim over areas he remembered scrutinising before. As he searched he knew that something was tugging at his thoughts. Something was jarring. But it was too faint for him to determine it accurately.

Having found nothing incriminating downstairs he moved his search to the upper floor two hours after entering the property.

As the stairs creaked beneath his tread he smiled with relief to think that he was not a cat burglar with the occupants upstairs in bed. The creaking stairs would surely wake them.

Beginning in Lily's bedroom he worked around the room geographically. He started at the door and worked around the walls back to the door examining the interior of every item of furniture meticulously. He then moved each piece of furniture and examined the floor beneath. He was annoyed with himself when he shifted the chest of drawers and allowed Lily's photograph album to fall to the floor with a noisy clump. He lifted it and threw it onto the bed. Having lifted sufficient floorboards to permit a good view of the area below he was beginning to feel better. He wanted Lily to be genuine. He did not want to find any incriminating evidence. He hoped, if there had to be a traitor that it was from within the German network.

Moving systematically from the outer to the inner areas of the room, Trubshaw was content that this room held nothing incriminating. Before moving onto the second bedroom he took the photograph album and replaced it on the chest of drawers.

It was as he was pulling the bedroom door to behind him that the thought entered his head. It was a memory of a thought in actuality; one which said, "such luxuriously thick pages". As the thought echoed in his head his heart sank. His mind raced. He snatched up the album and opened it. For a moment he fingered the soft, richly textured pages; one, then another, then another.

"Damn!" he bellowed.

His fingers tore frantically at the edge of a page. As he tore along it he saw that it was a double page. In here, as in an envelope, there was a space; a secret cavity. He peeled the two leaves apart and exposed the hidden interior.

He did not need to recognise the characters he was looking at to know what they were. Radio codes! He opened other pages. Geographical information about the British Isles. Another cavity showed an escape plan. In total the album contained all the information an agent would need once he or she became active in Britain. The information would be useful now in rounding up other agents. There were no names or contact addresses but some careful detective work would reveal Lily's web of treachery.

"Thick, luxurious pages!" The words taunted him as they ran across his brain again. How could he have missed it? In a sense he hadn't missed the clue. His brain had registered it but his consciousness had failed to scan it in his internal inventory.

One random thought suddenly led to another. His brain jarred and something else jumped into place.

"Creaking stairs!"

He ran to the stairs and set about ripping out the stair rods. He let them clatter down as he tossed each one aside and then he pulled away the linoleum. He recognised it as substantially expensive linoleum now. Incongruous in the context of this terraced house. The beam of his torch illuminated the wooden stairs and immediately he saw what he was looking for. A tiny catch clicked as he flicked it and he pulled towards him a stair-shaped door hinged atop the second step. Inside the exposed recess sat a transmitter in excellent condition. He knew all he needed to know now.

Returning to the downstairs sitting room he threw himself into a chair. He stared at the dull light bulb and mentally berated himself. He had made the easiest mistake of all to make. He had liked the idea of Lily and Sean as a team so much that he had lacked total thoroughness. Now Sean and the members of the network in Germany were all endangered.

Lily had obviously begun to work her treachery; hence the message from the apothecary. But they clearly had not identified her yet. He had to get the information to them immediately. Why? She had been so convincing. Her anti-Nazi credentials had seemed impeccable. As a sleeper she had pulled the wool over his eyes.

In the coming days, as he re-read his notes it would start to make sense to him. He had initially read the loss of her mother and brother as one of those unfortunate tragedies that occur in wartime. But a little military research revealed to him that despite popular recollection, parts of Germany had been invaded during the Great War. We all remember Belgium and France being overrun by Germany but few remembered that Alsace and parts of southern Bavaria, not to mention large tracts of eastern Prussia had been overrun by the allies. He had written:

> My original notes suggest Renate and Friedrich killed in accident whilst travelling into Freiburg in Alsace to visit Renate's dying mother. Military records confirm that Freiburg was under allied siege for most of the war and suffered many artillery bombardments.

Could this be it? Did a British shell kill her mother and brother? Resentment forged in early childhood against the British. The loss of a much-loved mother and brother. A desire for revenge. It could easily be the case. But what matter? He had failed. Now brave combatants were endangered and a vital mission was in jeopardy.

The resignation that he submitted was returned to him three times. But on his fourth attempt his request to be enlisted was granted. He completed basic training and was shipped out to join a Special Services Unit. His last administrative act before leaving his office for the last time was to write an instruction to the office in charge of homeland security. His communication ordered the release of former Detective Inspector Peter Herbert. Trubshaw was in Italy with his unit when news reached him that Former D.I. Peter Herbert had died of pneumonia in his prison hut on the Isle of Man.

Thirty-two

If Helga's dread of capture had been crippling, Adolf's prospects were considerably bleaker. As a member of the police force he was not truly Gestapo, but he took most of his orders from them. His was the worst possible kind of treachery. If caught his treatment would be extra special.

But Adolf had always expected this moment to arrive and he was fully prepared for it. He sighed with relief as he thanked God that his parents were dead. He had been an only child so there were no other family members to consider except his wife and their only son. He now congratulated himself for the hours he put in each week in his garden shed. Despite his wife's complaints, he had never neglected to spend some time every week working on his motor-bike. He had serviced it, fitted new parts, cleaned it and run the engine to keep it in trim. He had also collected, carefully and painstakingly, a full tank of fuel and several spare drums.

As he hurried home he knew he had one more task to perform for the group before vanishing from sight. At the corner of the avenue where he lived he knocked upon a house door and waited impatiently for it to be opened. A small boy of about ten years stood in the doorway.

"Hello, Adolf. My father's out."

"That's all right, Johann. It's you I wanted anyway."

"Me. What can I do?" asked Johann with surprise.

"Well I've got to get into work and I don't have time to deliver this prescription to the apothecary. If you will take it round there for me I will give you this."

Adolf unrolled a 100 deutschmark bill. It was not a massive amount but it was more pocket money than a boy of Johann's age and circumstances would see in a long time.

"Wow!" gasped Johann. And he shot into the house, reappearing in an instant in his coat and hat.

"Give it to me," he said. "I'll take it right now."

Adolf gave the boy the slip of paper with the carefully encrypted note and also the money.

"Thank you, Adolf," he called as he ran off down the street.

Adolf was unable to raise a smile as Johann ran away. Instead he turned and hurried to his own house. This was not going to be easy. His wife was a home bird. She would not like having to drop everything and leave. She would curse him for his treachery and the danger it had placed them in. But he had made up his mind that he would be firm and accept no argument. He was taking the boy with him and he knew she would follow.

In the end he had had to drag her out into the rear lane and force her astride the motor-cycle. She cried enormous tears at the thought of all she was leaving behind that had taken years to save for. But she straddled the pillion seat and hugged her son when Adolf placed him in front of her. He then got onto the driver's seat, kicked the engine into life and roared away from the house, away from the avenue, away from Munich.

From the moment he had decided to become a dissident, Adolf had prepared for this. In his minimalist luggage he carried several sets of identity papers that he had rifled away from criminals he had arrested. He had his life savings. He had a destination in mind and a planned route to get there. He was happy that the chaos of war would probably assist him in his plan of escape. He pointed his front wheel in the direction of his first staging post; the Sudetenland village where his father's family had originated.

Thirty-three

"Lily, is that you?"

Helga peered into the gloom of the cell at the silhouetted figure she was beginning to discern.

"How did you get here? Where's Sister Fa...?"

Before she could finish her question a large, gloved hand came around her shoulder and clasped itself over her mouth. She felt the immense strength of the arm around her neck and the other now encircling her waist.

In answer to her first question, the figure in front stepped forward. The facial features resolved themselves into those of Lily. Lily approached until their eyes were fixed together, their noses almost touching. A contemptuous smile flickered at her lips. She opened her mouth to speak to Helga but then seemed to think better of it.

A voice spoke softly and clearly in Helga's ear.

"Now my pretty! We have many exotic delights waiting for you back at headquarters. And you have many stories and names to tell us."

With a sudden movement Lily raised her right hand and struck out at Helga. Helga's scream was muffled by the leather glove smothering her mouth. Blood spurted from her neck as Lily withdrew her hand. Netzer pulled his hand away sharply and jumped back, tossing Helga aside.

"What the...?" yelled Netzer.

"Shhh!" urged Lily, placing a hand to his mouth. Her other hand still held a shiny blade now dripping red with Helga's blood.

"What did you do that for?" hissed Netzer. "She could have told us all we need to know. She could have led us up the network to the leaders of this conspiracy."

"Don't be ridiculous, darling. She is far too lowly in this conspiracy. Besides, I thought she had a gun. When she moved her hand I acted instinctively. I couldn't bear the thought of losing you."

Netzer lifted his eyes away from the bloodstain on his sleeve and looked into Lily's eyes. "Come here," he said. And he took her in his arms and kissed her mouth. As the kiss went on Lily's arms rose, circled his neck and they embraced as lovers.

Helga lay on the floor of the cell uselessly attempting to stem the gush of blood that poured from the wound Lily had inflicted upon her. Her eyes widened and dilated but not in fear. All fear was gone. As she slipped from consciousness she could not take her eyes away from Lily's face. Lily, who was unnerved by the stare, went across to Helga and turned her over with the sole of her foot. The woman's body slumped and gasped a final breath and then lay still.

Lily whispered, "We must get on before someone comes."

"You are right."

"What will you do with the body?" Lily asked.

The captain laughed, "The British will take care of that. Tonight she will be thrown into a burning building. Just another victim of bomber command."

"Good. Now get your men to remove this garbage from here. If Adolf Stern has been apprehended we have no reason to worry. We can carry on. The dissidents will be unaware that they are known to us. They can go about their mission and hopefully expose to us their networks, their chain of command. These people are nothing to us but they can lead us to the heart of the resistance in the upper echelons of the Wehrmacht."

"Never mind that," the captain whispered as he attempted to sweep Lily into his arms once more. How about another kiss? And when can we get together for some real lovemaking?"

Lily turned away as she pushed him from her.

"Stop it," she hissed. "There will be plenty of time for that all in due course. For now we have work to do."

The captain took hold of her elbow and jerked her round to face him.

"You're not going cold on me are you?" he asked.

Lily softened and put her lips to his.

"Don't be silly. I am yours always. But we have to get rid of this mess before it is discovered."

"All right," grunted the captain. He put his head out of the door and called out. Two men dressed in working clothes came in and he pointed at Helga's body.

"That thing," he said. "Get rid of it. Air raid casualty."

"Yes, Herr captain."

They bent down together and folded the limp corpse into a sack which they had brought with them and carried her out between them.

Thirty-four

The men in the guardroom stood to attention as Captain Netzer burst in. He glanced at the glove on his right hand with distaste as he realised there was a saliva stain there at the junction between thumb and index finger. Helga's mouth had been crushed there. He threw a desultory salute and the men returned with a sharp "Heil Hitler!"

He passed through to his office beyond. After a few minutes he called, "Schirach!" Corporal Schirach, a man of superb physique, jumped to his feet and walked into the office.

"Yes mein Obersturmfuhrer?"

"Where are they?"

Correctly inferring to whom the captain referred Schirach replied, "In room 12 Obersturmfuhrer."

The captain got up from his desk and walked towards the door.

"Come with me," he said.

Hauptsturmfuhrer Schirac followed Netzer through the guardroom, along a corridor and down three flights of stairs deep into the bowels of Gestapo headquarters. He stopped outside room 12 and allowed Schirach to open the door for him.

As he entered the two men seated at a table rose and saluted him. The air was thick with cigarette smoke. The Obersturmfuhrer paused and half turned to Schirac.

"Who said these men could smoke?" he asked.

Schirac swallowed with difficulty and replied, "I did sir."

Netzer turned fully to face him, "You shouldn't have done that," he muttered ominously.

"I am sorry, Obersturmfuhrer. It will not happen again."

"I hope not Hauptsturmfuhrer."

He turned to the men who were still at attention.

"Sit down men," he said. And then, as if to confound his previous remarks he took out a packet of cigarettes and offered the men a cigarette each. They gratefully accepted and took a light from the Obersturmfuhrer.

"You like smoking I think?"

"Yes Herr Obersturmfuhrer," they replied.

"I don't like smoking," Netzer said as he slowly shook his head.

The men froze and took their cigarettes away from their lips. "No, no," protested Netzer. "Do not misunderstand me. Please, continue with your enjoyment."

For a moment there was silence and slowly the men put their cigarettes back to their lips and continued to smoke.

"You were on guard duty yesterday in the area of the cells, correct?"

"Yes, mein Obersturmfuhrer."

"You were overheard discussing the prisoner in cell four."

The men looked at each other. So that's what this is about. The thought that passed between them was almost tangible.

"Is that why we are here, Herr Obersturmfuhrer?"

Netzer suddenly took hold of the table they were seated at and threw it aside and roared, "Yes. Yes, that is why you are here. Your incompetent behaviour has put a vital mission at risk."

The men jumped to their feet, spilling their chairs and backing away towards the walls of the room. Just as suddenly, Netzer's manner altered again.

"Calm down men," he soothed.

He righted the table and chairs and invited them to sit down again. The men did as they were told but the fear sat in their eyes.

"You know what I don't like about smoking," Netzer remarked gently.

The men were frozen in terror now.

"It gets in your eyes."

He looked at them, one to the other, as if expecting affirmation of his comment.

"People tell me," he went on, "That smokers cannot feel the irritation in their eyes because they are so used to smoke." He stopped and smiled at them. "They are immune to it, as it were." He directed his gaze at one of the men. The man immediately looked down. "You, for example," he said. "You cannot know what it is like for a non-smoker like me to feel the pain of smoke in my eyes. The Fuhrer is a non-smoker. I wonder if you would smoke in his presence and blow smoke into his eyes." Netzer got up from his seat again. "But do you know what?" he said. "I can give you an idea of what it feels like to be a non-smoker with smoke in your eyes."

The man he was staring at began to shake his head and tears appeared in the corners of his eyes. "Hauptsturmfuhrer," Netzer said, "Please assist me."

"Obersturmfuhrer!" affirmed the corporal.

"Place your cigarette on the table," Netzer requested.

The man did as he was told but he stood and backed away. Netzer's smile did not waver as he ordered, "Secure him, Hauptsturmfuhrer."

Schirach seized the man by his arms and secured them behind his back. He raised them so that the man was forced to stoop downwards. With the lighted cigarette in his hand Netzer took the man by the hair of his head and lifted his face upwards.

"Now my friend," he whispered as he held the lighted end an inch from the man's left eye. "This is what we non-smokers have to suffer every time you light up."

Slowly and deliberately he moved the cigarette towards the man's eye. First he watched it scorch the eyelash. Then he moved it towards the man's eyelid. The agonised screaming of a powerless victim caused even Hauptsturmfuhrer Schirach to struggle with his feelings. But then with a suddenness that startled his victim, Netzer pulled the cigarette away and started to laugh.

He moved away and approached the second guard who was sitting on the floor against the far wall his head in his hands. He took the second guard by the hair of his head and laughed into his face.

"You thought I was going to do it didn't you?"

He moved back to the first guard whose ribcage was trembling with panic.

"You actually thought I was going to do it?"

His laughter rose and then fell to a cold silence.

"Come, Schirach," he said. "Let's leave these men to ponder their position. Meanwhile I will ponder whether or not the Gestapo has room for indolents like them."

In the early hours of the following morning, Shirach was returning from a raid. A group of Jews had been discovered and they had been rounded up and delivered to the transportation unit. He felt good. A successful raid and more enemies of the state removed from the Fatherland.

As he progressed towards the canteen he found himself approaching a detail of men. They were engaged in carrying a body. As he drew level he asked one of the men, "What has happened here, Otto?"

"Obersturmfuhrer Netzer had a change of heart. He has carried out his preferred punishment on Gunther and Walter. He went into a furious rage when he was informed that Officer Stern had not been apprehended. Stern has disappeared."

"Where is the Obersturmfuhrer now?" asked Schirach.

"He's leading the raid to arrest the apothecary. He knows the dissidents at the convent were not contacted, but he cannot be sure that Stern did not get a message to the apothecary."

Schirach leaned forward and removed the blanket that was covering the face of the corpse. He suppressed an involuntary gasp when he saw the burnt out eye sockets. The hollow circles of charred flesh cast the visage into an expression of comic mockery. There remained a faint odour of cooked meat.

"And the other one?" he asked.

"The same," replied Otto.

"Where are you taking the bodies?"

"Obersturmfuhrer Netzer wants everyone to see them as an example. We are to sit them at a table in the mess room. They are to stay there tomorrow until midday. Then we must burn them."

"What about the families?" asked Schirach. "Have they been told?"

"The Obersturmfuhrer has taken a detail of men to arrest them. They will be delivered for transportation."

Schirach replaced the blanket on the face, nodded at Otto and the detail moved on.

Ilsa was putting on her coat and pinning her hat to her hair when the shop door tinkled open. She looked across wishing that she had locked it and turned the sign before getting ready to leave. A young boy bounded in, red-faced and breathless.

"I've brought a prescription," he said.

"You'll have to bring it back tomorrow. We're closed," she said.

"But it's from Adolf," the boy protested. "He said it's urgent. He gave me a hundred."

At the sound of Adolf's name Ilsa walked across the shop and closed and locked the door. Now she turned the sign to 'closed'. The boy handed her the prescription and she told him to wait. She took the prescription and disappeared into the back of the shop. In a moment or two she re-appeared, searched the shelves for something and chose a lollipop which she handed to the boy

"Well done," she said placing her hand affectionately upon the boy's cap. "The apothecary said he will deliver the medicine. You can go now."

The boy thanked her for the lollipop and skipped out of the shop. She locked the door behind him and walked through to the back. The apothecary was not there. She heard a sound from above and climbed the stairs.

In the gloomy room she found the apothecary at a radio transmitter, which he had brought out from under a floorboard. She listened as he spoke his message and watched as he signed off and packed the radio away again.

"What is it?" she asked, anxiety rising within her.

"We are destroyed," he replied in a hoarse whisper. "We must escape. If we are captured we will… It's unthinkable…" He was interrupted by the sound of cars screeching to a halt outside the shop. He ran to the window and saw Gestapo agents and a team of SS troops pouring out of one black saloon car and a truck. The sound of banging on the shop door was followed by the sound of the door being smashed in.

There was no precedent for the look that passed between the apothecary and Ilsa. Despair was inadequate as an accompaniment to their plight. Returning the radio transmitter to its hiding place and covering the removable floorboards with the rug and cupboard that routinely stood there, the apothecary rushed out of the room dragging Ilsa with him and pushed her into the room opposite. He just had time to close the door of the room they had vacated.

"Quickly Ilsa," the apothecary said in a voice that struggled to contain any expression. He took a key from the top pocket of his white jacket and used it to unlock a steel cabinet attached to the wall behind a desk. The pounding of boots on the stairs made him fumble as he reached inside the cabinet. A packet of capsules fell to the floor. He dropped to his knees to re-gather them and quickly removed two capsules from the packet.

"Swallow this!"

At the same moment as the door to the room burst open Ilsa and the apothecary swallowed a lethal dose of cyanide. The apothecary began to speak, "We won't see it now but this evil will be defeated."

"It's not fair," was all Ilsa could manage.

Obersturmfuhrer Netzer stood in the doorway, "Seize them," he screamed. Guards rushed past him and took hold of the dissidents. Ilsa felt their steely hands grasp her arms at the very same moment as the first excruciating knife of cyanide sliced through her.

In a few moments the wild-eyed Netzer was in possession of two corpses. His men could see the fury that engulfed him at being cheated of the chance to interrogate these two criminals. They made a mental note to steer well clear of him over the next few days if they only could.

Thirty-five

That evening Robert and Lily did not stir from their home. It was a quiet evening. No bombing raid. The silence of the sky twisted their nerves tight. Their ears strained to pick up the sound of the first enemy plane approaching from the west. They tingled with expectancy for the first explosion. But all night nothing came. There was to be no release from the tension.

Lily poured them both a drink of schnapps and as she handed Robert his glass she leaned and kissed him on the mouth. As their lips met her mind flashed images of her kiss with Captain Netzer. The sexual confusion aroused her and she quickly placed her drink on a side table and began to desperately kiss Robert. After struggling to rid himself of his own glass Robert responded and they fell into a passionate embrace. In a moment Lily was overtaken by physical desire. She fell on top of him as he lay back on the couch and they began to make love. The eroticism of being with Robert and letting her thoughts run to Netzer multiplied the intensity of the physical pleasure. Even as she luxuriated in the feeling her mind agonised over the choice she was playing with.

Thoughts of Netzer brought an intensification of the physical pleasure she was experiencing. But when she focused on Robert, the feeling was almost crippling. The words "I love you," poured out of her like a primeval instinct. Each time she said it, it acted as a trigger to say it again. Robert reached both hands up to her face and whispered "Shhh." With all his strength he turned her onto her back and re-entered her from on top. As their lovemaking entered its violently climactic rhythm, tears ran freely from Lily eyes. Robert collapsed on top of her and her arms encircled him. She began the "I love you" litany again but this time Robert said nothing. He lay with his face hidden in the curve of her neck thinking of Martha.

The doctor and his wife spent the rest of the evening mostly occupied with their own thoughts. They listened to some music on the wireless until it was interrupted by a propaganda speech by Himmler. Switching off the wireless they each read for a while.

Lily contemplated the extreme danger she had allowed herself to become embroiled in. The most frightening part of that danger was the way her mind was moving. She knew she had to face a choice and that she was becoming incapable of making the safe, sensible choice. Pausing in her reading she stared across at Robert. Looking at his serious expression as he concentrated on his novel she knew, even if she was reluctant to admit it yet, that the choice had already been made. The mortal danger for her lay in how to safely execute that choice.

Robert paused from time to time in his perusal of The Valley Of Fear by Conan Doyle, a favourite of his which he had read many times. As he paused he looked at the face opposite. This woman he now lived with as his wife; this woman who shared his dangerous mission. He could not remotely conjure up a repetition of the feeling he had initially felt for Martha. If that had been love, what he now felt for Lily had to be something else. But then, he reasoned, events in his life had turned him into something else. Maybe the love he had had for Martha was no longer available to him. Maybe this connection to Lily was all that was left. He knew in his heart that he could never re-capture the love between himself and Martha. That was dead and gone; as sure as Conny was dead and gone. The only things left for Sean and Martha to share from now on were recrimination and despair. As he looked at Lily he was thinking, so I will have to learn to live with this kind of love. It is probably better than no love at all.

"What happened at the convent?" Robert asked.

"Helga was right," Lily replied. "The strange thing is she wasn't there. When she left here we agreed to meet at the convent but she didn't appear. I obviously couldn't ask about her. Nevertheless, she is right. I found Totd's log book. He has written, 'God's representative – arriving early evening Tuesday week'."

"It's Wednesday today," calculated Robert. "That means he's arriving in less than two weeks."

"Wrong," interrupted Lily. "His entry was dated last Sunday. That means the Pope arrives next Tuesday, six days from now."

"Thank heavens. This waiting around is beginning to become a strain for all of us."

"We need to go over our action plan, Robert," Lily suggested.

"You're absolutely right."

He got up and poured out two glasses of schnapps. Handing one to Lily she took his arm and stopped him as he turned away.

"You're forgetting something," she said.

He was puzzled for an instant and then realised what she meant. He leaned down and kissed her. 'Why do I always have to remind him?' thought Lily.

"If he arrives Tuesday we do it Tuesday," stated Robert emphatically.

"Is that wise?" asked Lily.

"Wise," repeated Robert. "I don't think anything we are planning to do could be labelled wise."

Lily smiled wryly.

"Maybe not," she said, "But in the context of our actions is it wise?"

"The only thing I can say to that is we would be unwise to wait any longer. The sooner we complete the sooner we can get out of here. Everyday we are here brings us one day closer to discovery."

Lily sipped her schnapps and pondered.

"I suppose you are right. Next Tuesday it is then."

Having finished their preamble, Lily began a rehearsed procedure to make sure each knew exactly what the other was thinking. The questions she asked were ones they had contemplated and answered many times.

"How do we ensure that we are inside the convent on that night?"

"Well," said Robert, "That's the ground we have been preparing all this time. We are familiar faces in there now. We must continue the charm offensive. I will concentrate on Mother Superior. I already have her convinced that my vocation for the priesthood was only narrowly squeezed out of my life by my vocation for medicine. She believes I am the most devout lay individual she has ever met. I constantly refer to my devotion for our beloved Pope. I am convinced that she is planning to invite me, or both of us, to meet him. I can tell by the way she smiles, a secret "I know something you don't know" smile whenever we talk of him. I'm just a bit disappointed that we're still waiting for the invitation. But I tell myself that she is only being wise in delaying until the last minute for purposes of security. From now we continue to visit every night. We will attend mass and benediction together every night and we will take a gift for the Mother. Whilst he is here Pacelli is bound to say mass for the faithful. We are surely part of the inner circle now. We have to be invited. Mother has no reason not to invite us. I don't actually think she will be able to resist the temptation to show off in front of us her close connection with our beloved Father. In the meantime you must discover where Pacelli's apartment will be inside the convent. That shouldn't be too hard. I'm sure it will have one or two extra luxuries in it that you won't find in the nun's cells."

"What if the invitation does not arrive?"

"We turn up at the convent next Tuesday night anyway – unannounced."

"How will you do it?"

"I will overpower the target in his quarters and administer an overdose of adrenalin."

"After the completion of our mission, what do we do?"

"Tomorrow I will inform the apothecary of our completion date and he will make the arrangements for our withdrawal."

Lily looked down at her drink and sipped it thoughtfully.

"Very good," she said eventually. "I think we are ready."

Robert knew there was something they had not discussed. He had waited for Lily to raise the matter but he realised now that she was not going to. He placed his glass on the table beside his chair and looked carefully at Lily.

"You never told me about Vogts. What happened there?"

Lily's hand paused in raising her glass to her mouth. But only for the slightest of moments. Then she took a sip and placed her glass on the table top.

"You can forget about that. I have dealt with that situation. I spoke to the Trings and they confirmed that Vogts had been around asking if the man he had seen leaving their apartment had been a doctor. They had told him yes and he had gone away. I decided that the only thing I could do was call on him and ask him outright if he needed medical attention. I called at his house and he let me in. When he realised I was connected to you I could tell that he had become frightened. This confirmed to me that he had recognised you. I killed him. I had no option."

Robert got up from his seat and approached Lily.

"My poor girl," he said, leaning close down to look into her eyes. "Why didn't you tell me? You could be suffering a reaction."

"I was going to. Perhaps the trauma caused me to postpone reliving the event."

Robert leaned his head in and placed his lips upon hers. He felt the crinkled dryness of her lips and returned to his chair.

Thirty-six

"My nerves are destroyed." It was Mother Superior speaking over a cup of substitute tea that she held close to her face in both hands. "I've reached the stage," she said, "When I feel more relaxed when the bombs are falling all around us than I do listening to this fragile silence."

"I know exactly what you mean, Mother," said Frau Todt.

"It's the waiting," contributed Herr Todt. "We spoil the peace by constantly anticipating the arrival of the first bomb."

"You're right," said Mother. "We are sinful. We should be thanking God for the respite instead of eating up time with anxiety."

"We are only human," ventured Frau Todt.

"Well," declared Herr Todt, getting to his feet, "I am going to follow that advice and take advantage of this heaven sent pause to take a stroll in the garden. I will spare you ladies the scent of my cigar. One I have been saving for some time."

He left the Mother's office through the French windows and stood for a moment on the patio to light his cigar and study the sky. The women watched his figure recede into the gloom as he strolled along the path that wound its way around the garden. As he disappeared from sight they returned to their substitute tea and gentle conversation.

Behind an ivied wooden structure the head-teacher stepped up to the door of the shed secluded there and entered without knocking. The gardener did not speak as he entered. He had observed Todt's careful approach and was not surprised.

Todt spoke first, "Next Tuesday it is," he stated.

The gardener nodded in agreement.

"Good. I will be glad to have this task behind me."

"You sound troubled," Todt said.

The gardener put down a pot he had been planting with bulbs and stood up to look out of the dirty window. Turning back to Todt he whispered, "Something is wrong."

Controlled alarm brushed Todt's expression as he removed the cigar from his wet lips.

"Explain yourself!"

The gardener again turned to the window. Without looking at Todt he said, "Helga is missing. Adolf is missing. The apothecary is closed and I can contact no one from there. Sister Fatima has spoken to me. She feels the same. It is as if the network has been erased. Yet we are still here."

"When did you discover all of this? Why haven't you told me before now?"

"I was not sure. I still am not sure. I am telling you my worst suspicions. We need to make sure pretty damn quick and if I am right we need to vanish."

"But we are so close. In one week's time our work will be done."

"If the Gestapo know of us it will turn out to be the longest week of our sorry lives. One of us needs to inform the doctor and his wife in time for them to escape."

"Hell! What shall we do?" asked Todt, more of himself than the Gardener. Taking a long pull on his cigar and inhaling deeply, as if to re-assure himself through the sharp sting of the hot smoke on his throat that his senses were functioning properly. He proceeded to answer his own question. "I will pass your suspicions on."

Todt was thinking rapidly. The mission was the prime objective. Everything else was subordinate to that. "You have done well," he said to the gardener, "But now you must save yourself. You must disappear. You will be one less link in the chain that might lead them to us. I will inform the doctor and his wife and enable them to escape."

He took another lung destroying pull on his cigar. "Do you have a clear escape plan in waiting?"

"You can rest easy on that score Headmaster. The only unknown is when to activate it."

"Now! Immediately! And that is an order. The link to the leadership must not be discovered. You are the only one who knows that I am the link. You must go. Now, tonight!"

As Herr Todt walked as casually as he could back to the French windows the gardener opened the door and window of his shed to rid the interior of the stench of cigar smoke and began to step out of his overall.

Herr Todt did not immediately return to join the ladies in Mother Superior's office. Instead he walked silently towards the school building and his own office. He took care not to be seen. Inside the school he did not switch on the lights. Although it was dark he knew his way around this building better than a blind man. In his office he slid his heavy desk away from the wall it stood against. Taking a key from his pocket he slid it into the head of a flower on the wallpaper. Turning the key in the well-disguised keyhole he opened a door, approximately one-third of a metre square, standing at floor level. He reached inside and took out the receiver of a radio telephone. He dialled and asked to be connected directly to The Fox. After giving a complicated code sequence he waited for a full five minutes. Then, abruptly, he found himself talking to General Rommel.

Thirty-seven

Friedrich was already into his second beer when Robert arrived at their watering hole. On seeing Robert enter he ordered another beer and handed it to him after he had hung his wet raincoat over a chair arm and reached the bar. They sat on stools and sipped their beers as they chatted.

"She was the love of my life," concluded Friedrich, speaking through the froth on his moustache. "I am ashamed to admit it but in all honesty I must."

"What was her name?" Robert asked.

"Sadie."

"Sadie," remarked Robert with surprise, "But…"

"Yes, I know," interrupted Friedrich. "A Jewess. That is why I am ashamed to admit it. But if a thing is true it is true. The Fuhrer has taught us that much."

"What happened?"

"Well, it was after my discharge from the army in 1918. I fetched up in Warsaw. Don't ask me why. That's another story altogether. Anyway, I landed a job in a shoe factory. Nothing grand, just labouring. Hired muscle. Carting heavy crates from one floor to the next. Well Sadie worked in the wages office and I used to see her every Friday afternoon when she brought around our wage envelopes. I never dreamed she would look at me as a potential boyfriend, but I harboured fantasies. She was the most beautiful girl in the world. Some of the men took small liberties with her. Well we were a rough crew and she took it in good part. I used to boil inside when someone made a suggestive comment to her but I was too embarrassed to intervene. It would reveal my feelings you see."

Friedrich broke off his narrative to utter a deafening laugh and to clap Robert on his back, causing him to spill beer down his jacket.

"Can you imagine it, hey, Robert, my friend. Me, embarrassed. Me, shy. Hard to credit, hey?"

"Tell me more," said Robert, when he had wiped his jacket off. "What happened?"

"Well one day one of the men went too far. As she handed him his wage envelope he pretended to stumble and fell against her, placing his hands upon her breasts. Something happened to me when I saw the distress he caused register on her face. I snapped. Shyness and embarrassment flew out of the window. I took hold of him by the throat and I would have broken his neck. If she had not restrained me I would have ended my days on the Polish gallows. Well after that we took to going out. I saw my first cinematograph with her. I went to my first art gallery with her. Eventually we became lovers."

Taking a sip of beer Friedrich seemed to be at the end of his tale.

"Like I said," he concluded once more, "She was the love of my life."

Exasperated by the inconclusive ending Robert demanded to know, "What happened?"

Friedrich wrinkled his nose. He glanced down at the swastika insignia on his armband.

"Well," he replied, "It was at this time that I fell in with a group of German ex-patriots living in Warsaw like myself. They began my education. I realised an Aryan like myself and a Jewess could never be together." After a pause he quietly said, "I gave her up."

With that he lifted his glass and downed the remainder of his beer in one mighty swallow. Slamming it down on the bar he shouted, his good spirits returning in a flash, "Now then good doctor. You buy the beers and I will deal the cards. Give a poor man the chance to win some money from his friend, and I promise not to send you home penniless."

Thirty-eight

Lily walked through Marienplatz from Kaufinger Strasse to the Altes Rathaus. She stood before the golden statue of the Virgin and attempted to evoke some emotion within herself. She was trying to find some vestige of the religious belief she had once held. Something to encourage her to destroy this mission she had infiltrated. 'The one, holy and apostolic church,' she recited to herself. 'The blessed virgin', to whom she had prayed adoringly as a child. 'Hail Mary, full of grace,' the substitute mother figure that she had worshipped.

She turned away. Her efforts unrewarded. Nothing within her raged against the assassination of this Pope. She looked back now upon her fanatical hatred of Britain and the British as a deviant form of self-indoctrination. She bitterly regretted the contempt she had secretly harboured for her father and she longed to have one moment with him to let him know she loved him. Ironically, it had been Robert (or should she call him Sean?) who had dismantled her hatred of the British. That man who had borne arms against the British Empire and spilled the blood of its soldiers. Here was a man who had been hollowed out by the events that had crashed into his life; a man who did not feel anything any more; just thought and acted. A man who was certainly incapable of love, but who had fired the love within her like no man ever before.

She turned and looked around at the destruction evident everywhere. She looked at the pathetic people, starving both physically and emotionally. Afraid of each other's shadows. Gamblers who had risked all on the promise of a miracle cure only to discover that they had gambled away their souls. Now they faced retribution. How could it have taken the likes of Robert, a man with an interior void, to show her this world as it really is?

As she walked in front of the Altes Rathaus a Mercedes pulled up alongside her and Netzer's voice called out of the window to her.

"Get in," he said.

The ride to Gestapo headquarters had been a difficult experience for Lily. Netzer was full to the brim with desire and he could not keep his hands off her. Lily could not bear his touch today but could not let him think that lest she arouse his suspicions. She allowed his abuse of her with his fumbling hands and did her best to pretend she was enjoying it.

He threw his leather coat over her head as they walked from the car to the entrance and she kept it there until she was safely inside a cell. As Lily took the coat from over her head she had no idea what to expect from Netzer. Why had he brought her here? Could he have guessed her innermost thoughts – that she intended to help Robert complete his mission? How could he have? Nobody knew those thoughts. She was not even sure of them herself. All she knew was that she had begun a desperate game. If her actions and plans became known she would be as likely killed by Robert as by Netzer.

"Why have you brought me here? You are endangering my cover. And why have you brought me to a cell?"

"You are being interrogated, my dear. At least as far as everyone else is concerned. My handlers in Himmler's department want as few people as possible to know about your mission. They do not want it to get out that the Reich Government is prepared to use His Holiness as bait to trap the conspirators and a British spy. I am the only one here in the circle. As soon as we decide to strike I will inform my superiors here. Apparently the Fuhrer is extremely paranoid. He suspects everyone. Hence the secrecy."

"Anyway," he continued, "Have no fear, my love," Netzer soothed as he reached around her waist and cupped her breast in his hand. "We are safe here. I need to go over our plans with you to make sure you remain safe."

Over his shoulder Lily was looking at the Gestapo's infamous implements cabinet. Through a glass fronted door she could see steel implements of unusual shapes and sizes arranged in neat order. 'Manufactured in Dusseldorf' was imprinted into each one. She knew that the Dusseldorf factory produced these implements for all Gestapo/SS bases throughout Europe and North Africa. Dusseldorf factory workers knew exactly what they were manufacturing and why.

He moved away from her and seated himself at his desk. Anger flickered across his face. "Curse that Captain Vogts. And curse those two imbeciles who gossiped about him." He banged the desk with his fist. "Curse that blasted policeman Stern." He stopped his rant and looked across at her. "We haven't found him. So far he has made good his escape."

Lily composed herself, sitting upright and crossing her legs tightly. "Do you think I have been compromised?" she asked.

"I don't know," Netzer answered frankly. "I don't know. And that's what worries me. We are no nearer to the leadership of this conspiracy than we were at the beginning. I have to decide what I should recommend to Berlin now. My whole future depends on my decision-making here. With Stern at large, word could get to the good doctor that his mission is compromised. If we allow that to happen not only might we lose him, but *your* life could be at risk. Maybe we should move now to eliminate him. Maybe we should just take him in and interrogate him. See how well he stands up to our techniques before he tells us what he knows. Maybe he can tell us who is orchestrating this conspiracy."

Thinking rapidly Lily said, "You are right to re-assess our position in the light of recent events, my love. But let's be thorough. First, if Robert knew of the leadership then I would too. He and I have had to share all our information to survive thus far."

"Ha! I think not, my sweet Lily," ejaculated Netzer. "At least I hope not. Pray re-assure me that he does not know you are a double agent!"

"Of course he doesn't you fool. If he did I would not be sitting here. I would not be sitting anywhere. But apart from that! We have been jointly briefed. I know what he knows about this mission."

Lily shifted in her seat, uncrossing and re-crossing her legs.

"Putting that aside," she continued. "If we stop now all of our planning will have been for nothing. My years "sleeping" in England, waiting for a mission of sufficient importance, will have been wasted."

Netzer went to the door and shouted, "Schirach!" The sound of boots marching swiftly down the corridor preceded Schirach's arrival.

"Get us some food and drink. And don't bring any of that blasted substitute tea or coffee. Get some meat and cheese and red wine."

"Yes, Captain. Heil Hitler!"

"We have less than a week to keep the mission alive," argued Lily. "It is our only chance of uncovering the conspirators. We know that there are traitors at the highest level of the Wermacht. We could be less than a week away from exposing them. We are confident that there is a link to them from this mission. Remember what is at stake. If we abort this mission the conspirators melt away into the night. We set them free to plan another act of treason against the Fuhrer. We must go on as long as we can."

Lily looked into Netzer's eyes. She was assessing how close she was to convincing him. In her agent's mind she knew he was right. Now that Stern had fled, their knowledge of the mission had been exposed. How far and to whom was not yet clear. But Netzer, as the commanding officer, should clearly abort the mission and eliminate all known conspirators. However, as she argued with him she sensed she was close to convincing him to let it run.

"At any moment I can signal you to move in and finish it. Surely, to have come this far and to give up now would be madness."

"But how do we hope to proceed? In which direction are we to move to discover more than we already know? The apothecary is dead, as is his assistant. Stern has disappeared and, according to you, the good doctor knows nothing. "

Lily was beginning to panic. Her assessment of Netzer was proving wrong. She struggled to keep her thinking straight because her true agenda was to help Robert complete his mission safely and escape. She had no idea when this decision to tie herself irrevocably to Robert had been taken, but it was fixed in her now and was as immovable as concrete. She could try to persuade Robert that the mission was fatally damaged and that they should disappear whilst they still could. But within her she knew that, given the events that had crashed into his life, he could never even begin to resolve the turmoil within him if he decided to walk away from this mission.

With Netzer she had to doublethink herself back onto their original agenda and not give herself away. 'At least,' she thought, 'he has posed a practical question about how to move forward rather than how to abort.' So she had better give him a practical answer.

"What has changed?" she challenged. "Yes, you know about Vogts and Stern and the apothecary. But that information has not got through to the doctor yet. You and I both saw to that when we disposed of the teacher, Helga. If it had I would know."

A loud knock sounded at the door and in walked Schirach at Netzer's command. He placed a tray containing a bottle of red wine and a chunk of yellow cheese. Alongside, stood two glass beakers and a plate of gritty looking biscuits.

"Apologies, mein Captain. These are the only biscuits I can lay my hands on."

Netzer waved him away without looking at him. Lily considered the incongruity of the relationship between the giant Schirach and the arrogant Netzer, whose neck Schirach could break with one hand.

Maybe the act of pouring and tasting the wine made Lily's argument more palatable. Sensing success she pursued her point.

"The Pope is in no more danger than he ever was. From Robert's point of view nothing has changed. As long as he is in place and continuing with the mission there is still a chance that we will be led to the conspirators."

Lily was thinking about the gardener. She had never spoken about him to Netzer when she had first relayed information about the group. Should she now throw him in? Did she need to use him as a poker chip to keep Netzer in the game?

Netzer lifted a soggy biscuit out of his wine where he had been dunking it and lowered it into his mouth. Tossing a chunk of cheese into his mouth to accompany it he chewed as he considered. When he spoke he relieved Lily of the decision she thought she was about to make.

He said, "I think perhaps you are right. We will continue. Why not? War is a game. A great game. Let's play it! But you must inform me as soon as you know when the assassination is to take place. We must act to stop it even if we have not uncovered the identities of the conspirators."

Finishing a second beaker of wine in one swallow he got up from his seat and came around the table to Lily.

"Now let's spend some time doing what soldiers and female spies do best."

He pulled Lily to her feet and pushed her against the wall. His hands moved swiftly around her back and lifted her skirt above her waist. He slid both hands inside her panties and began to probe her with selfish pleasure. Being completely un-aroused, his attentions hurt her. However, she was determined not to do anything to upset him in case he changed his mind about allowing the mission to continue.

As he continued his attentions upon her she found herself thinking of the treatment she had undergone in Leicester gaol at the hands of Herbert and his colleagues. In her ear Netzer's breathing rasped and she could feel the sweat from his face on her neck. The odours of wine, cheese and stale biscuits enveloped her breathing. Netzer interpreted her gasp as a passionate response to his lovemaking. This was not the future she had imagined when she had first watched this young hero of the Nazi youth marching along the boulevards in his crisp uniform. What had happened to honour and heroism?

Reaching into his fly she forcefully took hold of him and with strong movements and a few mumbled phrases quickly brought him to a climax. It was her safest and quickest route to escape from this situation.

Netzer pulled away sharply. There was an immediate release of tension but when he spoke there was annoyance in his voice. "I didn't want that!" he complained.

She looked at his dishevelled, slumped form. His eyes were red rimmed with tiredness and the effects of alcohol. She felt no pity. She realised that she despised him. She went across to where he sat and took his face between her palms. She kissed him as sweetly as she could.

"Do you really want to conceive our child here, like this?"

He looked up at her sharply. The implication in her words worked on him. He took it as a declaration of commitment for the future. He stood up and held her tightly in his arms.

"Let's get this damned mission over with," he whispered hoarsely, "And then I'm going to marry you."

They kissed again and Lily knew she had succeeded in her aim.

Thirty-nine

Robert stepped out of the café where he had been eating a dry doughnut and drinking some chicory essence in the absence of any coffee beans on the premises. He was feeling a little disappointed with himself. He did not like to suspect someone without justification and his suspicions, on this occasion, seemed to have been unfounded.

He still believed he had justification for checking things out since he found himself cut adrift from the network he had been drafted into.He traced the disappearance of the network back to the day Helga had called at the surgery to tell them about the date of the Pope's arrival. Lily had dealt with that and he had thought no more of it. However, since then he had attempted on several occasions to enter the apothecary on the pretext of acquiring medication for his patients. Each time the apothecary had been closed. The last time he had been there two windows were broken and no attempt had been made to repair them, even temporarily. The shop had an air of abandonment about it.

As an agent he was trained to anticipate the worst, and in this instance he needed to assume that their network had been infiltrated and their cover was blown. The very worst possible scenario was that Lily was the traitor in their midst. He had forced himself to retain some scepticism about Lily. In his business no one could be one hundred per cent certain about anyone else. One or two tiny things had lodged in his mind and he thought about them now. They were attitudinal aspects of her and he knew they might be completely innocent, but he had pondered them as he had followed her into Marienplatz earlier that day and watched her stand before the statue of the Virgin. The first little thing had been her attitude to the Black American folk singer they had seen in London at the string quartet concert. He felt she had let slip an ingrained attitude, a deeply held prejudice that jarred with her persona as an anti-Nazi. Secondly, he had always wondered at the way she had not allowed the treatment she had received at the hands of the British authorities to affect her determination to become an agent. Most people would have decided that a nation that treated people with such barbarity did not deserve their loyalty. He balanced these thoughts with a recollection of his own contorted background and accepted that, in love and war, nothing was predictable.

Her account of the assassination of Captain Vogts had failed to convince him. Since then he had retained the position that he must be prepared to act as if she was a double agent. The conundrum lay in the fact that he had not been lifted by the Gestapo. However, it had been the arrival of Helga's body at the morgue that had cemented these concerns. Robert was working a shift at the hospital and had been the only one available to take a body down to the morgue after the mother of four he had been operating on had died. He had been due to go off duty when an emergency came in involving a train derailment and a dozen badly injured soldiers. Normally he would have stayed on, but his superior saw that he was sleep-walking following a forty-two hour shift and ordered him off site. As the staff rushed to deal with the incoming casualties he realised the corpse he had just finished working on lay abandoned on a trolley in the corridor. In an automated state he sleep-walked the trolley along the corridor to the lifts and waited for a car to come to ride him down to the basement where the corpses were stored.

Just as he was entering the lift another trolley came around the corner pushed by a porter and he held the doors allowing him to enter. Less out of interest and more as a means of keeping awake, Robert commented on the toe tag attached to the second corpse.

"Not for disposal!" he commented. "What's special about that one?"

"Cause of death," the porter replied. "She was found in a bombsite but some clever junior at the coroner's office discovered she'd been stabbed. Bombs are dangerous things but they don't usually go around stabbing young women. There will have to be an investigation. And a complete waste of time that will be. Who cares about one more murder in a world full of murder?"

Robert shrugged himself away from the wall of the elevator car and pulled back the sheet covering the corpse. Staring up at him he saw the blood-drained face of Helga.

"You're absolutely right, mein Herr!" he said "Who cares about one more death?"

As he drank his chicory essence and stared out of the cafe window at Lily, he saw the Mercedes skid to a halt beside her and a door open at the kerbside. He had no hope of following the car but he guessed where it would be going. He finished his drink and settled his bill. This could be the final piece of evidence he needed, or it could be an everyday snatch that the Gestapo indulged in. He walked out of Marienplatz and down towards SS/Getsapo headquarters. It was not an easy task to hang around outside this particular building for a couple of hours without attracting unwanted attention. Luckily he found a nearby bar open and he spent the time in there drinking beer and pretending to update some medical notes he had in his doctor's bag.

He knew there was an outside chance that he was wrong about Lily. Maybe she was undergoing some unimaginable interrogation right now. But something within Robert could not believe this. When a figure came out of a side door, head hidden by a Gestapo overcoat he easily recognised the shoes, legs and skirt of his wife. She was escorted to the same Mercedes and whisked away. If she is innocent, he thought, she will tell me of her encounter with the Gestapo when we meet up at home tonight.

Robert walked to his watering hole, ordered a beer and considered his options. If Lily was a double agent and had betrayed the network, he would have to act. To his knowledge the only members of the group still in place were Sister Fatima and the gardener. He would have to warn them and enable them to make good their escapes. He should eliminate Lily immediately. That was his duty. But the moment he contemplated it he knew he could never carry that action out. Something folded and died within him when he realised what he was admitting to himself. Here was Lily, possibly a truly evil individual. Working to betray the people she purported to support and who had taken her into their confidence. They had entrusted their lives to her and she was planning to sacrifice them all. But deep inside he knew that this was the only woman he would ever be able to look at again. He could look at her and he could survive her gaze because they both knew each other in a way that not even lovers did. In this war there were three sides now, and he and Lily were the third side. And so he hoped that the alternative possibility was the true one. He hoped that Lily and Robert were loyal comrades on this dangerous mission that, if successful, might shorten the length of the war. He hoped, but he could not convince himself.

As individuals they might be on opposite sides, but as a partnership they belonged to no one. Each knew the crippled husk that inhabited the interior of the other and each knew that no other one could survive in a relationship with either of them. They could never truly love each other but their intimate knowledge of each other was an acceptable counterfeit. Whichever version turned out to be true he guessed his future, if he had one, was with Lily

He was glad that he thought of himself as Robert now and not Sean. Using a different name worked on the inside as well as for the outside world. The Sean he had once been could not have acted and thought as he was doing now. But for Robert it was hardly a problem.

His assessment came out like this. The mission was all that was left for him in life. It did not matter if he died trying to succeed. In fact it would be a blessed relief. The only alternative was to walk away; disappear. But to what? An Ireland without Martha; without Conny. What would be the point in that? Part of him knew that his desire to assassinate this Pope was a substitute revenge for having failed to find and kill O'Shea. Perhaps every mission with a true motive needs an operative with a twisted motive to make it succeed.

He would warn Sister Fatima and the gardener to vanish and then he would ride the roller coaster until the end. If Lily was there to stop him there was no reason why the Gestapo should not have lifted him already. That was an argument in Lily's favour. If she was acting as a double agent they were stringing him out in search of something else. Most probably the German organisers of the plot, he reasoned. So he would play the game too. Forewarned he was forearmed and would be slightly better prepared when they made their move than they would expect him to be. If Lily attempted to prevent him from killing the Pope he would remove her then. That was the only circumstance he could foresee leading to Lily's elimination. But he would not take that action until he was absolutely certain that he had no alternative. To do so would bring the Gestapo down on him and terminate the mission anyway.

Friedrich pulled up a stool and seated himself beside Robert. Robert took out an envelope and handed it to him, "Here you are my friend," he said. "These should help relieve the headaches."

They drank their beers.

"Why do you think I'm getting these headaches, Robert?"

Robert laughed at the thought of the answer forming in his head.

"Well, my good Friedrich, Sigmund Freud would say they are the result of a latent trauma in your past. Probably a mild hysteria caused by the repression of your feelings for Sadie."

Friedrich grunted.

"How was work today?" Robert asked

Friedrich had previously told Robert that he was an administrator. The way he had said it told Robert much more. The vagueness used in contemporary Germany was always a signal of some Government involvement. It was a way language found to sidestep totalitarianism without falling foul of it.

"Big cargo today."

"Outgoing?"

"No incoming. Which is worse for me."

"How so?"

"Well outgoing there is one amount of paperwork per unit. Not so bad. But incoming there is one amount of paperwork for every item returning from that unit."

"Item? What do you mean item?"

"Think about it," said Friedrich in his helpful manner. "One unit outgoing might produce a dozen items incoming. A gold tooth! Six gold teeth. Who knows? A watch! A ring! Spectacles!" I tell you, the paper work it creates is horrendous."

Robert stared at his friend.

"No wonder you suffer from headaches," he remarked.

"No wonder at all," agreed Friedrich

There was a final contingency Robert decided upon and he set about organising that now. He retraced his steps to Marienplatz and then exited the square on the south side. He continued until he entered the residential area where the apothecary was situated. The terrace was occupied with children playing around a street light which had a rope dangling from it. There was a knot of mothers in housewives' wraparound robes chatting on one corner and the occasional cyclist and vehicle trundled over the cobblestones.

Robert walked straight past the apothecary noticing that it was still closed. The broken windows remained un-mended and there was a sense of increasing desolation about the place. Robert found his observations agreeable and turned at the end of the street to double back into the lane behind the row of houses in which the apothecary stood.

The lane was empty and he rapidly moved to the back gate of the apothecary and scrambled over it. He hurried across the yard and with three mighty bumps of his shoulder against the door, burst into the back of the shop. He spent the next forty minutes or so examining the property. He searched from the basement to the attic in the roof. He found that there was running water and a gas supply to a cooker. There was no electricity but there were candles and matches and there were tins of food. When he had finished he was satisfied that he could hideaway here for a short period of time if he had to. He also found a large variety of drugs still on the premises. He made a quick search and helped himself to generous amounts of diamorphine, sufficient cyanide to match his needs, sleeping pills, amphetamines and laxatives.

When he had finished he sat in the upstairs room where the apothecary and his assistant had swallowed their cyanide capsules and he dozed until it was dark. On waking he guessed the curfew would have started and he quickly left by the way he had entered and walked straight home, confident that his medical documents would satisfy any wardens or police officers out patrolling the curfew.

Lily was anxiously waiting for him when he entered the house.

"Where have you been," she asked.

Her anxiety and the scene they were enacting painted such an orthodox picture of domestic married life that Robert could not help but smile.

"What is amusing you? I have been worried."

"I'm sorry," he said. "You made me feel like a normal husband in a normal world for a moment. It made me smile."

He could see that his remark had hurt her and he put his arms around her and said into her hair. "I'm home now. You can stop worrying."

"We were supposed to be at the convent for Benediction. It's curfew now. We shan't be able to go."

"Damn the curfew. We have to go. Mother has got to invite us over next Tuesday to meet the Pope. Do we have anything to eat? I am ravenous."

"Yes. I bought some dried egg powder today. I will make you scrambled eggs. You can eat them with some rye biscuits."

Robert thanked her and went to wash. Lily did not eat with Robert. She sat opposite him as he devoured his light meal. What he would give for a big plate of potatoes, bacon hock and cabbage.

"You not eating, my love?" he asked.

"No, I ate earlier," Lily replied.

"You haven't told me about your day. Anything exciting happen to you?"

He lowered his knife and fork and paused to look into her eyes. She looked straight back.

"Nothing of interest. I went to town. I bought the dried eggs. I also got a ham bone from the butcher. I will try to get some vegetables to go with it tomorrow. I went to the convent school and examined some of the children. That's it. Not really exciting."

A tingle ran down Robert's spine. So it was true. She was a double agent. She must have killed Helga. A surge of adrenalin ran through him. So the game develops an infinitely greater complexity. He smiled at Lily and went back to his eggs.

After Robert had cleaned his plate, they slipped into their coats and headed out into the night. They both carried their medical identification cards and documents and were well prepared for any zealous curfew patrol they might encounter. Tonight, however, they were not stopped.

Robert and Lily managed to slip into the back of the chapel just as Father was raising the Monstrance and the altar boy was chiming the bell. They were seen arriving late by Mother Superior, but afterwards, in her quarters she forgave them when they told her about the awful day they had had and how their lateness had been unavoidable but they had been determined to come anyway.

Tonight Lily and Robert were alone with Mother Superior. Herr Todt and his wife had not attended Benediction because Herr Todt had been feeling under the weather. As they sipped the Mother's sherry around the log fire in the hearth, Robert and Lily kept the topic of conversation centred on religion. They discussed the importance of the church world-wide. They talked about the miracle of Fatima. They drew the talk around to the Holy Father in Rome and as that topic developed Robert got up to top up the sherry glasses. As he poured them he slid some powdered amphetamine into Mother's glass and returned to the fire. As the sherry and the mild amphetamine dose began to enter the nun's bloodstream she became ever more garrulous.

"I hope you won't think me immodest but I can boast that the Holy Father is a personal acquaintance of mine."

"No!" exclaimed Lily.

"Well, you do surprise me!" added Robert.

Mother leaned forward conspiratorially in her armchair and said, "I've been meaning to tell my exciting news for sometime now." She paused to sip her sherry. She looked down at it. "By the sweet Lord," she said. "This has never tasted so good." She sat back as if having forgotten why she had leaned forward in the first place.

"Um. You said you had some exciting news, Mother?" Lily prompted.

"Oh yes," replied Mother, sitting forward again. "Well, the Holy Father, himself, God bless him…" and at this she made the sign of the cross… "is coming here next week."

"The Holy Father coming he re?" exhaled Robert. "I don't believe it. Oh forgive me Mother. I did not mean to doubt your word. I meant to say such an honour is unbelievable to the likes of me."

Mother smiled at him forgivingly, "Well you can believe it now because it's true. And as two of the most devout Catholics in Munich I want you to be here to meet him."

The relief in Robert's demeanour was almost visible. Here it was at last. The invitation. The moment they had worked for all this time had just arrived.

"Well, Mother," he said. "I must say you overwhelm us with this honour. What do you say Lily?"

"Absolutely overwhelmed!"

Forty

Swiss Guards stood at either side of the vast double doors leading to the papal offices. From along the arched passageway a group of three men, escorted front and back by another two pairs of Swiss Guards, came between the tall marble pillars. The sun threw black lines of shadow across the shiny floor which echoed to the sound of the group's footsteps. Amongst the party of three, two were in military uniform and the third was in formal black suit and ceremonial red and yellow sash.

On arrival at the doors to the papal office the Swiss Guards crossed their lances barring the group's way. An exchange was barked between the lead guard with the party and one of those barring entry. The guards uncrossed their lances; stepped backwards opening the doors and the Spanish ambassador to Italy was admitted to the presence of God's representative on Earth.

Many formalities took place including the exchange of gifts. The item most prized by the Pope was a painting of the Madonna and child that Franco had recovered from the ruins of a church of San Francisco in Madrid. Franco's letter to the Pope claimed the church had been desecrated by the Anarchists but, in fact Franco's own artillery had destroyed the church. After blessing the party the Pope signalled the ambassador to accompany him into a generous recess within the enormous space of the office. There were comfortable chairs there and a table. The two men could talk here without being overheard.

The ambassador had with him a file which he handed to the Pope as they talked. The file contained Franco's greetings to the Pope and an outline of his plans for restoring Holy Mother Church to her position of ascendancy within Spain. He made reference to the restoration of the monarchy but claimed this would have to be postponed for the time being. Franco himself needed to keep executive control of the government whilst the task of mopping up the remnants of the hated Jewish-led communists, anarchists and other various atheistic groups which remained.

The file also contained a report on the position of monasteries and convents within Spain. Franco's notes declared his determination to restore to them their property, land and wealth.

Finally, Franco had outlined his plans in respect of social policy. Atheism would not be tolerated. Divorce would be outlawed. Divorces which had been granted during the Republic would be overturned. Divorcees would be compelled to honour their marriage vows and families would be re-united. The sanctity of marriage would be re-established. The role of women would be clearly defined and their disastrous excursions into the political and business life of the nation would be curtailed.

As the Pope read these monumental legislative drafts he nodded with obvious pleasure. The ambassador had time to take in his surroundings. He observed the symmetry of the apartments they were occupying. The opposite recess to the one they were sitting in contained an altar and he presumed the Pope would use it to say mass.

Having read the file the Pope placed it on the table and proceeded to thank the ambassador and to formally request that he relay profuse thanks to General Franco for his heroic work and his devout Catholicism. The rest of the conversation was dominated by a consideration of the evils of communism and how best to combat it. He made it clear to the ambassador that the Church would look favourably upon any actions taken by Franco to rid the world of this evil. He spoke of his pain for the Russian people and of his fervent hope that one day they would be returned to the Christian, hopefully the Catholic faith. The most important duty of all Catholics at this time was to do everything in their power, whatever their role in life, to bring about the destruction of communism. Holy Mary, the Mother of God was grieving in sorrow at the suffering of her Russian children and she instructed all Catholics to fight for their freedom.

The Pope called for a jug of water and informed the ambassador that he would now say mass for the assembled group, after which they would have proper refreshments. He picked up a silver bell and shook it. Its tiny peals ran along the pillars and walls and a young priest in his black cassock came.

"Ambassador," said the Pope, "Allow me to introduce the citizen of another neutral country and from another great national bastion of Catholicism. Monsignor O'Shea here is on a sabbatical from his native Ireland. His country has so recently been wrenched from the protestant clutches of the British Empire by the heroic actions of her brave sons. Monsignor O'Shea will assist me in the saying of mass."

Forty-one

Robert woke early and lay in the pitch black of the bedroom. The blackout curtains permitted no light to enter as well as no light to escape. Beside him in the bed he could hear the deep innocent breathing of a sleeping Lily. He felt the warmth of her body and became slightly aroused. He wondered at his ability to be aroused by the woman who planned to betray him.

He knew that the assassination plot should be aborted and he should eliminate the woman asleep beside him and activate his escape plan. Any other agent would be halfway back to England by now. But Robert knew he had nothing to go back to. This mission was his only purpose. In fact, he knew he dreaded its conclusion because then he would have to make choices he could not face. If he died in action it would be the best possible outcome for him. He only had to take care that this attitude did not ruin his efficiency. He did not want to die before making this Pope pay for his complicity with Nazism. He turned the sleeping Lily to face him and levered himself on top of her. Lily woke to find herself being made love to. Half dreaming she succumbed to the explosion of pleasure that Robert induced within her. Her pleasure was so intense that tears fell from her eyes. Robert wiped them away with the palm of his hand and kissed her face. As he succumbed to the climax of his pleasure the ice re-formed in his heart and he withdrew without speaking and went to the bathroom.

Having washed in cold water, Robert opened the window and looked out over the suburb to the skyline of downtown Munich. The gaps in the skyline gave the city the look of a badly maintained mouth in desperate need of a dentist. He knew, even as he finished shaving, the plan of action he was going to carry out. Returning to the bedroom, he dressed in darkness. Although Lily lay still he knew she was not sleeping. He could feel her eyes upon him. He thought of things to say to her; pleasantries; small talk. But his mood would not let him. He left the bedroom in silence. As he closed the door her voice came out to him on the landing.

"Robert, don't go. I want to say something."

He paused but he did not go back into the bedroom. After a moment or two he went downstairs, collected his coat, hat and bag and went through the front door. 'Goodbye Lily,' he thought to himself.

After a breakfast of black beech nut and acorn flour bread and black coffee at the hospital, Robert performed four operations that morning. The staff worked tirelessly to clean and reset the theatre after each procedure and Robert had the good feeling a successful morning's work gives one. He felt like the old Sean. Allowed an hour for lunch during a relative lull, he carried out part of the plan he had been formulating. His strategy was to disconcert Lily and whoever was controlling her. The only way he could think of doing that was to do the unexpected. Presumably they expected him to carry on as he had done so far. They could be forgiven for assuming he had no knowledge of the betrayal, otherwise they would have moved against him by now. So it was his intention to nonplus them. He would disappear. It was Thursday today and he had to remain at liberty until at least next Tuesday. By then he would have had the opportunity to carry out his mission.

He walked swiftly through the streets of the old town where Friedrich had first rescued him from his attackers, through Marienplatz, where women children and old men moved as if the sunshine was convincing them that there was no war and it had all been a bad dream, and out to the suburb where his home and surgery stood. If she were sticking to her own routines, Lily should be at the convent at this time.

Robert walked up the garden path and let himself into the house. There was a stillness hanging there that immediately told him the house was empty. Without hurrying, he efficiently collected together clothes and other items he would need and put them into a small suitcase. From beneath a board in his wardrobe he lifted an old towel and unfolded it. Wrapped inside was a black Luger pistol. He flicked open the chamber and checked the ammunition. He was in two minds about taking it with him. The whole point of this operation was that his assumed identity and his occupation would camouflage him from detection by the authorities. To be found with a gun in his possession would certainly arouse suspicion. But he told himself that he was departing from the agreed plan anyway and the gun was probably a sensible additional departure. He then made himself another black coffee and ate some rye biscuits. Collecting his things he walked down the hallway to the front door looking around him as if for the last time and went out.

During the afternoon he carried out another five procedures. Two of these he did for a colleague who was suffering from obvious exhaustion. Robert, who was tired himself thought, 'you don't know it but from now on you're all going to have to fill in for me.' When a break came at around 7:30pm he went to his locker and changed out of his surgeon's coat for the last time and left the hospital.

By 10:30 that same evening he was well into his cups alongside Friedrich. At a table in the middle of the bar the usual group of card players were talking intermittently between plays and bets. One of them was losing badly and betting food coupons to stay in the game. Friedrich had been telling Robert about an acquaintance of his who had been robbed by the Gestapo.

"I didn't know you still had any Jewish friends," said Robert, genuinely surprised.

Friedrich laughed. "You would think they would have to be Jewish wouldn't you." He paused to down another giant swallow of beer. "But Dieter's misfortune was to share accommodation with a Jewish family. Half Jewish actually. The children are meischlings. Dieter's neighbour Pedr, like myself, fell in love with a Jewess. He went one step further, however, and married the girl. Jews married to Aryans have not been relocated yet. Not all of them anyway. But, during a round up of Jews for transportation Pedr's wife and children were snatched. The Gestapo had enlisted some SS personnel to assist in the round up. That was probably the reason why things went as far as they did. Usually the regular police assist the Gestapo and they are not as brutal. As well as snatching the Jews the round up includes the confiscation of property. Anything valuable or useful is snatched. Well the SS got carried away and as well as ransacking Pedr's rooms they went through the other homes in the apartment block and confiscated anything they wanted there too. Dieter arrived home from his work of fire fighting to find his home had been burgled by the state."

"What did he do?" asked Robert.

Friedrich turned to look at him as if to suggest his question was superfluous.

"What can you do? If you speak out against the SS you are an enemy of the state. You might as well be a communist. Or a Jew even. You just have to thank them for robbing you and get on with life."

"What about Pedr's wife and children?"

"What about them?"

"Do you know what happened to them?"

Friedrich laughed ironically.

"Pedr got them back. Apparently the SS had gone way over the top as usual and rounded up a large group of Jews with Aryan spouses. The spouses all got together and marched down to Gestapo headquarters and demonstrated. I think it was a toss up between them being mown down and getting their loved ones back. In the end the gates opened and their spouses and children were released."

"What do you make of that Friedrich?"

"What do I make of it? I'll tell you what I make of it. If I was Dieter I'd want to know why the Jews went free and I didn't get my property back. If it wasn't for the Jews living in the apartment block none of this would have happened in the first place. Like the Fuhrer says, everything is their fault in the end."

"I didn't mean that," said Robert. "I meant why do you think they let them go?"

Wiping froth thoughtfully from his moustache Friedrich said, "That had me baffled for a while. But then I began to think there's been a lot of talk on the radio about terrorist groups plotting to assassinate our beloved Fuhrer. There's a lot of treachery afoot. I get the feeling that for the first time in my memory they were scared of angering the man in the street by gunning down a large crowd of Aryans."

Friedrich and Robert became suddenly aware that the room had gone very quiet and that others were listening in on their conversation. They said nothing for a while and Robert asked for more beers. Unfortunately the barman told him that the beer had all gone. There would be no more now for at least a week. They decided on two large schnapps.

When the level of noise had returned to its normal pitch Robert returned to the topic and asked, "Do you believe in this talk of assassination plots? If so, who do you think is behind it?"

Friedrich looked carefully around him before answering, "It's either the Wermacht or the Jews. Probably both."

" How can you say that?" asked Robert. "That sounds ridiculous."

"Oh, ridiculous is it," retorted Friedrich looking somewhat hurt. "We all know the Jews are behind everything. That's a given truth. Secondly, you're not telling me that there aren't some Jews left in the army. Some must have been overlooked. Why, I've heard a rumour that Himmler is a Jew. It's common knowledge that the Fuhrer's own doctor is a Jew. If this can be true, why not Jews in the Wermacht causing trouble?"

Robert could not answer this line of reasoning and so he let the subject drop. After a suitable interlude and two more schnapps each, he embarked upon his tale of woe.

"So, she has kicked me out. She accuses me of infidelity with a nurse and she won't let me back in the house."

All through his sad tale Friedrich had roared with laughter. He had ordered more drinks in a celebratory manner and kept clapping Robert on the back.

"You old dog," was all he said. And he said it over and over again. 'If he wants to believe that I have been bedding a young nurse, let him,' thought Robert. Now for the punchline.

"So I've got nowhere to stay," concluded Robert.

This was like the conclusion to a mighty joke and Friedrich thumped the bar in his mirth. Just as Robert had hoped and gambled, Friedrich drunkenly leaned on his shoulder and rasped conspiratorially in Robert's ear, "You have now, my friend. You're staying with me,"

Robert smiled inwardly. He had known ever since Friedrich had rescued him in the alley way when they had first met that inside this old bigot's chest there was a heart beating.

Forty-two

Friedrich lived in two attic rooms atop a four storey, terraced house in a narrow lane right in the downtown district. Why it had not been bombed Robert could not guess. A large number of its neighbours had. The main room that one entered immediately on going through the front door was a kitchen come lounge. There was a sofa bed with shiny wooden arms that would serve as Robert's bed for the next few nights. It was too short for him and gave him a stiff neck. But it was the best available and he was not about to complain. The second room was Friedrich's bedroom.

After sleeping heavily, thanks to the drink, and awaking with a throat that told him he had snored, Robert followed Friedrich in having a stand up wash at the kitchen sink and then they breakfasted on some tinned mackerel that Friedrich had acquired along with some black bread. Friedrich even made coffee, but there was a large proportion of sawdust amongst the ground beans.

After breakfast Friedrich headed off for work and Robert was left alone to plan his day. The first thing he needed to discover was how Lily would react to his disappearance.

He was not sure he would be any good at creating an impromptu disguise but he went to Friedrich's wardrobe and kitted himself out. Disguise was made more difficult by the fact that it was now July and the weather was good. Hence, people were wearing less clothes. The kind of disguise he had available to him required more clothing rather than less. In the end he was pleased with a workman's flat cap, an old jacket and a pair of sunglasses that Friedrich must have bought as a very young man. He blackened his face slightly with some ash from the fire and stepped out into the summer Munich morning.

The acrid smell of burning lingered in the air after the previous night's raid but the residential centre of Munich had been spared. Some industrial targets had been hit and the wind blew the smoke across the town.

Altering his gait with a slight limp he made his way back to his home. He sat on a bench at the entrance to a nearby park and pretended to be reading his newspaper as he watched the front of his home. Just after eight o' clock Lily emerged. He saw immediately from her face that she had slept little and from her dress that she had paid less than her usual attention to her appearance.

What would she do? If she thought the game was over she would surely drop her own pretence as Frau Hermann and take up her original identity. Maybe she had already communicated by telephone with the Gestapo and informed them of Robert's disappearance. Perhaps she was on her way to Gestapo headquarters now.

However, as he followed her he quickly realised that Gestapo headquarters was not her immediate destination. In fact he guessed she was heading for the convent, which suggested she was acting as if nothing had changed. Indeed she did go to the convent and from the amount of time she spent there he guessed she had carried out her normal duties with the children and sisters. After and hour and a half he saw Lily emerge. Robert followed her at a safe distance.

After she had walked a few blocks he guessed correctly that she was heading for the hospital where he worked. When she reached there he waited across the street. Through the glass panel on the upper half of the heavy oak door he caught glimpses of her talking to a receptionist at the main desk. Lily waited whilst the receptionist made a telephone call. Eventually the receptionist replaced the telephone in its cradle and shook her head. Lily turned away with a look of disappointment and came out through the front doors.

Hunching his shoulders, Robert looked across at her from the corner of his eye. At first she seemed undecided which way to go. Then she took a decisive step in the direction of their home.

Robert followed her and watched her go in. A few minutes later Inge came out through the front door. Her coat was on and she was carrying her handbag. Robert guessed Lily had told Inge that there was no need for her to stay. After ten minutes or so Robert decided that Lily was not going to re-emerge quickly and he walked as casually as he could manage to the end of the block and went around to the rear of the property. After making sure that there was nobody watching he slipped into the garden and approached the window to the living area. Peeping in, he saw that Lily was already in a bath robe. From the sound of running water he knew that she was about to bathe.

He made haste back to Friedrich's apartment and changed into his own clothes. He then hurried across town to the convent. He approached the convent through the school. Entering the lobby he saw a door marked "Head teacher" on the right hand side. He was about to knock when he heard voices from inside. The voices were low and there was an earnest sound to them as they exchanged short, sharp sentences. Gradually Robert tuned in to the frequency and realised he was listening to a conversation between Herr Todt and the convent gardener. They were discussing what Lily had just told them on her morning visit. As he listened Robert tried to decipher what it was they had been told. Lily had obviously communicated some concern about Robert's whereabouts for the men were speculating on what might have happened to him. He decided to join them.

The men were struck dumb in open-mouthed shock as he silently entered. Robert calmly removed his hat and hung it on the hat stand behind the door. The two men watched him as he pulled a chair across to the desk where they were sitting and sat himself down beside the gardener. They both faced across the desk towards the head teacher.

"I believe you have been concerned about me, gentlemen."

Neither spoke. Fear was coursing through their veins. If Lily's comments to them held any truth, this man could be a Gestapo agent.

Reading their expressions, Robert went on, "I can guess what Lily might have said to you. However, I am here to tell you that anything she might have said about me probably applies to her." He focused his attention on Herr Todt. "The fact that you are discussing me tells me that you are a sleeping member of our cell, Herr Todt. Tell me now. Does Lily know about you? It is obvious to me that you are the hidden link to the highly placed conspirators that the Gestapo are desperate to get their hands on."

It was the gardener who replied, "I don't believe she does know about Herr Todt. It was me she came to speak to. She has also been into the convent and asked if you had been here. Mother Superior is concerned for you. You ought to go through and see her before you leave."

"I intend to."

"It is unfortunate that you came upon us here. If you are genuine you are now in greater danger than before. To know the identity of our link to the leadership is a dangerous thing."

Robert gazed in contemplation for several minutes at the two men facing him. "Gentlemen, our plot is unravelling. For my part, I am almost certain that Lily is a double agent. You two must suspect both Lily and I. You would be fools not to. My advice to you both is that you execute your escape plans immediately. I cannot vouch for Lily's actions. She might at this very moment be informing her Gestapo contacts about our gardener. If they take you into custody it will not be long before they extract the identity of Herr Todt from you. At the same time you would be fools to trust me. I could be stalling you both right now in anticipation of the arrival of a gang of Storm troopers. In normal circumstances we would abort the plot now and all disappear into the night. However, I have an agenda of my own. I intend to go through with this mission at whatever cost. My mind is made up. Many better men than me have lost their lives in this war and I see no reason why I should not be prepared to risk mine."

The gardener and Herr Todt looked at each other but neither man spoke.

"You are right to look alarmed, my friends. You could well be in the company of a mad man. Hang on to the thought that you are still here and not in Gestapo custody and that this mad man is encouraging you to get out of here as fast as you can. If I am caught I will do everything in my power to dispose of myself before they can torture any information out of me. But by then you should be long gone."

Robert leaned forward and pressed his fingers into the polished desktop.

"Look, what I am saying to you is this. I don't have a future; nor do I want one. This mission is my sole reason for existing. For you two there is a future, now and after this damned war is over." He got up and collected his hat from the stand. "I am going through to see Mother now. I expect you two to be out of Munich within the next couple of hours."

Robert crossed the lobby and passed through double doors that led to the classrooms. He glanced through the glass panels that separated the classrooms from the corridor. Many of the desks were empty. He guessed most classes were about half full. He didn't contemplate where the other half might be. Each classroom boasted a Nazi flag across the back wall and a portrait of the Fuhrer above the black board. Several classes were being taught by nuns of the order, but many more were being taught by lay teachers. These teachers all wore Nazi insignia armbands. Robert experienced a wave of depression, but it only served to fuel his determination.

He exited the school building and walked across the lawn that linked it to the convent. He entered the convent through the rear door and made his way along the dimly lit corridors. He had to avoid bumping his head on low beams until he finally came to the front of the building and entered the more welcoming lobby area. Attaching a poster to the wall beside the front entrance was the Mother Superior. When she heard the door close she turned and caught sight of him. She showed surprise on her face but she moved directly towards him.

"Oh, sweet Mother of Mercy! Robert, you had me worried to death. Your poor wife has been here. She is out of her mind with worry for you. She thinks you might have been killed. Where have you been?"

Mother was holding both of Robert's hands in her own and he was surprisingly touched by her concern. He gave a wry smile.

"I think she's let her imagination run away with her. We had some dreadful emergencies to deal with at the hospital. I think we just missed each other. I tried phoning her but the lines from the hospital were down. Anyway don't worry. I'm going straight home after here and I'll put her mind at rest."

"Well thank the good lord you're safe and well. Come on in and have a drink and a chat. And then I'm sending you straight home to comfort your good lady wife."

She made them both a hot cup of chicory on the gas ring she had in her room. When it was ready she said, "We haven't any milk but this will do just as well." And she poured a generous measure of schnapps into each cup.

As they drank Mother was easily led by Robert into a discussion of the Pope's visit.

"Oh, you know," she said almost blushing," He's been here several times but I still get so excited at the prospect of a new visit."

She took a sip of her drink and Robert kept her company.

"I'm glad you'll be here, Robert," she went on. "He's not a well man you know. He needs constant medication. He will have his own doctor here, of course, but it will be a relief to me to know that you are here. I have great confidence in you, you know. I am not so sure of his personal physician. He is a man named Professor Ricardo Galeazzi-Lisi. I am afraid in certain circles he is known as 'the quack'."

"What are the Pope's major ailments?" Robert asked, genuinely interested.

"They are all to do with the digestion. The saintly man is plagued with terrible stomach pains and related bowel problems. He hiccups almost continuously. As well as that he has terrible problems with his gums. I believe they are becoming softer and collapsing. He is in danger of losing his teeth. He is terribly embarrassed by his complaints. He is frightened that he will lose the ability to address a great multitude if his gums deteriorate any more. How he retains his saintly dignity through all this infirmity is a tribute to his great holiness."

"I am sure I will be able to be of assistance to his Holiness."

Mother Superior beamed at Robert, "I am sure you will," she concurred.

"Tell me more about him," said Robert. "I am fascinated by him, just as you are."

Robert's flattery worked.

"Before I met him I have to admit that I was sceptical of his reputation. People spoke of his intense divinity. They claimed to be physically affected by his presence. Some claimed to be reduced to tears believing themselves to be in a Christ-like presence. I thought this kind of comment to be blasphemous. That was until I met him. Now I have to say I was affected in the same way. He exudes godliness. He has a child-like temperament which can charm the birds from the trees."

"What about his family?" asked Robert.

"His parents are both dead but they were devout and always closely connected to the church. He has three siblings; an older brother and sister and a younger sister. There have been some scandalous rumours concerning his siblings. In his younger days his Holiness was devoted to a female cousin of his, young Maria-Teresa. Maria-Teresa had the misfortune of being the child of parents who separated." At this point the Mother blessed herself and kissed the crucifix attached to her rosary beads. "There was no option for the poor, unfortunate child than to place her in a convent to hopefully rid her of the terrible example set by her wayward parents. In his saintly way his Holiness became devoted to her. He visited her regularly and took care of her spiritual needs. Maria-Teresa was cured of her deep melancholy and she was made whole again."

Mother sipped deeply from her drink and continued her tale.

"We know what human minds are made of and how willing human tongues are to spout unworthy thoughts."

'Including yours it seems,' thought Robert. But he allowed Mother Superior to continue.

"It was soon being alleged that his Holiness was developing more than a spiritual relationship with his cousin. Soon Maria-Teresa's father forbade the visits and the relationship was ended."

Again she strengthened herself with a stiff drink.

"As if that was not bad enough, another, even more scandalous story started being spread around. It was claimed that Maria-Teresa was not his cousin at all. Nor even a female! People claimed that his Holiness' elder brother Francesco had had a twin. This twin was retarded and as such a source of deep shame to the family. To hide their shame they had disguised the twin as a female child and parcelled it off to the family of Maria-Teresa. A fictional Maria-Teresa in this version of the story. When the child grew too big for its gender to be hidden anymore it was sent to the convent. This was why his Holiness is supposed to have devoted so much time to the individual in the convent: because they were brothers."

"That is a shocking tale. Where do you think the truth of it all lies?"

"I do my best to shut it all out of my mind. If the blessed man is good enough for God then I'm sure he's good enough for me, whatever the truth of his past is."

"A sound philosophy, Mother, if you don't mind me commenting. But getting back to his doctor, do you have real concerns for his Holiness in this Galeazzi-Lisi's hands?"

"Suffice it to say that I am more than happy that you will be in attendance during the Pope's visit here. God forbid that any mishap should befall him whilst in our care. I would be very grateful to you if you would

Forty-three

It was Friday evening and Robert was in Friedrich's apartment. He had eaten some bread and mixed some powdered soup. He washed it down with tea substitute and sat waiting for Friedrich to return.

When 8:30 came and went he guessed that Friedrich had gone straight to their watering hole. Robert got up and slipped his overcoat and hat on. But as he opened the door of the apartment to leave, the air raid siren sounded. He decided it made no sense to go out looking for Friedrich now. The bar would be evacuated and Friedrich would be down in the nearest shelter. Robert could not face the thought of a night in a shelter so he stepped back into the apartment, took off his coat and hat, undressed and climbed into his makeshift bed. The bombs had missed Friedrich's building so far. They could miss it again tonight. Within minutes Robert was fast asleep.

It was late the next morning when he was awakened by a loud knocking on the apartment door. Robert pushed back his blankets and went to the window. Down below the street showed no evidence of Gestapo or police activity. He went to the door and opened it enough to peer out onto the landing. An elderly, grey-haired man stood there nervously fingering his hat brim.

"Yes," inquired Robert abruptly.

"Oh! Pardon me. I was looking for Friedrich."

"He's not here."

"Oh dear," the man said. "Then the rumours might be true."

Robert's curiosity was roused now and he held the door open and said, "Look, you'd better come in."

The man shuffled nervously through the door and looked around him. Robert beckoned him over to a seat at the dining table and they sat down facing each other.

"What rumours?" asked Robert.

The man sat with his hat in his hands and looked at Robert.

"I don't know you," he said.

Robert looked at the distrust in the man's eyes. He was well used to it. To trust another man was the act of a fool in this modern Germany.

"I am a friend of Friedrich. He helped me out of a scrape once. Now he is helping me out of a bigger one. My residence was bombed out three nights ago. Friedrich is allowing me to share his apartment. He didn't come back last night. I assumed he was caught by the raid and went straight to a nearby shelter."

The man listened and watched Robert as he spoke. He was weighing Robert's words and manner. He reached a decision and said, "My name is Karl Belkin. I work with Friedrich. He is a good friend to me. I like Friedrich."

"Me too," concurred Robert. "He is a special man."

"Yes, I agree," said Karl.

"You mentioned rumours," interjected Robert. "What are these rumours?"

Karl leaned forward, lowered his voice and began, "I arrived late for work yesterday. My route was blocked by debris from the clearance work going on. If I had known it would not have been a problem. I could have easily taken another route. However, once I got into MagdaStrausa the police had cordoned the exit and I could not duck onto another route."

Karl noticed the impatience rising in Robert's eyes.

"At any rate," he hurried on, "When I finally got to work I noticed that Friedrich was not at his desk. When I asked around the office where he was I knew there was a problem by the reluctance I encountered. No one wanted to answer the question. Eventually, in the men's room, I cornered Mark, a good colleague of ours. He told me that the police had turned up at the beginning of the day and taken Friedrich away. He has been denounced as a Jew by a neighbour of his."

Robert struggled to take all this in.

"Where can this notion have come from?" he finally asked.

"It happens a lot," Karl replied, his voice a mixture of disappointment and resignation. "You annoy someone and they throw this allegation out. The police and the Gestapo take great pleasure in investigating any such claim."

"So, they will investigate and they will throw the allegation out. And then they will have to set Friedrich free."

Karl looked down at his fingers as they fiddled with the brim of his hat.

"Maybe," he muttered, "Maybe not."

"What do you mean?" asked Robert.

"Well," began Karl. But then he stalled as if unable to speak. Robert leaned forward forcing Karl to look him in the face.

"Karl, whatever it is, you must tell me."

Karl swallowed and stumbled on.

"It depends how you look at it. Karl is not a Jew. He's not even a meischling. But he is half a meischling."

"Wait a minute," interrupted Robert, "Half a meischling? What is half a meischling?"

"It means that one of his grandparents was a Jew, making his mother a meischling."

"Oh God damn! God damn! God Damn!" yelled Robert. "How stupid are the laws of the God damned country!"

Karl pushed his chair back and got up in fear.

"Be careful my friend. These walls could be listening to you."

Robert relented his anger and reached out to Karl to placate him.

"Please, sit down," he said. "I'm sorry. Please. I'm calm now. Sit down."

Karl reluctantly settled himself back into his chair.

"Well I don't know what else to tell you. I suggest you take care my friend. I'm surprised the Gestapo haven't been here already to check out his apartment. It usually gives them a good excuse to steal whatever takes their eye. If they find you here they may take you in as well."

'You don't know how close you are to the truth,' thought Robert.

"What will happen to Friedrich now?" he asked.

"It's hard to say. It could depend on the mood of his interrogator. Many meischlings are still at liberty. Unfortunately, as the progress of the war worsens things are getting tougher. At the end of the day he could be released or he could be shipped to a relocation centre."

"Did this Mark say where he had been taken?"

"Gestapo headquarters on…"

"Yes, I know where it is," interrupted Robert.

Robert stood indicating to Karl that it was time for this conversation to end and time for Karl to go. He got to his feet, placed his hat on his head and headed for the door that Robert held open for him.

In the emptiness of the apartment Robert tried to think clearly. Sounds from other homes came to him. Karl was right. The walls were thin. Try as he might he could not string together two clear thoughts. His calm was shattered and he was riding a tide of mounting anger. The conflict within him was causing a physical pain in his gut. He was desperate to take some action but at the same time he knew any action he took would compromise his ability to carry out his mission. The acute dilemma he felt caused him to pace frantically about the apartment. He felt he would explode without this frantic but pointless physical activity. For some reason Frau Hahn came back into his thoughts. That elderly Nazi patient he had been about to murder when Max had stepped in and saved him from himself. At the time he had castigated himself for succumbing to his emotions and planning to wipe out an insignificant nobody. Here, with Friedrich, he heard his objective voice saying to him, is another nobody. In the bigger picture of the war his fate was neither here or there. But this was the crux of his thinking that created the pain in his gut. If Friedrich did not matter then who or what did? A man who had stepped out of the dark and saved his life! How could he ignore this man's fate?

Robert felt that old Sean creeping up on him. That same Sean who had made the decision to murder Frau Hahn. That Sean, who against all his beliefs and instincts had known that to kill Frau Hahn was the only course of action he would take. He felt himself becoming deaf to the arguments that told him to forget Friedrich and he felt himself *wanting* to become deaf to those arguments. He made his decision. He would go into Gestapo headquarters and come out with Friedrich, or they would both die in the attempt. If he was killed the Pope would live and all of his work here would have been wasted. But he reasoned that their conspiracy was so far adrift of their planned course that it was probably bound to fail anyway. Lily had probably informed her handlers of everything she knew and it was only a matter of time before they caught up with him and disposed of him as only the Nazi machine knew how.

He had to act quickly. He had no time to devise an elaborate plan. No time for a disguise or a fake identity. The doctor persona would have to do.

Dr Robert Hermann stopped at the entrance to Gestapo headquarters and presented his papers to the two guards on duty. When asked what his business was he replied that he had been summoned to deal with a prisoner who had suffered an accident.

He was waved inside and went to the desk opposite the door. The wall behind the desk was a riot of Nazi insignia: the German eagle; the Gestapo badge; the shocking red, white and black of the Nazi flag; a giant portrait of The Fuhrer. Robert tried not to look intimidated. He repeated his mission to the officer at the desk who dealt with him. As the man studied Robert's papers, Robert studied his face. It did not resemble the poster faces of the master race that Robert had become used to in the streets. It was a tired, pale plasticine face. It portrayed the effects of too many days of idleness and too many pastries. When the man put his fingers to his cheek in thought, the tips of them disappeared below the surface fat. He summoned a guard and instructed him to lead the doctor to the prisoner in need of treatment.

In moments Robert could hardly believe he was walking along a network of corridors within Gestapo headquarters. If he had known how easy it would be he would have strapped a hundredweight of dynamite to his chest and blown the place to bits. At the end of a corridor lined with shiny white and green tiled walls he was taken through a metal gate which the guard unlocked with keys hanging from his belt. They then went down three flights of metal stairs. 'Each step,' thought Robert, 'is a step I might never retrace.'

Robert felt the fall in temperature as they descended and the echo of their footsteps rang out more clearly. Eventually the guard halted at a door and peered through the observation hole.

"Here you are, doctor. Friedrich Lehmann. Looks all right to me. I've seen a lot worse and no doctor sent for."

Robert shrugged as if to say, what do I know? The guard unlocked the door and let Robert in. As he stepped inside a cold shiver ran up his back as the guard stepped back and began to close the door.

"Just a moment," he said. "Where are you going? I don't want to be left alone with this asocial rodent."

The guard laughed and stepped back inside.

"Don't worry, Herr Doctor. I will only be outside in the corridor."

As he completed his sentence and turned to exit he felt a sharp prick in his neck. Robert had brought the syringe out of his pocket and swung it around the man's back and into the side of his neck just below his ear. Emitting a child-like yelp, the guard stumbled and then fell to his knees. A gentle push from Robert and he toppled forward onto his face.

Friedrich cowered in the corner of the cell. The cell was brightly lit. Too bright! Obviously a part of the torture process. Robert closed the cell door, disentangled the guard's keys from his belt and locked the door. He went across to Friedrich and bent close to him.

"It's me," he said somewhat unnecessarily.

"What the hell are you doing here?" whispered Friedrich

"I'm here to get you out. Now come on, help me."

Robert moved back to the prostrate guard.

"Come on," he said. "Help me undress him."

The two men worked in silence as they de-robed the guard.

"Now get out of your clothes. Quickly, man!"

Within minutes the guard was lying on Friedrich's cell bed, clad in Friedrich's old clothes, face turned to the wall. Friedrich stood as erect as he could manage in the guard's immaculate uniform.

"Here," said Robert. "Get rid of that face furniture."

He handed Friedrich a safety razor and Friedrich inflicted a painful dry shave upon his own face. Robert looked him over. He took some swabs out of his doctor's bag and cleaned up the blood spots on Friedrich's face.

"You'll have to do. Come on let's get out of here."

As they walked along the tiled corridor, Robert whispered instructions to Friedrich, "Take the keys. When we get to the top corridor and go into the lobby you walk well ahead of me. Whatever happens, keep walking. Don't turn round for anything. If someone tries to stop you, say you're hurrying to an incident under orders. Don't stop."

Robert paused to catch his breath and to listen for sounds in the corridor. He then went on, "You have a good friend called Karl."

Friedrich turned in surprise to hear that Robert knew this, but he did not interrupt.

"Go to his house. Tell him as much as you need to. Get rid of that uniform there and borrow some of his clothes. Then you must go to the apothecary in Beethoven Strasse. Do you know the one I mean?"

"Yes."

"It's closed now but you can gain entry through the back entrance in the lane at the rear."

Robert described the layout of the interior of the apothecary and where to locate the transmitter hidden there. He then handed Friedrich a tiny piece of paper. When Friedrich looked at it he saw a series of numbers.

"That's the frequency you must use," instructed Robert. "When you are connected you must utter three words only."

Friedrich stopped and stared at Robert. His visage portrayed a combination of puzzlement and fear.

"Are you listening to me?" Robert asked.

Friedrich nodded.

"You must say these three words – "A Pious Killing.""

Friedrich mouthed the words.

"Say them back to me," ordered Robert.

"A Pious Killing," whispered Friedrich.

"You'll do," grinned Robert. "When you manage to do that you will be given instructions on how to get out of Germany."

Friedrich's eyes opened wide.

"You'd better take that look off your face or we're going to have great difficulty getting out of here."

They stood at the gate leading into the lobby area. Gestapo uniforms were all around doing what Gestapo administration officers do.

"Unlock the door, then walk well ahead of me. Whatever happens, keep going! With any luck I'll see you at the apothecary in under an hour. Good luck my friend."

Friedrich made to speak but Robert stopped him with a hand to his mouth.

"Open the gate and get going!"

Friedrich reached towards the lock with the bunch of keys. His first attempt failed and as he tried a second key two other guards came running up the steps towards them. Robert felt his heartbeat race and then accelerate even further as Friedrich dropped the whole bunch of keys onto the metal landing.

The guards pushed in between them laughing and calling, "Out of the way donkey."

One of them slid his key into the lock and they ran through leaving it ajar. Now they only had the lobby to cross. They could see the daylight of freedom seeping in from the Munich street. Just a few metres and they would be out. Friedrich looked at Robert as if about to speak. Robert silenced him with a gesture.

"Just go," he said. "And as you walk do it with the arrogance of one of these deluded bastards. Whatever happens, don't look back. I will follow and I will meet you at the apothecary."

Robert hesitated as he watched Friedrich set off across the marble-tiled lobby towards the grand double doors of the entrance. 'My God,' he thought, 'he looks the part.'

When Friedrich was past half way to the doors Robert began his own walk to freedom. He tried to behave as he expected a doctor would under these circumstances and he approached the officer at the desk who had checked him in.

"You have finished, Herr Doctor?"

"Yes. There is nothing wrong with him that the relocation camp won't put right. I can't think why I was sent for to treat a common Jew."

Both men laughed and Robert turned to leave. As he turned, a door in the far corner of the lobby opened and into view came Netzer, followed closely by Lily. Robert froze momentarily. His eyes locked onto Lily's and hers onto his. Her mouth fell open in surprise and she suppressed a reflex to shout his name. But her expression was not missed by Netzer who turned to follow her line of sight. Too late, Lily touched Netzer's arm attempting to re-engage him in the conversation they had been having.

"Seize that man!" he screamed.

Robert reacted quickly and flew towards the entrance. The guards in the lobby reacted only seconds afterwards and in moments he was face down on the floor under the combined weight of four guards. Netzer took him by the hair and said, "Let him up."

He put his face close to Robert's and Robert flinched as he spat into it. So you like to visit our headquarters Doctor? Well, don't be in such a hurry to leave. We would very much like to entertain you."

Netzer pushed Robert's face away.

"Take him downstairs," he ordered.

In his office Netzer poured two large glasses of schnapps. He gave one to Lily who was seated in front of his desk. Netzer took a large swallow from his own glass and, placing it on his desk came to kneel in front of Lily. His hand slid between her legs and inside her skirt. He pushed aside her panties and roughly took hold of her pubic hair. Lily called out in pain but Netzer did not relinquish his hold.

"Now then my sweet Lily, I have a question for you do I not?"

He became invasive with his fingers. Lily's rising fear accentuated her dryness, increasing the discomfort.

"Why did you try to conceal the good doctor's presence? And why did you try to distract me?"

Lily made a big effort to assert herself. She slapped Netzer's face hard and pushed him away. She got up from the seat, re-adjusting herself.

"You damn fool," she screamed, looking down at him.

"What else should I do? I knew you would react in the idiotic way you did."

Netzer's expression showed surprise and dismay.

"What have you achieved?" Lily went on. "You've locked up the doctor. He was our only chance of uncovering the leaders of the conspiracy. How can he do that now? In one stupid reflex action you have undone all the work and preparation that went into establishing me as a double agent. Preparation that took years. You are a damned fool!"

Netzer got to his feet and took Lily by the chin.

"A fool am I? We'll see about that. Let's see how long it takes me to squeeze the information we need out of your beloved doctor."

"You are a bigger fool than I thought. If he knew, I would know. We were never told the names of the conspirators."

"So you say. But I'm going to find out."

Netzer arrived in the corridor outside Robert's cell and Robert could hear his voice as he spoke to the guards there.

"Don't kill him," was all he heard Netzer say.

As the two Gestapo men entered the thought that consoled Robert for what was about to happen was that the excitement he had created had so far led to the concealment of Friedrich's escape.

Forty-four

Robert was lying on the floor in the corner of his cell when Netzer eventually entered. Robert calculated that he had been in the cell for about twelve hours. He also calculated that he had at least one broken rib, two broken fingers and badly bruised kidneys. The bright lights and white walls of the cell had worked on his perception until there were times when he could not see the walls but felt the focus of his eyes slip into an unreal gleaming distance. Before he could react to Netzer's entrance an ice cold jet of water was turned upon him. He gasped at the shock and writhed to avoid the jet. But Netzer calmly sprayed him for a full five minutes. When finally the jet was switched off, Robert was thoroughly soaked. His body temperature had dropped significantly and he was wracked with shivers.

"Take him to my interrogation room," barked Netzer and the guards complied.

Robert waited an hour in another blindingly bright room. The temperature was akin to a refrigerator. He was tied to a chair with his hands behind his back and was therefore unable to move about to fight the cold. During his wait he had plenty of time to study the array of instruments that lined the wall opposite his chair; the same instruments that lined the walls of every SS/Gestapo establishment in Europe, manufactured by housewives in some foundry along the Ruhr valley.

When Netzer entered he was wearing a fur-lined hood, greatcoat and gloves. He sat down on a wooden chair facing Robert and pushed his face within an inch of Robert's. 'It is a form of dominant behaviour he obviously enjoys,' thought Robert.

"I am not even going to waste our time by asking you a question," he stated in a clam, matter-of-fact voice. "You will only refuse to answer and we will enter a silly bidding game until we find out how much pain you can endure before you decide to talk. So let me start with a marker for you. I'll just assume the first question has been asked and you have refused to answer. I will jump straight to the first application of pain."

He got up and walked to the rows of instruments on display.

"Let me see," he mused, as if choosing a chocolate snack. "None of these, I think. No, for my first move I will use this."

Removing a glove he revealed a screw-driver which had been concealed within it all along. Robert noticed how worn and rusted it was.

"Let's see how this works," said Netzer.

Moving swiftly to Robert's side he inserted the blade of the screw-driver into Robert's ear and slammed it with the heel of his hand.

Robert roared in pain. A sharp stab; a popping sound; a growing throb of agony; a hissing noise; a hot, wet feeling running onto his neck.

Netzer replaced the screw-driver within the glove and exited the cell. Two guards came in, released Robert from his chair and led him back to his cell. Before leaving him there, they jet-sprayed him with icy water for about five minutes.

Two hours later the guards returned. They lifted Robert up and dragged him back to Netzer's interrogation room. As Robert sat waiting for Netzer to enter he knew that hypothermia was beginning to deprive him of his full senses. His mind wanted to enter a numb featureless landscape where it could lie down and sleep. His hearing was irreparably damaged. He could hear noises but he knew all of them originated inside his head. He heard the outside world as if from under water. He would not survive much more of this. Netzer was undeniably good at what he did. If Robert needed a motivation to keep him alive, it was knowing that Friedrich was safe and he could now get back to his mission if he could only escape. It was keeping the word 'escape' in his mind, however ridiculous it seemed, that kept him conscious.

Netzer entered. He was again clad in fur.

"Don't look so worried my good doctor. I am not going to insult your bravery with any questions. Not just yet. I think we need a little more encouragement before we enter the questioning stage."

Robert could not prevent himself from glancing at the instruments.

"Aha!" laughed Netzer. "Curious, are we? But no we are not ready for the precision instruments yet. But look! Look what I've brought for you."

He removed his gloves. In one hand he held a small chisel. In the other he held a small sculptor's hammer.

"I love to improvise you know. Guard!" he screamed.

A guard entered and he was ordered to hold Robert's head still by taking handfuls of his hair. When the guard had Robert in position Netzer took up the hammer and chisel. As carefully as an artist working with stone he positioned the chisel upon Robert's left cheek bone. With an expert tap he hit it with the exact amount of force needed to split the bone apart. Moving quickly he repeated the act upon Robert's right cheek bone.

Robert screamed but it was a pathetically weak sound that emerged from his lungs. Meanwhile, the guard holding Robert let his head drop, turned and vomited in the corner of the room. Netzer went berserk.

"Get out of here you fucking girl!" As he screamed he kicked the guard all the way to the door and pushed him out. "Get your filth cleaned up and send someone to take this piece of vermin back to his cell."

Robert was thrown to the floor of his cell completely unconscious.

Lily had left headquarters as soon as Netzer had headed off to interrogate Robert. Any lingering doubts she had had about her loyalties were banished when she saw Robert being dragged away. The guilt she felt for revealing his presence to Netzer by her expression was unbearable.

She returned to their home. As she ate a meagre meal of black bread and hot chicory she made her plans. Her first objective was to get Robert out of the clutches of Netzer and the Gestapo. Next she had to initiate their escape plan. To do that, she would have to visit the apothecary and hope that the radio was still in its hiding place. Finally, if successful in her first objective she would have to force Robert to abort their mission. She went into their bedroom and pulled a case from the back of her wardrobe. From within the box she lifted two Luger pistols and a case of cartridges. She loaded each gun to its cartridge capacity. She placed one of them into her handbag and the other into the pocket of her overcoat, which she then put on. In the other pocket she placed the case with the remaining cartridges.

There was no heating in the house so she sat with her coat on, looking out into the street until dusk began to pull a blanket over the scene. When darkness had swallowed everything she got up from her chair and closed the blackout curtains. She went from room to room performing the same task. She opened the front door and slipped away along the darkened street.

By avoiding the main boulevards and circumnavigating Marienplatz she was able to keep out of sight of police, blackout wardens and Gestapo. She burrowed her way through the back lanes and alleyways until she came to the rear access parallel to Beethoven Strasse on which stood the apothecary. Although hindered by the length of her overcoat she quickly scaled the back gate and crossed the yard to the door. She noticed a pane of glass in the door was shattered and that the door stood slightly ajar. Just as she was about to enter she heard a bumping noise from inside and a soft curse uttered in profane German. Stepping back into the shadows she drew her Luger from her pocket.

Forty-five

The Papal train, having routed through Turin to avoid favouring red-tinged Milan with the Papal presence, had made its way through neutral Switzerland. Although a longer route than through the more direct Austria, it removed the Pontiff from the war-zone for a good part of the journey. Rumbling into Interlaken at 1700hrs local time, the Pope had left his palatial compartments for the short limousine drive to the cathedral where he had celebrated mass for a packed congregation. Although a neutral country several members of the congregation wore the uniforms or insignia of the German Nazi and the Italian Fascist parties. People either did not care or were too intimidated to object. The Pope welcomed one and all.

Father O'Shea served at mass. It was an activity he enjoyed as much, if not more than saying mass himself. He took a pride in his swift, efficient movements around the altar. He always anticipated the Pope's next movements and he believed he enhanced the act of the sacrament itself by his skilled assistance.

During communion, he and three local clergy administered the host to the multitude desperate to partake during the Pope's presence. The Pontiff sat in the throne at the right side of the altar, a benign expression on his face. All who gazed upon him, and they all did, felt blessed. His expression, though meditative, spoke of immense care and love. Each member of the congregation felt that care and love directed solely at themselves.

Before retiring for an evening meal with the Archbishop of Zurich, who had journeyed to Interlaken with the express purpose of outranking the Monsignor who was acting in charge of the local diocese, the Pope granted an audience with local Catholic boys. Father O'Shea met with the children in the crypt of the cathedral. He asked the parents of these children to wait in an ante-chamber whilst he briefed the children on manners and procedures when approaching the Pope. This he did in small groups of six in a side chapel.

Approximately one hour later the boys and their parents marched back into the body of the cathedral where the Pope awaited them in his throne, which was now positioned at the foot of the altar.

One by one the boys were guided by Father O'Shea to the feet of the Pope where he touched the back of each neck or the top of a shoulder to let them know it was time to kneel.

Kneeling, heads bowed and hands joined in angelic prayer, each boy felt the Pontiff's hand touch his scalp and the Papal thumb draw a cross on his forehead. The Pope's Latin prayer was all too soon over and the next boy was brought forward in the sure hands of Father O'Shea.

Forty-six

Friedrich stepped carefully through the back door of the apothecary into the pitch black of the yard. His knee was still smarting where he had cracked it against a corner of the counter. His feelings were a complete mixture. The fear and shock that had overwhelmed him when in the hands of the Gestapo still raced around his system. An unwanted thought would spring to mind and spark off a rush of emotion. Conflicting with these flashback feelings was one of immense guilt. He had heard the commotion that had flared as he walked out of Gestapo headquarters and he was pretty certain that Robert had been seized. He had followed Robert's strict instructions, but he knew deep down he wished he had turned round and stood shoulder to shoulder with him as they had on the night they first met in the alleyway. Into this conflicting mix spilled a massive amount of relief that he was out of Gestapo hands and had a chance to escape them and Germany forever. His shameful secret was out. Jewish blood, no matter how well diluted, mingled in his bloodstream. He could never again be the man he had been. Friends, colleagues and acquaintances would all look at him through different eyes. The hostility he had seen destroy strong, healthy men and women, would now be his to endure. And much worse! His administrative work told him that and he was no longer in any position to deny it.

As he pulled the door silently to, his ears prickled at the intimate proximity of a sound that invaded his soul. A cold, metal barrel was pressed to the back of his skull and a woman's voice said, "Don't make a sound."

All of Friedrich's conflicting emotions dissolved into disappointment and resignation.

"Open the door and go back inside."

With the gun at his head Friedrich obeyed and they walked together into the interior.

"Upstairs!" she ordered.

Friedrich led the way and soon he was back in the room where he had just replaced the radio transmitter in its hiding place. Pushing him in the back to clear a safe distance between them, the woman checked the blackout curtains were secured. She then switched on the faint light that hung bare in the middle of the ceiling. Friedrich saw her face for the first time. He did not recognise her.

"Who are you?" she said.

Friedrich did not speak. Emotionally he was working out an equation that would balance his guilt for leaving Robert to his fate if he refused to tell this person anything that Robert had confided in him. After the fear and humiliation it would be no terrible thing to die here defending Robert.

"Who are you and what are you doing here?"

Still nothing. Lily had an idea.

"Empty your pockets!" she ordered.

Friedrich complied. 'No drugs! Theft is not the reason he is here,' she thought.

Friedrich watched as the woman stared at him. She seemed to be making mental calculations.

"Okay," she said. "If that's how you want it, I will do the talking."

She lowered the gun but kept it cocked and ready.

"I am the wife of Dr. Robert Hermann. He is in the hands of the Gestapo. I want to rescue him from them. Now do you have anything to say?"

Friedrich was tempted but managed to hold fire. Her words had shocked him, but how did he know she was telling the truth?

"Still nothing to say? Well, my friend, listen carefully. I am now going to divulge things to you that no one should hear. If I am not convinced of who you are and what you are doing here by the time I have finished, you will have to die."

As if to emphasise her statement, it was immediately followed by the scream of the air raid siren. Another night of bombing was about to begin.

"Dr Robert Hermann and I are British agents. We have been planted here to carry out a mission vital to the Allies in pursuance of their war objectives. We are not married. I am German by birth. I lived in Britain for several years and volunteered my services to the British War Office when hostilities broke out. I think our mission is now forfeit. My remaining objective is to rescue Robert from the Gestapo and to get us away from here."

She paused as if reflecting on the words she had spoken. Then she raised the gun to shoulder height and pointed it at Friedrich's head.

"Now I need you to speak or I will kill you. I am counting to ten in my head."

A silence fell on the room. Friedrich began to count to ten in his head too. He wondered if they were counting at the same rate. When he reached five he had a sudden thought. All of this could be clever Gestapo lies. If it was, he would die *and* Robert would die. But that was going to happen anyway.

If, however, there was just a grain of truth in any of it – maybe, just maybe, there might be a way to save Robert.

Friedrich saw the woman's fingers tense and squeeze as the only words he could think to say fell from his lips, "A pious killing."

Lily immediately recognised the secret code name for their mission; the one they were to use when they wanted out. Only she and Robert knew it. Robert must have confided in this man. Her hopes rose slightly. If Robert trusted this man then maybe here was someone who could help her to rescue him.

"I've seen you before, haven't I?" Lily suddenly asked.

Friedrich shrugged.

"You were at headquarters earlier. That's it! I remember you now. You were leaving as Robert was seized."

Friedrich, determined to be careful with this woman, could see no reason to deny what she was saying.

"I was in custody. Robert rescued me. Unfortunately, he was seized as we were leaving."

"It's my fault," said Lily after a pause. "If I had not come into the lobby and glanced at him as you were leaving, Netzer would not have spotted him."

Lily lowered the gun and let it hang limply by her side.

"Look Herr, whatever your name is, I'm not going to force you to do anything. But I am asking you to help me do for Robert what he did for you. In truth we might all end up in Gestapo hands. But that's a chance I have to take. With you helping me I might have a better chance of success. You know what Netzer is capable of. God knows what torture he is subjecting Robert to at this very moment. Will you help me?"

Friedrich looked into Lily's eyes.

"I can think of nothing I would rather do," he said. "Tell me your plan."

It was about twenty minutes later when Lily and Friedrich left the apothecary. Lily had collected the drugs she thought she might need if Netzer had practised his arts on Robert. Friedrich led the way. He knew every short cut and back alley in Munich and he swiftly but cautiously led Lily straight to the home of Karl Belkin where a few hours earlier he had swapped his newly acquired Gestapo uniform for an outfit of Karl's clothes. The plan was to re-acquire the uniform, and as they hurried to their destination both Lily and Friedrich prayed to a god that neither of them believed in that Karl had not yet burned it.

Friedrich led Lily to the back garden of Karl's home and they knocked at the back door. Karl had been eating black bread and some thin broth at his kitchen table when they knocked. A sickness thudded into his stomach. He looked at the bundle of clothes rolled up on the floor and cursed his indolence for not burning it immediately after Friedrich had left. Rapidly he grabbed a damp towel, wrapped it around the bundle and kicked it out of sight under the mangle that stood beside the sink. He switched off the light and waited for his eyes to adjust. He then went to the blackout curtain and pulled it fractionally aside. He recognised the shape of Friedrich almost immediately. He experienced tremendous relief and immediately unlocked and opened the door and admitted his two visitors.

Friedrich and Karl looked at each other. Karl looked at Lily. Karl raised both hands and said, "I don't want to know anything!"

"Fine," replied Friedrich. "I just need the uniform back."

Karl's incredulous expression would have been amusing under any other circumstances.

"Friedrich," he said. "Are you mad? You've just had the closest brush with death you could ever have and survived. Now you're going back for more? Why are you not in Switzerland already?"

"I thought you did not want to know."

Karl raised his hands again.

"You are right! I don't!"

Friedrich took a few moments to get into the uniform again. This time he asked Karl for a small bag and he slipped the trousers and jacket into it that Karl had given to him earlier. With a desperately inadequate grimace Friedrich tried to express a fraction of his immense gratitude to Karl. He dismissed it with a flap of his hand and a reluctant, "Get out!"

Lily and Friederich walked with arms linked through the streets of Munich directly to Gestapo headquarters. They had no need to skulk along back alleyways. Friedrich's uniform was their curfew-breaking passport.

Friedrich placed his bag of clothes out of sight under a stairwell at the corner of the block. Lily handed him a loaded Luger.

"If I had a proper plan," she said, "I'd share it with you. The best I can say is if you need to - use it. If you start using it inside that building my best advice is to kill as many as you can as quickly as you can and then use it on yourself."

They walked on some more, their cold breath going before them.

"Just let me do all the talking. All you need to do is salute senior officers and say 'Heil Hitler,' if required."

As Lily and Friedrich approached the desk sergeant, Netzer was walking along the basement corridor below towards the interrogation cell where Robert had been recently re-installed. As Netzer had ordered he was tightly tied by his hands to the back of the chair in which he was seated.

Netzer looked down on the man in front of him. Robert's head slumped on his chest. He could see Netzer's boots as his torturer walked up and down in front of the array of tools hanging on the wall.

"Now then Doctor Robert Hermann, or should I say Doctor Sean Colquhoun? What instrument of truth should I select for you today?"

Robert felt totally disassociated from the sound of the name his parents had given him at birth. It was as if Netzer had mentioned the name of someone they both once knew. It convinced him, though, that he was right about Lily. She had betrayed him; she was a German sleeper. His considered decision was that the best option left to him was to die quickly. He had nothing to gain from clinging to life whilst in the clutches of this monster. The only way he could think to hasten on his own death was to enrage Netzer; to incite him to go further than he intended. He knew what he wanted to do and he was sure Netzer would give him at least one chance.

Netzer moved behind Robert and took hold of his hair. Wrenching Robert's head back he forced him to look at the various tools on view.

"Don't be coy, Doctor. I'm sure you would like to help me choose."

Robert felt Netzer's breath on his neck as Netzer stooped close to his ear.

"What's the matter doctor?" he hissed. "Are you hard of hearing today? Is this the ear that was unfortunately injured the last time we had a chat?"

A fetid odour of stale food and stomach disorder washed into Robert's nostrils. Employing his favourite mode of dominance, Netzer moved his head to Robert's other side and, with his mouth almost touching Robert's other ear he yelled, "Or was it this one?" He walked away to the wall laughing loudly. He picked up a hand drill and came back. "Maybe today," he mused, "You will experience a little eye trouble."

Again, taking a handful of Robert's hair he yanked his face upwards and brought the drill close to his left eye. "You can close your eyelid if it makes you feel better. But you need to know that I have seen this drill bit enter through the eyelid like a bayonet into a bowl of water. I have to confess, it is always a lot messier than my simile suggests, but it is definitely as slick. But look, my good Doctor! See, I have put the drill on the table. Maybe today is the day I should begin with a question or two. Perhaps you are ready to talk. It will not take us long to find out. As soon as we know we can decide whether my drill goes back onto its hook or gets to work."

Leaving the drill on the table Netzer moved towards Robert. He spread his hands in mock appeal.

"You know, Doctor, we men of the Gestapo take no pleasure in the vital work we have to do. We are honourable men. It is because we are honourable that we are prepared to undertake the dirty tasks. We are men. We know what must be done. We do not flinch from our painful duty. We do not burden lesser mortals with the details of our heroism. Save me from this duty and at the same time save yourself from an intolerable fate."

As he delivered this speech Netzer drew closer and closer to Robert. Indulging himself once more in the power to humiliate, he put his face as close as possible to Robert's. He wore an expression of mock friendship. Robert had seen sweeter smiles on the face of a serpent.

But this time Robert did not recoil from the nauseous odour of his breath, nor did he flinch from the malevolence of Netzer's dominant stare. This was in fact, the moment he had hoped for.

In one swift, reptilian-like dart he lunged forward and sank his teeth into Netzer's face. He had intended to clamp his teeth onto the prominent nose but Netzer's reaction had been quick enough to evade that attempt. However, Robert got lucky and grabbed a secure purchase on Netzer's top lip. He focused all his strength into that one physical effort and closed his jaws like a vice. In that one split second of activity the tables were suddenly turned.

In anticipating this moment Robert had wondered if the touch of Netzer's lips to his own would be repellent. Here was the moment of truth, and the answer was no. This was as sweet a kiss as he had ever known. Netzer's actions now worked to his own disadvantage. His attempt to scream came out as a child's startled yelp and his instinct to pull back resulted in his top lip tearing right off and pulling a large chunk of his right cheek with it.

Robert tasted the warm blood and saliva that exploded from Netzer's face and it stimulated him to further action. Disoriented by the immeasurable pain and reacting without thought, Netzer stumbled forward, his face bumping Robert's, instinctively trying to prevent further tearing of his face. With animal ferocity Robert pushed with his feet, rising with the chair attached to his imprisoned arms, and lunged again at Netzer's face. With the force of the collision between them Netzer toppled over backwards with Robert falling on top of him, his teeth already sinking deep into the wound. With the added assistance of his body weight Robert gouged his teeth into Netzer's eye socket and bit ferociously on his eyeball. He felt the liquid jelly spurt into his mouth and he shook the eye out with a vicious tear.

Completely engulfed by an animalistic rage he raised his head and from his bloody mouth he uttered a barbaric roar. As he roared and spat out the cartilage, mucus and blood he was distantly aware of the sound of the cell door opening. He triumphantly turned to face his death, rags of Netzer's face still dangling from his mouth. He waited for the hot lead to enter his brain or his heart. But as he slowly ceased his victory roar and the blood and liquid cleared from his eyes he found himself looking at Lily and Friedrich.

Friedrich stepped swiftly past Lily into the cell taking a bayonet from the one of the hooks on the wall as he went. He leaned over Netzer and inserted the bayonet into his throat. The honourable man from the Gestapo gurgled like a fountain for a few seconds and then fell silent. Friedrich then helped Lily to get Robert upright before untying him. As his bonds were being released Lily hissed to Friedrich, "Someone's coming. Do something!"

The echo of boot heels bounced along the corridor. Friedrich stepped out of the cell closing the door behind him. Coming towards him strode two Gestapo agents in their field-grey, office uniforms.

"What's going on?" the older of the two asked. He noticed blood on Friedrich's sleeve. "Is everything all right?"

Friedrich fingered his collar and released a deep sigh.

"I think so. Herr Gruppenfuhrer Netzer is busy interrogating a suspect. You may have heard the suspect's responses."

The two men stared at him for an instant and then sniggered nervously.

"We should have guessed. Good old Netzer – protecting the state and the leader with his usual enthusiasm."

The younger man touched his companion's elbow.

"Come on; let's get out of here before he asks us to join him."

They wished Friedrich good luck and hurried back along the corridor out of sight.

Inside the cell Lily was dressing Robert's facial wounds. The cuts made by Netzer's chisel were turning septic and she bathed them with an antiseptic fluid. The violent stinging the fluid induced made no impression upon Robert's consciousness. Turning away from Robert to search her bag for the M B 760 anti-infection serum she did not see Robert rise from his chair and step towards her. She turned to find his hands slipping around her throat and beginning to tighten.

"What ar…" she gasped before Robert's hands squeezed the breath out of her.

"You treacherous bitch," he spluttered. "You might have destroyed our mission but you will not live to enjoy your success."

As he began to apply the necessary pressure to break her neck he felt a sharp, cold blade push into the side of his throat.

"I do not know much about your business Robert my friend," he heard Friedrich say, "But, for now, you will let her go and we will all leave this house of death together. When we are clear you can do what you want. But I have to tell you – without her we would not be here and you would undoubtedly be dead."

Robert released his grip and slumped back into his chair. Lily bent over and retched. She snatched at the air for oxygen and eventually achieved enough equilibrium to continue. She rolled up one of Robert's sleeves and injected him with the M B 760. She then began to undress him.

"Undress Netzer!" she ordered Friedrich.

Friedrich obeyed without hesitation and in a few moments Robert and Netzer were dressed as each other. Lily gave her instructions, "I know a rear exit that Netzer habitually uses to remove the remains of suspects who do not survive his interrogations. You are Netzer!" she instructed Robert. "Netzer is you."

The three of them looked at the bloody skeletal frame exposed where his face had been.

"No one will recognise that," she said coldly. "If anyone asks we reply with Netzer's favourite rejoinder in these circumstances –'we are taking out the garbage'."

Robert was too weak to assist in carrying Netzer's body. He went ahead having been pointed in the right direction by Lily. Lily and Friedrich carried Netzer between them. They passed locked cell doors and turned right at a T-junction. At the end of the corridor was the door to the outside world. It was about thirty yards distant when it opened and in stepped two Getsapo agents returning from operations. Lily instinctively knew this as they were not in uniform. Gestapo agents in the field did not wear uniform when operating within the fatherland.

They approached Robert first but they could see beyond to Lily and Friedrich and the corpse they were carrying.

"Heil Hitler, Gruppenfuhrer. More garbage to be disposed of I see."

The two men chuckled. Not knowing what else to do Robert kept his face low beneath the brim of his hat and barged between them cursing loudly. The men were shocked. Before they could react, however, they found themselves looking into the remains of what had once been a face. The horror of the sight silenced any protest they might have been contemplating. Netzer had truly excelled himself this time.

Beyond the door they found themselves in an outside compound. Lily and Friedrich laid Netzer on the ground at the feet of Robert who propped himself up against the wall. They both went to the far end of the compound. They tried three of the cars parked there before finding one with the keys in. In moments Lily was driving them away from SS Gestapo headquarters and back to the surgery. Robert and Netzer sat side by side in the rear. Sitting in the everyday environment of an automobile and released from the insanity of Netzer's domain Robert was subject to deep self revulsion. In the moments before death, as he had fully anticipated in that cell, his behaviour had had a valid motivation. Now he was disintegrating psychologically at the thought of his actions.

Forty-seven

The rest of that Sunday and all the next day saw the newly formed gang of three playing cat and mouse. In reality they played mouse, but there was little evidence of cat. The freedom to pursue his own investigations in his own sadistic way had made Netzer the dangerous animal he had been. But, conversely, now that he was dead (or temporarily missing as was thought by his colleagues) there was no one in a hurry to follow up his unfinished work. Lily was fairly sure that she was the only other individual fully briefed on the papal assassination plan and on the monitoring of the resistance support group acting as enablers for Robert. Netzer had in fact successfully destroyed the resistance group, but he had failed on two major counts; one, the leadership conspiracy had not been exposed and two, the assassination plan was still on track – just.

It had been left to Friedrich to dispose of Netzer's body. He took no pleasure in his task. Under cover of night he took the corpse into the garden and by a corner of the wall had placed it in a shallow grave. In order to make identification of the corpse as difficult as possible he had been obliged to strip the corpse of clothes and burn them. He had then carried out the morbid task of pouring acid onto crucial parts of the body to obliterate distinguishing characteristics. The face; the SS tattoo; the hands; and various spots where individual marks such as moles resided.

An hour after he had finished this necessary endeavour a loud knocking came at the front door. The three of them were sitting in the living room having finished a meal of liverwurst, cabbage soup and ersatz bread. They had no clean water to drink so they were making do with unsweetened ersatz coffee. The knocking startled all three. Lily got up from her seat and went to answer the door.

Standing in the gloom was a man she knew as Arne Lahm. Herr Lahm was the block warden. In the neighbourhood he was known as the rat. This was because he was always sniffing around and he belonged with the garbage. As a member of the party he received a nominal payment to monitor the behaviour of all occupants of the six blocks of houses that sat astride this part of Heydrichstrasse. He had been the one who suggested the patriotic re-naming of their road from the more acceptable Haselnubstrasse. Despite the name of Heydrich now attached to the strasse, the hazelnut trees still adorned its pavements. Herr Lahm stood their in his crombie and trilby with a swastika armband decorating his right sleeve. He offered a crooked smile to her, which exposed two missing lower teeth.

"Good evening Herr Lahm. How good of you to call. Can I help you?"

Being aware of the man's zealotry Lily applied all the formal politeness she could muster.

"Neighbours have reported unusual activity in your garden area," he said. It was neither a question nor an accusation, but it left Lily momentarily dumbstruck. For want of something else to say Lily heard herself inviting Herr Lahm inside. She led him into the waiting area for the surgery and asked him to give her more details about the so-called unusual activity. Herr Lahm informed her of the observed digging in the garden by one of their more attentive neighbours.

"I will get my husband for you," she said and left the room.

Moments later Robert entered the waiting room and approached Herr Lahm with his hand out. He shook hands with him enthusiastically and invited him through to their living quarters.

"Have a seat Her Lahm and let me pour you a drink. I have some schnapps."

"You are very kind Herr Doctor. A small measure would be most welcome."

As he handed the glass of schnapps to Herr Lahm, Robert remarked, "You have noticed my injuries, Herr Lahm. But you are too polite to comment."

"Please forgive me Herr Doctor. I did not mean to appear rude."

"I am not offended Herr Lahm. Let me explain. During the last air raid I was called out to attend an emergency. It was at an address not far from Marienplatz but it meant walking through the narrow lanes of the asocial housing that festers to the east of that district. Having been the victim of an attack there not so long ago I decided to take my dog with me. Unfortunately, as we were progressing past the primary school building it was hit by a bomb. I took some of the debris in my face. Hence the disagreeable sight you now see before you. Sadly, Kaiser, my dog, had run on ahead and caught the full blast of the explosion. He was killed. I am assuming that the unusual activity you have mentioned to my wife was when I buried him in the garden."

"A dog? I didn't know you had a dog,"

"But of course! I have had him since I moved in here. You do surprise me. You have such an encyclopaedic knowledge of this area; surely you knew I had a dog."

Not happy to expose a lack of knowledge, the block warden was nonplussed. Robert decided to gamble.

"Would you like to come through and inspect his grave, Herr Lahm?"

Herr Lahm hesitated long enough for Robert to contemplate how he would kill him if he said yes.

"No, Herr doctor, that will not be necessary. I will finish my schnapps and leave you in peace."

He tipped his glass and drained it. He placed it on the occasional table that stood by the door and turning, raised his arm in salute.

"Heil Hitler!" he exclaimed.

"Heil Hitler!" returned Robert with all the enthusiasm he could muster. He showed Herr Lahm out and urged him to get on home swiftly and safely.

Herr Lahm, Block Warden, did return home immediately. But he spent a restless, sleepless night and arose the next morning determined to satisfy his curiosity. He made a number of calls to houses close to the home of Herr and Frau Doctor. He never tired of the thrill he experienced when he observed the combination of fear and dismay on the faces of those who answered to his knock. Expressions turned to relief and then puzzlement when it became apparent that his enquiries were about the doctor and his wife and not about themselves. Puzzlement because, no, no one had ever seen a dog. If the doctor and his wife possessed a dog it had never been seen.

So, it was as Herr Lahm had suspected. The dog burial story was a lie. What lay behind this seemingly meaningless subterfuge?

Lily's main concern was to administer medical care to Robert. Apart from his physical injuries, which were substantial, he was suffering from shock. Lily and Friedrich assumed the shock was caused by Netzer's treatment of him. Friedrich himself was still working hard to obliterate his own memory of his time in Netzer's hands. In fact, Robert was struggling to recover from the shock of his own behaviour. In that cell, for a few brief minutes, he had become a cannibalistic monster. When his back was completely against the wall he had metamorphosed into a fiend. The seismic, psychological shock lay in the fact that during the metamorphosis, he had enjoyed himself. He had never experienced such a heightened form of blood lust – had not known it was humanly achievable. Now he shook from the inner core of his being. There had to be a route back from the monster he had briefly become and passing through a dark tunnel of traumatic shock was probably the only way.

Lily believed the strength of Robert's subconscious would sort through the shock, although she kept him mildly sedated throughout Sunday and all of Monday. She worried most of all about the fractures and open wounds in and on his face. If left untreated infection could set in and prove fatal.

On closer inspection she discovered that the fractures to his cheekbones and sinus cavities were in fact clean. Netzer's sadistic use of a sculptor's chisel had proved beneficial. The instrument was of such high quality that the bones split in neat, straight lines. She did not need to perform any painful manipulation procedures to set them in place. They would knit and heal naturally if kept free from infection.

She continued to administer MB 760. During her days at Leicester Royal Infirmary this had been hailed as the new wonder drug and all hospital staff had been crying out to get sufficient quantities of it. Winston Churchill had gone on public record in praise of it, claiming it had saved his life when he had succumbed to a bronchial infection. But even as it had been arriving into the hospital pharmacies talk was already spreading that it was not as effective as its proselytisers claimed. Already there was talk of a newer, stronger, miracle medicine that would alter infection treatment forever. Some said that humanity was about to win the final battle in the war against infection. The end of infection was in sight. Alexander Fleming's penicillin was the great hope of the future, but he was struggling to find a company prepared to find a way to produce it in sufficient quantity to make a difference.

Lily had a supply of penicillin but she did not know if she had enough. She was sufficiently knowledgeable about the new medicine to know that it would be better not to give the patient any penicillin at all rather than not give enough or not continue the dose for long enough. But how much was 'enough' and how long was 'long enough'? These were the things she did not know. So she trusted the MB 760 throughout Sunday and Monday morning and afternoon, hoping that Winston Churchill knew what he was talking about.

Her concerns proved superfluous when she entered Robert's bedroom on Monday evening to find him injecting himself with a dose of penicillin. She started across the room and began to scold him. She stopped herself when he raised his eyes to meet hers. As their eyes met she recognised the hatred in his. The look was like a blow and she turned away. When Robert spoke his voice carried none of the emotion his face had shown.

"Tomorrow is the day," he said.

"I know," replied Lily.

"We need to agree a plan."

"Yes."

"What about Friedrich?" asked Robert. "Is he still here?"

"Yes."

"Do we need him? Shouldn't we send him on his way. We do not need to endanger him further."

"I agree," said Lily. "But if you want him to go you will have to tell him. I have told him many times and he takes no notice of me. He wants to help us."

"Does he know what we are about to do?"

"I do not think so. He knows we are subversives. He knows we are part of the resistance. He wants to help us."

"Go down," ordered Robert. "Send him up. Tell him I want to talk to him."

Lily waited downstairs. She could hear the men's voices from above but she could not make out what they were saying. After just over an hour they both came down. Lily looked at Robert. He answered her with a shrug. She looked at Friedrich, "Well?" she asked.

"As I said to your husband, my good Lily, I did not know I had a grudge against the Pope, but if Robert says I have, that's good enough for me." And he shrugged again. "I think," he continued, "I have persuaded your husband that I might be of some use somewhere along the line."

Lily looked at Robert. He shrugged. That was it. Lily was getting used to this particular male form of communication.

They shared a meal of tinned meat followed by tinned pears. They sat down to discuss the following day's activities and then retired to their beds. Lily went straight to the guest room at the back of the house. She made no attempt to share a bed with Robert that evening. In the eerie silence of a bomb-free night she cried herself into a short, fitful, hallucinatory sleep.

Forty-eight

The arrival of the Pope's train in the Hauptbahnhof coincided with the imminent departure of a troop train for southern Poland. Alongside Wermacht troops waiting to embark were uniformed Waffen SS. As the Pope's train slid to a halt at the terminus the troops crushed cigarette butts beneath their heels and following the barked orders of their officers, they placed their caps on their heads and came to attention.

Until this moment they had only been aware that an important friend of the Third Reich would be arriving. Now some of the more devout Catholics amongst the troops recognised the Pope's insignia on the side of the coaches. Word soon spread and even the most committed atheists amongst them were hurrying into position driven by curiosity to see this unique individual.

All the doors of the three coaches opened to the platform simultaneously. Half a dozen Swiss Guards stepped smartly out of each door and formed a human cordon between the train and the rest of humanity. In their blue doublets and berets they looked particularly non-threatening in comparison to the battle-hardened troops all around them. Clerical members of the Pope's entourage then descended to the platform and unrolled a purple carpet. Finally the Pope's immediate coterie stepped from the train followed immediately by the Pope himself. The last man off the train, directly in the shadow of the Pope, was the former curate from Cork, Monsignor O'Shea.

His feet hidden by his long flowing robes, the Pope glided over the carpet towards the exit from the platform where the Wermacht and Waffen SS officers stood waiting to greet him.

There were no handshakes and no kissing of rings. The officers saluted and then politely bowed. The Pope acknowledged their greetings with a slight tilt of his head. Whilst this was happening O'Shea was being assisted to light the incense in a thurible he was carrying. The Pope turned and stepped off the purple carpet. He walked behind the protective line of Swiss Guards and along the lines of troops standing at attention. As he went his hand worked the sign of the cross, constantly blessing individuals as he passed them. Twice he stopped in front of individual soldiers who wore the marks of battle on their faces. Speaking softly in Latin he caressed the blemish with his warm soft hand.

On returning to the platform barriers he took the thurible, which was now smoking abundantly, from O'Shea. Turning to the ranks before him he waved the thurible high and, clanking the gold chain from which it hung, blessed those about to embark for duties in Poland and beyond.

Those amongst the crowd who understood Italian and had ears strong enough to pick up his soft words would have heard him assure the troops that Mary, the Mother of Our Sweet Lord Jesus blessed them and the holy mission they were about to undertake. If they were successful in returning atheistic Russia to Jesus, Our Lady would intercede on their behalf and their place in heaven would be assured.

Mother Superior and representatives of the convent had been asked to stay away from the Hauptbahnhof so as not to unnecessarily advertise the whereabouts of the Pope's accommodation. So, following the formalities the Pope and his entourage climbed into three cars and set off through the streets of Munich to the convent.

As a fervent devotee of Mary, the Pope insisted on being driven first to Marienplatz. Here, without his loyal Swiss Guards, who were being accommodated at a local police barracks, he walked about amongst the populace, which was going about its business. Before arriving at the statue of Mary he paused to speak to and bless one or two individuals. The crowd that gathered to watch this unexpected visitation was visibly lifted. Many would talk ever after of the saintliness and godliness that emanated from this slight, fragile man.

Having knelt and prayed before the statue he returned to his car and the entourage continued on its way. En route to the convent, the Pope insisted on stopping twice more. Each time it was at the site of a bombed church. In each case he got out of the limousine and knelt to pray for the restoration of God's house.

Finally, just before midday on Tuesday 13th March 1944 the Pope's entourage swept into the grounds of the convent and crunched to a halt outside the grey-pillared entrance. Mother Superior, who was waiting on the steps with her senior nuns, could not suppress the full flush of colour surrounding the beam that had taken control of her mouth.

Forty-nine

The mood at the home and surgery of Dr. and Mrs. Robert Hermann was starting to undermine the fragile equilibrium of Friedrich. He was struggling to deal with his own recent experiences and what they signified for his opinion of himself. The deep shame he felt was all directed against himself. How could he possibly come to terms with being a Jew? Half of the time he wanted to vehemently deny it. At others he felt self disgust when he fleetingly acknowledged the truth of the allegation. Everything he had learned to hate was what he had turned out to be.

These feelings would be suddenly swamped by ones of relief at the thought of the narrow escape he had had. Of all people he had a pretty good idea what happened to Jews who were relocated to the so-called work camps. That had nearly been his fate.

Then his dislocated mind would fixate on the love of his life. He cringed when he recalled how he had related the tale to Robert. How Friedrich, the superior Aryan had ditched Sadie the Jewess. In the company of his German ex-pats all those years ago in Warsaw he had confidently asserted his racial superiority and turned his back on the love of his life. Now, not only was he forced to face the fact that he was not an Aryan but a lowly Jew himself. He was also forced to admit that, even back then, he had known all along. What kind of man was he? Capable of mental self-deception powerful enough to get him to deny the very fabric of his being. Capable of turning his back on love in order to fit in with the flow of the tide. Had he ever really known himself? Could he ever really know himself?

Into this maelstrom of self loathing spilled the evil atmosphere that existed between Lily and Robert. As they finished some cabbage soup and dry bread, washed down with a hot chicory coffee, Friedrich had had enough. He roughly pushed his plate away and stood up at the table.

"I'm going upstairs," he growled. "Give me a shout when you two have decided whether you're on the same side or not. If you ask me, whatever you've got planned won't work until you sort that out! One thing I know – without Lily, you'd be a dead man now Robert. You'd better factor that in to your calculations." With that he left them to it.

They slowly finished their tasteless meal and found themselves looking across the table at each other. Robert spoke first.

"Why did you get me out? Friedrich is right. You saved me. But it's the only thing that doesn't make sense."

Lily opened her mouth to speak but Robert went on as if not noticing.

"I know you are a German agent. There's no use denying that. You must be extremely important for the Reich to have invested so much time in you. Concocting your story; transporting you to England; allowing you to 'sleep' for so many years. Well it's paid off. You've infiltrated the mission and, but for your intervention, it would have been destroyed by now. Why did you not let Netzer finish me? It's the one aspect that doesn't make sense."

Robert stared at her. Lily met his stare and did not flinch.

"If you will let me," she said calmly, "I will explain."

Robert sat back in his seat and waited for her to continue.

"You are wrong about the success of my mission. I have not succeeded. My instructions were not to foil your plan but to discover who in the German establishment or Wermacht was involved in the Resistance. I know about Robert Hermann. I know about Sean Colquhoun. You are risking your life in the employ of the power you once found the most repulsive on the planet. You took up arms against the British Empire. Now you are willing to make the ultimate sacrifice for that same Empire. You should understand all about how a change of heart can come about. I too grew to hate the British and their Empire. British guns deprived me of a mother and brother in the Great War. Growing up I agreed with everything the Nazis stood for. My father and I disagreed on just about everything. His love of democracy blinded him to the deficiencies of the Weimar Republic. While he was fighting to establish that fragile state, I was secretly joining the Nazi societies open to girls. Nazi dogma had an attitude to women that I saw as traditional respect and at that time in my life I was convinced of its correctness. Although the Party wanted women out of public life I found it possible to make contacts with boys and men in the Party structure. So when my silly father was making himself a target for the Brownshirts, I was able to arrange our escape to England through those contacts. My father never knew that his argumentative daughter had been the one to save him from Nazi justice. However, the price I paid for his life was to agree to act as an agent of Germany in Britain. Until war was declared they had no use for me. But then I was instructed to volunteer myself for active duty with the British Secret Service. They thought that my father's history would make me most acceptable to the British. The Gestapo would have been proud of Peter Herbert, the police inspector assigned to my case. Despite Herbert, I managed to convince Andrew Trubshaw of my reliability... and the rest is well-known to you."

"A disloyal elite in the Wermacht has long held the view that the war cannot be won. With even a little encouragement from Roosevelt and Churchill they might have been able to persuade more of their number that a negotiable peace was possible and that therefore it was time to get rid of

Hitler. Unfortunately for them, no such encouragement was forthcoming. The network of state intelligence is so thorough that they have been unable to raise their heads above the parapet. Since Stalingrad, however, it is becoming increasingly obvious that the war cannot be won by Germany, and the Resistance is becoming bolder. My mission is to do everything possible to enable you to carry out your mission in the hope of flushing out those elite conspirators who want to bring down the Reich and negotiate another Weimar peace."

"Everything possible?" interrupted Robert.

Lily grimaced ironically.

"Everything except let you kill the Pope."

"So that's why you saved me from the clutches of Netzer? In order to carry on with your mission."

Lily dismissed him summarily.

"Now you are being ridiculous. I'm sure I'd be telling you all of this if that was my aim. Robert! Wake up! I have turned. I no longer serve the Reich. Just like you turned from your Irish rebellion activities to become and agent of the crown, so have I turned."

Robert leaned on the table closer to Lily. He cupped her chin roughly in his hand.

"If you have turned, tell me, who do you work for now?"

As if he were squeezing them out of her glistening eyes with the physical force of his grip, the tears began to flow.

"You," she whispered. "You, you damned fool, you!"

Robert released his grip and for a few minutes they sat in silence. Eventually he said, "I really don't understand. You haven't been converted to the Allies' cause. I can't believe that. I don't really believe you've rejected Nazism. Attachments and beliefs formed in youth are the hardest to break."

"You broke with yours," she countered. "Catholicism, Irish Republicanism."

"You're not completely right there," he argued. "Catholicism, yes. Irish Republicanism, no. I might not agree with current government policy in Eire, but I still believe in republican democracy. I have elected to fight with Britain against what I see as a terrible evil. I have first hand experience of your beloved Nazism. I have to fight it. If it succeeds I do not want to survive." The vehemence with which he spoke had left him breathless and he was forced to pause. Into the silence Lily interjected a quiet comment accompanied by a flush of embarrassment on her face.

"It is not *my* beloved Nazism."

She struggled to continue. Her statement hovered as a reproach to Robert. "I was doing what I thought was right," she finally went on. "Just as you were." Looking down at her hands which were playing with a piece of stale bread, she continued, "Once we arrived here in Munich and things got underway I began to realise that I was not doing things I ought to." She tossed the bread onto the tablecloth in front of her. "I was holding onto information I should have passed on. I was deceiving my superior, Sturmbannfuhrer Netzer. I began to ask myself, why? In the end one answer kept coming back no matter how hard I tried to push it away. Robert. I was doing it for Robert. I wanted you to win. I wanted you to succeed. Against all of my training and beliefs I wanted your mission... our mission to succeed. I believe in you. I..." she choked and reached to wipe away a tear with a gesture of annoyance, "...love you."

Lily glanced up into Robert's face. She had no way of knowing if the look confronting her was of pity, love, contempt or hatred. The bruising and distortion caused by Netzer did not help. She put her face in her hands and let her tears flow.

Robert in fact was experiencing all of those emotions in turn. He got up and walked about the room. His agent's brain was weighing up his options based upon his current knowledge. If Lily was not lying she was one of the century's great actresses. Lying or not, the present state of play meant that he needed to behave as if he believed her if he was to carry on with his mission. He was no longer working to a prepared plan. He was being opportunistic. Keep moving forward. Take each opportunity as it comes. If it goes wrong it does not matter. He has little else to live for once this mission is completed. But all his training told him that an agent with nothing to lose was inevitably a bad agent. Turning away from the window to face Lily he said, "You don't love me; no more than I love you."

"Why not?" Lily demanded, more sharply than she had intended.

"Because people like you and me can't be loved. As far as love goes we are like radio receivers that have been switched off."

Lily lowered her voice but replied with firm assertiveness, "That's just an expression of self pity. If I say, 'I love you,' I love you!"

He moved around the table to her side and pulled her out of her chair into his arms. He held her tight, his hands around the back of her head.

"Okay, I believe you," he whispered.

Lily sobbed onto his chest as she held onto his back like a forgiven child. When she had finished crying she looked up into his face and whispered, "I know you don't, but one day you will!"

Fifty

Haupsturmfuhrer Schirach had gone beyond the sense of relief that always overtook him when his Sturmbannfuhrer – one Alois Netzer – was away from the office. He had now reached the stage where he was beginning to wonder where he could be. The beloved Sturmbannfuhrer was a law unto himself and in many ways he was a loose cannon. But that is what the state had decreed the SS must be. Hitler's merest opinion was a manifestation of the German will. The courts had stated as much. The SS and the Gestapo operated on behalf of that will. They stood outside the jurisdiction of the law and the courts. Sturmbannfuhrer Netzer always took his freedom to act for granted. However, although Schirach had his reservations about Netzer and his methods of operating he was nonetheless loyal to his superior officer. Netzer's absence from duty had stretched to the point where Schirach began to worry. It was not so much his absence as his total disappearance. Schirach usually received communications from Netzer when he took off on one of his projects. But not this time. Schirach had tried his home – a decision he had been reluctant to take knowing how jealously his superior guarded his privacy. However, his wife Marlene said she had not seen him herself. She did not seem unduly concerned but Schirach guessed that she too might experience a sense of relief whenever Netzer went absent.

It was on the morning of Tuesday 13 March 1944 that Schirach was approached at his desk by a Gestapo officer who dealt with denunciations and informants. This particular individual had become disillusioned with his fellow Germans. Ninety percent of the denunciations he dealt with had their roots in family or neighbourly jealousies. However, the information he had just received from a local Block Warden had intrigued him. His curiosity was aroused because the information pertained to a certain Doctor Robert Hermann. This was interesting because the rumour around headquarters was that Sturmbannfuhrer Netzer had tortured the said Doctor to death just before he had gone missing. Although Netzer had deliberately kept Schirach in the dark about this, one of his many projects, Schirach was never completely ignorant of what his blind eye was supposed to ignore. He had seen Netzer in the company of the doctor's wife and he knew that she was collaborating with Netzer in some way.

Having read the brief notes the desk man had taken, Schirach's interest was sufficiently aroused to ask the Gestapo agent to send the Block Warden in to see him. As the warden approached his desk, Schirach decided to stand. It was not a show of respect. Like most Germans he despised these low level party activists. Although useful to him in his duties he considered most of them to be repulsive snoops. He stood to get a better look at this specimen as he approached and to let the Block Warden absorb Schirach's superior physical presence. He stretched to his full six feet three inches and brushed his palm through his thick black hair.

Full of his own importance, the Warden began to address Schirach before he had fully arrived at his desk. Schirach turned aside and flicked at a speck of dust on the upper sleeve of his jacket. The snub silenced the Warden and he removed his hat and stood waiting to be acknowledged. Schirach turned back to face his visitor and noticed now the bald head above the round face. The man's face, chin and neck had all blended into one. This pink oval reminded Schirach of those children at school he had always steered clear of because they could be relied upon to tell tales to the teachers and get others into trouble.

With a movement of his hand Schirach gestured for the man to sit.

"What is your name?" he asked.

In a manner that Schirach could not help but find amusing, his visitor leapt to his feet, raised his right arm in a perfectly executed Nazi salute and virtually screamed, "Block Warden, Herr Lahm, mein Haupsturmfuhrer Schirach!"

Not altogether sure that this spherical character would not denounce him to the front desk, Schirach was obliged to stand and return the salute.

Again Schirach gestured and they both took to their seats.

"Now Block Warden, Herr Lahm. Tell me about this incident you have reported to the desk officer."

"But I have already…"

"Please," interrupted Schirach, "For my sake. Tell it directly to me. I would rather hear a Block Warden's account first hand than get it second hand from a desk officer."

Herr Lahm went over the details. Schirach could see that the man enjoyed his duties. He swelled with importance as he took control of the conversation.

"And this neighbour of Herr and Frau Doctor, is she reliable?"

"Oh extremely reliable mein Haupsturmfuhrer. She has been a loyal party member since 1934."

"Excuse me for doubting you, Block Warden Herr Lahm, but you see I do not think this neighbour can be as reliable as you claim. You see our information is that this doctor…" he picked up the file that had been brought to him… "let me see, ah yes, Dr Robert Hermann…" he put the file down and looked straight into the eyes of Herr Lahm… "is dead!"

Herr Lahm's round oval face and neck flushed a bright red and he shuffled uncomfortably in his seat.

"But, with respect mein Haupsturmfuhrer, that cannot be. I was talking with him myself only yesterday. I must say his face was badly injured. He had obviously experienced some major misfortune, but I can assure you, he is not dead."

"And how do you know the man you spoke to was this Dr Robert Hermann?"

Herr Lahm smiled a self-congratulatory smile, "Mein Haupsturmfuhrer, please. I am a Block Warden. Do you not think I know the residents in my area? Of course it was the doctor. I have known him since he moved there."

Despite himself Schirach was interested.

"All right, Herr Block Warden. You will have to indulge me and tell it all to me just one more time. I have to be quite certain in my own mind what you are telling me."

Herr Lam's instinctive reluctance melted under Schirach's fierce glare.

"You are an important source for me on this issue," said Schirach in a mildly placatory manner. This appealed to Herr Lahm's vanity and he plunged enthusiastically into his recount.

When Lahm had gone Schirach wrote a short list:

1. Doctor is killed and body disposed of.
2. Neighbour sees strange activity in doctor's garden.
3. Block Warden speaks to 'dead' doctor.
4. 'Dead' doctor has severe facial injuries.
5. Strange activity was doctor burying dead dog.
6. Doctor does not have/has never had a dog.
7. Block Warden obnoxious but reliable.

He read through this list several times but he had known as he was writing it that there were enough contradictions here to warrant further investigation. He looked at his watch. 1:30pm. He began to weigh up many considerations. His first thought was to doubt the Warden despite his reliable record. It was just too unreasonable to think that the doctor had managed to get out of Netzer's clutches. The reality of Netzer's work was one of stunningly brutal efficiency. Secondly, if the doctor had escaped, why had the alarm not gone up? Thirdly, if a dog has been buried in a back garden, who gives two shits?

However, how can a dead doctor talk to a Block Warden? Moreover, if the doctor is not dead and no dog exists, who or what was buried in that garden? He knew he had to follow this up but he still hesitated. To interfere in one of his Sturmbannfuhrer's projects without being invited was asking for serious trouble.

It was as he sat pondering this dilemma that a desk officer came through and handed an arrest document to him.

"What's this?" he asked.

"A report has come in through Gestapo denunciations from Geretsried."

"What the hell do they want? It's over twenty-five kilometres away. They've got their own people down there haven't they?"

"Well yes, but there are complications. I think they're hoping you will take over the case, but if not they need your advice."

"What complications?"

"The Gestapo group down there have received information that a local family is sheltering two Jewish children. These children should have been transported along with their parents, the allegation goes, but this family has saved them from the camps and is claiming they are cousins from Hamburg whose parents were killed in a bombing raid. The denouncer claims to know these children because her husband worked with their father when they were both junior clerks in a solicitor's office until 1933. She and her husband ceased their acquaintance with the Jewish couple when they realised the folly of such a relationship, thanks to the spiritual guidance of the Fuhrer."

Schirach was becoming impatient with this saga and interrupted the desk officer.

"If they broke off relations with these Jews as long ago as 1933 how can they possibly know their children? How old are the children?"

"Nine and ten, Hauptsturmfuhrer."

"Well, for heaven's sake, they weren't even born then."

"My Gestapo colleague in Geretsried suggests that the informant is manipulating the facts to protect herself and her husband. His best guess is that these two couples have in fact remained close friends, particularly the two men. He has no doubt that the woman knows the children very well."

"Well then," snapped Schirach, "Why is she coming forward now?"

"Well, if I may say so Hauptsturmfuhrer…"

But Schirach raised his hand to silence his colleague. He knew what was coming. The woman had succumbed to the anxiety that must have haunted her every breath. To know about an illicit harbouring of Jews and not to speak out was equivalent to conspiring against the state. She had cracked.

"But you are not explaining why the Geretsried officers cannot deal with it. You said there was a complication…"

"Yes, indeed, Hauptsturmfuhrer. The family allegedly sheltering the Jewish children is the family of a Wermacht officer. Oberleutnant Bleibtreu. Oberleutnant Bleibtreu is currently on active service in Greece with his Panzer division."

"Okay, leave it with me," Schirach concluded, taking the file from the desk officer. 'It's not such a bad assignment,' he was thinking. 'It postpones for a few hours the need to decide what to do about the Netzer situation.'

Fifty-one

As his driver and partner in this investigation, Untersturmfuhrer Sepp Dortmuller, took them south along Princeregentenstrasse, across the River Isar, Schirach decided to put the Netzer situation to his partner.

"Netzer is a law unto himself, Tomas," replied Dortmuller when Schirach had completed his recount. "He could be anywhere. He has a mistress in Dachau and another in Penzberg. He often allows himself some recuperation time on completion of a difficult case. One, shall we say, where he develops his skills to the ultimate level."

Schirach's mouth twisted in an ironic grin. He was not surprised that Netzer's private affairs were so well known amongst the lower ranks. He was mildly surprised that Dortmuller was so open about his knowledge. Maybe it was the state of the war. There was a growing feeling that the tide was turning against them. The glorious victories of '39 and '40, the stunning brutality of the blitzkrieg, were long behind them now. Victories were coming at greater and greater cost and were thinner on the ground. Such thoughts were, of course treason, but everyone secretly shared them. Maybe the realisation that the Thousand Year Reich might be about to crumble after barely eleven years had opened minds to a more sceptical view.

"You know he won't thank you for interfering, whatever you do," concluded Dortmuller.

Schirach was not unhappy. It was the advice he had been hoping to receive. Now he could push it out of his mind and concentrate on the business in hand.

The river Isar was high and fast flowing on its way to the mighty Danube. The melting snows were sourcing it with its annual surge. Schirach wound down his window and smelt the freshness of the water on the air for a few minutes. It was a relief to get out of the city and to ride along beside the free-flowing water.

"Are you too hot Hauptsturmfuhrer?" asked Dortmuller in a mock formal manner.

"No, Sepp," Schirach replied apologetically. "I just felt the need for a taste of fresh air. It's been a long time."

They drove the rest of the way in silence. Dortmuller chain smoked all the way. It was a habit Schrach had never acquired but he was content to inhale the wisps of blue smoke that came his way. Arriving in Geretsried just before 1400hrs they headed straight for Gestapo headquarters. The local unit had commandeered the Catholic parish priest's presbytery because it was the best house in the locality. Crunching to a halt at the top of the drive,

Schirach and Dortmuller alighted from their vehicle and took in their surroundings. Even just this little way south of the city the view of the mountains was spectacularly improved. They seemed unmoved by the war. Their indifference seemed a source of optimism to Schirach.

After a short briefing from the head of the unit, Schirach and Dortmuller headed east out of the village towards the family farmhouse of Oberleutnant Bleibtreu. They were both aware of the level of distaste current at Geretsried HQ towards them. Evidently this Oberleutnant Bleibtreu was a highly respected member of the village community and a hero of the Wehrmacht to boot. He had been awarded the Iron Cross during the invasion of France. No one was keen to support the two big city SS men in their task. The Gestapo unit head had made it obvious that all of the opprobrium was directed against the denouncers. Schirach did not rate their chances of remaining outside the camp system very highly.

The farmhouse was in fact an expansive country house and the approach, through an avenue of birch trees, signified a certain grandeur. As they drew to a halt outside the front door two dark haired children ran across the lawn to meet them. They were half attracted to the newly arrived car but half still engrossed in their game of tag. They continued their game around the car and in and out of Schirach and Dortmuller until the house door opened and an attractive woman in her late thirties stepped out. She was dressed in a yellow woollen cardigan and a green, flared skirt. She wore high heels, though her legs were bare. She was obviously not dressed for cleaning or cooking and the visitors were given the impression of a woman comfortable enough to have domestic help.

"Children!" she called. "Stop that and come inside at once."

Schirach studied her face. There was just enough embarrassment, or was it anxiety, there to suggest that the allegations against her would hold water. However, once having ushered the children inside she stepped confidently out to meet her visitors.

"Good morning, gentlemen. To what do I owe the honour of a visit from the SS? My husband is not here at the moment if you are hoping to see him."

Schirach stood to attention, clicked his heels and formally presented himself to Frau Oberleutnant Bleibtreu.

"We may be seeking to interview your husband shortly, but for the moment I am sure you can provide us with the help we are seeking. I wonder – can we go inside?"

"Of course! Forgive me my poor manners."

She pushed open the door and preceded them into the house. Before following, Schirach delayed Dortmuller and asked, "What do you think?"

"Guilty as charged," he replied under his breath.

"Why?"

"Did you see the colour of their hair?" asked Dortmuller in response. "Black! A complete giveaway."

"Sepp, your hair is black. Just like theirs."

"No, not just like theirs. Theirs is Jewish black, mine is German black!"

Both men laughed as they entered the house.

It had taken Schirach less than an hour to break the children. They had a well-rehearsed story but his experience in interrogations had soon found the cracks in it. Dortmuller had used the field telephone in their car to order a vehicle to come to deliver them to Dachau as the first stage of their confinement. Meanwhile Schirach was completing his interrogation of Frau Bleibtreu.

"What I can't understand is why. You have everything. Land, wealth, your husband is a loyal member of the Wehrmacht. It doesn't make sense."

Frau Bleibtreu spoke calmly when she replied, "You are quite right, Haupsturmfuhrer. It doesn't make sense. It makes no sense at all. But then I might ask you why you are a Nazi. And your answer might not make sense to me."

Schirach had no answer. He simply raised his arm and gestured her towards the car where Dortmuller was waiting.

"I want to see the children," she demanded.

But her response had disturbed Schirach and he petulantly refused. He took her by the arm and dragged her forcibly to the car. From the room where he had locked them, the children could be heard calling.

"Please. In the name of all that's good and holy. Please let me see them!"

But he was deaf to her plea.

On the way back to the city the rain began to fall. The river was grey and in full flow. Schirach had no desire to open his window and breathe the air this time. Dortmuller's smoke filled the car. Both men were silent. Schirach began to think about the Netzer case again.

Back at his desk, Schirach telephoned Berlin to inform them of his actions and to recommend the arrest of Oberleutnant Bleibtrue as soon as hostilities in Greece allowed.

Fifty-two

Lily and Robert sat side by side halfway down the right side of the convent chapel. Friedrich sat at the back on the left. He was still in uniform and he carried the Mauser that Lily had given to him. She had introduced him as SS Standartenfuhrer Schmidt and explained that he had been assigned to them to ensure their safe conduct across the city. Mother Superior accepted the explanation without question and with less interest. Her mind was entirely preoccupied.

The congregation sensed an unusual expectancy and there was more than the usual amount of whispering. Even from behind Robert could determine the delight on Mother Superior's shoulders and he did not begrudge her. 'Enjoy it while you can,' he thought. 'After tonight you are going to be infamously linked with the source of your joy for all time.'

A sudden hush descended and, on an invisible signal, the congregation rose. Robert was anticipating looking for the changes in the slight figure he expected to emerge from the sacristy. The figure he had encountered once before in Berlin when the future Pontiff had met the future Fuhrer. But his search for the Pope as he emerged into the chapel to lead Benediction was abruptly curtailed when his eyes fell upon O'Shea. O'Shea? Surely not? How could it be?

Even in those flamboyant embossed and embroidered robes there was no mistaking him. Each gesture, each movement, each turn of the head and tilt of the shoulder was scorched into his brain like a brand. He felt himself succumb to an involuntary flinch that jerked his whole body. For an instant he thought he was going to rush the altar. Lily looked at him, concerned. She took his arm and held it tightly. He felt his knees go weak and his mouth filled with saliva. He pulled away from Lily's grip and slumped to the pew. He sat with his elbows on his knees and put his hands together as if in prayer.

Meanwhile the Benediction had begun. Scents of incense and sounds of bells. Call and response in the deep growl of a Catholic congregation. Echoes in the beams of the chapel roof. The gleaming Monstrance held aloft. Held aloft in the Papal hands. The pale, thin, Papal face below the Host. The Host that will become the living, breathing Jesus whenever the Pope and all his priests on Earth perform the miracle of the Mass.

Even for Robert, who was struggling for sanity, the service ended in an instant. The Pope and his entourage were exiting into the sacristy.

Outside the chapel the congregation gathered in the cold night air striving to extend the event, unwilling to admit it was over and time to go home. Robert heard similar comments being shared within the several groups that clustered from the wind in the shelter of the chapel wall.

"God bless him. He sounds so gentle. He hardly looks strong enough to lift the Monstrance. God gives him strength. Such a soft voice. A saintly presence."

Mother nodded at the various groups as she moved towards the convent entrance. As she passed Robert and Lily she stopped.

"So pleased you are here. You will come in of course."

Before they could reply, the wind blew the boughs of a tree exposing Robert's face to the light of the moon.

"Sweet Mother of God. What has happened to you Robert? I would not have recognised you but for Lily. Your face has been..." But she stopped herself.

Robert pulled the brim of his hat lower over his face. He managed a smile, "I got too close to an unexploded bomb whilst treating a trapped child," he effortlessly lied.

"God bless you!" she said. "Follow me in."

They waited in the nun's common room. There were Lily and Robert. Friedrich was there, introduced by Lily, when necessary, as an SS Orpo assigned to them. Fraulein Todt was there, stricken and bereaved since the disappearance of her husband. An elderly, round-backed man in a black suit stood around smoking and looking bored. Doctor Galeazzi-Lisi, Robert correctly guessed. There were no members of the local Church hierarchy present. To invite one would have necessitated inviting all of them in order of seniority. The Pope needed these visits to be low key. He was here to refresh himself. He would ride every day in the grounds of the convent and he would have no formal engagements. Two senior nuns handed around glasses of water. The main body of nuns was excluded from this informal gathering. The Pope was in the chambers allocated to him being ministered to by members of his entourage and refreshing himself before going to meet the faithful.

When he was sufficiently refreshed Pope Pius XII, the man Sean Colquhoun first met as Cardinal Eugenio Pacelli, left his chambers and went to the office of Mother Superior. He was accompanied by Sister Pasqualina, two blue bereted and doubleted Swiss Guards and Monsignor O'Shea.

Mother rose from her seat as he entered her sanctum and got down onto her knees at his feet. She kissed the ring on his hand and he beckoned her to rise.

O'Shea paid close attention as Mother ran through the names of those in the small party waiting to meet the Pontiff. The Pope himself appeared uninterested. When Mother had related the full list he glanced at O'Shea. O'Shea could find nothing to object to and so Mother walked along to the common room and invited the group to her office.

They moved along the dimly lit corridor like a group of schoolchildren sent to see the Head. Doctor Galeazzi-Lisi went directly in, but the rest of them waited at the door to be announced by Mother. The two senior nuns were first to enter the presence. Robert almost envied them the sense of fulfilment they were obviously feeling. After Fraulein Todt, it was Robert's turn. Mother spoke to him before announcing him.

"Look carefully at the blessed man. Cast your doctor's eye over him. See what you can determine. I am going to ask him to let you examine him."

Robert smiled down into Mother's face. He could hardly believe what an ally she had become. When he entered, Mother accompanied him across the floor of the office right up to the Papal presence.

"Holy Father, this is Doctor Robert Hermann. He is a hero of the Munich bombing raids. You can see from his injuries that he risks his life doing God's work, ministering to the sick and wounded. He has become a valued friend to the Convent and a faithful parishioner."

At the sound of the word 'doctor' Galeazzi-Lisi had cocked an ear but just as quickly lost interest. O'Shea hardly glanced in the Doctor's direction. He failed to recognise Sean Colquhoun. Robert kept his head bent in deference to the Holy Father and away from O'Shea's gaze. Robert kept his eyes firmly fixed on the hem of the Pope's robe. He knelt, took the Papal hand and kissed the ring.

"Our beloved Mother Superior speaks very highly of you," the Pope said in fluent German.

"She is too kind, Holy Father," he replied in his deepest German voice.

"No, you must not be modest. Your work is furthering God's purpose. You are helping to maintain hope and order at home whilst the Wermacht struggles to defeat the Soviet atheists. Your own small contribution could well aid the return of Russia to the Christian fold. This is the fervent wish of Mary, the Mother of Our Lord Jesus."

Throughout this brief exchange the Pope hiccupped continuously and Robert could not mistake the stale, pungent odour on his breath. Robert became aware of the fierce stare he was being subjected to from Sister Pasqualina. She scrutinised his every facial movement. She was obviously repelled by his injuries. At least that's how it felt to Robert. He managed not to flinch or blush under the examination.

"Thank you, Holy Father. I am pleased to do whatever I can."

Robert got to his feet and moved to the back of the room well away from O'Shea.

As Lily was presented to the Pope, Robert moved silently around the perimeter of the room until he was standing beside Mother Superior.

"You are right to be worried about the Holy Father," he whispered.

Mother turned her head and cocked an invisible ear to listen.

"My guess is he is being treated for a stomach or bowel complaint with chromic acid. I've been reading up on it since you told me about his medical problems. It is a brutal form of medication probably doing more harm than good. It is used by dentists as an antidote to chronic gum disease. It is probably causing all of his digestive problems."

Mother turned fully to look at Robert. Her expression was one of deep gratitude and an ironic satisfaction in being vindicated in her suspicions of the Papal physician.

"If you can arrange for me to conduct a private examination of the Pope, I might be able to effect a more accurate diagnosis."

"I'll do what I can."

If the select audience had been expecting any further intercourse with the Pope and his entourage, they were to be mistaken. Sister Pasqualina summoned Mother Superior to her side and with a few brief snapped phrases informed her that the Pope would now be retiring to his quarters. He was tired from his journey and as the Mother was only too well aware, he was a martyr to bad health. The Pope walked from the room with Sister Pasqualina, Father O'Shea and Doctor Galeazzi-Lisi following in his wake. The two Swiss Guards outside the door snapped to attention as he emerged and followed him to his quarters.

Robert walked to the door of the office and observed their progress. They turned left at the chapel entrance, along the dimly-lit, blacked out corridor. Halfway along the Pope stopped at the foot of a set of stairs. He turned and with a swift movement of his right hand, blessed his followers.

"You will leave me now," he said in Italian. "Take your rest. Monsignor O'Shea. You will wake me at 5:30."

O'Shea had barely time to reply before the Pope had taken to the stairs.

"Good doctor," he said to Galeazzi-Lisi, "you will accompany me."

Galeazzi-Lisi shouldered his way through the group and took to the stairs in pursuit of his patient. Robert went back inside the office and going first to Lily he whispered, "Prepare the drinks." She nodded and left the office. Robert then went to Mother. "Mother," he insisted. "We must decide how we are going to get the Holy Father to let me see him."

"You are right but I do not see…"

"I have an idea," Robert interrupted. "Doctor Galeazzi-Lisi will be finished administering to the Pope in a few minutes. You must tell the Swiss Guards that there is a meal waiting for them in a nearby room. Whilst they are eating I will enter the Pope's room and carry out an examination. Now Mother, as soon as Doctor Galeazzi-Lisi comes out, invite him to your office and keep him occupied for ten minutes or so."

Mother looked worried.

"Are you sure, Robert? It feels like deception."

"With the very best of motives, Mother. I might be able to help the Holy Father. If not, we have done no harm."

Robert gave her his most reassuring smile. She nodded.

"You are right. I will take the guards into the ante room beside the Holy Father's quarters and we will feed them there."

"Don't worry about the food, Mother. Lily is taking care of that."

Somewhat taken aback by this comment, Mother hesitated momentarily.

"The guards, Mother," Robert reminded her and she set off along the corridor to climb the staircase to the Pope's quarters.

When Mother Superior explained to the guards that they would be as close to the Pope in the ante room as they would be standing at his door, they overcame their reluctance and went with her to be fed. Mother left them there to wait for Doctor Galeazzi-Lisi to complete his ministrations to the Pontiff. The Swiss Guards relaxed in the ante room, one of them taking a look along the landing at the entrance to the Pope's room every thirty seconds or so. Within five minutes Lily entered with a tray of food and drink.

"Here we are at last," she said as she pushed her way in. She placed the tray on the table and started to lay out the food. There was black bread, French cheese, tinned pears and tinned milk. Black chicory steamed in the two enamel mugs she placed at the elbow of each guard. Both men went for the drink first, each pouring a generous portion of thick tinned milk into his mug before adding the hot liquid chicory. Neither man had time to taste more than a first mouthful of the French cheese before succumbing to the powerful drug Lily had mixed with the chicory.

So far so good.

Lily went to the door of the ante room, opened it a crack and peered out. After a few long minutes Doctor Galeazzi-Lisi emerged from the Pope's room and Mother immediately intercepted him. Galeazzi-Lisi wore his usual bored expression. He was mildly interested by Mother's suggestion that he must be very tired and probably in need of a brandy before retiring. He nodded agreement and followed Mother back to her office. As they passed along they did not notice Robert moving out of the shadow of the chapel door to wait at the foot of the stairs.

Lily ran silently along the landing to the top of the staircase. She gestured down the stairwell to Robert. She then went back in and sat with the guards. If anyone came along she would find some way of distracting them and preventing them from entering. Robert mounted the stairs three at a time. He tapped his breast to check his inside pocket. The bulge beneath his palm told him that his emergency pack was there. His hand remembered the shape of the syringe and the phial of diacetylmorphine contained within. On reaching the top of the stairs he began the short walk to the Pope's chambers. A wave of euphoria swept through him. With a sense of disbelief he realised that he was moments away from accomplishing his mission. It would be his last mission, he knew that. The man who killed the Pope would not be employable hereafter. So, here he was, moments from the culmination of his active career. As that thought hit he reached the Pope's door. He did not knock. His hand reached out to lift the latch. As his thumb pressed the lever and the latch rose Lily came to the door of the ante room just in time to catch sight of his back as he slipped in.

Fifty-three

Lily remained at the door of the ante-room. Half in, half out. A grunt from one of the sleeping guards startled her. She went over to them and checked that they were still unconscious before going back to the door. Seconds passed. Where was Robert? Had he finished and come out while she was checking the guards? How could he be taking this long? The deep silence and gloom of the corridor intensified each moment, lengthening them to infinite proportions.

Suddenly, as if no time at all had passed, there he was stepping out into the corridor, placing his trilby onto his head. She closed the ante-room door and ran to him. He turned to receive her into his arms. He answered the unspoken question.

"It is done!" he said. "We must go!"

But as they turned to walk the length of the corridor a voice called out to them.

"What is done?" it said. In the hollow emptiness the voice flew like a dart. They turned instinctively, both incapable of disguising the startled guilt etched on their faces.

They heard footsteps as the figure stepped out of the shadows towards them. A black clad figure emerged. Robert stared into the gloom desperately trying to decipher the features on the approaching face. Too late, he realised that in his determination to know who was approaching them, he had allowed the stranger a too-clear look at his own face.

"Oh my God," the voice suddenly said in English. "I know you!"

'O'Shea,' thought Robert. With the speed of a serpent he darted across the floor towards the priest. With fear rising to a crescendo in his voice O'Shea screamed, "What have you done? Why were you in the Pope's room?"

Robert became aware on a secondary level that doors were opening along the corridor. Sister Pasquelina emerged from her room just as Robert's fist smashed into O'Shea's face, knocking him to the ground. Robert had made an unconscious decision that this was the opportunity he had dreamed of. O'Shea at his mercy! He would now kill him with his bare hands.

More doors opening! Mother's voice calling out! Sleepy faced nuns appearing from their cells. His fist smashing again into O'Shea's face! Blood spurting from his nose and lips like juice from a tomato. Screams and shouts and Lily's hands tugging at him - pulling him away. But she is not strong enough. Nothing will stop him now. O'Shea is going to die.

Suddenly he is spun around and pushed against the wall. He pushes himself upwards to find himself face to face with Friedrich. Friedrich the SS man.

"Enough!" yelled Friedrich.

Lily took her opportunity at that moment. As Friedrich turned to look at O'Shea. Lily rushed forward, grabbed Robert's arm and dragged him away.

"What is happening?" screamed Mother.

"Stop them," shouted Galeazzi-Lisi. "Don't let them get away. Call the police."

Before anyone could formulate a coherent thought to precede action, O'Shea let out a hoarse cry.

"The Holy Father. Check the Pope."

A number of nuns clasped palms to their mouths. Mother stumbled and had to be caught by Friedrich. Galeazzi-Lisi knew that he had to be the one to act. He entered the Pope's chambers, immediately followed by Sister Pasqualina. Soon morbid screams could be heard coming from within.

"Mother of God, what is happening here? We will be cursed for all eternity," Mother sobbed. And then, suddenly remembering Robert and Lily she shouted, "They're getting away. Stop them! In the name of Jesus, stop them!"

At this point Fraulein Todt came along the landing. "What's happening? Why were Robert and Lily running down the stairs?"

Friedrich took hold of her, "Which way did they go?"

"They were heading for the entrance but when they saw me Lily pulled Robert away towards the cellar."

"Mother," said Friedrich. "You must help me. I have to apprehend those two assassins."

Mother turned to Fraulein Todt, "Which cellar did they enter?"

"The south cellar, just beyond the central hall."

Mother turned to Friedrich, "But they can't get out of there. That witch Lily thinks it will be open as it usually is. But tonight it is locked. With His Holiness here we took no chances."

Friedrich pulled the Mauser from its holster. "If the cellar is locked we have them trapped like rats. Quick, come with me to lock the door they entered. Then I must use your phone and summon assistance."

Friedrich was navigating his way through the scenario he had rehearsed with Robert and Lily many times during their preparations for tonight. It was a strategy designed to give them maximum escape time.

Mother's eyes glistened and her nose started to run. The distraction in her face was painful to observe.

"Mother," urged Friedrich. I must apprehend them. Come with me. The rest of you wait here. My colleagues will be here shortly."

Friedrich took Mother by the elbow and instructed her to lead him to the entrance to the cellar. She retrieved a key from beneath her tunic and handed it to Friedrich. He inserted it into the lock and turned it. The culprits were trapped. When he had done so Friedrich slipped the key into his own pocket.

"Now, quickly, let's go to your office."

They hurried along the corridor to Mother's office and once inside Friedrich went to the telephone. Before dialling he said, "Get me the key for the outer door to the cellar."

"But why would you wa…?" Mother began but Friedrich interrupted her.

"Don't waste time!" he snapped.

Mother responded obediently to his authoritative manner. She slid open a drawer in her desk and handed a brass key to Friedrich. Friedrich dialled a spurious number and then spoke whilst keeping his hand upon the telephone cradle. He spoke briefly giving the details of the situation and finished by adding, "Be quick. I am going to confront them now."

He turned to Mother and said, "Stay here in your office and wait for me."

She watched him go. Her restlessness and sorrow would not let her sit. She paced backwards and forwards rubbing her hands in anxiety.

Friedrich reached the cellar door and opened it. Stepping inside, he carefully closed and locked the door behind him. Beginning his descent he called out, "It's me, Friedrich. Where are you?"

A light came on and Lily and Robert appeared before him. This part of the plan had been agreed upon to allow them a head start before the hue and cry after them began in earnest. They would enter the cellar where Friedrich would apprehend them and shoot them dead. Friedrich would then placate the others by informing them that the culprits were dead and that he would deal with the bodies whilst they waited for the Police SS, who were not coming. Telling Mother that he was removing the bodies they would make their escape. However, the cellar door was not supposed to be locked. It had caused a complication, but he seemed to have overcome it.

"Mother took the precaution of locking your escape route to improve security for the Pope," Friedrich explained.

"Where is the key kept?" asked Robert.

"I have it."

"Well done, Friedrich," said Lily. "Let's get out of here."

"Okay," said Friedrich with finality. He walked past them to the outer door and unlocked it. He looked outside and saw the steps leading up to the garden. He went back in, closing the door behind him. He lifted his Mauser and pointed it at Lily and Robert. Just before he squeezed the trigger he said, "I'll be back in a minute. Wait by the door. Now put your fingers in your ears." He pulled the trigger twice. The noise was a physical blow on the chest. At the top of the stairs when he re-emerged into the corridor, Doctor Galeazzi-Lisi was there.

"Where are those useless Swiss Guards?" asked Friedrich.

"They have been drugged," the doctor replied. "What has happened down there?"

"The criminals are dead," Friedrich replied. "Resisting arrest. Go and tell Mother that the assassins are dead and I am removing the bodies to the outside. Have the police van come to the back to collect them. Tell her my instructions are for everyone to stay in their rooms and to wait for my colleagues to arrive. Anyone disobeying my instruction could be accused of obstructing the SS in the execution of their duties. You go and work on those Guards. Wake them up whatever it takes."

"When I left Mother she was on the phone to the Police. She sounded angry. They said there had been no earlier report from here about the assassination," said Galeazzi-Lisi.

Friedrich swallowed before replying, "Useless incompetents! What can you expect from the imbeciles we are left to work with when every good man is doing his duty on the Russian front?"

As soon as Galeazzi-Lisi was out of sight on his way back to Mother's office Friedrich opened the cellar door and entered. Taking the cellar stairs three at a time, calling, "It's me!" as he went, he bounded across the cellar floor to the rear door. Robert and Lily were at his side.

"We do not have long," he whispered. "Mother took it upon herself to call the SS."

The moon shone brightly in a star-filled sky, illuminating the convent grounds. The air-raid sirens started to whine as Lily said, "This way!"

"No!" ordered Friedrich in contradiction. "You follow me. I know every back lane in Munich."

They ran across the grounds towards the gardener's shed. As they skirted the greenhouse, which stood adjacent to the shed, they were startled by a movement in the shadows and a voice cutting into the night.

"Over here," it called hoarsely.

The three fugitives halted and froze. Friedrich reached for his gun.

"There is no need for that, comrade," the voice continued.

Before their eyes Herr Todt stepped out of the shadows. Robert stepped forward and put a hand on his shoulder.

"What are you doing here?" he asked. "I told you to leave Munich. I expected you to be well on your way to Switzerland by now."

"I couldn't do it. I set off but it felt wrong. I felt if you could risk your life then I could do the same. I also did not realise I would be unable to leave my wife behind. I had allowed myself to believe that she was a stupid woman because she had swallowed the Nazi lies. But I realised that made her no more stupid than sixty million others. Her allegiance to the Nazis would not save her from their retribution for my treachery. I discovered I wanted to be with her. So here I am."

Fifty-four

Schirach stood with Dortmuller in the fine drizzle that was descending onto the garden of the surgery of Doctor and Frau Hermann. Two labourers had just finished digging out the mound at the bottom of the garden. They were not happy about having to work outside whilst English bombers flew high overhead unloading bombs, even if they were concentrating their drop several miles away over the industrial sector. BMW and Seimens were taking a pounding tonight.

There was no dog corpse in the shallow grave. But they had just exhumed a human male corpse. The facial disfigurement was horrendous but it had not been insufficient to hide Netzer's identity from Schirach. As fellow SS men they had often trained at the gymnasium together. A wart on the left hand side of his torso, just below the rib cage, was a distinguishing feature that Schirach was familiar with. The shock of finding the indestructible Netzer like this was affecting both Schirach and Dortmund. One of the world's constants had been removed. The world had become a shakier place. With a rush of guilt Schirach knew that his postponement of decision-making regarding this case was over. He needed to get into top gear immediately. His problem was that Netzer had kept him completely in the dark about his Doctor and Frau Hermann project. Besides, as far as he was aware, not only was Frau Hermann working with Netzer on this project, but she was also his lover.

Schirach was in the process of deciding that his starting point would have to be Netzer's files, to which he would now have unfettered access until a replacement for Netzer was appointed and, following that, a thorough search of the surgery and home of the doctor and his wife. His thinking was interrupted by Dortmuller who called from their car where he was speaking on the field telephone.

"Haupsturmfuhrer!" Dortmuller's tone could not disguise the urgency in his voice.

"What is it?" called Schirach as he began to run towards the car.

Dortmuller dropped the telephone into its cradle and began to run to meet Schirach. The men came together and Dortmuller gave Schirach a message that made his stomach turn.

"It's the convent. The Sisters of Perpetual Succour. They've called in an emergency. According to reports the Pope has been assassinated. They've named Doctor and Frau Robert Hermann as the culprits. Both suspects are reported dead."

Feeling a sickness swell up in him, all Schirach could scream was, "Everybody mobile! Follow me!"

Three black Daimlers screeched away from the surgery and headed for the eastern outskirts of the city.

Todt turned and headed down the path towards the fence at the southern end of the grounds.

"Come on," he said. "I have a car waiting. I will drive you to the Hauptbahnhof. After that you are on your own and I shall return for my wife."

They headed off into the night. Herr Todt drove without headlights. They were passing through a wooded area which lay between the convent grounds and the residential area, which marked the outskirts of suburban Munich. Ahead of them searchlights sliced across the skies and a burst of anti-aircraft fire painted a bloody light upon the night, throwing the Munich skyline into a macabre silhouette.

With a sudden swerve, Herr Todt pulled the car off the road into an opening between the trees. A blaze of headlights ate up the road they had just exited as three SS cars screeched towards the convent.

"You were successful?" was all Herr Todt asked.

"We were successful," replied Robert.

As the car made its way through the outskirts of Munich Herr Todt said, "Under the passenger seat there is a file. In it you will find paperwork that should assist you in your escape. There are identity papers and passports. There are also documents explaining your reasons for travelling. You will need to look through them and rehearse your new identity in your mind. If you are questioned it will be no good having to read your papers to explain who you are. There is another problem. I was not expecting a third party."

He glanced across at Friedrich who was next to him in the passenger seat, "Our friendly SS man here."

"Don't worry about me, headmaster," said Friedrich. The SS guard who kindly loaned me this uniform also passed over his ID papers."

"That is useful," replied Herr Todt. "But I'm not sure they will see you safely all the way to Spain. You might need to find some other form of ID before you reach your journey's end."

For the rest of the ride to the Hauptbahnhof, Robert and Lily scrutinised the paperwork they had been assigned. If Robert's distinctive facial injuries were known to the SS they were not sure that new papers would help disguise their true identities, but they had no alternative to fall back on. With the added complication of Friedrich's predicament to consider as well, they would surely need to improvise.

"These papers," said Robert, "authorise us to travel to Spain to recruit and train Francoists who wish to become non-combative medics in war zones. What if we choose to get out through Italy? Will our papers allow that?"

· "Certainly not," responded Herr Todt. "Your escape route is over the Pyrenees to Spain. Once there you declare yourself the citizen of neutral Eire. Lily is your wife."

Robert raised his head to look at the section of Herr Todt's face available to him in the rear view mirror. This man knew much more about him than Robert had realised. He wondered just how high up he was in the conspiracy.

"Wrong, Herr Todt. My destination is Rome."

"Rome!" exclaimed Herr Todt. "Why on earth wou…"

"You don't need to know the answer to that. I have unfinished business and it is of a personal nature. However, my two colleagues will be taking the Spanish route."

"I'm going with you!" declared Lily abruptly.

Before Robert could dismiss this suggestion he was anticipated by Friedrich.

"Me too!" was all he said.

Silenced and at a loss for a reply Robert accepted the inevitable.

Ten minutes later they were parked two hundred metres from the entrance to Hauptbahnhof. The doctor, his wife and their SS escort stepped out. Their farewell to Herr Todt was nothing more than a moment's glance. It was not a lack of gratitude; it was a complete incapacity to express the gratitude his actions deserved. War mutes all emotion.

Fifty-five

The chaos caused by the air raid, which had now finished, made entry to the station and then the train itself easier than anticipated. Although they had had to stop the vehicle several streets away from the Hauptbahnhof, there was no one to intercept or question them. They hurried past whole blocks ablaze as fire-fighters struggled to contain the inferno. There was no more than a cursory examination of their papers at the ticket office. Friedrich's uniform carried the most weight. It would be a brave railway employee who would challenge the authority of that uniform. The downside was that there was no guarantee that the train would be leaving Munich at all that night, although the official who informed them of this was quite happy to take their money for the tickets.

As the post-raid silence settled upon the city, Robert, Lily and Friedrich sat aboard the train. They had little to say to one another. The carriage was unheated and their breath was visible whenever they sighed or exchanged a word or two. There was nobody else in their compartment, but a trio of men in large crombie overcoats and identical briefcases had boarded the train further along the platform. The compartment next to theirs was occupied by a family and one other man. Father, mother, two daughters and one son. The other man was perhaps ten years younger than the man and wife. Somewhere in his early to mid twenties, prematurely thinning hair and thick spectacles perched on his nose. Lily could not guess what might be the purpose of their journey to Rome. Or perhaps they were bound for one of the intermediate stops en route.

Robert was awakened from a doze by the sound of a train braking alongside theirs. From the darkness of their compartment he could see the lights of the adjacent train. On board there was a great deal of activity. From the robes worn by the men and women rushing to and fro he knew they were priests and nuns and could make the logical supposition that this was the Pope's train being readied.

Suddenly the echoing silence in the cathedral of the platforms was invaded by the screaming of sirens and the screeching of brakes. The coarse gunning of engines continued to reverberate when the sirens had fallen silent. The convoy of vehicles disgorged its passengers, who jumped into action. Foot soldiers spread out around the station taking up armed defensive positions. The clatter of soldiers' boots rang out accompanied by barked orders.

The looks that passed between Lily, Robert and Friedrich expressed their mutual fear of imminent capture. If they had not been taken so completely by surprise, they might have taken some action, attracting unwanted attention. Fortunately, their inability to move gave them time to realise that they were not the subject of this military manoeuvre. Through the window of their compartment and through the two windows of the adjacent train they could see a stretcher being carried from the back of an ambulance towards a carriage door. The cluster of clergy and military officials shuffling along with the stretcher made clear identification impossible, but in Robert's mind there was no doubt. Here was the body of Pope Pius XII being delivered for transportation back to Rome.

One of the businessmen from further down the train stepped onto the platform and walked along towards a railway guard. As he passed by their compartment Robert noticed the father from the family next door joining him.

"Inquisitive fools," he thought.

An SS officer from the convoy saw them talking with the guard and lighting up cigarettes. He screamed orders at the nearest soldiers and they rushed the group of three, rifles aimed at their heads. Robert, Lily and Friedrich watched from behind their curtains as the three were spread-eagled out on the floor. The officer who had spotted them screamed questions at them. The father lifted his head up to answer and was met with the butt of a soldier's rifle. Their pockets were searched and the officer scrutinised their papers. Taking in the information on the paperwork the officer turned his gaze to the train they had come from.

'Stupid bastards,' thought Robert.

"Quick," he said. "They're going to search the train. Come with me."

He hurried out of the compartment and along the corridor with Lily and Friedrich right on his heels. At the end of the carriage he turned left towards the door facing away from the platform. Tugging at the leather strap he lowered the window. He took a careful look up and down the track to make sure there was no one there before opening the door and jumping down between the trains. He turned and took Lily by the waist, lowering her to the gravel and then assisted Friedrich by offering him a shoulder to lean a hand on. Robert then carefully closed the door.

"Okay," he whispered. "Under here."

They ducked under the belly of the train and squatted uncomfortably in silence. The train above them began resounding with the banging of boots, the slamming of doors and the barking of orders. The young son in the family compartment looked away from the window and said to his mother, "Look mama! There's an SS man going under the train."

His mother put her arm around him and said, "Shush, darling. I'm worried about papa."

The younger man kept his eyes on the book he was reading. Just then the door to their compartment was flung open and her husband was thrown in. His face was already bloodied and beginning to swell around the left eye. The curved imprint of a rifle butt was showing. The young wife leapt up and caught him in her arms. "What has happened to you?" she screamed. But the SS officer who followed her husband in interrupted her.

"I am Untersturmfuhrer Kremer," he said. "Do you have a complaint to make about the state of your husband?"

The woman bowed her head. She knew that to complain about any activities of the SS or the Gestapo was considered an offence against the state. "No mein Untersturmfuhrer. I merely wanted to know how my husband had fallen and hurt his face."

Kremer gave her a knowing look and then demanded her papers and those for the children. As he scrutinised them the little boy tugged at his mother's coat and repeated over and over again, "But it's true. I did. I did see one."

"Please, my darling, shush."

"What is the purpose of your journey? Why is your whole family leaving Germany?"

The woman looked at her husband but he could not speak. "My husband is a linguist. He has been ordered to the Reich embassy in Rome. He works on translating documents. It is quite normal for families to accompany state servants on long-term postings."

"And who is this?" he asked turning to the young man in the corner of the carriage who now had his book face down upon his knee.

"I am also a linguist," the man answered nervously. "Herr Lindow and I are colleagues. We are additions to the embassy staff in Rome."

"Why are you not in the Wermacht?"

With a nervous push of his spectacles and an embarrassed frown he replied, "My eyesight. I failed the medical."

Kremer finished with their papers and handed them back. He turned to leave. At the door he paused and turned back. He looked at the boy and approached him. He was not surprised to see the mother enfold her son protectively in her arms. Suddenly the boy became afraid and hid his head in his mother's chest.

"What did he see?" asked Kremer.

"He said he saw an SS officer outside the train."

Kremer was nonplussed by this response and failed to react for a moment. The boy attempted to lift his head and turn his face towards Kremer. He wanted to tell the man what he had seen. Very firmly but with little display of strength, his mother pulled his face back to her bosom.

"He probably meant you," she ventured.

This seemed to satisfy Kremer and he went out.

Underneath the train Robert was peeping above the edge of the platform. He watched jackboot after jackboot dismount from the carriages and heard them batter away at the double along the platform. When all was clear he turned back to Lily and Friedrich.

"I think it's safe to get back on board. Come on!"

He crept past them into the space between the trains.

"Lily first," he hissed. Lily stooped out and he whispered, "I'll lift you so that you can climb in through the window." She nodded.

He bent down and wrapped his arms around her thighs. He lifted her so that she could easily pull herself through the window and open the door for them.

"Okay Friedrich. Me next. You follow on."

Robert jumped up onto the train using his knees and elbows to lever himself in. He turned and reached down a hand to assist Friedrich. As he did so his eyes were distracted by a movement in the Pope's train. It was a figure in the facing compartment. It was reaching up to place a box onto the overhead rack. In the lit compartment the figure could not see out but looked at its own reflection in the window. Robert found himself looking straight into the face of O'Shea.

Fifty-six

At six the following morning the Pope's train laboured out of the Hauptbahnhof. Two hours later the Munich-Rome international commenced in pursuit. Apart from the arrival of more passengers nothing else had occurred during the long wait.

It was Lily who raised the issue that they needed to resolve quickly. They were speeding south through outer Munich. From the tracks they had a comprehensive view of the city they were leaving. They ran between burnt out buildings, some still alight. They passed through suburbs where whole blocks of domestic accommodation were bombed out. They ran alongside roads choked with refugees heading south, hoping to find safety in the Bavarian countryside or over the border in Austria.

"How are we going to pass the checkpoints?" asked Lily.

The question was so vital to their survival and, at this present moment, so unanswerable, that Friedrich and Robert both grunted in a perverse laugh.

"Well," mused Friedrich. "We all have papers. Yours would be fine if we were going to Spain. As we are bound for Rome they are really not much use. They might fool some unconscientious border guards with the help of my SS authority. But then my authority might not hold out."

"We have papers that allow us to go to Spain," grunted Robert. "We are on a train to Italy. They are useless!"

Nobody spoke as several miles rattled by.

The first scheduled stop was at a small town called Rosenheim. It was still in Germany. Innsbruck was the stop after that inside Austria. There should not be any major problem at the Austrian border because the Anschluss in 1938 had absorbed Austria into the Reich. 'However,' thought Friedrich, 'it would be better to be safe than sorry.' He got up from his seat attracting the immediate attention of Robert and Lily.

"I have an idea," he said. "I will be back soon."

Placing his SS hat upon his head and drawing himself up to his best SS height he went out of the compartment. In the corridor he adjusted his balance to the rocking of the train. He then went the length of the carriage asking all passengers for their papers. In the third compartment he entered he was followed in by a railway official; a ticket inspector.

"Excuse me, mein Herr," the official began. "What is happening here?"

Friedrich bowed to the occupants of the compartment and excused himself. He took the official by the arm and guided him into the corridor. He put his face up close to the official's and spoke with controlled anger through gritted teeth, "How dare you question me in the pursuance of my duties! What are you? An asocial who questions the activities of the state?"

The man was clearly shaken by the reaction he had sparked. He climbed down apologetically and begged forgiveness. As he watched the man, Friedrich was thinking 'so this is what we have reduced manhood to in our era of Aryan superiority.'

"Get a grip of yourself, mein Herr. You were only doing your job. I can inform you that there has been an incident in Munich that could have international repercussions. I have been assigned to this train to monitor the passengers and to ensure cowardly conspirators are not on board. I will be checking the papers of all passengers. Do you have any objections?"

"No mein Herr. I am a loyal follower of the Fuhrer. I have been a party member since 1933."

'Yes,' thought Friedrich. 'When every coward signed up.'

"Go about your business," he said, "And report anything suspicious to me."

"Certainly, mien Herr, Heil Hitler."

"Heil Hitler!"

Friedrich found what he needed in the compartment right next to his own. When he walked in the occupants gasped. The first to speak was the young son.

"You see mama! I told you I was right. That's him, the one I saw."

"Be quiet, Willy," his mother snapped.

"Papers please," demanded Friedrich.

The mother fumbled with her bag. Her husband was slumped in the corner by the window. His face was as white as a ghost and from the stench in the compartment Friedrich guessed he had been sick.

The papers were handed to Friedrich and he read them carefully. Looking at the parents he guessed their ages were not too different from Robert's and Lily's and so it proved. Their papers would fit.

"Thank you Herr and Frau Lindow. Everything is in order."

He handed everything back to the woman and nodded at her with a faint smile. Turning to the young man he snapped, "Papers!" The young man handed over his papers. Friedrich read them carefully and looked intently into the man's face. In a voice that came out much more high-pitched than the nervous man had intended he said, "They have been checked already."

"Have they!" retorted Friedrich with no hint of a question in his tone.

Friedrich stood outside the compartment. He considered the permutations. There were two men and a woman. Unfortunately the age of the family's male companion was too young. If Friedrich took Herr Lindow's papers and Robert the male companion's, both ages would look wrong. If Robert took Herr Lindow's that would be just about acceptable. But that would leave Friedrich with papers describing him as thirty years younger than he really was. He was probably better off keeping his SS ID for now.

Soon the train began to slow on a long wide curve into Rosenheim. As the station approached Friedrich once again entered the compartment of the family of five. As soon as he entered he saw the look of dread pass over all the faces save that of the young son who knew no better.

"Pardon me once more, mein Herr and mein Frau. But I need you to accompany me. This is merely a formality I assure you."

A desire to protest flickered across the expression of the mother but she immediately curbed it. The husband was still too dazed to make a coherent response.

"Come on children," said the mother with mock cheerfulness. "I'm sure the officer will deal with us courteously and have us back in our compartment in the wink of an eye."

"You will need to bring your papers with you. I have arranged for confirmation of your need for travel to be telegraphed from Rome. It will be confirmed and as you say mein Frau, you will be back in your compartment in the wink of an eye."

"What about Otto?" she asked looking at their young companion.

Friedrich looked at Otto.

"I do not need him," he replied. "This is just a spot check mein Frau. A mere formality."

The mother was re-assured and as soon as the train pulled into Rosenheim the family disembarked with Friedrich. Before disembarking Friedrich beckoned the bemused Otto to him and suggested politely, "I would move as far from this compartment as you can if I were you and make no reference to your former travelling companions."

Otto nodded vigorously, quickly gathered his belongings and, after stealing one guilty glance at Fraulein Lindow, scuttled away down the corridor towards the front of the train.

"If you would be so good as to follow me we will have this matter concluded in minutes."

Friedrich crossed the platform and entered the station house with the family in tow. He beckoned them to a bench and requested that they sit.

"Your papers please!" he instructed.

Frau Lindow reached into her bag and pulled out a brown envelope. Friedrich examined the contents, slid them back into the envelope and slotted them in to the inside pocket of his jacket. He then went to the station office and asked for the station superintendent. The superintendent invited him into the ticket office and from behind the glass they spoke about the family.

"I have suspicions that these people are conspirators. There has been an incident in Munich. News will not have reached you yet. I have played a deception upon them. They think they will be re-boarding the train but I have arranged for the train to leave without them. You will be apologetic when it does so and assure them that it has been a dreadful mistake. Within fifteen minutes colleagues of mine will arrive to take them into custody. These people might be innocent, but I cannot take that chance."

The superintendent nodded, barely able to keep the excitement out of his eyes. "You need have no fear. I will keep them pre-occupied until your colleagues arrive."

"Excellent. You are a credit to the Fatherland, Heil Hitler!"

"Heil Hitler!"

When Friedrich emerged from the superintendent's office and walked out of the station house without looking at or speaking to the family the mother started to call out to him. To ask what was going on; to protest. But some instinct made her bite her tongue. Even when the train jolted forward and began its slow acceleration out of the station she remained stuck to her seat, a kind of dread inevitability descending upon her.

Looking back out of the train Friedrich saw the young boy and girl come to the door of the station office and watch the train leaving. He wondered for a moment if he had deceived a good German or a bad one. He would never know.

Fifty-seven

Untersturmfuhrer Kremer was entering headquarters as Schirach and Dortmuller arrived back from the exhumation of Netzer.

"What the hell are you doing here?" demanded Schirach.

A shocked Kremer replied, "We have carried out our orders Herr Haupsturmfuhrer. We await further instructions."

"Report!" snapped Schirach.

"My instructions were to clear the Hauptbahnhof, verify the facts as reported, check all security issues, such as other departures and effect a speedy departure for the Papal train. We did all this. The Vatican officials claimed diplomatic immunity for the train but I insisted on verifying the facts of the report. I am afraid it is true. The Pope has been assassinated."

"Has the train departed for Italy?"

"Yes, Hauptsturmfuhrer. We ensured its departure."

Schirach visibly relaxed and started to turn away. Then he visibly stiffened and turned back to Kremer.

"Why did you not escort the train?"

"Direct orders from Berlin; from Himmler himself. We were to disassociate from the train as soon as possible. It is obvious the Allied propaganda machine will make the most of the Pope's assassination on German soil. We want as little involvement as possible. Those were Himmler's orders."

Turning to Dortmuller, but in truth asking the question of himself, he muttered, "Is that sensible?"

Unsure if the question was directed at him, Dortmuller merely shrugged.

When Lily awoke it was dark outside the window and the train was making good progress. She had no idea how long she had slept. Opposite her Friedrich was dozing, his head slumped into his folded arms. The train began to decelerate. Robert was at the opposite end of the facing bench. He was gazing into space and delicately fingering the slits where Netzer's chisel had pierced his cheeks. It was not an unwelcome sign. If the wounds were becoming itchy they were healing. Lily smiled to think that Netzer's meticulous care of his instruments of torture had meant that the wounds were so clean and precise that healing had begun very rapidly.

Her gaze was distracted by lights outside the train window. She realised their train was drawing into a station. It was certainly not Innsbruck. The station was just a few buildings either side of the dual tracks with a couple of sidings looping around the backs of the buildings. This was an unscheduled stop. The station nameplate had been removed. Steam billowed around the window as the train shuddered to a halt. Gradually the steam cleared and Robert joined the awakened Friedrich and Lily at the window.

There was minimal activity outside on the platform. As far as they could see there were no passengers waiting to board. A signalman hurried past carrying a lamp towards the front of the train. Friedrich touched Robert's arm. "That's it," he said pointing through an archway between the two buildings on the platform. There, on a siding shone the lights from another train.

"You're right," breathed Robert. "It's our brother train on this journey to oblivion. The Holy Father's cortege."

Robert turned and headed towards the compartment door. Lily reached out and caught the sleeve of his overcoat.

"Where are you going?"

He stopped and gently lifted her hand away from his arm.

"Well," he whispered, "I've been wondering all journey if I would get another chance to complete some unfinished business with that train, and it seems fate has provided me with an ideal opportunity."

"You mean O'Shea, don't you," said Lily accusingly.

"Yes."

"This is why we are compromising our escape travelling to Rome. We should be well on the way to Spain by now. But no, you have us riding to Rome to carry out some personal vendetta of your own."

Robert's face showed the accuracy of Lily's claim.

"You are right, Lily. I shouldn't involve you and Friedrich in this action. You two should make your own plans. I cannot let it end here. I know I am taking ridiculous risks. But for me it is a simple equation. Although this action will probably lead me to my death, the fact is I would rather be dead than live not having carried it out."

Friedrich shrugged his shoulders and re-took his seat. Lily realised that the only person who might lend her support in this confrontation had just opted out. Something manifested itself in her understanding about this man Robert, and her relationship to him. She knew that something structural had collapsed inside him. The other stark fact manifesting inside her was that she did not want to be without him. She would accept him on any terms. So, eventually, she too shrugged and sat down.

As Robert turned to exit the compartment Friedrich said, "Don't you think you should tell us what you intend to do and what, if anything we can do to assist."

"Nothing. Just be here. If I don't get back on board meet me in Rome. Shall we say at the Spanish Steps?" Then he was gone.

As he scurried across the platform space and through the archway, Robert saw the Pope's train start to move off. He guessed that the train they were on had been halted to allow the Papal train priority. He boarded the train through the last door and pulled it to behind him. Already the train was clear of the station. The space at the end of the carriage where he had boarded contained the WC and he slipped inside to contemplate his plan of action. He guessed he would be conspicuous. His fellow travellers on this train would be clerics, nuns and Swiss Guards plus a few known civilians. Even if he had been able to pose as one of these civilians his facial bruising would attract unwanted attention. Just as he was resigned to the fact of taking his chances and moving through the train in search of O'Shea the door handle of the WC was rattled.

"One moment," called Robert in his flawless German.

"I'm sorry," came back an Italian male voice.

Robert cautiously opened the door and stepped out backwards into the corridor. The Italian priest waiting there raised his biretta and said, "Grazia."

However, as the priest was entering the WC he felt a blow to his back and found himself flung against the basin, banging his elbow. For a moment the shock made him believe the train must have jolted, but the large forearm now around his throat immediately relieved him of that misapprehension. The words that he next heard hissing in his ears filled him with fear. In schoolboy Italian, Robert said, "Take off your robes."

The terrified cleric was spun round to face his assailant and he felt a large hand grip his throat like a vice. He undid the buttons on his cassock and let it fall from his shoulders to the floor. Underneath he was wearing woollen long johns and a vest. Robert almost laughed. The sight reminded him of his father.

"Take off your biretta!" he ordered.

The man did as he was instructed, the biretta falling to the floor. Robert then forced the man to turn around and made him look at the floor. He quickly pulled off his overcoat and dressed himself in the cassock. He placed the Biretta onto his head. He turned the man round to face him again and said, "Put the coat on!"

The priest put the coat on.

"Button up!" ordered Robert.

When the coat was buttoned Robert suddenly gripped the man by the throat again. He leaned his face against the priest's and hissed, "Do you want to die or jump?"

Complete incomprehension chased fear across the man's visage.

"Die or jump," repeated Robert, "…from the train."

"Jump," croaked the priest.

"Okay!"

They waited. After several minutes Robert sensed the train was slowing as it encountered an incline. He opened the door and checked the corridor. Still grasping the priest by the throat he dragged him across the corridor to the exit door. Without pausing he flipped open the window, reached out, grabbed the handle and turned it to fling the door open. With no time to react the priest found himself being propelled out into the freezing temperature of the Bavarian night.

Robert calmed his breathing and checked his cassock and biretta. He pulled the ridiculous headwear as low as he reasonably could, bowed his head and stooped his shoulders to disguise the fullness of his height. He pushed himself along the walls of the swaying corridor and headed towards the front of the train.

Each compartment he passed he scanned for any sight of O'Shea. The passengers, all members of the Papal entourage, seemed to be numbed out of their shock by the tedium of travel. In some compartments nuns dozed; in others priests of all ranks smoked up a thick fog. In still others, nuns and priests knelt on the floor in front of their seats and said the rosary. No sign of O'Shea!

It was when he reached the connection between the third and second carriages that Robert guessed he was getting close. Standing at the connecting door was a Swiss Guard. The Guard caught sight of Robert from halfway along the corridor and Robert could not turn around and retreat without attracting unwelcome attention. He continued to move slowly along the corridor towards the Guard, desperately trying to think of an excuse for being there. He was rescued by the contents of the priest's cassock pockets. His hand closed around a packet of cigarettes and as he reached the Guard he pulled them out and offered him one.

"I was hoping you had a light for my cigarette," ventured Robert.

Fortunately he was a German-speaking Swiss and he replied, "No I do not, Father, but if perhaps you can spare one more," he smiled. "My partner through the connection will oblige us both."

Robert gave the Guard another cigarette and he opened the connecting door and stepped through the gap. Robert placed his foot in the doorway to prevent it slamming closed. When the Guard opened the door at the far side of the connection he could see right into the Pope's carriage. It was not like the others. There were no compartments and no corridor. It was kitted out like a state room with carpet, desks and comfortable armchairs. High ranking clergy were standing and sitting in clusters, deep in earnest conversation.

And suddenly there he was. O'Shea! Robert felt his nerves tighten like wire and his mind go red with anger. Then O'Shea moved across the carriage and disappeared from sight. The far door closed and the Guard was standing in front of him again offering him a lighted cigarette. Robert took it and used it to light one for himself. He sucked in the smoke and felt himself go light-headed. As a non-smoker his throat could not handle the onslaught. Fortunately, he managed to control the impulse to cough up his lungs and gathered himself enough to say.

"Will you please pass a message to Monsignor O'Shea. Tell him a group of priests and nuns would like to report to him on the content of an important conversation they have been having about the current situation. We are positioned in the first compartment of the carriage behind this one we are in."

"Certainly, Father. Would you mind if I smoked my cigarette first or is this an urgent message?"

"You smoke your cigarette, Son. We have plenty of time before we get to Rome."

Robert smiled at the Guard and turned away from him. He moved back down the corridor cursing the cigarette and the Guard for asking for time to smoke it. Still, it gave him time to have a think about what he would do when O'Shea came along the corridor into his hands.

Fifty-eight

In the station building at Rosenheim, train superintendent Meuller was beginning to reflect ruefully on the efficiency of the security services. The SS Orpo officer had told him that SS colleagues would be here to check on the Lindow family within fifteen minutes. After twenty minutes he had telephoned Munich SS Orpo Headquarters and asked why they were taking so long. He had found himself in a complex conversation which he only began to understand when he realised they did not know what he was talking about. Eventually he had been asked if the Papal train had passed through Rosenheim. When he had replied in the affirmative things had begun to happen. But that was over twenty-five minutes ago. He thought he had waited long enough but he was too afraid to lock up and go home. It had already been a long day for him. He had put in two shifts because his co-superintendent, Gunther, had cried off sick. Meuller knew that Gunther had tuberculosis and should be fired. So, if he took the money he should do the work. Why damage Meuller's health with over-work?

He was locking up his office when Kremer arrived with his detachment of men. Superintendent Meuller found himself confronting a wild-eyed, unshaven Untersturmfuhrer.

"Where is this family?"

Superintendent Meuller was immediately intimidated and glad to throw the attention of this man away from himself and onto the Lindows. Kremer looked across the station hall at the family sitting there. Already fear and uncertainty had turned their appearance into a family of refugees. The children's clothes were creased and hanging awkwardly from them. The father was white-faced with concussion and had vomit stains on his coat front. The mother was trying to hold the unit together.

Kremer, still angry at the way he had been spoken to by Schirach, leaned towards SS Orpo Heines and said, "What do you think of her?"

"Very nice," replied Heines.

Having worked with Kremer many times before, Heines guessed where this was going and he hoped he was right.

"You remember our training, Heines. We do not exist to investigate crimes against the state after they have occurred. We exist to act to prevent crimes against the state happening in the first place."

Heines nodded, the embryo of a smirk emerging on his face.

"This family could indeed be innocent. But for us to establish that fact could take up valuable time. In the end, if they prove to be guilty, all of that time will have been wasted. Therefore it is in the interests of the state that we assume their guilt."

"Agreed!"

"Very well! Tell Schmidt and Essen to question the father and the children. You bring the mother to this office."

Turning to Superintendent Meuller he barked, "Open up your office and then get out of here."

Frau Lindow was escorted into the office by Heines and courteously guided to a chair in front of the desk. Kremer sat on the front edge of the desk and Frau Lindow had to brush against his legs as she sat down. The only light in the office came from the hall through the windows. Kremer's face was a patchwork of shadows.

"Please take off your coat Frau Lindow," ordered Kremer.

Frau Lindow was surprised and was about to ask why when she thought better of it. She removed her fitted coat and hung it on the back of her chair. She was wearing a shaped, red, woollen cardigan with large red buttons to the neck. Her calf-length skirt was tight and black.

The moment she was seated Kremer fell upon her, pinning her to the chair, his hands like clamps upon her shoulders.

"What do you know about the assassination of the Pope?" he hissed into her face.

His breath evidenced a lifetime of stale ash from his throat.

"The Pope!" she exclaimed in utter disbelief. "Are you mad? I know nothing of any assassination. We are the victims of a theft. Our papers have been stolen."

"I am afraid I have to assume you are lying."

He took her by the arm and lifted her roughly out of the chair.

"Heines. Help me," he ordered and together they ripped her cardigan and skirt from her.

Standing in her underwear and stockings, she crouched in fear. Between them they picked her up and threw her on her onto the table. The back of her head cracked against the telephone and it fell noisily to the floor. Kremer unbuttoned his trousers whilst Heines ripped her knickers from her, burning her thigh with the friction. When Kremer had finished Heines began. When Heines had finished he ordered her to get dressed and went out to join Kremer in the station hall.

As Heines emerged from the office, Schirach and Dortmuller arrived. Schirach glanced past Kremer to where Heines was tucking a shirt tail into his trousers and smiling over conspiratorially at some of the men. Schirach immediately pushed past Kremer and Heines and burst into the office. He switched on the light and saw Frau Lindow crouched down beside the table. She was using her torn knickers to wipe blood away from between her legs. There was also blood in her hair on the back of her head.

Schirach burst out of the office and took hold of Heines. He threw Heines to the floor of the hall and kicked him, between his legs, with all the force he could muster. Heines screamed in agony and fell onto his back. Methodically and with complete control, Schirach took hold of the man's feet and proceeded to stamp repeatedly on his testicles. He did not stop until Heines had lost consciousness. Kremer watched with accelerating alarm but found himself incapable of speech.

Schirach went back to Kremer. He controlled his breathing and then calmly said, "Your men say the boy saw an SS Orpo on the tracks between the trains in the Hauptbahnhof. Have you checked this out?"

Kremer swallowed carefully. Yes, he remembered the little bastard saying something about an Orpo back in Munich.

"Yes, Hauptsturmfuhrer. We checked this at the time but found nothing. However, I followed this up back at Headquarters. I could find no record of an escort being assigned to the scheduled Rome train."

"Damn you Kremer!" screamed Schirach. "You've missed something here. You've possibly let the Pope's assassin slip through your fingers."

Schirach took a breath and composed himself.

"You'd better come good from now on," he added.

Schirach turned and stormed out of the station hall.

"Come on Dortmuller. We have to catch that train."

The men ran out after him. In the relative emptiness of the hall Kremer felt his breathing gradually returning to normal. A voice startled him. It was the Superintendent.

"What is to happen to the family?"

Kremer looked at the man. He wore the armband of the volunteer SS member.

"Get two colleague volunteers, commandeer transport and deliver them to Dachau."

Before the Superintendent could speak he added sharply, "Tonight!"

The superintendent hid his resentment and turned to go. As he did so he caught sight of Heines lying unconscious on the floor, a dark red stain seeping through the crotch of his trousers.

"And what am I to do with him?"

Kremer walked over to where his colleague of three years lay. He looked down upon him for several moments. Then he turned to stare fixedly into the face of the Superintendent and said, "Him too!"

Fifty-nine

The Papal train had not been rolling long since its last stop when Robert could swear it was slowing down again. From where he stood at the end of the carriage he could see O'Shea now emerging from the state room ahead. He looked puzzled and stopped to speak to the Guard to whom Robert had spoken. After a moment or two in conversation, during which the Guard pointed down the carriage towards where Robert stood, out of view, O'Shea began a slow progress along the corridor. The irregular braking of the train caused him to stumble and roll using the walls for support.

The train's deceleration did not please Robert. He had hoped to finish his business here as the train sped through the night. When a train slowed or stopped you could guarantee a certain proportion of passengers would be roused to wander around whether they were alighting or not.

O'Shea stopped and slid open compartment doors as he progressed through the carriage. Each time he received a negative response to his enquiry, 'did someone want me?' he inched closer to his appointment with destiny. As he reached the last compartment in the carriage and received the same response, the train finally shuddered to a halt. O'Shea stepped across the corridor and peered into the night beyond the window. He was less than a metre away from Robert's grasp, moments away from death. Robert could hear activity from the compartments as people started to question why they had stopped, seemingly in the middle of nowhere. He hesitated before stepping into the sight of the passengers in the last compartment. Someone stepped into the corridor beside O'Shea and asked, "What is happening?"

"I'm sure it's nothing," replied O'Shea. "Go back to your seat and do not worry."

The cleric returned to the compartment and Robert decided to act. Disguising his voice by deepening it, he said in Italian, "You can see from here, Father. Through the open window."

Unaware until then of any presence behind him O'Shea was startled. Robert kept himself in the shadow of the corner but permitted his form to be visible to O'Shea.

"What was that you said?" asked O'Shea.

Robert did not reply but stepped further back towards the door. He saw O'Shea begin to move towards him. A rush of murderous anticipation flooded his being. Then a shout came from the far end of the corridor. The sound of running footsteps pounding along the train towards them.

O'Shea turned to look along the corridor and then moved back towards the state room. The moment had slipped through Robert's fingers. Amongst the shouts he could hear German voices and he could only guess that the Germans were searching the train. He opened the door and jumped down onto the tracks.

Robert tumbled down an embankment and scuttled away into a small copse that separated the tracks from a field of potatoes. He took off his cassock and berretta and lay them down. He went as far into the copse as he could without emerging into the field and lay down. The earth immediately transmitted its deathly cold through his clothing to his body.

The lights of the stationary train glowed above him; a distant source of warmth. He saw silhouettes behind the blinds and could surmise the progress of a search party from the front end of the train to the back.

The sound of boots crunching on gravel and coarse breathing told him that soldiers were moving along outside the train and that they had a dog with them. As they drew level with him the dog began to get excited. It tugged at its leash and yelped. The dog-handler yanked its leash with mighty force and cursed the dog. His companion asked, "What's the matter with him?"

"Rabbits! Damn him. He's crazy for rabbits!"

The men both laughed and dragged the dog along towards the rear of the train. They crossed over and walked back along the far side to the front.

After what Robert calculated to be fifteen minutes, the activity aboard the train settled down and some ten minutes after that the train jerked into life and pulled away. When the train had moved off Robert crept out of the copse to the top of the embankment. Three hundred metres or so along the track he could see that there was a level crossing at which an ADGZ armoured car was parked, along with two saloons. Why were they stopping the Papal train when it was obvious it had been cleared by Himmler to return to Rome? It might well mean that they were searching for himself, Lily and Friedrich. If so, would they wait to stop and search the one they were on?

The sound of gunning engines and the plumes of exhaust fumes collided with the cold night air. The SS men, for that's who he guessed they were, swung themselves aboard the ADGZ and, along with one of the saloons, accelerated away.

Giving them time to disappear and waiting some time more to make sure no guards had been left behind, he then crept along the embankment towards the crossing. He could see the light from the crossing attendant's cottage. Coming around, creeping up to the window he could see the attendant leaning over a stove and then turning to pour boiling water into three cups. Leaning further in he already knew what he would see. Seated at a small table were two SS storm troopers, who had obviously been detailed to stop and search the next train. So, he wondered, how was he to stop the following train and warn Lily and Friedrich? He knew they could not be far from Innsbruck, but that did not mean safety. Austria was a part of the Reich and a pro-active Nazi society. Hadn't Hagan rejoiced in 1938 when the Anschluss had been concluded? He considered his options. As far as he could see he had two. One, he could walk into the cottage now and shoot the three men dead, then stop the train at the level crossing gates and re-board. The problem was the driver and the rest of the crew would want to know why the train had stopped and go looking for the crossing attendant. Two, he could wait for the storm troopers to stop and search the train and hope that they were fooled by Lily's false papers and Friedrich's false ID. If he waited to see what happened he might have to execute the storm troopers as they led Lily and Friedrich into custody. But he would have to be careful not to be seen. Then they would be cut adrift, on the run in the Bavarian countryside. He decided his best outcome would result from the search of the train not identifying Lily or Friedrich. Everything else led to basically the same outcome, so he might as well let fate run its course.

Someone inside the cottage lifted the door latch. Robert melted away into the darkness. The three men came out and the crossing attendant walked back along the track swinging a large oil lamp. The storm troopers went to the crossing gates and closed them.

The train boasted no lights and Robert could only make it out as a bigger shadow amongst the darkness. Quite clearly, though, he could hear the squeal of the brakes and the loud protests of the ice cold rails. He scurried across the tracks, bent double and approached as close as he could to the road across which the train ran. He came to a stone wall and hid himself there with the storm troopers in clear view. He drew the Mauser from his pocket and waited.

When the train had screamed to an agonising halt, the storm troopers walked alongside and spoke to the driver. One waited at the first door until the other had reached the door at the end of the rear carriage Then they moved along the train towards each other.

All was calm for a while. Then, all too quickly, activity exploded. There was shouting and the clunk of doors being opened. Halfway down the train first Lily and then Friedrich were tossed off the train. The storm troopers jumped down behind them. With rifles pointed at their heads Lily and Friedrich were ordered to get to their feet and were marched towards the waiting saloon. Robert, watching this, made a snap decision. If he wanted to avoid killing the crossing attendant, it was his only option. He shot out from behind his wall and climbed into the back of the car. He lay on the floor covered in his black crombie overcoat. He heard Lily grunt as she was slammed against the body of the car, inches from him. One of the storm troopers tied their hands behind their backs whilst the other covered them with his rifle. In the meantime, the crossing attendant had opened the gates and waved the train through, unaware of his close brush with death.

As Lily and Friedrich were tossed into the car they stepped and stumbled over him and then sat with their feet on him. In the rural darkness the storm troopers were unaware of him. For the first mile or so the storm trooper not driving kept his face turned to the back watching the prisoners. Robert stared fixedly at the man from beneath his coat.

As soon as the man became tired of twisting around Robert took hold of Lily's calf. He tapped the word 'friend' in morse code and she understood. He then manoeuvred himself into a position behind the passenger seat. Lily suppressed Friedrich's surprise reaction with a sharp nudge.

Suddenly, there was an explosion of noise inside the car, deafening all of the occupants. The driver felt his heart shift in shock. He shot a glance across at his partner. His eyes fell upon his partner's stomach, which seemed to have exploded outwards. There was blood, stomach matter, undigested food and shreds of clothing plastered onto the dashboard in front of him. His head lolled on his shoulder. Robert had shot him through the seat into the back, the bullet making its exit through his stomach.

The driver felt a cold, hard metal press into his temple and a voice ordered, "Stop the car!"

When the car was stationery, Robert got out first and then ordered the driver out. First he instructed the driver to untie Lily and Friedrich and then he took him to the side of the road and shot him in the temple so that he fell into the roadside ditch. Lily and Friedrich brought the other corpse and tossed it into the ditch on top of its companion. In minutes they were driving away from the scene in the direction of Innsbruck across the border.

As they entered Innsbruck, Friedrich was at the wheel and Lily sat with Robert in back. They parked several blocks away from the Hauptbahnhoff and Lily walked arm in arm with Friedrich to reconnoitre the station and find out about the trains bound for Rome. Lily and Friedrich had the same feeling about Innsbruck. It was relatively undamaged, particularly in comparison to Munich, and they both experienced a fleeting nostalgia for their pre-war lives. At the station Friedrich discovered from the ticket desk that the train for Rome had been diverted to the Westbahnhoff, many blocks to the south, and they quickly made it back to the car.

"Why don't we just drive into Italy?" asked Friedrich.

"You're forgetting," responded Robert. "Those SS men identified you both on the train. The identities we stole have been seen through."

Friedrich and Lily looked at each other. Robert saw the look.

"What?" he asked.

Both were reluctant to reply.

"What?" repeated Robert. "Come on, I need to know."

Friedrich spoke up at last, "Our identities held good," he confessed. "They believed Lily's papers and my uniform and explanation was enough to fool them. They were pretty useless at their jobs to be honest. But I gave us away. It was my stupid temper again. One of them accused a woman of being a Jewess and gun-butted her in the face. I took a swing at him. The two of them overpowered us and guessed who we were."

"So you're saying that they weren't looking for you. They did not know to check for the linguist and his wife?"

"That's right."

"And those two are dead."

"Right again."

"So our identities are secure for now."

Robert tapped his lips.

"All right then," he said after a moment's thought. "Drive on Friedrich. Let the SS guard take the linguist and his wife to Rome."

Sixty

The linguist, his wife and their SS minder negotiated their way through German occupied northern Italy and arrived in Rome after two days hazardous travel. It gave them plenty of time to talk, though to get information from Robert was like pulling teeth.

Robert preferred to question Lily about her decision to turn.

"How could you suddenly ditch decades of belief, years of training and yet more years of waiting to be activated?"

Lily had no immediate answer, but Robert was not going to be put off by her silence.

"You were better than most," he persisted. "You convinced me. You convinced Trubshaw. You passed his tests. Come on, Lily, I want to know why!"

"You know why," she suddenly hissed.

"But I don't," he argued disingenuously.

"Yes you do," she snapped but there was embarrassment in her tone too.

There was a silence and then, as if suddenly lighting upon a satisfactory answer to his questioning Lily stated, "Call it a Road to Damascus conversion."

"You wouldn't like to elaborate would you?" asked Robert with more than a hint of sarcasm.

"I had a school friend when I lived with my father in Berlin," began Lily. "She was a devout Catholic. She made her confession every week on a Saturday and attended mass and took communion every Sunday. More than that, she went to benediction each Friday after school and said her rosary before going to bed. When she was sixteen her parents took up a three year contract in South Africa and they left her with her maternal Grandparents. Her mother had been brought up as a Lutheran and only converted in order to be able to marry my friend's father. On the day she moved in with her Grandparents, who were of course still Lutherans, she immediately ceased her Catholic worship practices. Her Grandparents did not attend church regularly and it just seemed rude to inconvenience them by asking if she could go to her church. When I asked her how difficult it had been to deny her religious principles she said she had not given it a moment's thought. She said it was as if they had never existed. She speculated that maybe her beliefs were just habit, held onto in the absence of anything else. As soon as her context changed, so did her principles."

At this point Lily paused and turned to stare into Robert's eyes.

"So in answer to your question," she concluded, "Maybe my context changed."

Robert said nothing in reply but looked at Lily for a long time as Friedrich guided their vehicle through the rocky alpine terrain.

Although Robert had been reluctant to communicate too much to the others about his plans, by the time they reached Rome this much was known by all three. Robert was going to assassinate O'Shea and they would make good their escape via the underground route to Argentina that was already established for senior Nazi collaborators who were beginning to doubt the survival of the Thousand Year Reich. What they didn't know was that Robert had another motive for getting to Rome. He intended to find Grete, Lisa and David and take them away with him to Argentina.

They had had time to agree a plan of sorts. As the papers they carried had held good so far they intended to keep these identities. The one weakness in that plan was the position of Friedrich as an SS officer. He would not be expected to remain with the linguist and his wife now that they had arrived in Rome. Therefore he had to put away his uniform and SS identity. Maybe it would come in handy later on, but for now he had to acquire another identity and all three of them put their minds to this. Robert and Lily quickly agreed that they would venture out after dark and ambush a likely candidate, steal his clothes and his papers. Luckily, in German occupied Italy, everyone had to carry papers. Friedrich surprised them, however, when he objected to this plan.

"Don't you have any feelings of guilt about the last people we did this to; the linguist and his family? Do we know where they are now?"

Both Robert and Lily looked at each other, suddenly shocked to realise that they had come so far along the road they had chosen to travel that no such thought had entered their minds. Their cold, uncaring approach caused them both to take pause.

"What do you suggest, Friedrich?" Lily asked.

"I suggest that we at least take a little trouble to select a deserving case. Someone in league with the Nazis; a bureaucrat or a collaborator."

"All right," grimaced Robert. "We'll do what we can."

"And listen," interjected Friedrich. "I can't be an Italian. I will be exposed the moment I open my mouth."

"Now you are getting too choosy!"

Lily and Robert sat drinking Austrian beer in a café beside the corner of Via Veneto and Via Boncompagni. It was early evening but already dark and the passing trade from office workers on their way home was dwindling away.

They had already taken in a beer near the Teatro delle Arti. They had been asked for their papers there and after finishing their beers had made an unhurried exit. No one suitable so far!

Aware that lingering too long in any one place would attract unwanted attention, they drained their glasses and decided to give up on their task for the evening.

It was as they walked back through the unlit streets towards Via Cavour and the Stazione Centrale on their way back to the southern district where their lodgings were located that an opportunity arose. Their attention was drawn to the perimeter of the classical ruins of the Baths of Diocletian by the sound of raised voices. The voices echoed menacingly in the relative emptiness of the night and Lily and Robert had no problem locating the source.

Silhouetted against the ruins of the Baths, two off-duty German soldiers were laying into an old man with drunken fury. The man took the first two or three blows to the head and kept his feet, but several more and a brutal push saw him fall and crack his head on the stone wall behind him. The soldiers took to kicking him and he very soon ceased moving.

Lily had reached out and grabbed Robert's arm when he had instinctively made a move to go to the man's aid.

"You can't get involved," she hissed. "It could blow our cover! Look! Over there! Several spectators are taking an interest. There will be a crowd here soon."

The soldiers continued to abuse the lifeless figure saying that that would teach him to call them Nazi scum. One yelled to the other, "He's a very good Bolshevik now, isn't he. Yes because he's a dead Bolshevik!" And the two of them laughed at their own wit.

Eventually, even in their drunken state, the soldiers arrived at the conclusion that they were wasting their energy. This man was not going to feel pain ever again. Pausing to bend and get their breath they picked up their caps which had fallen due to their exertions, and headed off, arm in arm, singing a victory song.

Lily held tightly onto Robert's arm. Beneath her hand she could feel the flexing and tensing of his muscles as he fought with himself not to get involved.

"Get over there!" whispered Robert. "Quickly, before that crowd gets too close. Get his papers! Wait till I come back."

Lily grabbed his shoulders.

"No! No! No! Robert you can't."

But by the strength Robert applied to the grip he took on her forearms, Lily knew there was no way of reasoning with him. There was almost a pleading in his eyes when he said, matter-of-factly, "I've got to."

Once the main action had subsided, the crowd slowly drifted off and Lily was left alone with the corpse. She managed to move him into a shadowy corner of the ruins. She relieved the man of his papers. He would not need them now. She had the corpse half undressed when Robert returned. She could not help noticing the blood on his hands and something bulging under his overcoat. They hurried away from the site of the Ancient Roman Baths and burrowed into the residential area to the south. In an alleyway somewhere behind them, two representatives of the invincible Wehrmacht lay in their underwear, on their backs each presenting two gaping smiles to the leaden sky.

"You'll have to be an Italian and that's all there is to it," declared Lily to an incredulous Friedrich. "You can't use the papers of the dead soldiers. If you were stopped you'd have to explain why you were roaming the city."

"But I don't speak one word of the language."

"Well there's your answer then – don't speak one word. Play dumb!"

This comment roused Robert from a bout of melancholy and with a humourless grin he muttered, "That will do us all a big favour."

It was the first time he had spoken for a day and a half and Friedrich took the opportunity to try to engage him in conversation.

"Do you think you could explain to us why we are here risking our lives when our mission has been accomplished? Who is this O'Shea to you and why are we planning to assassinate him?"

Under Robert's stare Friedrich looked to Lily but she, realising that Friedrich had already put his foot in it, looked away. A silence intensified until at last Robert spoke. Looking from Lily to Friedrich and back, he moved uncomfortably in his seat. He placed his hands on the table in front of him and leaned forward in his chair.

"It's personal," he muttered. "You two ought to make good your escape now and forget about me."

"A bit late for that," stated Friedrich matter-of-factly. "We are already here in Nazi occupied Rome."

Suddenly Robert stood up, knocking his chair over backwards and shouted, "You know why, Lily. I've told you about my son. I haven't told Friedrich my pathetic story. Perhaps you will fill him in on the details. All I can say is the man who abused my son is here in Rome and I'm not leaving while he lives. O'Shea – that man of God, that blessed disciple of Jesus, that devout Christian – O'Shea is the priest who abused my son."

The shocked silence seemed to intensify Robert's despair.

"O'Shea abused my son," he repeated, his voice suddenly retreating to a whisper, "And I let it happen. Now he's dead and he died thinking the world a terrible place. A young child should not have to think like that, even if we know it to be true."

For an instant Robert was Sean again and became wracked with uncontrollable sobbing. Instinctively Lily moved towards Robert to enfold him in an embrace. Robert pushed her away and, grabbing his coat and hat, went out into the Roman night. Lily attempted to follow him but Friedrich restrained her. He held her like a child as she cried in his arms.

Sixty-one

Robert walked beneath the walls of the Vatican and crossed over to the ghetto. He had been here every morning since arriving in Rome. Looking over his shoulder he knew that the Pope's living quarters were behind the windows above him. These were the windows Eugenio Pacelli had ordered shuttered when the Jews had been rounded up in October 1943. He had preferred not to witness the brutality of the regime that he had climbed into bed with.

Robert wondered what feverish activity was happening in there. From a safe distance he had observed frantic comings and goings in and out of Vatican City. Official German Mercedes cars filled with diplomats and generals sped to and fro between Wehrmacht headquarters and the Papal Throne room. But no announcement yet! No newspaper headlines screaming –"Pope Assassinated" – or –"Allies Murder Pius XII".

The Germans were keeping a tight lid on the news. How to distance the Axis from the assassination would be exercising their minds. Maybe they were working on a modern resurrection to make the problem go away. This thought brought a half smile to Robert's taut lips. But it slipped away suddenly as he turned his footsteps into the ghetto and an image of Grete entered his mind.

Many of the apartments and tenements were empty now. Gradually, poorer Italians were moving in to occupy vacated premises. Some even found themselves the proud occupiers of fully furnished rooms if the Nazi looters had failed to get round to the property left behind.

Robert had established for himself a mindless routine of door to door enquiries. He spoke broken Italian with a heavy German accent and was able to pass himself off as an official of the Reich administration. The replies he received varied.

"You should know – you took them all!"

"Why don't you fuck off you bastard."

"I'm so sorry my friend. I would love to help you but I know nothing."

Robert was not that concerned with the verbal replies he received. As each individual responded he studied their faces intently. He was looking for some tell-tale sign that would give the respondent away. Some facial flicker that would signal to him that the name was familiar. After two or three hours of this he would give up, leave the ghetto and hang around St Peter's Square, hoping to catch sight of O'Shea.

However, a few days previously he had made a breakthrough. Going from occupied house to occupied house, he had finally found someone who had known Grete and both of the children. The someone was an old Italian male who had married a Jewess and lived all his married life in the ghetto. He was alone now. His wife had been deported. No, he did not know where she was, but he lived in hope of hearing from her.

Robert's desperation stepped in at that moment and he stooped to a level he had not considered himself capable of.

"Perhaps I could do a deal with you," he said.

"What do you mean?"

"Maybe I could exchange information with you. Your wife can be traced."

The spark of hope that ignited in the man's eyes burned a shaft of guilt into Robert, but he could not go back now.

"Tell me what you know and I'll see what I can do."

The man, whose name was Antonio Bruccialo, remembered when Grete and the children had arrived. He was familiar with Grete's relatives, who had been neighbours of his for many years.

"Can you tell me what happened to them?" Robert asked, making a decided effort to keep the impatience out of his voice.

"Well," said Antonio Bruccialo, "No I don't think I can."

"Why not?"

"Because I never saw her."

"What do you mean?"

"I mean, I saw her aunt and her husband and I saw my wife that day."

"Which day do you mean?"

"The day they were all taken away. I saw her aunt and uncle. I saw my wife."

Here the man began to weep and he paused to wipe his eyes, "I watched them as they were herded onto the train. I saw many, many of my friends and neighbours. I watched them all being crammed into the cattle cars. But what I am saying is I didn't see Grete and her children that day. I didn't see them getting onto the train."

"So, maybe they escaped the round-up. Is that what you are saying?"

"Maybe I am," nodded the man. "Maybe I am."

After almost an hour of frantic questioning, the man finally gave Robert a name and an address where he might get more information about Grete and the children. As he was turning to leave, Robert fingered the brim of his hat and asked, "Why have you told me this? Maybe I will find them and send them where the others have gone."

The man looked Robert up and down: hesitated. Then he said, "My money says you're no German. The Germans are never as desperate as you. You my friend are a desperate man. For Grete and her children I am glad. But for me it is not so good. You should not have awoken my hopes. Not even for the few moments I was foolish enough to believe you. You, my friend, I will always despise. You forced me to make a choice I should not have to make. I chose to betray an innocent family in order to perhaps help my wife. The fact that you are a fake does not help me. If you had been a German agent you might have found news of my wife. The fact that you are not is good for Grete. But can it be good for Grete to have a friend such as you? I don't know."

Excitement and anticipation caused Robert to spend a sleepless night. He did not make love to Lily but he allowed her to make love to him. He tried desperately not to think of Grete as Lily spent her passion upon him.

"Is anything the matter?" she asked as they lay side by side in the dark.

"We need to plan our escape from Rome. There are rumours that the Vatican is assisting the passage of Nazis out of Europe to South America. We need to make our arrangements to join them. Tomorrow, you and I will track O'Shea, but Friedrich must find out how we can join the Nazi escape route."

"Is it a good idea for us to travel to South America with a shipload of Nazis?" asked Lily.

"In this instance I think they will be more concerned to hide their true identities than we will be.

"I have heard of a priest with the sobriquet 'Father Rat'. He is apparently the chief organiser of the route to Argentina."

"Argentina," mused Robert. "How do you fancy a new life in Argentina?"

Lily rolled towards him, wrapped her arm over his chest and her leg over his waist.

"If I am with you, I don't care where we go."

Guiltily Robert kissed her on the forehead and whispered, "Go to sleep."

Since arriving in Rome he had begun to feel more and more inadequate. The sense of achievement on completing his mission had evaporated as each day had passed and no announcement of the Pope's demise had been made. If the Church did not announce the death of Pope Pius, then his mission had been futile. Unless, of course, papal policy changed in his absence and the encyclical was published. Also, his activities in Rome were so badly organised that his sense of discipline and order were falling apart. He no longer thought of himself as an Allied undercover agent. His mission for them had been completed and he had voluntarily cut himself adrift.

His actions were now self-motivated and independent. The need to eradicate O'Shea was irresistible, but his pursuit of Grete was a secret mission of his own that he had tacked on to their journey to Rome. By not sharing this mission with Lily and Friedrich he felt he had betrayed them. But he could not bring himself to tell them. For Lily it would be a slap in the face. Although he knew they would never love each other as he had Grete, and, as he now realised, Martha too in a different way, he had no desire to hurt her. They shared the same damaged persona. They knew the hollowness of each other. They could tolerate each other's emptiness and deep melancholy. They still shared the same bed and their physical love was brutal and selfish and they accepted it equally. But... Yes there was a 'but'. He had an addictive need to find Grete again to see if the fire of real love could be re-ignited within him.

The only semblance of organisation he had brought to the team was a simple division of labour. Friedrich's role was to investigate and plan their escape from Rome. Robert and Lily would find O'Shea.

Lily and Robert would walk out each Sunday, like a conventional, married couple and hear mass in St Peter's Square. After mass on their second Sunday in Rome it was announced that the Pope himself, newly returned from his diplomatic efforts to bring about peace, would say mass the following Sunday.

Sixty-two

The address was a café bar at the southern end of the ghetto. It showed evidence of once having been a smart and probably prosperous establishment. The exterior wall surrounding the window was lined with shining ceramic tiles in green, red and white, and the interior was wood panelling and red leather booths. However, the whole interior was now shabby and neglected - in need of a good spring clean. One or two tears in the red upholstery had not been repaired and some splintered panels were hanging away from the walls. Robert walked in and ordered a coffee.

"We have ersatz!"

"That will do fine."

The man steamed the combination of coffee, dust and nuts and presented the thick, black concoction to Robert.

"Anything to eat?" he asked.

"A bowl of pasta, nothing more."

Robert ate and drank at the bar. Three other tables were occupied; one with an elderly couple; one with two women and one with a young man – should have been a student but was probably a soldier on leave.

When the proprietor, a man with a wide moustache and receding hair, ceased serving at a table and sat opposite Robert polishing cutlery, Robert leaned forward and said, "Antonio Bruccialo recommended your café to me."

"How is Antonio?"

"He seems in good enough health but he remains morose since he lost his wife."

"Ah! Poor Antonio! His wife was a diamond. She was the most beautiful woman of her generation. Sweet Rachel! Such a loss! But tell me my friend – what is Antonio to you?"

"Antonio has agreed to help me."

"But why would he? You are German are you not? Antonio despises all Germans, with good reason. You might have been our allies but you always worried the shit out of us. Now you are our masters."

Robert leaned closer and keeping his voice as low as he could, said, "I am not German. I am Irish. Antonio guessed that and agreed to help me. You can trust me."

"I can trust nobody!"

"Well perhaps you are correct there, but…"

As he spoke Robert pulled his wallet out of his pocket. He pulled several lire notes out one after the other.

"…there is a price for everything."

The man took a handful of notes and said, "What do you want?"

"I want you to take a message to Grete Hidberg."

The man's eyebrows rose.

"What makes you think I know this person?"

"Antonio seems to think you do. Tell her Sean is here. Don't forget. Sean is here. Tell her I want to meet her. I will be here in your café tomorrow at noon. If she doesn't want to come I will go away and leave her alone. But tell her Sean is desperate to see her."

"How will she know it is truly this Sean you claim to be?"

"Tell her I am the man who taught David to use a Hurley stick."

Sixty-three

When the door to the café swung open Robert did not immediately recognise the woman who slipped in. It was not just the headscarf that hid most of her face. It was the cultivated invisibility: the deliberate insignificance; an air of non-existence that worked to make her almost not there at all. When she sat down opposite him she did not look at him. She made no attempt to appear acknowledged. It was as if she had been there all the time like the chairs and tables.

The moment most longed for is always the most disappointing. Robert would have disputed that word –'disappointing'. Unexpected, surprising, wrong even. This scene had been played out a million times in his head and this was like none of them. However, this was real. Maybe Grete's complexion was drier and more creased – but it was real. Maybe her eyes were duller than he had remembered – but they were real. And if her hair had been shorn and needed washing, at least it was real.

"Grete?"

It was all Robert could manage. When he spoke her name she looked nervously around her. A couple near the window studied the odd couple.

"Can we walk?" she asked, and without waiting for a reply stood and left the café. Robert spilled some coins on the table and hurried after her.

They walked for a long time in silence. At one point Robert attempted to take her hand but she pulled away and hurried her steps. In time they arrived at the river and Grete found a bench and sat down. The wind gusted in the trees and whipped her headscarf about her face.

"Why have you come?" she asked in some irritation.

"Grete? I had to. You know I did."

"I know no such thing."

"Don't tell me you don't remember what we meant to each other."

She looked into his eyes for the first time before answering.

"What did we mean to each other, Sean?"

The longing in her voice was manifest. For a moment she was lost for words. There was too much that needed to be said; too much lost time to make up. It was not possible to encapsulate all of it in the next few sentences. Her expression melted slightly, as if recalling something akin to Robert's memory of that time. But then her expression fell and she said, "Whatever we were then, we are not that now."

"But then why did you come to meet me? You need not have. You could have stayed away. That must mean something."

"But I did have to come. You have been trawling the district asking questions about me. You were making my life intolerable. Eyes were beginning to pick me out. I am a fugitive. I have to be invisible. You were making me the most talked about woman in this part of Rome."

She then looked into his face, but there was no anger in her eyes. He saw uncertainty there and fear and excitement. He also saw love. He reached out and took her hands. She held onto them tightly.

"I cannot put my children's lives at risk. It concerns me that I am here at all. I worry that you mean too much to me, Sean. What kind of mother am I to risk my children in order to satisfy my need to see you?"

Robert was stricken with guilt. After a moment or two he said, "Forgive me. I wanted to help you. I still can."

It was then that she leaned in towards him and they kissed. It was a moment he had longed for so many times that he was not sure this was not just another of his fantasies. His hands and arms were hungry for her. He embraced her passionately and she responded. He felt glad that they were in Italy and not puritanical Germany.

When she whispered, "I love you." It was an arrow of fire to his heart.

The words, "I love you," fell from him as an unconscious reflex. He had said them before he knew he was going to. As they drew apart the sudden dreadful realisation of what he must do descended upon him.

"Let's walk," he said

Walking along hand in hand Robert imagined himself married to Grete. One, ten, twenty years. It was a nice moment.

"Give me your address," he said.

As she wrote it onto the piece of paper he had given her he gave her his instructions.

"Carry on as normal. Do nothing. You have escaped their attentions for this long. There's no reason to think that they are on to you now. Is there a telephone number I can get you on?"

She took the piece of paper again and wrote a number on it.

"It is the shared phone for the apartment block. I take the children to school at eight in the morning. I go straight to work in the laundry. I am there at ten minutes to nine. I stay there until eleven and then I walk to the Past shop where I work throughout the afternoon. I get home after the children. They arrive home by three in the afternoon and I get in at six."

Robert kissed her again.

"Wait until you hear from me. I will telephone if I have to. But I might just turn up. Pack your things ready to leave. Necessities only, I'm afraid. But don't worry. There will be a new life waiting and we will have little use for the old things. If it is not me, whoever comes will use the phrase 'Hurley sticks'. That way you will know you can trust them."

That was it. Suddenly they knew that this encounter was over and both were afraid. Robert pulled her into his arms and they kissed for one last time.

"Be brave," he said.

"Ciao," she retorted and they both smiled. She moved quickly away along the embankment.

Robert walked away thinking of Conny. He also thought of Martha. His duplicity with her had led to one tragedy. Here he was right at the commencement of another duplicitous deception. From the moment the words, 'I love you,' had escaped from his lips he had known that he and Grete could never be together. He did love her, and that was the problem. Maybe if he didn't he could deceive her into entering his dark world. Like he had deceived Martha! Like he was deceiving Lily in a similar if not identical way! Because he loved Grete he knew he had to get as far away from her as possible – for her own sake.

Grete crossed the Tiber swiftly, taking the bridge to the southern district where she had her apartment. Neither Robert nor Grete looked back. If they had they might have noticed Hauptsturmfuhrer Schirach move slowly away from his position against the parapet above the Tiber. As his eyes followed Grete, another man moved to stand by his side.

"Follow her. Find out about her. Then report back to me."

Sixty-four

Father O'Shea, closed the door on his apartment inside Vatican City and headed across the avenue to the Pope's offices. The sound of Croatian voices carried along the colonnade towards him. An increasing number of apartments and safe houses within the walls of the Vatican had been allocated to Croatian Fascists who had fled after the collapse of the Ustashe regime in their homeland under the increasingly successful onslaught from Tito and his Yugoslav battalions.

O'Shea was content for the Vatican to support these Catholics and help them to escape retribution, but he found their presence tiresome. They had compromised the peaceful atmosphere of the Vatican and diluted the sense of piety he usually felt when living there in normal times. Pretty much the way the Jews had when some of them had been allowed to find refuge within the holy walls. He sought forgiveness from God as soon as he thought it, but he could not prevent a fleeting feeling of pleasure to know that they had gone. Not that he was an anti-Semite. Not in the German sense. Nor after the fashion of dear old Brian Hagan back in Dublin.

O'Shea had other reasons for the discomfort he felt. The brutal assassination of the Blessed Holy Father had plunged him into fear and depression. The fear was gradually receding but the depression was more persistent. The most unthinkable action in the history of the world; and performed by an Irishman no less. He knew a major slab of his black depression was caused by the knowledge that his own past sins may have contributed to the actions of the assassin. He was also sure that the assassin had unfinished business and that he was the object of that business.

He reached his desk in the Papal suite of offices and sat down to work on the Pope's diary of meetings and events. He worked conscientiously although he knew any itinerary he worked out was a fiction. Each day, as diary secretary, he re-allocated dates that had been missed and re-arranged appointments for future dates that he knew the Pope would never complete.

The frantic comings and goings of the bishops, cardinals and officials of the Swiss Guard filled the offices with an intensity of activity he had never known before. Baron Ernst von Weizsacker, Hitler's ambassador to the Holy See, was a regular visitor. This very morning he marched in as the Brazilian Ambassador Pinto Accioly was coming out of the Papal chamber. Ambassador Accioly's face clearly showed the outrage he was feeling. He stepped in front of Weizsacker, halting his progress.

"If you are responsible for denying access to the Holy Father, you will be held responsible."

A flicker of rage flashed across Weizsacker's face but he controlled himself and spoke calmly, "The Vatican remains an independent state and I have as much influence here as you."

"Don't think I am a fool, Herr Weizsacker. I want you to know that I am here to petition His Holiness to issue an unequivocal denunciation of German atrocities with respect to European Jews. The time for Papal neutrality is gone. Catholic opinion around the world is outraged."

"You are entitled to petition His Holiness on whatever issue you choose."

"Don't patronise me. The world knows you Germans administer Rome. Perhaps you are controlling the Vatican too. Why can I not have a Papal audience? Why is the ambassador of a Catholic country ushered into the presence of his companion, Sister Pasquelina? Mark my words Herr Weizsacker, the world will not forgive you." With that Accioly turned from Weizsacker and approached O'Shea at his desk.

"Sister Pasquelina instructed me to leave this petition with you. I trust you will ensure His Holiness receives this with the utmost urgency." With that he turned on his heel and left without further comment.

Ambassador Weizsacker entered the Papal chambers without announcement or introduction. During the three and a half hours that Weizsacker remained within the Papal chambers, O'Shea became bored enough to prise open the lightly sealed envelope and to extract the petition from inside.

The petition was a strongly worded denouncement of German atrocities in Europe. The accompanying letter claimed that the world now had sufficient evidence to prove that the allegations of mass murder were true. Eye witness accounts had reached Britain and the USA. The Vatican could no longer hide behind German denials. The petition demanded that the Pope issue a statement unequivocally condemning German practices of slave labour and mass murder. The statement the Pope should issue was presented in draft form. An appendix confirmed that all Allied and many neutral countries, including several significant Catholic countries, had agreed the draft. The world was waiting on the Pope. O'Shea filled his time making notes countering the arguments in the draft.

1. Eye-witness accounts unreliable.
2. German denials had ring of sincerity.
3. What about Russian atrocities?
4. If a Papal statement destabilised Germany, how would the spread of Bolshevism be prevented?

5. The Pope could never abandon the Catholics in Germany who had remained true to the faith.

6. Abandoning position of strict neutrality would necessitate relinquishing an invaluable position to hold in the event of a negotiated peace.

He attempted a separate list noting the dangers of refusing to issue the statement.

1. Alienating millions of Catholics in countries like Brazil.

2. Being seen to be sympathetic to Nazism – particularly dangerous if Germany were to lose the war.

He got no further with this list, not just because his heart was not in it, but because Weizsacker emerged from the inner sanctum and shocked him with the following statement.

"Pope Pius has asked for you!"

Before O'Shea could gather his senses Weizsacker had strode across the office and disappeared through the outer door. O'Shea sat wondering whether or not he had misheard. After all, they all knew there was no Pope Pius. Not any more.

Convinced that when he entered the Papal chamber he would be told to leave again he, nevertheless, could not prevent himself acting upon the words he thought Weizsacker had spoken.

He turned the great handle and pushed the door. It slid smoothly open. Mind numbed with expectation he slipped silently into the room. There were no lights on but a rack of candles flickered in the far corner. To the right and beyond the candles he could dimly make out a figure. The figure was dressed in Papal robes, as if ready to say mass. As he stepped closer, O'Shea gasped silently. He felt his breath catch in his throat. In front of him, in the gloom, stood his beloved Pope Pius XII. O'Shea fell to his knees. He was burdened down with thoughts that sprang from the deepest regions of his religious mind. One word echoed around his bludgeoned brain.

"Resurrection."

He began to experience a feeling of dizziness and disorientation. He believed he was experiencing a sacred religious episode. His thighs and calves trembled, even though he was already on his knees. His head was too heavy for his neck muscles to hold. He crumpled to the floor, forehead pressing upon the carpet. And then the Pope spoke.

A shaft of cold steel shot through O'Shea's being. It was the Pope; but it wasn't the Pope. The voice was close but there was enough difference in the pitch and the emphasis for O'Shea to know. A new word entered his brain.

"Reincarnation."

Not part of the Catholic canon, but if God willed it, O'Shea would accept it. If the Cardinals had decided on this path with God's good guidance, then O'Shea would accept it.

The figure rose and came towards him. Pope Pius spoke again, "Father O'Shea. You must get to your feet. The Cardinals say we have work to do. You will attend me in saying mass."

O'Shea rose and stood before the figure approaching him. He observed the gait and heard the tones of the Pope's simpleton brother who had, until now, lived an isolated life in a Sicilian monastery. O'Shea had once accompanied the Pope on a visit to the monastery. He had not been introduced to the papal sibling but he had caught a good glimpse from across a quadrangle. His existence was not known to the world at large, although rumours had survived from the days of their childhood. O'Shea bowed, took the hand offered to him and kissed the Papal ring. Together they walked through the Vatican to the room with the balcony over St Peter's square, where they said mass together to the congregation below.

When the Pope had delivered the final blessing and bid the congregation go in peace, the crowd applauded and cheered, so relieved were they to see His Holiness once more.

Sixty-five

Down below, at the edge of the square, Robert and Lily watched in disbelief as the Pope said mass. They looked at each other, silently expressing a mutual 'how can this be?'

"It's not him!" whispered Robert.

Although he had whispered, a nun standing alongside them immediately turned and stared at him. She then moved swiftly away and Robert watched her approach a Swiss Guard. It dawned on him at that moment that the crowd contained an unusual number of nuns and Swiss Guards. Before she could turn and point him out he took Lily by the arm and pulled her behind a column. Telling her to stoop, they scuttled away from the square.

Later, as they sipped an ersatz coffee at a pavement café they saw several men and women being escorted away from the square by Swiss Guards.

"That's what nearly happened to us," he said to Lily nodding at those being dragged away. "The good old Catholic Church never changes. It knows what it is good at and it plays to its strengths. Forcing its own view of the truth upon others has always worked in the past. Why not now?"

Lily watched Robert, elbows on his knees and head in his hands.

"What are you thinking?" she asked.

"I'm thinking that that was O'Shea with him up there on the balcony. And if it was, I know that he will eventually be bound to come out of the walled city, and when he does I have a good idea which exit he will be likely to use."

"And what do you propose to do?"

Robert finished his coffee and put down his cup.

"I intend to go and wait for him and then I'm going to kill him."

"In that case," said Lily, finishing her own coffee, "I'm coming with you."

Robert could see from the set of her face that it was pointless arguing with her, so he simply nodded.

"What are you smiling at?" he asked her.

"Nothing much," she replied. "It's just that I noticed a light in your eye that I haven't seen for some time."

"What does that mean?"

"It means," said Lily, "That you've stopped planning and you're ready to act."

Robert smiled at that and they left the pavement café together.

Sixty-six

Haupsturmfuhrer Schirach extinguished his cigarette beneath the heel of his shoe and followed after Robert and Lily. In a grey suit and trilby he looked less formidable than in his uniform. Nonetheless he was a determined and relentless pursuer and now his prey was within sight.

Schirach followed at a safe distance and only when Robert and Lily were established in their position opposite the staff entrance to the Papal apartments did he peel away to a public telephone box to make a call.

When he returned to his observation position he spotted his subjects and then checked his watch. In approximately ten minutes, a snatch squad would be in place and these two British agents would be history. Assassination had been an option, but he had decided against it. Arrest and interrogation before execution; that was his preference – especially for the traitor Lily Brecht. It was important to have them dead rather than allow word of their mission to get out, but he was confident that he could organise their removal from the world into the limbo of his custody before eliminating them permanently. Schirach was one of the few people on the planet who knew that Pope Pius XII was dead. Despite that knowledge he was quite content to be told that Pope Pius was now alive and had never been dead. What are facts when you are dealing with Christ's representative on Earth? He had a simple, methodical mind. He was no philosopher-scientist and had no desire to be one.

Just then a door opened at the base of the Vatican walls and out stepped O'Shea. O'Shea moved swiftly. Just as swiftly Robert and Lily got to their feet and hurried after him. Schirach found himself hurrying after them. He was annoyed! His support team had not arrived and he was pursuing them on his own. He could assassinate them but he was not totally confident that he would be able to arrest them on his own.

Robert and Lily hurried after O'Shea through the streets, which were now subject to a fine drizzle of rain. As pursuers they had little thought of being followed themselves. As they gradually gained on O'Shea, Schirach was gaining on them. He had his pistol in his palm inside his jacket pocket.

Turning into a cobbled lane which ran down towards the river, Robert decided that this was to be the scene of his final revenge on O'Shea. O'Shea, hair and robes flapping in the wind, was halfway down the lane when Robert spurted ahead of Lily and moved up on him. Before he could catch him O'Shea surprised them by stepping into a doorway and disappearing inside a building. Robert stopped, cursed and looked up at the sign above the door.

Red Cross? What the hell did O'Shea want with the Red Cross? Lily came to Robert's side and said, "What's going on?"

"I don't know. I was so close."

"Shall we go in?" Lily asked.

Prompted by the question and the need to make a decision they looked up and down the lane. Halfway down the slope, walking swiftly towards them was a man in a grey suit and trilby hat. As they turned to look the other way a group of schoolchildren in black uniforms turned at the bottom of the slope and swarmed around them as they proceeded up the bank.

The man in the grey suit stopped suddenly. Robert did not recognise the man but some kind of indecision showed on his face. Robert recognised a potential danger and was appalled at his carelessness in his blinkered pursuit of O'Shea. Pushing Lily by the waist he hissed, "Quick, this way." And using the schoolchildren as a shield they slipped away to the bottom of the lane and fled around the corner.

Schirach made a brave attempt to push his way through the children, but by the time he made it to the corner Lily and Robert were long gone.

"All right my good doctor. We will have to make more careful plans to get our hands on you. Perhaps I will speak to this cleric you seem to be so interested in."

Sixty-seven

Hours spent in the apartment were heavy and slow. Lily had been unable to speak to Robert for several days. She knew something must have happened, but whenever she approached the matter with him he warned her off with a look.

"I know what keeps taking O'Shea into the Red Cross office." It was Friedrich who just dropped this into the silence that had pervaded the room.

Robert and Lily looked at him. He was sitting in a thin grey overcoat and his face was unshaven. Lily thought he looked unwell. Realising they were waiting for him to explain Friedrich continued, "It's a front for Nazis wanting to get to Argentina. Bishop Alois Hudal is a Nazi sympathiser. He is running an organisation that is releasing hundreds of Nazis. They are escaping to Argentina and various other South American countries."

Lily was aghast.

"How is he doing that?" she queried. "Are you serious?"

"He provides hiding places and false passports. He then provides tickets on liners going to South America. Mainly Argentina."

"Is this official Vatican policy?"

"It's not official. But they sure as hell know what's going on. The Vatican sponsors an institution known as the College of San Girolamo degli Illirici. It started out as a theological college for Croatian priests. But now it is a refuge for fleeing Croatian war criminals. The Vatican is struggling to find anything wrong with Pavelic's attempt to create a completely Catholic Croatia by murdering all non-Catholics in the country. Unfortunately for them Tito is proving rather more successful as a leader than Pavelic. So Croatian butchers are turning up in their droves at the college. They come with lots of plundered gold so they can pay handsomely for the hospitality they receive. Hudal's partner in this enterprise is a theological professor known as Father Krunoslav Dragonovic. He and his minions do all of the administration. I believe the Vatican is projecting the end for Catholic Croatia and wants to deploy the wealth and personnel to Argentina, for which Pope Pius XII has such an affection. For him it has the perfect regime. Catholic, military, pseudo republican. Very much like Spain. Ostensibly Dragonovic devotes much of his time to the Red Cross. But his office is a pure front. It is a base to which fugitives can flock. They probably believe they are saving the world from Bolshevism by releasing the Nazi virus into the future. They also believe they are saving good Catholics.

Anyway, the good news is I may be able to get us a passage on the next ship embarking. It's a Uruguayan liner called The Montevideo."

"Good work, Friedrich. Keep at it. We need to be away from here as soon as we can."

Friedrich smiled. Praise from Robert always meant so much to him. Lily could see that he was pleased and she touched his shoulder affectionately as she walked by his chair to make tea. She felt the sharp bone of his shoulder protruding through his skin and his coat, but made no comment.

Sixty-eight

Schirach was in poor spirits. He had missed his chance to snatch the doctor and his wife. He was working on a safer plan to do just that. But also, on his way to work he had been forced to pick his way through the rubble that littered the streets following the Allied bombing of Rome last night. For the first time he was allowing his mind to consider the idea that the fatherland might lose the war. It was not good for his blood pressure.

A knock came at the door to his office and an underling stepped in.

"What do you want?" he snapped.

The soldier snatched his hat from his head and barked out a Heil Hitler salute.

"Pardon mein Haupsturmfuhrer. The woman you asked me to investigate. The one you saw associating with the doctor."

Schirach's eyebrows raised and his expression lifted slightly.

"Well?"

"I have discovered several things of interest."

The man stared at Schirach as if seeking permission to continue. Schirach impatiently waved a carry-on gesture at him and the man continued.

"She lives with a Roman family in the Testaccio area. She has lived with them since October 17 1943."

"But that's…" ejaculated Schirach.

"Exactly, mein Hauptsturmfuhrer," interrupted Keppler, for that was the informant's name. "The round-up of the Jews."

"Is she…?" began Schirach, but again Keppler interrupted him.

"Indeed she is. Jewish! A Berlin Jew to be precise. Migrated to Rome following the suicide of her husband in about '36 I am informed."

"Excellent. Anything else?"

"Yes. She has two children, a boy and a girl. They attend a Catholic school in the Testaccio district."

"How did they escape the round-up?"

"They were aided by their current landlords; a childless couple, both doctors. Both Catholics and natives of Rome. Signor and Signora Marino."

"You have done well, Keppler," said Schirach as he came around his desk and put on his coat and hat. "Come with me. We will round up these Jews and their disloyal hosts."

Pausing at his telephone to order a small commando unit to meet him at the Piazza Berberini, he left his office and took to the stairs, enthusiastically pursued by Keppler.

Grete, covered in dust and sweating from exertion, stood with a spade full of glass in her hands and tipped it into a large bin that stood in the middle of the store. She wanted the Allies to win the war, and quickly, but she dreaded the air raids and the sights they left the morning after. There had been an initial reluctance amongst the Allies to bomb Rome. But after Mussolini had been deposed and then re-instated by Germany as a puppet in the north, that reluctance had been overcome. The growing significance of the Italian Partisans leading the resistance against what was now a puppet state of Germany, acted as an encouragement to the Allies to raise the odds. Since the Americans first bombed Rome on July 19 earlier in the year, Grete had never become used to the horror they delivered. Last night's raid had caused only collateral damage to the pasta shop where she worked, but it still meant a whole day clearing out debris. In the adjacent avenue a family of twelve had all been killed. Her boss and proprietor of the shop, a short, round bellied, red-nosed Roman called Silvio Corato came in. He put his arm around Grete and took the spade from her.

"You must take a break," he said. "We cannot open today. So we have no need to rush. You go take a lunch break now and then we will finish up this afternoon."

Grete wiped her face with her forearm, only smudging it further.

"If you say so Signor Corato."

"I do say so. Now go and get something to eat and we will carry on in an hour or so."

Grete went into the back of the premises where there was little damage. Signor Corato walked to the door of his shop and tossed the spade full of debris onto a pile that had accumulated in the gutter. Before turning back into the shop he looked across the street and nodded towards a man in a grey trilby and a black overcoat. Grete washed her hands and face at the small basin in the rest room. The cold water stung her face but she was pleased with the refreshment. She put her coat over her shoulders, for her exertions had left her too hot to wear it yet, and picked up her handbag.

She picked her way over debris as she walked down the street to the corner. As she turned into Via Di San Basilio a gust of wind caught her coat, lifted it from her shoulders and tossed it to the ground. She turned to pick it up but found herself beaten to it by a smiling male. He was tall and good-looking and he wore a grey trilby and black overcoat. Grete knew immediately that he was a German and her heart stopped. The man said politely, "Permit me Signora.!"

But as he spoke Grete's mind was thrown into total confusion. At first trucks came to a screeching halt. Storm troopers jumped down and ran to surround her. Then she thought she heard Lisa and David calling to her. She looked at the man with fear and apprehension and she then swung her gaze in a panic, sure now that she could hear her children.

Suddenly the man spoke in German, "You are not hearing things, Jew bitch."

A shaft of steel shot through her heart. She had not been subject to such abuse since leaving Berlin. She felt all her hopes beginning to implode.

"Your Jew children are over there."

Grete followed the man's stare and saw the faces of Lisa and David pressed to the inside of the window of a military vehicle. Every dream she had dared to dream was exhaled with the desperate, "No!" which she screamed as the wall of storm troopers parted and she ran between the muzzles of their rifles, across the avenue towards the faces that called to her from behind the glass.

As she looked from the vehicle out onto the streets of Rome for the last time she did not cry, nor did she respond to the anxious questions coming at her from Lisa and David. She felt a numbness. She was irrationally worried about Signor and Signora Marino. They had been so kind and helpful. It had not been easy for them. When Grete and the children had first arrived in Rome to stay with Aunt Rebecca and Uncle Isaac, she had been forced to adopt a more Jewish way of life than she had been used to. Both she and Raul had converted to Christianity during their early years together in Berlin. Now, in order to fit into the ghetto, the children had gone to the Jewish school and they had celebrated the Sabbath by attending the temple every week. That meant there were people who could identify them as Jews when the round-up came. The Marinos had risked their lives to take them in. She and the children had reverted to a Christian lifestyle, albeit Catholic in deference to the Marinos. They had been their saviours and she hoped and prayed that her misfortune would not spread so far as to encompass them.

She did not see Signor Corato standing in the doorway of the café watching as she and her children were driven away.

Sixty-nine

The holding station was a disused brewery at the western edge of Rome. Grete and the children were housed with twenty-four other captives, including Emilio Marino and his wife, Maria, in an old railway truck. They were kept locked inside and fed with bread and water twice a day. The competition for food was furious and most times Grete failed to secure any for her children before the men grabbed it for themselves or their families. Emilio Marino sometimes secured some for them but Grete was aware of an understandable feeling of resentment coming from Maria because of the position they now found themselves in.

In the day time they sweated in the heat and at night they shivered in the cold. It was the hardest and worst time for Grete. She had loved Sean but now she blamed him. She came close to despising him for bringing her children to this. She had been surviving without him. Now her children would die.

When Robert had turned the corner on his approach to the café he was overtaken by a posse of military vehicles. He had frozen in fear, expecting them to screech to a halt beside him and for storm troopers to leap out and seize him. But he had been mistaken. The vehicles had screamed past him and skidded to halt someway beyond the café.

Robert had stepped into the shadows and watched events unfold. He didn't have long to wait. Storm troopers had disembarked from the back of the trucks and surrounded a couple standing on the pavement. The man wore a grey trilby and a black overcoat. The woman had been Grete. Screaming inside with frustration, self-directed anger and guilt, he had turned and sprinted back to the apartment.

Seventy

"What about these?" asked Friedrich. He was holding up the German uniforms that Robert had acquired on the night the two soldiers had killed the Italian Bolshevik.

"Of course," said Robert. "It's an idea. It might work. What do you think Lily?"

Lily seemed reluctant to respond. They had been discussing a plan to rescue Grete and the children from the holding station. This had necessitated an explanation from Robert about Grete and the children, who they were and how he knew them. Lily's intuition had told her that there was something more than he had told them and, of course, she was right.

"They might be useful in getting us in," she said eventually. "But why are we taking such a dreadful risk? I thought we were here to kill O'Shea. How many more missions are you going to dream up for us? And one other thing Robert. If you want our help I don't think you should treat us with the contempt you have been showing us."

"What on earth do you mean?" asked Robert.

"You just bumped into this Grete. That's what you told us. Please, Robert, don't take us for fools. Not if you want us to risk our lives for you."

Caught out in embarrassment, Robert looked to Friedrich. Friedrich looked away. Obviously he felt the same as Lily, although he would never have said anything. In that moment of embarrassment Robert reached a decision he had been pondering for some time.

"You are right. I have not been totally truthful. But I am not going to go over the past now. I will tell you the future, though. That's if everything works out. When we have Grete and the children we are going to send them on their way to Palestine and then we are going to get out of this corrupt continent and sail to Argentina." He paused to look at them. They made no response. "All right! We are agreed? The 'two birds with one stone plan'?"

Lily and Friedrich both nodded.

"Let's do it!"

Dressed in the uniforms, Robert and Friedrich walked ahead of Lily in the direction of the Vatican. Lily and Robert waited in the shadows opposite the walls of the Holy City and watched Friedrich stride confidently in through the administrative workers' entrance. As soon as he had entered, Robert disappeared into a side street in search of a car.

Inside the corridors of the Papal buildings, Friedrich showed the letter Lily had forged for him, to the Swiss Guards who challenged him. The letter explained that Friedrich was investigating information they had received that a Papal secretary, Monsignor O'Shea was being pursued by Allied agents and that his life was in danger. The letter worked and he was allowed to pass through to the secretary's office.

O'Shea looked up from his desk when Friedrich entered, "How may I help you?" he asked.

Friedrich handed O'Shea the letter without speaking. When O'Shea had finished reading it he looked up and said, "This is true, but I must ask you again, how can you help me?"

Friedrich spoke, "My superiors are concerned for your safety. They are convinced that you are in imminent danger. I have been ordered to escort you to Gestapo SS headquarters where a detailed plan of protection has been worked out. We would like you to consider it. We hope you will accept our protection."

O'Shea's natural suspicion was countered by his surprise and gratitude that the German authorities were showing such concern for him. After a moment's hesitation he said, "Thank you. If you will wait outside I will join you in a moment."

Friedrich nodded, clicked his heels and went into the corridor. As he stood there he was trying not to convince himself that he should make a run for it. For all he knew, O'Shea was alerting the guards and they were already on their way to seize him. But, he told himself, that was the risk he had agreed to. So he waited. After a very long five minutes, the office door opened and O'Shea came out.

"Very well," said O'Shea. "Let's go."

Robert sat in the driver's seat, his collar turned up and his cap pulled down to his eyes. Lily sat in the rear, her scarf draped loosely over her head covering half of her face. Friedrich led O'Shea to the car which stood in the shadow of the Vatican's walls. He opened the rear door for O'Shea and ushered him inside. As O'Shea settled into his seat beside Lily he felt the hard, cold muzzle of a pistol pushing against his kidneys. Friedrich slammed the rear door, jumped in beside Robert, who put his foot to the floor, and away they sped, out through the suburbs of Rome and through the surrounding countryside.

At first O'Shea had screamed in horror when he realised who his captors were. But Lily had silenced him by pushing the muzzle of the pistol into his mouth. When he had calmed down she explained to him what he was going to do.

The old brewery was partially destroyed thanks to allied bombing, and the site was now surrounded by derelict wasteland where worker's housing had once stood. It was late afternoon when they pulled up at the gates in the barbed wire fencing that had been erected to enclose the holding station. Rail tracks ran into the old brewery yard, along which trucks had once collected barrels of Italy's finest beer. At the end of the track, in the brewery yard, stood the truck containing Grete, the children, the Marinos and the other prisoners. The inmates were not a precious cargo and so security was no more than adequate. An elderly German Wermacht captain was in charge of half-a-dozen Carabinieri. The whole deportation programme had been run down following the main round-up of Jews. Besides, every German able-bodied man was on the front line defending northern Italy against the allied advance, and every able bodied Italian soldier in this sector, had been incarcerated or massacred by his former ally.

Robert brought the car to a halt at the gates and the Wermacht captain stepped forward, accompanied by two Carabinieri. Friedrich got out and opened the rear door for O'Shea.

Under Friedrich's watchful eye and aware of the gun pointed at his back from the car, O'Shea introduced himself and offered his Vatican credentials to the captain. The captain bowed formally and welcomed O'Shea and his companion to the compound. He turned and shouted orders to the gatehouse and another of the Carabinieri ran to swing the gates open. O'Shea and Friedrich climbed back into the car and Robert drove through the gates and pulled up inside the old brewery yard. As the captain and one of his Carabinieri walked up to the car, all four occupants got out and waited.

"Come, follow me inside, Monsignor O'Shea," called the captain and he passed them and entered the giant oak doors that led into the last remaining wing of the brewery that was still habitable and where he now had his office. A Carabinieri stood guarding the office door.

The four visitors followed the captain into his office, where he sat behind his desk and invited O'Shea to occupy the only other chair in the room. Suddenly rising he moved around the desk and approached Lily, who was standing beside Robert by the doorway.

"Pardon my rough Bavarian manners, Signora. Please take my seat. I have been too long in the army. My soldierly ways have blunted my behaviour."

"Please, captain," replied Lily. "I am fine here. You need to conduct your business with the Monsignor. Please keep your seat and forget about me."

Lily's faultless German had surprised the captain as he had assumed that she was Italian.

"Pardon me again, mein Frau. I had mistaken you for an Italian."

At this point Robert spoke up, also in his own faultless German, "We three are seconded from Fatherland security to the Vatican. Our current task is to ensure the Monsignor is successful in his mission. I am sure the Monsignor will explain everything to you."

The captain nodded slowly as if trying to weigh and sift the information he was receiving.

"Very well, Monsignor," he said turning to O'Shea. "How can I help you?"

O'Shea hesitated and glanced around at his three captors.

"Well," he began, "It has been brought to the attention of the Pontiff that two Catholic children may have been delivered to you in the last twenty-four hours or so. They were accompanied by their mother, who may or may not be a Jewess."

"How is this?" interjected the captain. "Catholic children of a maybe, maybe not Jewess. I don't think I understand. I am a simple soldier. You will have to spell it out more clearly for me."

O'Shea shifted uncomfortably in his seat and once more glanced around at his captors.

"Well," he coughed, "It is not as complicated as you might think. The woman might be a Jewess. That still needs to be verified. But the children are definitely Catholic. The Vatican has documentary proof of their baptism. You see their father, now deceased, was a Catholic of Austrian descent. Unfortunately, some sons of the church disregard the best advice and enter into mixed marriages. This was possibly one such unfortunate example. But, whatever the regrettable circumstances of their birth, the stain of original sin was washed from their souls and they have been received into the Catholic communion. They should not be here. It is the Pontiff's own wish that they be returned to the Holy City and placed under the direct care of the Church. A good Catholic family will be found for them. They will be adopted and brought up in the sight of God's grace. As for the mother, a thorough investigation will be carried out and, if it is proven that she is a Jewess, she will be returned to you for deportation."

The captain listened carefully and when O'Shea had finished he reached for some papers that were lying in a tray on his right hand side. He scanned the papers in his hand and then said, "I know the family you are speaking of. She is an extremely handsome woman this Frau Hildberg."

Lily felt Robert bristle at this comment and touched his arm to defuse his rising anger.

"But," the captain went on, "I have no evidence of a Catholic heritage in this family. The name Hildberg suggests a Jewish husband rather than an Austrian Catholic."

O'Shea responded quickly and impressed Lily with his dexterity of thought.

"Exactly, my good captain! That is why we think the confusion has arisen. The name is quite common among the Jewish population, but it is not exclusively Jewish. There are examples of Hildbergs of pure German or Austrian extraction going back centuries. I believe a branch of Himmler's extended family was called Hildenberg, which is of course another form of the name."

This seemed to mollify the captain, who was thinking that this was a remarkably unimportant family and one not worth falling out with the church over. He slowly got to his feet, obviously coming to a decision.

"You have persuaded me, Monsignor O'Shea. Please, bear with me for a moment. I will have the family delivered to this room immediately."

He barked orders at the Carabinieri, who hurried into the room. As the captain gave his instructions, Robert walked over to O'Shea and spoke to him quietly in Irish.

"Tell him I must accompany the Carabinieri to ensure we get the right people."

Overcoming his shock at the sound of Irish so close to his ear from a man he once considered a friend and who he now considered the most evil and dangerous man on Earth, he nodded. The captain agreed to O'Shea's request and Robert left with the Carabinieri.

The Carabinieri's boots echoed along the brick-tiled corridor as Robert followed him below the high windows. Robert fancied he could detect a faint odour of malt coming from the very walls, but it may have just been a suggestion in the mind.

At the end of the corridor they stepped out into bright, late-afternoon daylight and, immediately, Robert saw the railway truck at the end of the yard where Grete and the children were. Robert followed the Carabinieri up to the door of the truck and watched as he put a key into the large chain lock and threw the doors open. Light spilled into the truck and the occupants all covered their eyes from the glare. The stench of human waste drifted out and the Carabinieri covered his nose with his sleeve and made some indignant comment. He shouted out the name Hildberg.

Robert recognised Grete and the children but they could not distinguish his features as their pupils tried to adjust to the light. All they perceived were two silhouettes and the sound of their name. Eventually, Grete persuaded the children to accompany her to the door of the truck and Robert helped them down onto the ground.

"Say nothing," he hissed into Grete's ear. But as he lifted David down, the boy threw his arms around his neck and shouted, "Uncle Robert!"

The Carabinieri looked at Robert and asked, "What did he say? Does he know you?"

Fortunately the Italian did not understand German and so Robert could just shrug. Before David could say anything else Robert put him onto the ground, shook his shoulders and roughly ordered him to shut up. David immediately began to cry and went to his mother.

"What is happening," Grete asked anxiously. "Why are you here?"

"Be quiet woman," he snapped. "You are coming with me."

As he herded the family of three together and pointed in the direction he wanted them to walk, Grete suddenly pulled away and rushed back to the door of the truck.

"The Marinos!" she cried. "The Marinos must come with us."

Robert ran after her and pulled her away from the truck.

"You must come now," he shouted in as officious a manner as he could manage.

Grete struggled as he pulled her away and the Carabinieri began to lose patience in the situation.

"What is going on here?" he asked Robert as he began to un-shoulder his rifle.

Robert roughly pushed Grete towards her children and went across to the Carabinieri. He palmed his hands in a calming gesture but he could see that the Carabinieri had made a decision and he continued to raise his rifle. Robert sprang like a snake and pushed the rifle upwards into his face. The rifle fell to the floor and Robert seized the Carabinieri in a headlock. Using his knowledge of anatomy he squeezed the man's throat until he lost consciousness. Throwing the man over his shoulder he hurried with him to the truck and threw him in. Climbing into the truck after him Robert was again overcome by the stench of human waste. He pointed at the man nearest to him and demanded his belt. Using the belt, he trussed the unconscious Carabinieri's arms tightly behind his back and then, taking a woman's scarf, which was lying on the floor beside her, he tightly tied the Carabinieri's legs together. He then took a rag that was lying on the floor and stuffed it into the unconscious man's mouth. Getting to his feet he looked around him.

"Signor Marino," he said. In the dark he was still having difficulty making out the features of the twenty-five or so people in there.

"Signor Marino," he called again, impatience rising in his tone.

A man got to his feet at the back of the truck and shuffled forward towards him.

"Are you Signor Marino?" Robert asked.

The man nodded.

"Where is your wife?"

From the same dark corner a woman got to her feet and came towards them.

"Come with me," he ordered.

Robert turned and jumped down from the truck. The Marinos had not moved.

"Now!" he barked and they obeyed him. He helped them both down and taking them on each side of him by the elbow, marched them towards Grete and the children.

"We do not have time to waste," he hissed at them. "Just follow me as quickly as you can."

So saying, he let go of the Marinos, took David and Lisa by the hand and marched back towards the captain's office. Grete and the Marinos ran to keep up with him. As they walked back inside the building Robert realised that the absence of his escort and the presence of the Marinos had changed the situation. There was no way they were going to get out of this holding station without a fight.

*   *   *

When Robert had left the office with the Carabinieri escort, Lily and Friedrich had settled down to a nerve-wracking wait. The captain asked if they would like some tea but before O'Shea could say yes, Lily snapped, "We do not have time. We must get these people back to the Vatican for proper identification."

"As you wish," said the captain with a shrug. He returned to his seat and reached out for the telephone. His hand hesitated over the receiver as the sound of pistols being cocked grabbed his attention. He looked up to see the soldier and his woman accomplice pointing barrels into his face. His stomach churned as he realised he had been duped. The captain looked at the cleric, Monsignor O'Shea. O'Shea read his thoughts.

"They are heinous assassins. I am their captive. They are going…"

"That's enough," barked Lily. "Not another word from either of you."

And they waited.

*   *   *

Approaching the office, Robert knew he had to deal with the guard standing outside. Halfway along the corridor he stopped and turned to Grete.

"Stay here," he said. "I am going to go ahead and speak to the guard. When I signal, come quickly to join me."

Grete just nodded. By this time she was numbed into obeying his orders. Robert went ahead and approached the guard. He leaned close to whisper conspiratorially. As the guard tilted his head to listen, Robert clamped his hand over the man's mouth and simultaneously brought his knee up sharply between his legs. The man crumpled into Robert's arms. Robert span him around and with one hand across the man's chest and one tightly gripping his chin, he snapped his neck with one sharp pull. He lowered the guard to the ground and beckoned the group to join him.

When he entered the office he could not at first see Lily and Friedrich. He saw the captain sitting opposite O'Shea. Both sat in complete silence. As he moved into the room Lily and Friedrich stepped out from the space behind the door. Robert ushered his party inside and Lily shut the door. She answered Robert's unspoken question and he answered hers.

"The captain was going to make a telephone call."

"The Marinos. They sheltered Grete and the children from the first round-up."

Lily nodded. She then stared at Grete closely for the first time. Robert did his best not to notice her expression.

"Watch them closely," Robert said to Friedrich and then pulled Lily to one side.

"There's a dead guard outside. Help me pull him in before someone sees him."

As they dragged him in, O'Shea groaned and blessed himself. It was more a groan of self pity than outrage at an atrocity. Conferring secretly once more with Lily, Robert said, "There's one guard trussed up in the truck. I think he'll be unconscious for a good while longer. Then there are the four guards at the gate and the captain."

"What are we going to do with them?"

"Well our ruse with O'Shea has crashed. There's only one way out of here. We have to get rid of them all."

After a pause Lily nodded.

"You're right. But we need to do things in the right order or we are going to end up in the truck."

"Okay. Let's think it through. Four guards at the gate are too many for us to deal with in one go. Two we can manage. Then there's the captain."

"And O'Shea," added Lily.

"Yes," mumbled Robert looking across at the worried priest. "Then there's O'Shea."

Taking his pistol out, Robert walked over to the captain and stood behind his seat. Placing the barrel against his temple he said simply, "Call the gate and get two of your men up here immediately. Tell them they are to escort the visitors out of the camp."

The captain slowly reached for the receiver. He lifted it to his ear and dialled one number. Through the open window they could all hear the external telephone bell at the gatehouse ringing.

"No smart ideas," warned Robert, tapping the barrel gently against the captain's temple.

The ringing stopped and a voice spoke on the line. The captain gave the instructions he had been told to and then replaced the receiver. In a moment the sound of boots at the double coming up the yard could be heard. Friedrich and Robert moved the body of the dead guard to a corner out of view from the doorway and then stood back against the wall alongside the door. Lily stood behind the captain where she could pick off either the captain or O'Shea if she needed to.

The sound of boots in the corridor. A loud knocking at the door. After a prod from Lily the captain called, "Come!"

The door opened and two elderly Carabinieri stepped up to the captain's desk and stood to attention. Robert and Friedrich jumped forward and took one man each around the neck. A flash of steel in each hand and a sharp drag of metal upon throat. Friedrich's victim fell like a stone. He tipped to one side and fell onto O'Shea's lap, his blood spilling voluminously onto his cassock. O'Shea leapt to his feet in fear and disgust. He then fell to the floor as Robert and his guard stumbled in a death struggle into Friedrich, who in turn had bumped O'Shea. Witnessing this horror, the captain's face froze into a permanent mask of anguish as Lily sliced his throat open with one sleek slash. Grete, the children and the Marinos hid themselves in a huddle to avoid witnessing the carnage going on around them as Robert and his stubborn victim still wrestled in a death dance that had embroiled Friedrich. Finally, the stubborn Carabinieri fell to his knees, overcome by loss of blood and Robert and Friedrich were able to disentangle themselves from him. He tilted forward on to his face and gave up the ghost.

Struggling for breath, Robert said, "Quick! Everyone to the car!"

He quickly scanned the room. His heart froze.

"Where is O'Shea?"

His eyes went from Lily to Friedrich and back again.

"Where is O'Shea?" he repeated.

"He must have crept out in the melee," said Friedrich, wiping blood from his hands.

In a frenzy, Robert made a dive towards the door but Lily's scream halted him in his tracks.

"No!" she yelled.

Robert turned to look at her.

"What is more important?" she asked. "O'Shea or...?" And she looked at the huddled group in the corner of the room. Robert realised, in his despair, that she was right. He stood, torn for a moment between two courses of action and then almost reluctantly repeated his first instruction.

"Everyone to the car!"

Lily ushered them all outside into the corridor and then closed the office door behind her. They hurried along the corridor to the large oak doors and stepped out into the now fading afternoon light. Lily climbed in on the driver's side and the Marinos got in beside her along the bench. Grete and the children climbed in the back. Robert and Friedrich marched ahead of the car in their blood-stained uniforms, out of the brewery yard and along the dusty path to the gatehouse. The two guards ahead, the only two now left at the holding station, were laughing at some joke. Robert and Friedrich approached them swiftly. They were surprised at the sudden appearance of these two Germans and had insufficient time to raise their rifles when they saw the pistols pointed at them. Two shots rang out and two Carabinieri fell to the dust, head wounds spilling blood like red surf onto dark sand.

The car arrived as Friedrich opened the gates. Robert leaned into the car and said to Lily.

"I must go and finish off the one in the truck. If I don't he could raise the alarm before we have sufficient time to get away."

Lily nodded and switched off the engine. Robert turned and ran back up to the old brewery yard. He had no need to go through the old building. He could follow the tracks around the side to the spot where the truck stood.

When he got to the truck he could hear shouting in Italian. Somehow, the guard had managed to expel the gag from his mouth. He was ordering a middle-aged woman to untie his bonds. She was untying the scarf around his legs as Robert climbed into the truck. When she saw him she stopped and stepped away. With his leg bonds loosened the Italian scrabbled away from Robert screaming, "No! No! No!"

Like a man about to cut a cabbage head from his allotment, Robert calmly approached the frightened man, reached around his throat and opened it with his blade. There were now approximately twenty to twenty-five men, women and children in the truck. There was no reaction from them. They stared like so many cynics at something they had seen a thousand times before. As he jumped down from the truck Robert turned and said in German, English and Italian,   "You can go! You are free!" Then he turned and ran all the way back to the gate.

From an upstairs window in the old brewery building, the cowering figure of O'Shea watched as his nemesis jumped into the car at the gate and sped away. After waiting over an hour for his courage and strength to return, he slowly picked his way through the derelict building and began his long walk back to civilisation. He walked for half an hour before reaching a village. He was dimly aware that he should have telephoned the authorities from the brewery but nothing could have prevailed upon him to linger in that place. On arriving in the village he immediately went to the church and knocked at the door of the priest's house. He was ushered inside by the housekeeper and given permission by the parish priest to use the telephone. He informed the Vatican authorities of the crimes he had witnessed and they informed the German SS. After another hour a Mercedes screamed to a halt outside the village church. Schirach and Dortmuller got out. They collected O'Shea from the priest's house and then sped off towards the old brewery.

O'Shea refused to move out of the gatehouse and so Schirach and Dortmuller went on alone to inspect the carnage. The light was fading now as night began to reclaim the hemisphere. Shadows became one with the night as Schirach and Dortmuller finally approached the old railway truck. The door was still open and the stench reached their nostrils well before they reached it. Covering their faces with their sleeves to look inside, they were shocked to find one bloodied corpse and twenty to twenty-five men, women and children staring out at them. The traumatised captives had waited to be told what to do. They had not been able to trust the word of the assassin who had lied to them about freedom.

"Close the door!" ordered Schirach.

Dortmuller tugged at the door and slid it to.

"Lock it!"

Dortmuller lifted the heavy chain through the padlock and snapped it shut. Schirach marched away and Dortmuller followed him. He scouted around the yard until he found the thing he was looking for. He had guessed that a railway truck terminus would need to have a fuel bin. Filling a bucket each with fuel, Shirach and Dortmuller returned to the locked truck. They splashed the contents of their buckets over the walls of the truck. One or two voices from inside could be heard to moan, "Oh, please, no." Schirach took a cigarette lighter from his pocket and held the flame to the fuel-soaked walls. The flame caught and licked its way greedily over the truck. Moans turned to screams as Schirach and Dortmuller walked away back to the gatehouse.

*   *   *

When the car arrived at the fishing port, Robert refused to get out. He was unable to go through another goodbye with Grete. He struggled to harden his heart whilst it was breaking. Lily and Friedrich escorted the Hildbergs and the Marinos down to the dock. Robert did not turn to watch them go. He did not see Grete try to walk back to the car to say goodbye to him. He did not see Lily restrain her and force her to walk on towards the dock. Money changed hands and the skipper of the fishing trawler agreed to deliver them to Palermo and there to guide them into the hands of the allied authorities who would support them in their desire to emigrate to Palestine, after which Lily and Friedrich returned to the car. No one spoke on the long drive back into Rome.

Seventy-one
Three weeks later

Panic reigned in O'Shea's breast even though he knew exactly where to go. He had been to the catacombs many times. He had often guided visiting clerics through the passageways and delivered a potted history to them. He knew his way around and he knew a way in but would he make it in time. The Red Cross office - the one fronting the underground exit route for Nazis and Fascists to make their escape to South America — had been the obvious location for tonight's plan. His superiors in the Vatican had made it clear that he was no longer required in Rome. He had been appointed to a parish outside Buenos Aires where he would oversee the development of primary Catholic education in the region. But he needed to travel under an alias to avoid his own personal grim reaper - Sean Colquhoun. Colquhoun and his cohorts had been waiting for him and the chase had begun.

It had been a long time since he had run so far and so fast. Until now his fear had propelled him but now he was breathless and exhausted. The cold night air burned in his lungs and his cassock was wet and sticky with his sweat.

His fear of Sean Colquhoun was overpowering. His nose ran and he sniffed back tears like a terrified child. To know that this man was dead set on snuffing out his life made him angry, terrified and frustrated. He longed to be able to strike back at this evil that pursued him Maybe tonight. .

He fell against the entrance he had chosen and put the key nervously to the lock. It was an entrance not used by the public.

The sound of running feet made him rush and he fumbled with the key. Two pairs of feet; a man's and a woman's. Who was this female fiend, he wondered? What evil had possessed them both, her most of all, to want to murder a man of God? What a ridiculous question, he realised. These two had assassinated His Holiness. Why would they balk at the thought of murdering a humble Monsignor like himself!

He cursed the key for its lack of co-operation and begged God's forgiveness at the same time. They must not catch him here. Not yet. His very veins were racing when at last the key turned. 'I've done it,' he thought triumphantly. He pushed the heavy door open and tugged at the key to retrieve it from the lock. The cursed thing caught in the lock and fell from his fingers to the damp paving stones. The running feet were just around the corner now. He just had time to reach out of the doorway and pick up the key. There was no way he could leave it there. It would give him away immediately. He stepped out and stooped down. The scrape of feet caused him to glance up towards the corner just as his hand closed around the key. There was Colquhoun sliding to a halt. He was certain the Colquhoun had seen him. He grabbed the key, turned and bolted into the tunnel. He heard Colquhoun's voice.

"Lily, quick! He's here!"

O'Shea slammed the door enclosing himself in the pitch black of the tunnel. No time to mess with the key attempting to lock the door. He could hear Colquhoun's hands on the other side of the door, even now turning the handle. He shot away into the darkness. 'Colquhoun saw me,' he thought, 'but I know my way through the catacombs – blindfolded.'

Robert held the door open for Lily and she entered to stand alongside him. From where they stood there was only one passageway along which O'Shea could have gone. Robert pulled a torch out of his pocket, flicked it on and said, "Okay, let's go."

Together they hurried along the cold, dark tunnel. Occasionally, Robert bumped his head on a rough overhang. From time to time the sound of running feet ahead of them could be heard.

O'Shea was gambling between speed and care. He had already fallen twice and was sure his pursuers had heard him. His cassock slowed him down and he was at the edge of his endurance. The realisation that he could not outrun these relentless pursuers was fast seeping into his crazed mind. But as he stumbled forward he knew he only had to make it so far. About thirty yards further on there was a fork in the passage. The fork itself led nowhere, but halfway along it there was an alcove big enough to hide a man. That is where he must go. Dressed in black and deep inside that alcove he would be hard to spot, even with a torch. He didn't have to outrun them. If he could reach the alcove beyond the fork he knew he would be safe. His only concern was that they would catch him before he got there.

Having made up his mind he felt a sense of relief, although it was a very relative thing. He took care not to stumble again, even if it meant sacrificing some speed. He walked with a measured and quiet tread. As soon as he reached the fork he ducked into it and went straight to the alcove where he crawled to the far end and curled himself into a black ball against the black rock. 'Now,' he thought. 'Keep coming Mr Coquhoun and let's see what happens.'

He heard his pursuers approach the mouth of the fork and he heard their footsteps cease. Voices came to him but with the effects of echo he could not make out their words. Then he heard more footsteps. He was sure they were not getting closer to him. They grew fainter and then they died altogether.

A feeling of elation swept over him. As soon as it had passed, a feeling of dread re-invaded him. Then he was victim to a triumphant sensation. His emotions went up and down like this but there was a gradual yet growing conviction that he had outsmarted his would-be assassins yet again. Now it might be their turn to feel fear. The utter and endless silence of the catacombs persisted. He had heard no sound since their footsteps had died away. How many minutes ago? One? Ten? He had no way of knowing. That was puzzling him. Surely he should have heard something by now. He realised that the longer he stayed where he was, the less able he would be to gauge the passing of time. He also knew that the longer he waited, the greater the likelihood of his pursuers' return if something had gone wrong.

He uncurled himself from the ball he had become and slowly, stiffly straightened himself up. With great caution, feeling his way along the cold wall, he moved stealthily out of the alcove and back along the passage towards the entrance to the fork. In the utter silence he felt confident that he was alone. In his thoughts he offered a prayer to God for preserving him from the evil that his pursuers had intended.

As he approached the junction with the main tunnel he was determined to take no chances. He crept silently along the wall to the corner. Pressing himself hard against the rock he craned his neck to look and listen along the tunnel his pursuers had taken. Nothing! Creeping further forward he paused again to look and listen. Again, nothing! But then! A click! And a flashlight blinding in his face. And then as it fell away Colquhoun's face six inches from his.

"Good evening Father O'Shea. It's been a long time."

O'Shea remained uncharacteristically calm.

"I have nothing to say to you, Colquhoun. You have committed the worst crime known on Earth. You will rot in hell."

"Well you're going to have to save a place for me there because that's where you are going right now. You can spend the rest of this evening explaining to your God what you did to my son."

"I did nothing to your son," retorted O'Shea a level of fear registering in his voice. "I loved your son."

Robert reached out wildly and grabbed O'Shea by the throat.

"Don't you dare speak about my son in that way. Don't you dare mention him again."

O'Shea recovered himself somewhat and, pulling himself as much as he could from Robert shouted, "They are here! Come out! Come and arrest them!"

Robert and Lily froze. What was this? Robert and Lily listened intently. Nothing!

"Nice try, O'Shea. But that was your last gambit."

Robert bounced O'Shea off the wall and took him from behind. With his arm around O'Shea's throat and his hand upon his chin he braced himself to snap his miserable neck in one swift movement. O'Shea emitted a pathetic, childlike cry of protest.

Lily and Robert were both instantly blinded by a searchlight which blazed into life, bathing them in stark, white light. As their eyes grew accustomed to the glare they began to decipher uniformed figures approaching them from all sides. In the shock of the moment Robert had let slip his hold on O'Shea and he was now wriggling free of Robert's clutches. Robert and Lily were seized by two officers apiece and flung against the wall of the tunnel.

"Good evening Herr Doctor. I've been waiting to meet you for a long time," said Hauptsturmfuhrer Schirach.

Robert estimated twenty men surrounding them. There was no escape.

"You have been here all the time," he stated.

"Correct," returned Schirach.

O'Shea scrabbled to his feet, his face wet with tears and snot.

"What the hell took you so long, you bastard, Schirach. He could have killed me. Kill them!" he screamed. "Kill them! Kill them!"

Schirach turned to look at O'Shea

"I heard what this man said to you, man of God. You deserved to die. I don't know why I stopped him. Get out of my sight before I change my mind. And remember, holy man, do not be in Rome in the morning."

O'Shea glanced at Colquhoun. The depth of hatred in Robert's eyes was bottomless. A wave of fear swept over O'Shea and he collected the skirt of his cassock in his sweaty palms and ran out of sight towards the entrance they had used minutes earlier.

Schirach nodded to a group of his men and they bound Lily and Robert by their hands in seconds.

"And now," continued Schirach, "We will make our way to my temporary headquarters in this eternal city."

At his command the detachment headed off towards the entrance O'Shea had used. Robert tried to get close to Lily but his captors would not allow it. He called back to her.

"Lily, I'm sorry. You didn't need to be involved in this. It was my folly. Tell them everything they want to know. We have nothing to hide now."

A guard pushed the butt of his rifle into Robert's face and ordered him to shut up. For the rest of the procession through the catacombs, Schirach spoke quietly to Robert so that he could not be overheard.

"Your mission has been a complete failure. Oh, maybe you succeeded in killing the Pope but sadly for you the world will never know it. His idiot brother has been excavated from his secret obscurity. He will be Pope Pius XII now. All Papal decisions will be made for him. He will keep right out of politics from now on. This is exactly what the Fuhrer has always wanted. The Fuhrer would thank you personally if he hadn't ordered your immediate execution. As for your collaborator, Lily Brecht. You beg her to tell all in a vain attempt to save her from the intricacies of our interrogation techniques. But as a German citizen, and an agent of the Third Reich, she has committed the crime of treason. It would not matter if she were to sing her secrets from the top of the Brandenburg Gate, her treatment will be specialised and prolonged."

As they emerged from the catacombs and were shepherded towards the waiting vehicles, Robert experienced despair. This was his fault. He had finally hit bottom in his long fall from sanity and civilised behaviour. The young man who set off for Germany in his twenties with a mission to save lives had come to this. A killing machine! All hope gone! All optimism fled! And, worst of all, he had dragged Lily into this situation. She had proved herself his true ally. She had played her part in the success of their mission and then his own personal folly had led them on this wild goose chase to find and kill O'Shea and to seek out Grete. At least Friedrich was not caught up in this disaster. Hopefully he'd found a way of getting them out of Italy and would now use that route to save himself.

Robert was in between Schirach and a young commando in the rear of the lead vehicle. Lily was in a similar position in the second of the three vehicles that now made their way through the dampened streets of Rome back towards the heart of the city. Robert was too deep in thought to pay much attention when his vehicle came to a shuddering halt.

The driver leaned out of his window and yelled at someone ahead on the street. After that things happened so quickly Robert only retained a sketchy memory of events. The first thing he was aware of was the sound of gunfire and glass bursting all over him. When he looked at Schirach a red bullet hole had appeared in the centre of his forehead. Out of the back of his head there was a bloody cavernous mess. Turning to his other co-passenger he saw another red bullet hole, this time where the man's left eye had been moments before. Then he heard a wild blaze of continuous gunfire.

Keeping his head down as much as he could, all he saw was the driver of the vehicle slump over the steering wheel as he was hit in the neck. After an eternity of gunfire, which rose to an insane crescendo, an insane silence fell upon the scene. In a moment two men dressed in the garb of Italian merchant seamen wrenched open the rear doors of his vehicle.

These were Italian Partisans - the true Italian heroes of the war. Robert held out little hope of explaining to them that he too was an enemy of the Germans. He expected to be shot. All he could do was raise his hands and show them the binds that held him. But then a truly surprising thing happened. One of the men leaned in and pulled the blue cravat away from his face. Robert found himself looking into the eyes of a dirty, unshaven Andrew Trubshaw.

"Come on, Colquhoun," Andrew said. "We need to get moving if we're to get you out of here."

Trubshaw then surprised Robert. He handed his machine gun to one of his men and drew his pistol from a shining, brown, leather holster.

"But before that there is one more task to perform."

Robert watched in astonishment as Trubshaw walked towards the scene where the second vehicle had come to a halt. To his horror he watched Trubshaw approach Lily as she was being pulled from the back seat. As he approached he raised his pistol and pointed it directly at Lily's temple.

Robert screamed, "No!" His animalistic cry was enough to make Trubshaw pause and turn to look at him.

"Andrew!" gasped Robert. "No – you've got it wrong. She's one of us. Don't shoot her. I know she started out with them. But you've got to believe me. She's turned. She's with us."

Trubshaw exhibited a reluctance to believe Robert. His pistol remained hard against Lily's temple and he was obviously contemplating pulling the trigger. He had spent so many months longing for this moment. He had been humiliated by her successful deception. He felt personally responsible for the deaths her activities had led to. But here was Robert, who had worked alongside her for all these months, pleading for her life. Slowly he lowered his pistol.

"You are a very lucky woman," he whispered into Lily's ear.

Lily, shaking with shock and fear was dragged to join Robert and the whole group ran into the Roman night.

Seventy-two

The Montevideo slipped through the Straits of Gibraltar and headed south-west into the open Atlantic. Gran Canaria was the first scheduled stop on the seven week journey. Friedrich lay in his cabin. He would not survive the journey. Severe hypertension was compounded by the guilt that assailed him for his years as a clerk in Munich. Two days out from Buenos Aires he would succumb to a massive stroke. He was not sad. He had played his part in helping Robert and Lily and he truly had no desire to begin a new life in a new world.

Robert and Lily were on deck. The sea was black ahead of them. To their starboard side no lights revealed the position of Gibraltar, although the lights of Fascist Spain could be seen. The white surf that was pierced by the ships bow attracted Robert's gaze and he realised as he looked further ahead into the black, Atlantic night that he was thinking of O'Shea. Somewhere out there, two days ahead of them, O'Shea was standing on a similar deck cutting through the same surf.

"Your frown tells me you are thinking things you have no need to."

Lily put her arm inside Robert's and leaned against him. He kind of smiled. He did not mind her demonstrating affection. It only reminded him that he felt none. He turned and looked at her the way a camera looks at a subject. Pulling her to him he kissed her and felt the curves of her warm body against him. With her he could master this pretence. Deep inside he hoped she was practising the same self deception. Without her there would be nothing – not even pretence. He made do with what he had.

"I know what you are thinking," she said. "It is not so bad. Perhaps it is what we need to keep us going. I don't fool myself that we are starting anew. Life's not like that for you and me anymore. We are outside of normal life."

Robert wiped away a moist bead from below her right eye. He did not interrupt her. He was thinking of Grete and her children and wondering if they were safely on their way to Palestine. He thought about Martha and a child who would never know her father. He thought about a dead child too.

"O'Shea gives us purpose." Lily continued. "And when O'Shea is done with there will be plenty of work to do in Argentina if this shipload of Nazis and Ustashes is representative of the traffic flowing between Rome and South America."

Robert pulled her to him and looked out over her head to the white face of the moon. He saw the expressionless visage riding over the waves as a reflection of himself. He wondered if it would be enough.